A Splendid Sin

Michelangelo: *A Novel of the Renaissance*

A Splendid Sin

Michelangelo: A Novel of the Renaissance

ALANA BOLTON COOKE

CLOUD
INK

First published in 2019
Published by Cloud Ink Press Ltd, Auckland
P.O. Box 8988, Symonds Street, Auckland, 1150
www.cloudink.co.nz

ISBN 978-0-473-45776-1

Cover design: Rachel Stevens

Book design and typesetting: Craig Violich (www.cvdgraphics.nz)
Printed by yourbooks.co.nz

For Peter, David and Felicity with love and gratitude.

FORMATION

ONE
Caprese, 1481

Lodovico loomed over Lionardo and Michelangelo's bed and shook them awake. The boys climbed out of bed and their father ushered them into the hallway.

'You must come and see Mama, she is very sick,' he said as he led them towards their parents' bedchamber. Michelangelo and his older brother, Lionardo, held their father's hands as they padded down the hallway towards the light. The brightness from so many candles in the room blinded the boys. They rubbed their eyes, trying to adjust. They knew their parents' room but were rarely invited in.

As Michelangelo's vision cleared, he saw his mother, Francesca, lying in the large bed. A tall man stood beside the bed, reading prayers out of a book. Michelangelo recognised the priest from the village church. Lodovico's brother, Francesco, stood to one side, not looking at the children but at his sister-in-law. In the corner stood a cot, the very one Michelangelo and his brothers had occupied as babies. He looked up at his father, trying to ascertain what was happening, but was astonished and frightened to see him crying. Something awful was happening. Lodovico bent and picked up Lionardo and took him to his mother's bedside. Michelangelo saw her raise her hand to touch him. Lodovico, still crying, took the boy away and turned to lift Michelangelo but the little boy avoided him and ran to his mother's bedside, tugging at the sleeve of her nightgown.

'Mama, Mama, what's happening?'

Francesca always answered his questions but now she didn't

even look at him. Lodovico lifted Michelangelo up so he could see his mother properly. Francesca reached out to him as Lodovico held him close to her. She tried to bring him even closer but was too weak. Michelangelo could see her face was very white.

'My darling,' she whispered.

Lodovico put him down and lifted her off the bed, holding her close in his arms. After a few minutes he laid her down again.

Michelangelo screamed, 'Mama. Mama. Mama!' His mother was lifeless in the bed, her dark hair lying over the pillow.

Francesco took the children from the room and put them back to bed. Lionardo was sobbing but Michelangelo had stopped crying. He lay beside his restless brother. He could hear his father and brother talking with the priest in the hallway. Then there was silence. He crept out of bed and down the hallway into his parents' room. His mother was still there, in the bed, covered in a sheet. The room was lit now by a few candles and he tiptoed over to the baby's cot and peered in. The infant boy with a shock of black, matted hair slept on his side, still swaddled in tight coverings.

'You took my mama away. I don't like you,' Michelangelo said to the baby. He reached into the cot and twisted the baby's soft ear. The baby screamed. Francesca sat up, the sheet falling from her body.

'Michelangelo, what have you done?' She looked at him with eyes no longer alive but blank.

'Sorry, Mama. Don't go!' he screamed, running to the bedside. She looked at him in silence and lay down again, her limp body flattened onto the mattress, a billow of dust around her in the light like gold dust, angel dust. Michelangelo ran out of the room towards his bedchamber before his uncle and father saw him. He climbed in beside his brothers and, with the baby's cries still echoing throughout the house, he lay in bed and trembled. His mother was dead and with this unwanted certainty, he eventually fell asleep.

The next day the house was silent, the windows closed and shuttered, the drapery drawn. Francesca was lying in a long box in the front salon. Michelangelo could not bear to look at her. She looked stiff and cold, no longer like his mama. The boys watched as their father and uncle and some local men from the church carried her outside. They watched the procession from the window as it wound its way towards the church. Then she was gone.

A wet-nurse was found for the baby, Sigismondo, while the other children, caught in the miasma of their father's sorrow, quietened and kept away from him. He had become a stranger with unkempt hair, a black beard and red eyes swollen from weeping. Michelangelo did not like his new father and whenever he had to pass his parents' room, he skirted the space to walk on the opposite side of the hallway, just in case he saw his mother again, alive, yet dead.

An emptiness surrounded the children, bored into them. Sometimes Michelangelo took a big sniff and tried to smell her presence in the kitchen or the salon where they used to gather around the tall chimney place with the fire lit. The smell of Hungary water, tinged with rosemary, lavender, jasmine and tumbling white roses from the fields which she always picked and arranged in vases in the villa, had gone. After some time, Michelangelo ventured into his parents' room and stared at the bed as if she were suddenly going to appear before him. But she had gone for good.

How would they live without her?

TWO
Settignano, 1484

Michelangelo stretched his legs to climb up and stand on the wooden kitchen stool. With a piece of charcoal he sketched a satyr on the kitchen wall of the villa at Settignano, half man and half goat, hooves and a thick hairy coat, ugly and frightening. Lodovico had told him about the satyrs from Greek mythology and warned that if he didn't behave, they would come and get him. His father hadn't told him that satyrs also had a benign side, playing musical instruments and dancing with nymphs. How old was he? Eight? Nine?

The satyr he had seen in his father's book frightened him but he found if he looked at the pictures in the book just before bed time, he didn't dream about them. So he decided that if he drew one, he would be less frightened and would never have nightmares again. It worked. He drew his fears out on scraps of paper and looked at them before he slept. His father found them, raged about him drawing and threw them away and Michelangelo's nightmares returned. So he tried again, this time on the wall because there was no paper in the house; his father had forbidden it.

Lodovico walked into the kitchen, caught Michelangelo by the arm and dragged him off the stool. He told him to bend over and belted him with a birch stick. Backside stinging, Michelangelo ran from the house, all the way down the dusty road, around the corner and over the fields to the home of his former wet nurse, Mona Basso. His sobs echoing in the confined yard, he skirted the house and ran into the barn where they kept the animals, the coolness a relief against his hurt body and his tear-stained face. He climbed the ladder into the loft and buried himself in a pile of hay.

'Michelangelo! Where are you? I saw you run in here.'

Michelangelo listened. He recognised the voice of Bernardino Basso, his friend, the boy who refused to grow.

'I'm up here, Dino. I don't want to come down. My father beat me and if my uncle knows about it, he'll beat me too.'

'We won't tell them you're here Angelo. Come down. Papa is coming.'

Michelangelo scrambled to the edge of the loft and looked down. He knew for certain that Piero Basso would not beat him.

'Come, Michelangelo,' called Piero. 'We have fresh baked bread and nutty cheese in the kitchen, and fresh milk. Come on, you must be hungry. Boys are always hungry,' called Piero, standing beside Bernardino in the shaft of sunlight from the open door of the barn. Dust motes swirled around them. Gold flecks from Mama, thought Michelangelo. They were painted in sunshine like angels. He would like to know how to paint sunshine. His tummy rumbled, he had not eaten since breakfast.

'You won't tell Papa I'm here?'

'No, but come, what's the matter?'

Michelangelo climbed slowly down the ladder and stood before Piero and Bernardino. He was shaking and his bottom and legs were stinging but he felt the light, reassuring pressure of Piero's hand on his shoulder and his kind face bending down to him.

'Come, Michelangelo. Come with us, and we'll help.'

He walked out of the barn between the two, towards the stonemason's house where he had spent much of his young life. Soon, as he entered the familiar kitchen with its bright hob and flickering flame, he felt better.

'Oh, Michelangelo, what happened to you? Look at your legs! Have you been whipped?' Mona shook her head in alarm, glanced at Piero with eyebrows raised and enveloped the boy in her arms. He felt her warmth, her softness and love and suddenly cried out for his mother. Mama had been dead three years but it felt like yesterday. Mona wrapped him in her arms and crooned, 'Shh-shh….'

'Papa beat me. I drew on the kitchen wall,' Michelangelo sobbed. 'He told me not to draw or carve stone anymore, and I did.'

'Why doesn't he like you drawing, Michelangelo? You are very good at it,' Mona bent over the boy and took off his shirt. She turned him around and covered her mouth with her hand.

Bernardino and Piero were silent as they looked at Michelangelo's back and lower legs. The boy knew he was scarred, not only from this beating but from others too.

'He doesn't want me to draw because he doesn't want me to become an artist He tries to take it away from me but it's all I want to do. I like drawing! It makes me happy,' Michelangelo sobbed.

'Take your shirt and hose off. I will clean your back and legs and apply some salve to help you heal,' Mona said gently.

Piero took the boy aside, peeled off his clothes and wrapped him in a blanket. After Mona applied some ointment, Michelangelo and Bernardino drank warm milk and devoured the bread and cheese, vaguely aware of Piero talking quietly to his wife.

'Bernardino, do you still have the stone animals Michelangelo carved for you?' Piero said, joining the boys.

'Yes, Papa.'

'Fetch them. We'll take Michelangelo home and you can show his Papa his carvings.'

Mona hugged Michelangelo, and the three of them walked down the road towards the villa of Michelangelo's father. Arrow-sharp cypresses on either side of the road pierced the sky and fell in long shadows across the cobbles in the afternoon sun. Fields of barley and maize rolled beyond the road, giving way to vineyards heavy with blue grapes ready for harvest. Beyond them stretched rows of olive trees that flashed silver as they were laced by a breeze. In the distance, a blast of red poppies seared a hill before disappearing into the blue dimness of valley. The colours became imprinted on Michelangelo's brain. This was Lodovico's land where, during the height of summer, Michelangelo and Bernardino loved to run and jump and climb the olive trees, then lie under the grey-green foliage in the shade. But now the late afternoon air chilled Michelangelo as a flock of swifts in a feeding frenzy, with rapid darting flight, flitted from tree to tree, their calls high and strident. Michelangelo was nervous despite Piero's reassuring hand on his shoulder.

At the door, Piero removed his cap and bowed to Lodovico di Buonarroti Simoni, the former podesta of Caprese and Chiusi which was not far from Florence in the Tuscan Hills. His had been a civic office, a former mayor. He liked being bowed to but he gave Piero a curt nod. Michelangelo hung back, his view of Lodovico blocked by the bulk of the stone mason. Bernardino stood quietly beside him.

'You brought him back. I wondered where he was. I should have known he would have run to you.' Lodovico made no effort to curb the impatience in his voice as he showed the three into the house. 'He has been disobedient. I told him not to draw anymore and he deliberately disobeyed me.'

'His drawings are very good, Signore Buonarroti,' Piero said, as he stood cap in hand. 'He is talented and carves well — animals and people. He's only a child and yet he can do this.' Piero drew out of his pocket some figurines including Bernardino's stone rabbit, holding them up so Lodovico could see them clearly in the light. 'These have been carved in the soft sandstone found here in your Settignano quarries,' Piero said.

Lodovico nodded impatiently, 'I know the stone. It's macigno.'

Piero nodded. 'When he visited us some time ago, he gave these to Bernardino, and look at the detail, how well he captures the fur of the rabbit, how crisp the carving is. This is the work of a child, yet how fine it is. Polished to perfection.'

Michelangelo watched as his father took the rabbit in the palm of his hand. The carving seemed alive, the face, ears and nose of the rabbit were almost twitching. Lodovico turned it around, looking at it intently.

'Imagine what he could achieve if he received the right tutelage?' Piero continued.

Lodovico took Piero aside so the boys could not hear him.

Michelangelo's brothers Lionardo and Sigismondo stood behind their father. They had witnessed the beating and Sigismondo cried at the violence; he was too young to understand what was happening. Michelangelo disliked Sigismondo and found the now three-year-old simple-minded and demanding of his father.

The men's voices were quiet but Michelangelo could hear what was being said.

'There's a reason I don't encourage him in drawing. I don't want him to be an artist. It is below our station in society. Art doesn't pay well unless you are very successful and it's not an honourable profession. You know what is said about artists, they love boys, not women. Look at Leonardo da Vinci; he cultivates young men and uses them as he pleases. He doesn't hide it. He has no shame. Florence is rampant with sodomites. I don't want my son to be part of that.'

'I can understand your anxiety, Signore, but if you take charge of your son's schooling and he is guided by you and living with you, then surely there will be no harm done, and his talent will flourish. To have such ability go to waste is a sin.'

Lodovico remained silent.

'My own father,' continued Piero, 'didn't have enough money to give me a career. I ended up as a quarry worker, carving out stone and marble for sculptors when I would much rather be a sculptor.'

'Are you sure it was not you who carved those figurines?' Lodovico narrowed his eyes suspiciously and looked hard at the stonemason.

'No, Signore, they are your son's work.'

'But you taught him?'

'A little. How to handle a mallet and chisel, types of marble. All I know.'

Lodovico's eyebrows formed a straight black line across his forehead. 'We are returning to Florence soon,' he said, half turned away from Piero as if in dismissal. 'There the boys will have adequate schooling, and religious instruction and this nonsense in Michelangelo's head will disappear. But I shall decide when we are there whether he has tuition in the arts.'

Piero bowed to Lodovico and patted Michelangelo on the shoulder as he and Bernardino were shown out of the house. After closing the door on the visitors, Lodovico sternly ordered Michelangelo to go to bed. 'No supper tonight!' he added.

Michelangelo obeyed, glad he had eaten at the Basso's. He was looking forward to returning and living permanently in Florence. It was full of art, churches and buildings. There was bound to be someone there who would teach him to draw, sculpt and paint. If only he could convince his father.

THREE
Florence, 1487

Florence enchanted Michelangelo. Lodovico occasionally took the older boys into the city when he had business to attend to. The time spent there was never long enough. When Lodovico had finished for the day, they would climb into the family carriage and set off home, to Michelangelo's dismay. One day, he persuaded his father to include Bernardino on their journey to Florence. His father hesitated because Bernardino was deformed and he did not want to be associated with such abnormality. Michelangelo finally persuaded his father and Bernardino happily joined Lodovico and the boys.

As the day went by, Michelangelo wondered if he had done the right thing. Bernardino kept up with him and his brothers but Michelangelo became aware of people staring. Some talked behind their hands, some pointed and some laughed, others blessed themselves. Michelangelo glanced at Bernardino; he was aware and, perhaps, hurt but he didn't seem to notice as he trotted happily alongside Michelangelo.

They had spent the day looking at everything around them – the ochre colours of the crowded buildings and the uneven roof lines of terracotta tiles within the city walls. The sight of the Duomo, Brunelleschi's Dome, the Campanile and the carved doors of the Baptistry took Michelangelo's breath away. Lodovico had to grab him by the arm and pull him away. As far as Michelangelo was concerned, Florence was paradise.

Wide-eyed, the boys watched the rush and bustle, noise and colour of people in the streets and in the piazzas. The smells coming from flower stalls, food cooking in shops and stalls and the heavy odour of horse dung. The people paraded in a tumult of colour. Merchants, officials and clergy, noble men and women dressed in shiny, smooth silks and plush velvet; the women with tall headdresses, the men with soft hats, cloaks and caps. Everything looked prosperous.

'People are rich here, Papa,' said Michelangelo, impressed by the milling crowds.

'That's because of the wise governing of Florence by Lorenzo de Medici, Il Magnifico,' answered Lodovico.

'Is he a prince, Papa?' Michelangelo asked.

'No, not a prince by birth, but he is a princely figure,' answered Lodovico. Michelangelo wondered if the magnificent man would be his sponsor but said nothing to Lodovico.

'Where does he live, Papa?'

'He lives in the Palazzo Medici.' Lodovico pointed across the road towards the fortress-like façade of the building facing the street.

Michelangelo studied it carefully. Perhaps one day he would visit the palazzo.

His eyes weren't wide enough to take in everything around him. As they passed tall buildings, Michelangelo glimpsed the sluggish Arno running through and dividing the city.

Michelangelo wanted to explore the churches with their art, to walk amongst the crowds of people in the Piazza della Signoria and gaze at the Palazzo Vecchio, Florence's town hall. He longed to run down the narrow cobble-laid streets, narrow lanes and tight alleys, past merchants' and nobles' houses, civic buildings and churches but his father, as usual, was in a hurry. Lodovico impatiently and frequently turned and called to the boys to hurry up as they dawdled behind.

To Michelangelo, the city buzzed with a life of its own. He noticed the play of light off the buildings and the dark shadows between, where light never seemed to penetrate, yet the air, to him, shimmered like gold in the light, brimming with promise. His promise. His excited heart tumbled within him. This was where he wanted to be.

Bernardino followed Michelangelo, listening to every word as

Michelangelo explained and pointed things out to him. Exhausted, both boys fell asleep on the way home. Michelangelo felt he had done the right thing in asking Bernardino along. He may be short, but he had an inquisitive brain and an artistic soul. And Michelangelo was grateful for his adoring company. Perhaps Florence did that to people.

~

Shifting to Florence was no hardship for Michelangelo. To his delight, the Buonarroti house on the Via dei Bentaccordi was not far from the gothic Santa Croce Church. On his own, Michelangelo entered the church and his eyes widened with delight at being in the presence of great art works. The church seemed to stretch before him forever and soar to the heavens above his head, making him dizzy. Santo Croce was crowded with tombs, chapels and statues. He saw Donatello's wooden crucifix and closely studied the interior frescoes painted by great painters, Giotto and Gaddi and the domed Pazzi Chapel by Brunelleschi. Once again Lodovico had to drag him out of the church but any opportunity and Michelangelo was back inside copying and studying. He knew his father would not be pleased. He sat cross-legged before Giotto's paintings and quickly copied them. Absorbed, he did not hear the rapid footfall of his father until the man was upon him.

'Out. Home. Now,' Lodovico hissed, pointing towards the entrance of the church.

Michelangelo didn't argue as he gathered his chalk and papers and clambered to his feet. He had been warned. He knew what was coming. He ran ahead of his father down the nave of the church and out the door, his father close behind.

After a silent family supper and evening prayers with Lucrezia, the boy's stepmother, the boys were sent to bed.

Buonarroto, Michelangelo's favourite brother, and Lionardo lay beside him on the bed.

'Why is Papa so against you drawing, Michelangelo?' asked Buonarroto, looking at Michelangelo staring through the rooftop window at the sky above his head.

'You're not going to stop, are you?' said Lionardo.

'Papa's beatings haven't stopped me before,' Michelangelo said, feeling soreness on his back from the latest beating.

'But why do you keep doing it?' asked Buonarroto.

'Papa wants me to be a Florentine dignitary, not an artist. I could never do that, it's too boring. He's really scared I won't get married and have children. I can't help it. I want to draw everything I see,' answered Michelangelo. 'Will you get Auntie Mona's salve out of my drawer and put it on my back?'

Buonarroto climbed over Michelangelo and out of bed. He found the pottle in the drawer and came back to Michelangelo. 'Turn over,' he said. Michelangelo did. 'Your back looks awful.' Buonarroto took a scoop with his finger and smoothed it over the painful weals. 'But how can you get married and be a papa? You're just a child yourself.'

'Not now, later, when I'm grown up.'

'Go to sleep, you two, or I'll call Papa in here,' threatened Lionardo.

Michelangelo and Buonarroto kept quiet until Lionardo went to sleep. Michelangelo wondered how he could get around the problem of his father's intolerance. He needed to find a tutor who would teach him art. There must be someone in Florence who would persuade his father that his talent must be nurtured. He lay on his bed and looked up through the window at the clear Florentine sky. The stars were bright and close enough to touch.

'One day I will be up amongst the stars, and Papa won't be able to touch me,' thought Michelangelo. He fell asleep.

PART TWO
1510–1534

THE MEETING

FOUR
Rome, 1510

Bernardino remembered the stars. Michelangelo had told him about the stars on the ceiling of the Sistine Chapel and he wanted to see them. On a winter's day, Bernardino arrived in Rome to seek out his friend, the famed sculptor Michelangelo. The Roman sky was a brilliant blue, and the icy air smelt fresh and stung his nostrils. The city was full of noise, horses neighing, the clip-clop of their shoes on the cobbles, the cries of hawkers, shouts, laughter and chatter. Bernardino clutched his knapsack and trudged through the crowded streets, grateful for the warmth of his cloak around him. He was conscious of his size even more than he'd been in Florence. He seemed to be surrounded by a world of knees, hosed legs and long skirts. The bodies of people stretched into the bright sky above him. He was light on his feet and dodged and darted, accompanied by the startled swearing of passers-by.

Rome was not new to him; he had been before when Lodovico and Buonarroti had visited Michelangelo in Rome. They had taken him along at Michelangelo's request, much to his delight. He found the city crammed within its ancient Aurelian walls, full of new buildings erected out of the ancient Roman rubble. The Colosseum stood near the Imperial Forum, its arches home to a variety of vagrants, and the Forum stood proudly nearby with its arches and columns, the surrounding area full of toppled stone. Trajan's Market was noisy and bustling, and Bernardino noticed the people weren't as grand as in Florence; there seemed to be many beggars around. Life and important buildings appeared centred around the ancient basilica of St Peter and the accompanying Papal Palace. It was built over the area where Peter had been crucified, not like his Lord and leader, but upside down on the cross, as he deemed himself not worthy enough to be crucified in the same manner as Christ. Through it all, ran the Tiber, sometimes clear and clean after recent rain and other times stinking and cloudy with filth and garbage.

It wasn't that long since he had seen Michelangelo in Florence and the artist had told him if he ever needed help to come to him in Rome. Bernardino had heard Michelangelo had left Florence in a tearful fury because Pope Julius had ordered him to stop working on the tomb he had commissioned for himself. Julius stopped supplying him with money then ordered him to come to Rome to paint the ceiling of the Sistine Chapel. Bernardino had received a long letter from Michelangelo in Rome complaining about his treatment by the Pope. He also told him that Julius was supplying the architect, Bramante, with money so he could start rebuilding the new St Peter's. To someone he could confide in, Michelangelo's fury knew no bounds. He wrote:

I'm a sculptor, not a painter. It was Donato Bramante's idea
for me to paint the chapel. He knew I wouldn't want to do it.
He and Raphael are jealous of my work and my sculptures and
they know I'm supposed to be working on the Julius tomb. Now
I'm taken away from it. Frustration!

Michelangelo had been in Rome for some time and Bernardino wondered if he would still be furious. Knowing Michelangelo as he did – yes, most probably he would be. At last, he found the Piazza Rusticucci not far from the Vatican. The piazza was a cramped square space in the midst of rows of houses and shops.

Bernardino knew where Michelangelo lived and worked. He skirted the piazza and walked behind the church, Santa Caterina delle Cavallerote, to Michelangelo's house and workshop which was in a narrow street close to the great overhang of the Vatican's wall. Relieved to be there, he knocked on the door only to be told by one of the boy apprentices that the Master was at St Peter's in the Sistine Chapel, producing the most ambitious painting in Rome.

Gritting his teeth to cope with yet more walking over rough cobblestones, Bernardino made his way back to the crowded piazza in front of St Peter's Basilica. The Vatican Palace and the Basilica appeared to be a jumble of medieval buildings in the process of being demolished and rebuilt. The whole edifice was surrounded by building materials scattered over the surrounding streets.

Carpenters and stonemasons crawled over the building site, creating a cacophony of shouts, banging, tapping and sawing. Pope Julius was determined that his tomb, the one Michelangelo had designed and started to sculpt, needed a new basilica to house it. The old basilica was in a state of disrepair and could not house Michelangelo's construction. The Master had written to Bernardino that his current work was thirty-four feet wide and fifty-feet high, with forty-five life-sized statues. Bernardino realised that, despite Michelangelo's unhappiness at leaving the tomb commission behind, he was part of St Peter's historic renewal.

The guard at the door to the Apostolic Palace did not seem pleased to see Bernardino who tried to persuade the guard that he was Michelangelo's greatest friend and brother, which to his chagrin was met with ridicule and disbelief. Red-faced and humiliated, he was rescued by a passing priest whom Bernardino recognised as the chaplain of the Florentine cathedral, Father Giovanfrancesco Fattucci, and one of Michelangelo's friends who frequented the house in Florence.

'He is, indeed, the artist's brother,' Father Fattucci said to the guard. 'It's not that long ago that I met him in Florence.'

How could Fattucci forget him? Sometimes Bernardino's distinctive appearance came in handy. The priest insisted the guard admit him. The guard was still unconvinced. Was this short, stocky person with the bowed legs and large head really a 'brother' of the great sculptor? Fattuci again assured the guard who Bernardino was.

By the shield of Florence emblazoned on his soutane the priest was of some importance and he couldn't be challenged. Eventually, the great door into the Apostolic Palace was opened but not before the guard blessed himself as he ushered the pair inside.

Bristling, Bernardino would have dearly loved to have kicked the guard in the shins, something he was good at and normally did if anyone riled him. However, if he did he would probably end up in the Vatican's dungeon or locked up in the Castel Sant'Angelo. Instead, he walked with the priest down the marble-floored corridors filled with frescoes on the walls, towards an anteroom dominated by large double doors. Bernardino could hear noises of workmen coming from rooms around him. Already there was a great spiral staircase within a tower in the Vatican Palace designed by Bramante, which Michelangelo had told him about. Pope Julius was cementing his legacy to the Church and to Rome. Once more a guard tried to stop him and added to Bernardino's discomfort, and again the priest was insistent. The guards relented, opened the large door and ushered him inside. He bowed with thanks to the priest who bowed in return then disappeared back down the corridor. Bernardino turned to find himself, for the first time, in the vast chapel usually reserved for the Pope and cardinals for their Mass and ceremonies.

The place was cavernous. Michelangelo had told him it had been built in the time of Francesco della Rovere, Pope Sixtus IV. As Bernardino looked up at the large vault, he searched for the traditional medieval painting featuring gold stars on a blue background which Michelangelo had described to him. To his dismay, it was covered with a layer of plaster. He liked the ceiling full of stars as he had seen in other churches and had wondered about the stars in this great vault. He was disappointed. He had imagined himself up amongst them, looking down upon the earth. But they had gone.

Scaffolding and ladders half-filled the large space, reaching high above him. He tipped his head further back and squinted into the dimness illuminated in places by the light of many candles and lamps. On platforms above him, Michelangelo's helpers mixed paints and fixed cartoons in sections to the ceiling that had already been covered in intonaco, ready for painting before the plaster completely dried.

Some Bernardino recognised, as Michelangelo preferred to employ men from Settignano because he trusted them more than others. Bernardino's old childhood friend and 'almost' brother would be up there, somewhere, with his assistants. He hoped Michelangelo would be pleased to see him.

The Master's reputation for wearing dishevelled clothes, having wild ways and a bad temper preceded him. Bernardino knew him of old. The ranting didn't scare him. Bernardino's mother taught him to look after himself, to be clean, to wash, to cook and eat the right foods. Michelangelo had not been blessed with the mother Bernardino had and, after leaving his father's home and living on his own, he had quickly lapsed into untidiness and squalor. He was too busy concentrating on his art to worry about niceties.

His head tipped back, Bernardino wondered what would be painted on the ceiling. The space was so vast, like the arc of heaven, that Michelangelo and the workers could only prepare and paint a small section at a time.

'Michelangelo.' Bernardino's voice reverberated back to him as he heaved his short frame up onto the first rung of one of the ladders attached to the scaffolding. He stayed there, clinging to the next rung, searching for Michelangelo somewhere up near the roof. He couldn't tell if his voice had reached the Master's ears high up in the vault so, calling as he went, he continued to climb, dragging himself up by his hands, his legs swinging with the effort. A bombastic roar, a sound he remembered from his days in Florence, echoed down the ladder. He stopped climbing and stared upwards towards the noise.

'Bernardino, what are you doing here? And how did you get past the guard? No one is allowed in here to see my painting. Even the Pope himself has to ask for permission.'

'The guard didn't believe me. He thought I was a work of the devil. My persistence scared him. He blessed himself,' Bernardino called back, still unable to see Michelangelo. The voice of the Master seemed to come from behind a layer of drapery. Bernardino recognised the rumbling laugh.

'He was most probably right, he should have kept you out,' came the voice from heaven.

Laughter echoed around the chapel as the others up above joined in.

Bernardino resumed climbing and reached the level close to where the Master's helpers were working. Michelangelo was up on the next level, paint splattered over his shirt, face, hair and apron. He towered over him at the top of the scaffold's ladder, looking down. It was very high up, and Bernardino wondered how he was going to get down.

'You have broken into my work time. Go. You are not to come here. No one is to come here. Why are you here?'

'Mama has died. I can't work as a stone-mason, as you know, and my brothers sent me to Rome to see if I could be of use to you.'

Michelangelo growled under his breath and shouted down. 'Mama? Your mother, dead? The one who fed me with her milk, held me close as a boy, dead? God rest her soul.' Suddenly sobered, he made the sign of the cross.

'Yes, one month ago.' Bernardino also blessed himself, his eyes filling with tears. He wondered if this feeling of hurt and loss would ever leave him. She was the only one who'd treasured him, calling him her precious little one. He knew she'd treasured Michelangelo too, and when Michelangelo went to Settignano, he always visited her.

There was silence from the ceiling. Then Michelangelo's voice echoed down again.

'Your brothers are about as useless as mine. Well, you certainly can't draw, paint, or sculpt, I know that. What else can you do?'

'I can cook, Michelangelo.'

'What? Standing on a chair?'

More laughter. The sound echoed, annoying Bernardino. The whole of the Sistine Chapel and the workers need not know about his lack of height.

'If necessary,' Bernardino replied. Michelangelo could hurt when he wanted to.

'God in heaven. As if I haven't got enough to worry about, now there's you, falling from the chair into the fire and killing yourself.'

Bernardino saw the helpers stopping their work to turn and stare at him. Smirking grins stretched the paintwork on their faces, making them look like clowns in the marketplace. Bernardino cringed, despite being used to ridicule throughout his life. The sharp sting he once felt at rejection was now a dull ache, often exacerbated by an amused, mocking glance, a thoughtless comment, or someone pointing and sniggering. He would have to endure ridicule until the day he died.

'Go back to the house and wait for me. I will talk to you then.'

Michelangelo turned away in dismissal and disappeared under drapery out of sight. Bernardino looked down at the floor nearly sixty feet below, and his stomach turned at the thought of climbing back down there. The climb up had been difficult, now going down seemed an impossibility with his short legs. He would be swinging on every rung. He needed a pole to shimmy down but there were no poles in sight.

One of the assistants came over, looked at Bernardino askance and blessed himself with the sign of the cross.

'Come, I will lower you down in the basket we keep for hauling supplies,' he laughed.

Bernardino frowned; he hardly looked like a 'supply'. The helper, someone unfamiliar, not from Settignano, smelt of oil paint, stale sweat and plaster as he bent and lifted Bernardino off his feet.

'We didn't know the Master knew anyone like you,' he said, putting Bernardino into the basket. 'He usually demands physical perfection in his associates.'

'Really? You're not so perfect,' Bernardino looked at his helper up and down as he bristled with silent anger and heat flooded his face. 'People usually keep their friendship with me hidden, ashamed to reveal to others that they could be friendly with such an insignificant person, such as myself, but Michelangelo has always been my friend.'

The helper shrugged and swung the basket over the side. 'Hold on,' he instructed.

Bernardino closed his eyes and clutched the roughly hewn cane, feeling a jerk as the basket was released. For what seemed an endless time, the basket descended to the marble floor below. Only when it touched solidity did he open his eyes.

'Show me, Bernardino.' Michelangelo's voice echoed above him. 'Show me that you can look after me, my house and my apprentices.'

Bernardino tipped the basket and rolled out. He looked up towards the ceiling. Michelangelo was up there somewhere but Bernardino couldn't see him for platforms, dancing candlelight, scaffolding, draperies and ladders. It could have been the voice of God Himself coming from the firmament.

'Show me what you can do,' boomed the voice again.

FIVE
Rome, 1532

Bernardino looked up. Michelangelo Buonarotti Simoni, Count of Palatine, stood in the doorway. His silhouette blocked out the Roman sun and surrounded him with a golden aura.

'Master, did you enjoy your ride in the country?'

'I did, Bernardino. It's invigorating. I love riding,' the Master said as he removed his riding cloak and gave it to Bernardino.

The sound of the horses's hooves clattered in the entrance as one of Michelangelo's apprentices led the Master's horse to the stables behind the house.

'Come, sit down,' Bernardino said, pulling up a chair. 'Let me help you remove your boots.'

Michelangelo nodded. 'Sometimes… I need time to myself to think, relax, distance myself from work, create new ideas, banish all my troubles, get my affairs in order in my thoughts and decide what I want to do next,' he said, lowering himself into the chair.

Bernardino nodded. Michelangelo had loved riding since boyhood. Today the Master's eyes held a faraway look, his cheeks flushed, his expression open.

'Are you happy to be back in Rome, Master?' Bernardino was slightly puzzled. 'You normally don't like being here.'

'Rome is Rome. Untidy, dirty, full of ruins and beggars. And yet for all that, it is sublime. The lovely wide straight roads, the carefully designed and executed buildings in the newer part of the city. The architect, Peruzzi, has outdone himself. There is so much here. So much past, so much future. This time, to me, it is ravishing, captivating, riveting, and inspiring.'

Bernardino raised his eyebrows at such praise. Usually, Michelangelo couldn't wait to leave Rome and travel back to Florence. He was gazing at Bernardino from beneath a shelf of overhanging brow, and Bernardino knew he wasn't the reason for such a soulful look. The Master's voice had shaken with some hidden emotion, and Michelangelo didn't usually fight his feelings. If he was displeased, the entire house knew it; if anything worried him, they knew that too; if he was angry, sad or depressed, his face would convulse even more than it already was. Michelangelo raged whenever he wanted to, laughed – though not very often – and groaned and moaned and shouted. He even cried readily but then it was fashionable for an artist to be melancholy and it suited his face. Occasionally, annoyed about some misdemeanour, Michelangelo would kick Bernardino out of the room, making sure it wasn't the kitchen since Bernardino cooked his meals. Once he had even kicked him out of the house when he was in one of his moods. When Bernardino returned Michelangelo always had him back, relieved to see him. Bernardino liked to think so, anyway.

Michelangelo's chair scraped on the marble tiles as Bernardino bent on one knee, grasped the leather of one of Michelangelo's riding boots and pulled with all his weight. The boot came off with a rush. Bernardino, balancing on his short legs, was ready and staggered back, clutching the boot. The second boot was even harder and Bernardino ended up on the floor.

He squinted up at the man's craggy face, illuminated by the light of the dying day shining through the high windows in the hallway. Bernardino could remember that face before its even features had been squashed by a ferocious blow from a fellow artist apprenticed in Lorenzo de Medici's court. Now, his brow bulged and his eyes were deep set behind the flattened nose. Very rarely was his expression relaxed and glowing with happiness as it was now.

Bernardino pushed the boots aside.

'Rome is never sublime, Master,' Bernardino shook his head. 'The streets are rough and dangerous. They stink of urine, the ruins are overgrown with weeds. The older buildings are slung together like drunkards holding each other up. The people's speech is lewd, and they'd rob the eyes from out of your head. They certainly don't respect the teachings of the church. Mind you, the church's hierarchy leaves much to be desired. How can you say this place is wonderful when I know, and you know, that most of the time you're glad to be out of it and back in Florence?'

Michelangelo leaned towards his friend. 'Not all of Rome is like that, Dino. Parts of it are fine indeed. Peruzzi has done a good job rebuilding after the Sack destroyed many fine buildings and houses. Rome was certainly a sad place then. You remember how it was when we returned.' Michelangelo shook his head. 'No, Florence holds no sway over me now. That irascible Duke Allesandro de Medici hates me. You know I had to go into hiding in Florence to get away from him. I'm sure if I stay there for much longer he'll have me killed.'

Bernardino shifted on the floor at the Master's feet. 'I heard a rumour in the marketplace that Allesandro is the illegitimate son of Pope Clement.'

'Perhaps. Or of Pope Clement's uncle, Lorenzo. Such rumours abound easily. Look what's said about me!' he said heatedly. 'It's a relief to be out of Florence. I have to return there to finalise details of Pope Julius's tomb then I think we will leave for good. As much as I love Florence, I want to leave and come back to Rome.'

'This decision is sudden, Master,' Bernardino said, not entirely surprised.

Michelangelo often sprang things upon his household.

'No,' Michelangelo's eyes, set deeply under his heavy brow, were brooding as they looked down upon Bernardino. 'I have been thinking about it for some time but there's someone who has helped me make up my mind. I have met my beginning and my end. I have met the epitome of beauty. I have met the meaning for my existence. It is in Rome. *He* is in Rome.'

Another young man thought Bernardino, keeping his face

impassive. He might have guessed. The Master was being poetic again. His poetry was good, almost as good as his sculpture and painting. When he wasn't busy doing those, he was writing poems in his leather-bound notebook. The one he tied with leather ties in a tight knot, the cover stained with paint and marble dust. However, Bernardino was startled. To claim he had met his meaning in life was astonishing. Surely, his art was that meaning? His sculptures, frescoes and paintings? Yet Bernardino knew Michelangelo had another love, the love of beauty, especially that of young men and now there must be another perfect youth. Michelangelo often exaggerated but that was who he was – his whole life was an exaggeration expressed in his art.

Definitely another youth, Bernardino thought with a smile.

'I shall bring you something to eat in your salon, but first I will wash your feet.'

A short time later, in an adjoining room off the salon, Bernardino knelt at his feet as Michelangelo placed one foot at a time into the bowl, and Bernardino bent to his task, scrubbing firmly. Michelangelo sighed and closed his eyes as Bernardino kneaded the flesh of his foot, the heel, instep and toes. Embedded dust and dirt slipped away and the feet revealed themselves. They were long, slim, sinewy and strong, much like the man himself. The floor was cold under Michelangelo's feet as Bernardino wiped them dry and placed each foot in soft house shoes. Even the Pope would not have had better treatment.

Michelangelo shivered. 'These floors are freezing in the winter. We are not as clever as the old Romans, Bernardino,' commented the Master. 'They knew how to heat their houses by running hot water in channels through the stone floor.'

'Perhaps that's what the old Roman furnace in the garden was for.'

'Probably, and the channels are more than likely under the earth and beneath the house, and it would be impossible to dig them out now.'

Bernardino wondered at the word impossible. It was one Michelangelo rarely used. The usual sigh came with a word of thanks as Bernardino climbed to his feet and lifted the basin of water.

'Why so tired today, Master?'

'I didn't sleep well. My mind was reeling with excitement! My friend Bartolemeo knows Tommaso de Cavalieri's family. I'm going to write to Tommaso and Bartolomeo will deliver the letter for me. I know of the name of Cavalieri from Florence too. I think Tommaso's grandfather was a banker there, though the family has Roman roots.'

'Where does Tommaso live, Master?'

'On the Capitoline Hill.' Michelangelo bent down to Bernardino. 'No one must know about this,' he instructed in a low voice.

'Of course, Master. No one will know.'

The craggy face softened into a relieved expression as Bernardino put a stool under Michelangelo's feet and carried the basin and clothes out of the hallway and into the utility room behind the kitchen. Before he reached the door, he turned and looked at the man in the chair – Michelangelo the greatest sculptor in Christendom, his chin resting on his chest, was snoring softly.

~

Bernardino laid a cloth on a table in the dining salon in front of the open windows. Michelangelo appeared in the doorway rubbing his eyes from sleep. The reflection of rays from the low sun, muted by the grimy glass of the lead-lined window, cast a yellow glow over the cloth. Bernardino placed dishes of fruit, olives, salted meat, cheese and bread on the table before Michelangelo, then ladled broth into a bowl. At least Bernardino could make sure he was eating well despite the Master's protests that he did not need much food. The truth was that if left to himself, Michelangelo would hardly eat at all. He was the same with sleeping, working until late at night in his workroom on some project, then falling exhausted into bed, sometimes fully clothed, boots and all. Bernardino knew he didn't wash regularly because his Master's clothes stank with stale sweat and plaster and it was his task to wash them.

The workshop in the back part of the house reverberated with hammering and tapping of mallet and chisel, along with the murmurings of the apprentices. There were four of them today, including Michelangelo's favourite, Febo. This cramped house in the Piazza Rusticucci was temporary, while Michelangelo's usual residence in the Macello dei Corvi was being repaired after being damaged during the Sack of Rome. Michelangelo looked forward to when they could return to the big house, given to him by Cardinal Aginensis of the de Rovere family, not far from the old Forum and Colosseum of imperial Rome. The cardinal had given him use of the house as a favour, to give him room and comfort while he completed the tomb of his uncle, Julius II. The cardinal had since died but the de Rovere family allowed Michelangelo to stay on.

The last time Michelangelo had lived at the great house, as Michelangelo called it, he and Bernardino had heard rumours of the strained relationship between Pope Clement and Charles V of Spain. They sensed trouble coming and had locked the house and fled to Florence. Later, upon their return, they found Rome destroyed by Spanish troops. Even the Vatican had been attacked. Pope Clement, fearful for his life, had taken refuge in the Pope's castle, the Castel Sant'Angelo. The devastated streets were littered with rubble, the houses torched, and broken into. The house on Macello dei Corvi had not come through unscathed. Sword marks and fire stains covered the outer façade and the interior had been ransacked. The doors and shutters over the windows had been broken open, and the usually light and airy vestibule was full of dumped, broken furniture, dirt and broken glass. Floors and walls were covered in pigeon droppings, furniture had gone, windows were broken, frescoes on the walls had been damaged.

At least it hadn't been burnt to the ground as a few surrounding houses had. They both loved the house, Michelangelo especially, with its large workshop and garden. The de Rovere family had promised to repair it for him and Michelangelo would soon be able to move back in.

'Has everything been alright in the workshop?' Michelangelo always asked this after coming back from riding.

'Yes, though I'm not sure how much work has been done.'

Bernardino poured the wine, the Master's favourite, Trebbiano.

'Join me, Bernardino. Have some wine.'

Another surprise. The Master never liked eating or drinking with his servants, although Bernardino was almost a brother to him. Bernardino didn't hesitate, he lifted the carafe and poured the rich red liquid into a second cup, waited until the Master drank his and quickly swallowed it, feeling the warmth fill him. He had not eaten yet.

Bernardino sat on the stool beside Michelangelo and waited. The Master would tell him, because he was the only one Michelangelo confided in, apart from one or two friends in Florence and Rome.

'I have met my life,' Michelangelo quietly admitted, half to himself, half to Bernardino.

If he asked any questions, the Master would withdraw into himself and never reveal what was on his mind, so Bernardino remained silent and waited.

The setting sun cast long shadows over the piazza and onto the ochre stone facade of the house, dimming the rooms facing the street. Outside horses' hooves clattered over cobbles and voices called to one another. The crack of the driver's whip echoed past the house, accompanied by the rumble and creek of cartwheels. Bernardino climbed on the chair near the windows to shut them. The apprentices would be finishing in the workshop soon and tumbling into the kitchen, looking for food. He had to cook for them too.

'He is beautiful to behold,' Michelangelo said.

How old? Bernardino wanted to say. He stayed quiet. The rest would come.

'He's twenty-two and perfect, a young nobleman. He's what I have been waiting for all my life.'

Bernardino sighed. Again?

'I have seen the young man,' he commented congenially, knowing what would please Michelangelo. 'He is indeed very handsome, the talk of Rome with his good looks and aristocratic manners. Very gracious.' Then he cautioned, 'Master, you must be careful. Your love of beauty inspires your art. You bury your desire and burial is transferred and released in your work. Many do not understand that. Already the rumours fly that your youths please you in ways undesirable and that the practice of art is not the only thing you teach them.'

Bernardino had been a witness. Both he and Michelangelo pretended he knew nothing. He never told anyone what went on in Michelangelo's private life. There were enough rumours flying around about him anyway.

'Ah, Bernardino. Always with my welfare at heart. Thank you for your concern but it's unnecessary. There's nothing to fear. I abstain from sexual intercourse as much as possible. For me, sometimes the beauty and desire become too much and then I confess to my dear friend, Father Fattucci, and try to start afresh. Sex can weaken and enslave a man. I have been warned about it. So, I don't indulge. We are only human, aren't we, Bernardino?' Michelangelo leaned down and patted Bernardino on the shoulder.

'Some say you are divine, Master.' Bernardino smiled up at him.

Michelangelo smiled back. 'Well, that's better than saying the opposite, as so many do.'

His voice trailed away and Bernardino knew he was thinking of Febo, his present favourite apprentice.

'As soon as I can I will finish my business in Florence, shut down the workshop and leave for good. Rome, this blessed city, calls me even more now and Florence is a sad and sorry place with Allesandro de Medici's new regime.'

'Some say it's better,' Bernardino said, thinking about the gossip he'd heard in the market.

'Perhaps. I doubt it. I must finish Pope Julius's tomb, I have already been paid to do so. It worries me. It's a dilemma. Pope Clement demands my attention to finish the library in Florence and I have to complete the statues for the Medici tomb too. There is much to do. I will shut down the workshop there and transport the figures for the tomb to Rome to work on them here. Somehow, I must satisfy Pope Julius's relatives who are as conceited as he was and want him remembered.

I yearn to be in Rome, to be near Tommaso. That's necessary for my art. He's my inspiration, my joy,' Michelangelo murmured. Then, as if he'd suddenly remembered, he leant forward and looked down at Bernardino. 'You will be with me, of course?'

What if I don't want to move permanently to Rome? thought Bernardino, nodding automatically.

Michelangelo reached across and took the servant's hand. 'I can't do without you.'

'Yes, Michelangelo, of course.'

Bernardino was the only one who would do everything for Michelangelo and had done so for years. However, Michelangelo sometimes did not know he existed, ignoring his presence completely as he came home at all hours of the day and night to find food waiting for him, with warm water and fresh towels laid out so he could wash. There was never a word said and sometimes the meal remained untouched and the water unused. Bernardino just shrugged. He was used to Michelangelo's strange ways. Bernardino put up with his tempers and frustrations, washed his linen, made his bed, emptied his chamber-pot, ran messages and delivered letters, poems and sketches and put him to bed when he'd drunk too much wine. Always discreet, he shopped in the market, haggled with the market stall-keepers, supervised and fed the apprentices and serving girls, and ran the household. Bernardino also ignored the shouted insults of people regarding his size. They knew him, of course, knew that he was the confidante of the "Divine One", who, in their eyes and gossip, was far from divine. That was shouted about regularly too. Michelangelo, wrapped in his world of creativity, seemed oblivious to all going on around him. The Master couldn't do without Bernardino, especially with a new romance occurring.

'What about Febo? Will he stay with you in Rome?' Bernardino wondered how the spoiled apprentice would react when he found he'd been superseded by someone of noble blood. Febo de' Poggio, the street boy, was not noble. Even Michelangelo called him his 'little blackmailer'.

The Master's face collapsed inward further. Bernardino knew the signs: worry, distress and frustration over his complicated relationships which dissolved the expression on his face and highlighted the hills and valleys of his torment. It was never far from the surface.

Michelangelo shook his head.

Surprised, Bernardino kept his face straight. How was the Master going to get out of that one? Michelangelo had often extolled the virtues of the handsome young man who'd shared his bed for some time. The Master loved him and usually Febo brought a brightness to his eyes and a rare smile about his lips. Michelangelo had willingly put up with the incessant demands for money, clothes and anything else Febo wanted. His inspiration, Michelangelo called him. Now someone else inspired him.

As if summoned, the door to the dining room opened and Febo appeared. He glanced over to Michelangelo, leaning towards Bernardino, holding his hand. Michelangelo let his hand drop.

'Master, Rome? Are we going to stay in Rome?' Febo's face was flushed and scarred with red chalk, his fingers stained. Bernardino thought he looked much like the satyr that Michelangelo had drawn on the wall in his father's kitchen. Bernardino watched Febo wipe his hands carefully on a cloth attached to the bib of his apron. So, he'd been listening at the door; this did not surprise Bernardino. Febo had always stirred uncertainty in Bernardino's mind but then he, too, listened at doors. Sometimes it was the only way he knew what was going on.

'I do prefer Rome to Florence. There's so much going on here,' Febo said eagerly.

Bernardino stood and balanced on the tip of his toes to clear the dishes as Michelangelo pushed them towards him.

The Master held out his arms to Febo who immediately rushed to him, kissed him on the cheek and knelt beside him. 'Would you like that, Febo?' The Master benevolently stroked the curls on the young man's head.

Dishes in hand, Bernardino stopped at the doorway, marvelling at the softness in Michelangelo's voice. It was a rare occurrence and perhaps only Bernardino and one or two of the apprentices ever heard such tenderness. It was possible for the Master to love two boys at a time; he had done it before. This new love must be special. He wanted Febo out of the way.

Bernardino quietly closed the door behind him and made his way down the darkened hallway to the kitchen, his soft shoes squelching on the flagstones. He wasn't surprised by Febo's response. Rome's delights lured him as well. The Master wouldn't risk having two loves compete in the same place – not in Rome. It had happened before in Florence where sodomy was rampant despite being punishable, even with the death sentence. People gossiped but ignored it. Michelangelo's sexuality endangered him; he could be punished and abandoned by the religious hierarchy. There were laws in Rome against love between men, just as there were in Florence. Bernardino, forever watchful, made certain Michelangelo's activities were protected by himself and Michelangelo's sympathetic friends.

Michelangelo had been aware of the sexual activities in the Medici court but had assured Bernardino he had always kept himself apart from those involved. Rumours ran wild about the activities of Lorenzo and his friends. As far as Michelangelo was concerned, the meetings were full of friendship and knowledge. The strongly spirited preacher, Fra Girolamo Savonarola absolved Lorenzo regularly. Savonarola spent time and many fiery sermons protesting the state of morals in Florence, as well as the inadequacies of the Church and its clergy and Michelangelo had listened with interest. Rome was a different matter. Rome had many prelates with strong views on morality who looked down on the decadent Florentines, although there were also prelates who openly flaunted their sinful ways. The ecclesiastical society was corrupt and had been for some time. Too many Popes had produced bastard sons or conferred honours on eager brothers, nephews and sons who inherited ecclesiastical wealth along with office.

Europe was stirring with discontent and Michelangelo was aware that Friar Luther had started a movement to leave Rome's corruption.

His call was being taken up by the northern countries. In England, Henry the Eighth's wife, Queen Catherine, couldn't produce a male heir. He too had begun using Rome's corruption as an excuse to discard both Church and Queen. Perhaps it was time for a change in the Church.

The present Pope Clement VII, nephew of Lorenzo de' Medici, was largely an exception to corruption and Michelangelo admired him. Michelangelo remembered their youth together in the Medici court. Guilio, as he was known then, had become his friend.

The lamps and candles in the kitchen flickered when Bernardino entered the kitchen, then guttered as the door from the back of the house burst open in a rush as the apprentices tumbled one after the other into the room, vying for places at a table already set for them.

'Is it true the Master's going to stay in Rome?' one asked.

'There is much to be done in Florence first, so we have to go back there. Really, I don't know. Now, you know the rules about mealtimes. You don't get anything to eat until you have washed and tidied yourselves up,' Bernardino said, re-lighting snuffed candles with a taper from the kitchen hob.

They grumbled but knew Bernardino always enforced Michelangelo's orders. The kitchen grew quiet again as the young men disappeared through the hallway door and ran to an outside back room to wash. The water and soap would be ready for them and clean towels to dry themselves; Bernardino made sure of that.

He looked around the warm kitchen and set Michelangelo's dishes aside. The maid Vincenza would wash those later.

Although Bernardino liked Rome, he preferred Florence and the surrounding Tuscan hills where one could readily escape into the countryside. There, he and Michelangelo had enjoyed their early childhood.

Bernardino particularly remembered the stone rabbit Michelangelo had given him. He was conscious of the joy and envy it provoked because, as hard as he tried, he could not find the mysterious inner being locked in the smooth slab of stone. That had been a long time ago and the stone rabbit was back in the Basso's house in Settignano.

Michelangelo had done much and come far with his art since then. Bernardino was proud to be close to such a man, even if it meant living in Rome. And since the Sack, the city streets had improved and new buildings had arisen. Something about Rome had undoubtedly changed the Master. Or perhaps Michelangelo was really in love this time, not just a lover of beauty.

SIX
Rome, 1532

The Master woke and stared at the wood and plaster ceiling above his bed. The house was silent. What had woken him? Febo snored softly beside him, his long, slim frame stripped of the covers. In the bright moonlight slanting through the shutters, the laxity of sleep had softened Febo's features. Still youthful, he had a woman's beauty, and Michelangelo had often sketched his perfection in wonder. Febo's skin was smooth, his limbs muscular, and he had yet to be hardened by the toughness of life. It was the inner beauty of youth that Michelangelo found so alluring and inspiring. He strove to bring the beauty of youth out in his sketches, sculptures and paintings and he was never entirely satisfied he could capture the exquisite tenderness, the softness of the skin, the beauty in the boy's expression.

Febo had crept into his bed as many of the apprentices did at the end of the day. Michelangelo turned his back on most of them and fell asleep but Febo was different. He made no advances to Michelangelo. Instead he curled up and slept facing him, his head resting on his bent arm. Michelangelo had stretched out his hand and touched Febo's rounded shoulder. Febo had woken and snuggled into the Master's arms, stirring him. Michelangelo shut out the thought, threw back the covers and climbed out of bed. The boy hardly moved. Michelangelo would return to Florence again. It would be better if Febo was not in Florence, Rome or anywhere near him. He knew too much, demanded too much, and his beauty paled in comparison to what he'd recently encountered.

Michelangelo threw a gown over his shoulders against the cold of the room and, padding to a table in a corner alcove, lit an oil lamp and found pen and paper. There was only one young man he really wanted. He felt consumed by his passion and knew that unless it was controlled, it would cause problems. This young man was an aristocrat who could trace his family name through centuries, back to the Imperial days of Rome. Michelangelo needed Tommaso's love to inspire his creativity. He could not afford to frighten him away.

I, too, have noble blood, Michelangelo thought, or liked to think, although to look at him no one would know. Many years ago, his father's family had been noble but fallen on hard times. His mother's family, the Rucellai, had been a noble family.

'When I look in the mirror before me I see nothing but ugliness, Bernardino,' he'd said once, in a fit of desperation about his looks. 'That swine Torregiani marked me forever. Look at me. Grotesque, uneven, bashed, mutilated. Forever disfigured. Just because I taunted him, mocked his works. We were sketching in the Brancacci Chapel in Santa Maria del Carmine. His blow was so fast I had no time to duck. Hit the floor unconscious. I have been left with the legacy of it as he said I would. My looks frighten people away.'

Michelangelo's disfigurement had been so bad that when Bernardino first saw him after the attack, he'd walked right past, not recognising him.

Bernardino would soothe him. 'Your soul is noble, Lord, and your great mind is revealed in your art.'

'I was handsome once.'

'You are still handsome, Michelangelo.'

Michelangelo shook his head in disbelief. 'My face causes fright. How could any young man love me?' his voice was pained.

'He will see your soul, Master, as you see his.'

Michelangelo turned towards his old friend, his brother.

'Bernardino, where did you come from?'

'Settignano, Master.'

'There must have been something special in your mother's milk, Bernardino.'

'Yes, look at us. Just look at us.'

They had both smiled into the mirror on the wall before them and laughed.

SEVEN
Rome, 1532

I do not want you physically, Michelangelo thought, although he knew he was deceiving himself. His adoration was coupled with the physical need to express that desire. Yet, because it offended the Church, he could not willingly give into temptation. Tommaso was his link to the supernatural, to God. That had been taught to Michelangelo all those years ago in Florence by the finest scholars, implanting Plato's wisdom, which he put into practice as much as he could. To gaze upon such beauty was to gaze at the beneficence of God. Yet, he had to hold his passion within, somehow. Not touching, not caressing when he desperately wanted to. That sublimation inspired his creativity. If he expressed his desire openly, the young prince might flee and, the muse gone, Michelangelo would be bereft.

It was Tommaso's angelic face he wanted to capture, his perfect body to immortalise. The sculpture of *David* had arisen from his observation of the young bodies of the men who modelled for him, not to mention his own, but that had been many years ago when he too had been slim and well-formed. He had learnt about anatomy the hard way in the Santo Spirito Convent in Florence. The memory of those secretive, nauseating nights dissecting the dead to learn how the muscles worked had stayed with him. Those men had been dead, their tissues lax, yet he had appreciated their sacrifice, so he could learn about the musculature of the body. The knowledge gained had transferred into his sculpture of the perfect male, *David*.

Now Michelangelo was in his late fifties and had grown slim and grizzled. His body was splattered in paint, plaster, and every crevice filled with stone dust. His hands were still pliable, his fingertips sensitive, but only in the service of his art.

Oh, yes, Bernardino tended him as a brother should. He filled the bath with water warmed on the kitchen hob's hot charcoals but the opportunities for such luxuries were few and far between. There was barely time to paint, sculpt and tutor his apprentices to get them to a level where they could assist him. Yet, Tommaso looked so clean, his clothes fresh and perfumed. Michelangelo knew that to please the young man, to make him his muse, he himself had to be clean, not smell the way some of his apprentices said he did. They can talk, he thought. Some of them hadn't washed in the whole year they'd been with him, despite Bernardino's persistent threats. I must bathe. Bernardino will draw water from the well and heat it for me.

Michelangelo stared into the lamp's long, steady flame. He had heard reports of Tommaso and remembered seeing him once when out walking with Bernardino. His good looks were well known but it was not the only thing that attracted people to him; it was his courteous, gracious manner.

They met at a gathering of prelates and notables at the Palazzo Cavalieri.

Michelangelo had been invited to the palazzo and only the persistence of his friend Bartolemeo Angelini and the promise he would be there had persuaded Michelangelo to go. Social gatherings did not interest him. He feared a loss of energy and drive if he socialised too much; he felt too much interaction with people took something away from his creativity. However, this night he was glad of Bartolemeo's insistence. After being introduced to Tommaso and his father, Michelangelo felt he'd been struck by a blow. He stared at Tommaso, dazzled by his perfection and beauty. In an effort to calm himself, Michelangelo walked out onto the marble balcony adjoining the salon. The sun had set and the sky was ablaze with orange and yellow. He watched the shifting clouds – dull grey and purple against gold, above the ochre buildings of Rome. As the garden of the palazzo dissolved into shadows, he turned to look once again into the salon at the young man greeting each guest in turn.

Tommaso was tall and well built, his physique slim but solid. He was dressed in a dark-blue velvet cape over his doublet and breeches, which only enhanced his stature. Conscious of proportions, Michelangelo noticed Tommaso's head was well formed, his hair dark brown and curling to his shoulders. Not unlike many in the room, Michelangelo thought as he looked around. He turned to look again at Tommaso and his heart leapt anew. This man was special, the most perfect physical specimen he had seen, and that was with his clothes on! Michelangelo undressed him in his mind. The young man looked straight at him and Michelangelo felt his face heat up, wondering if Tommaso could read his thoughts. He bowed to him and Tommaso bowed back before he turned to greet more guests at his father's side.

Michelangelo's heart beat hard, his breathing grew rapid. To look at such beauty made him tremble; this young man would inspire him to even greater heights in his art. Michelangelo searched the growing crowd of people in the room for his friend Bartolomeo but didn't have to search far. His friend bustled up to him in greeting, took him by the arm and pulled him gently into the salon to mingle with the guests.

'I'm so pleased to see you here, Michelangelo. I know you don't like such occasions but the young Lord Cavalieri wanted to meet you. He hopes you will teach him how to draw and paint. He admires you greatly.'

Michelangelo looked at his friend with gratitude. 'Bring him around to see me, Bartolomeo. I am most taken with him.'

Bartolomeo placed his arm around Michelangelo's shoulders. 'I thought you would be, my dear friend. The young man is of noble blood and it's revealed in his physical stature and presence, wouldn't you say?'

'Yes, he is what I have been waiting for.' Such beauty, Michelangelo thought. If he is someone with talent or a lively mind, I am bound to fall in love with him, perhaps fall prey to him in such a manner that I am no longer my own.

Bartolomeo smiled knowingly. 'He's well-mannered and highly learned and knows much about your work and the arts. He's also educated in the ideals of Facino's Platonic thought. How exceptional, true, chaste love can exist between men. He knows you were educated at the court of the Medici under the tutelage of Masilio Facino and Pico della Mirandola. That has helped form you and from that has come your art. He knows and understands this. He's pure in his habits and thoughts and his sensitivities are heightened by the very ideals you hold dear. He thinks you are exceptional. I have known the family for years, and Tommaso from boyhood.'

'I can't help but look at him. He's perfect in every way,' Michelangelo sighed. 'His beauty is a divine gift.'

'That perfection will help you create even greater works of art, my dear friend. I look forward to seeing your next sculpture.' Bartolemeo bowed slightly.

'How does Ficino put it?' queried Michelangelo, his head on one side as he recalled Ficino's commentary that praised love between males. "The man enjoys looking at the beautiful youth; the youth enjoys the beautiful mind and soul of the man. It serves both because the youth, as he admires the man, becomes beautiful in soul, while the man, already beautiful in soul, only looks upon the beautiful youth."'

Bartolemeo, already versed in Ficino's philosophy, nodded gravely.

Michelangelo glanced around the room full of Roman nobility and clergy. 'I see Reginald Pole has returned to us from England.'

'Mmm.' Bartolemeo frowned, looking over at the slight young man dressed in clerical black, talking to some cardinals. Turning his back on the group in case Pole recognised he was being talked about, Bartolemeo said quietly, 'He wanted to get away from King Henry. The King offered him the Archbishopric of York or the Diocese of Winchester if Pole would support his divorce from Catherine of Aragon. Pole thought it better to leave. The times for the Church in England are grim under Henry's rule. He seems determined to marry the Boleyn woman. Some say they have already married secretly.'

Michelangelo studied Pole's fine, smooth-skinned features. The cleric carried himself like a prince, erect and autocratic looking. A handsome man, still youthful, and one he would like to sculpt.

'He is a cousin of the King and I have heard he has a claim to the English throne,' Michelangelo said.

Bartolemeo nodded. 'That's a problem for him. He could be regarded as a threat to Henry. He has even been touted as a future husband for Princess Mary, Henry's daughter by Queen Catherine. Pole regards Henry as the anti-Christ. There's talk amongst the English clerics of reform in the Church and his name has been mentioned as part of that,' muttered Bartolomeo.

Michelangelo caught the cleric's eye and nodded to him in recognition. Pole nodded back and approached them. As he drew near, Bartolemeo bowed and withdrew.

'My Lord,' Michelangelo bowed.

'You are well, I trust?' Pole asked in perfect Italian.

'Yes, well, thank you.'

'There are rumours you are safer in Rome than in Florence,' Pole said.

Michelangelo raised his eyebrows. 'I'm amazed you would have heard that.'

'Nothing much escapes the papal court. The city is confined and word travels fast, true or untrue,' replied Pole. 'I know that Pope Clement will be pleased to have you here in Rome. He's a great admirer of your work and always tells us of his young days with Lorenzo de Medici and, even then when you were just a youth, how good-looking and talented you were. Perhaps you could visit him? After all, you were both young together in the Medici court. I believe he may have another commission in mind for you.'

'I have done some work for Clement, and I have seen him many times, which has been my honour, but not lately. I still have much work to do on the tomb of Pope Julius.' Michelangelo was alarmed, thinking of the amount of work involved in sculpting the figures for the tomb and his unfinished work in the Medici Chapel and the Laurentian Library in Florence for Clement. He did not want any more commissions. 'I was disrupted from finishing the tomb when Pope Julius demanded I return to Rome to paint the ceiling in the Sistine Chapel. I must return to Florence to finish my business there and complete the statues for the tomb. I shall be away for two or three months. However, it would be good to see him again, as it is some time since I've had the honour. He was always a friend to me when I was at the Medici Court.'

'Well, then, there's the reason,' answered the cleric. 'When you do see him, don't be shocked at his appearance, he is unwell and burdened by his care of the Church. As you most probably know, the business in England with the Church under threat has distressed the Pope. As far as the Church is concerned there is no way around the problem in England. Many of the King's courtiers feel threatened by the changes and turn their support away from the King. By now, most probably, the great statesman and good man, Sir Thomas More, has resigned from his position as Lord High Chancellor. Being the cautious, learned man More is, he's refusing to speak on the matter of Ann Boleyn. He thinks keeping silent will make him safe, as does Bishop Fisher. He too stands with More and refuses to speak, frustrating the King. They are both influential, good men with strong reputations and they are in danger. The times are evil in England,' muttered Reginald Pope, shaking his head.

'I have heard of Thomas More and read his book *Utopia*.' Michelangelo mused thoughtfully, half to himself, half to Pole. 'Your own family is in England, my Lord?'

'For the moment they are safe, but they have to be very careful. They are deeply Catholic, especially my mother. I pray for them constantly.' Pole sighed unhappily.

The evening had passed quickly, despite Michelangelo's reluctance to mingle, and he was relieved to find most people came to him and engaged in conversation. Yet the whole time he spoke to Reginald Pole and other guests, he'd been aware of Tommaso standing not far from him talking to guests. Any spare moment, his eyes fixed on the young man as he mingled with guests. He was taller than Michelangelo, nearly six feet tall - although the heels on his shoes were not high. When

Michelangelo bowed his farewells to the guests and his hosts at the end of the evening, it was an effort for him to tear his eyes from the young man. Tommaso greeted him again with a smile and Michelangelo saw God in his smile. Michelangelo's face tingled with warmth and he couldn't stop the corners of his mouth rising. Smiling. Something he did not do often. He realised he was happy. He took Tommaso's hand on leaving and held it firmly within his own, relishing its warmth and strength. He broke the handshake reluctantly.

'If there's a time you wish to approach me, perhaps to teach you art, or just in friendship, please don't hesitate,' he said. Tommaso bowed, thanked him and smiled in return at him.

His heart beating fast, Michelangelo walked out into the night. The touch of Tommaso's hand had been enough to send his senses reeling and his skin blazing with desire. Rome's darkness fell softly upon him as he walked through the streets, hoping his racing thoughts would calm. Torch bearers held torches aloft and guided people in the darkness. Sure-footed, Michelangelo avoided them as he headed towards the basilica's piazza. He passed squatters lying in alleyways and doorways. Usually he would kick them out of his way or throw them a coin. But now he was hardly aware of them. All his senses were stimulated. The world had become an inspiring place.

~

I must write to him, Michelangelo thought later, sitting at the table in his bedchamber. Febo quietly snored in the bed nearby. The flame in the oil lamp flickered, casting long shadows into the darkened room. I must express my adoration; I have to try and hold onto him. How would I sculpt him? He closed his eyes against the brightness of the flame and imagined the contours of Tommaso's face beneath his fingers, the high-brow and long straight nose, the pronounced cheekbones and finely hewn jaw, the soft, brown, heavy-lidded eyes, his fine skin. Michelangelo's fingers traced Tommaso's profile in the air. He imagined running his fingers over the large closed eyes, long dark lashes, arched full brows, and upturn of his sweet firm lips. The slim length of his torso, broad shoulders, slim arms and long legs. He is divine. Michelangelo ached with desire.

He shook himself. I must write, he thought. He must not forget me.

My dear Lord,

You have come into my world and changed it forever. My thoughts are awhirl, my heart beating like one newly born, strange, vigorous, and excited at a glimpse of life. How can I ever be the same again, now I have looked upon your dear young face, astounded by your beauty? You are my muse, the one I have been searching for; never dreaming, always hoping, I would come across that which would influence my creations and satisfy my desires. You are that soul. You are the living embodiment of my desire. What I have dreamt about and looked for the whole of my life has presented itself before me in the presence of your youthful masculine beauty. I wish to behold you again, once more gaze on your perfection; to breathe in deeply and become enveloped in your perfume. Will you come to me? Will you tolerate the musings of someone much older than yourself but someone who can make you immortal through art? My heart is burnished with the desire to hold you, grasp you forever, keep you close to me. How can I live here and not be near you? My Lord, may I come to you? You are an extension of my mind, my arm, my fingertips; I will make you immortal.

Michelangelo looked up from his writing. He thought, I can't write that, he would laugh at me. He is not long out of boyhood.

He pushed the paper away. He would rewrite the letter in daylight then give it to Bernardino to deliver to Bartolomeo who would understand the necessity of urgency. Michelangelo would do some sketches and decide which ones to send to the young noble, something he would understand and appreciate, that would show him the meaning of the affectionate letter.

The youth in Michelangelo's bed stirred, his arms outspread on the pillow as if beginning a difficult climb. Febo, yes, Febo, Michelangelo thought. Young and handsome also. Febo knew too many of his secrets, but he would not know this one. Bernardino had already been warned to stay silent about Tommaso de Cavalieri.

Febo, as if sensing Michelangelo looking at him, turned on his side, his shirt riding up his body. Michelangelo smiled at the sight of the lax genitals. He reached for his pen and did a quick sketch. He would use the sketch later, in some painting or sculpture. He dropped the pen and his hand fell to his own lap where he felt the swelling grow beneath his touch. He moaned softly, his eyes on Febo, his thoughts on the young Cavalieri. How he longed for him. How could he control that longing?

Michelangelo withdrew his hand and sat up, staring into the darkness beyond the circle of light. There comes a point where you progress or withdraw, he thought. He knew if he gave in to such desire he would lose the sublime muse necessary for his art, his divine gift. Michelangelo's suppression of desire, through Tommaso, would fuel his artistic expression. First though, Tommaso had to be caught. But would the young man understand what Michelangelo wanted – a pure, chaste love? And did he really want that? No, but it had to be. Would Michelangelo be able to resist such beauty? His desire forever sublimated, simmering beneath the surface of his mind, manipulating his arm and hand to create? If he kept himself away from Tommaso, would he be able to create? If he gave into his desire and seduced him, would he be able to create? The questions tumbled through his mind. Somehow, he had to find a way to encourage the young man and his friendship and yet keep him himself apart so that Tommaso remained pure and unsullied, for that was part of the attraction. This nobleman had been pampered, protected and was innocent and virginal, everything Michelangelo desired in a youth. Michelangelo was walking on a narrow ledge, one slip and it could all be taken from him.

He banished Tommaso from his mind and felt his body relax. He put out the lamp and climbed into bed beside Febo, who stirred and put his arm over Michelangelo's chest, his leg resting on his Master's leg. Michelangelo fell asleep and dreamt of Tommaso.

My dearest Lord Tommaso,

My mistake was writing to you before you wrote to me. I thought a quick note might kindle our friendship sooner. However, I had no sooner started to write than I began to doubt my wisdom and I feared you might be angry at my impertinence hence the writing became harder. However, I had put my heart in my words so I decided to continue....

It was the letter's tenth draft. Was that enough or did the missive require further refinement? Michelangelo checked the drawings he had done for Tommaso. If the young man was educated as everyone said, he would quickly ascertain the meaning. Before he signed the letter, he added a postscript.

Usually I would title my drawings that I send to you, but out of respect I feel it is better that I don't.

A coded postscript, hopefully one Tommaso would understand. Michelangelo sat back in his chair. Tommaso would either accept the letters and drawings or ignore them. Michelangelo would just have to wait, and the waiting felt like an eternity.

EIGHT

'Bernardino!' Michelangelo's call echoed throughout the house.

Bernardino, busy preparing vegetables for supper with Vincenza the maid, at first did not hear him.

'He's calling you, Bernardino,' Vincenza said.

'Bernardino!' the call came again. Bernardino looked up.

He slid off the high stool, wiped his hands hurriedly with a cloth and went in search of the voice. The last time he'd seen the Master he'd been in the workshops, up a ladder as usual, covered in dust and chipping at a block of marble.

'Yes, Master,' Bernardino called.

'I'm in the salon,' came the voice.

Bernardino entered the room and found Michelangelo sitting at the scrivania in a pool of sunlight.

'I have finished a letter and some sketches to be sent to my Lord Tommaso. Will you take them to Signore Angelini for me, please? He will deliver them. I trust him.'

He handed Bernardino a sheaf of papers carefully rolled, tied and sealed.

'Now, Master?' Bernardino asked with false cheer. He had too many chores needing completion in the kitchen to run errands.

'Yes, now. At once.'

Bernardino guessed what the papers contained – love letters, poems and sketches, a gift to the young Cavalieri. A token of hope. He headed back to the kitchen and removed his apron. 'I have to deliver a message for the Master.'

'For his latest love?' Vincenza asked without looking up.

Bernardino raised his eyebrows in surprise. She was the sister of a grocer at the market, near the big Roman house, and the daughter of a Settignano family. Vincenza had always appeared to respect Michelangelo. She lived mainly with her brother but had a servant's room within the house so she did not have to walk home in the dark. She said it was more comfortable than her room attached to the grocer's shop.

'I'm just the messenger. And you must not speak like that about the Master.'

'Well, who's it to?' She stopped peeling and put down the knife, hand on hip, head tilted, her eyes narrowed like a suspicious fishwife.

'I told you, it's none of my business or yours. I just have to deliver it to Signore Angelini,' he turned peevishly from her challenging stare, 'who delivers the Master's letters for him.' Bartolomeo Angelini, Michelangelo's good friend, would do anything for him, including carrying love letters to his latest love but he wasn't going to say that to Vincenza.

The maid smiled but the smile didn't reach her brown eyes as she studied him carefully. 'It's alright, Bernardino,' she said. 'It's well known what goes on in this house.'

Vincenza was young, with a good bosom beneath the shift of her blouse, her skin unlined and firm, her arms long and capable looking, her dark hair caught up beneath the white linen cap on her head. She was a steady worker though there was something about her he didn't trust. She had quickly linked herself to Febo although she knew he was Michelangelo's favourite. Bernardino had watched with dismay as Febo, unbeknown to Michelangelo, sneaked into her bed at night. Bernardino wasn't going to tell the Master and upset him. He decided he would watch Vincenza closely. She had been hired simply because she came from the area where they had both grown up. To Michelangelo, people of Caprese and Settignano, within the outer radius of Florence, were to be trusted. The community of the area was close-knit. Michelangelo cherished this loyalty. Bernardino's own link to the Master was stronger than most; as babies and toddlers they had shared the same breasts. That alone established Michelangelo's trust for him but could he trust everybody?

'It's not alright. Mind what you say, it's gossip you're alluding to.'

Vincenza shrugged, picked up the knife and resumed peeling vegetables. 'Rome is full of gossip, Bernardino. You just have to walk through the streets and market to hear the latest talk about the Master.'

'Well, you must not take any notice.' Bernardino shrugged on his outdoor cloak.

'I know what goes on behind closed doors. The presence of pretty Febo and his way with the Master is not confined to this house,' she said.

'Whatever do you mean?' Bernardino hoped she didn't include him in what went on behind closed doors.

'Don't look so alarmed, Bernardino. I don't mean you,' she laughed. 'Now that would be something to see.'

Bernardino turned away.

'Febo is known to frequent the inns and taverns while the Master is working and he has a loose tongue, as well as another part of his body,' Vincenza said, still peeling. 'He dresses like a prince and draws attention to himself. There are spies everywhere in Rome, reporting to the Holy See. Surely you know that? Even here in the Master's house.'

Bernardino turned and looked at her. 'In this house?'

'There are many apprentices here. Do you know everything about them? Their backgrounds?'

'The Master employs them. He usually judges them by their talent.'

Vincenza laughed. 'He tries to keep things quiet, but you know how rumours get around.'

'What is there to gossip about?'

'How much he likes the boys in his bed.'

'A scandalous lie,' Bernardino growled, incensed.

'Well, you should know.' She shrugged, avoiding Bernardino's glance. 'You must admit, he's never happier than when he's surrounded by his apprentices, day and night. He's a child of the Medici's and we all know what went on in that court.'

'He's a Buonorotti not a Medici but he owes a lot to Lorenzo the Magnificent who took him into his house and treated him like a son. Mind your tongue. Your talk is dangerous. He has great regard for the Medici family, especially Il Magnifico.'

'You know more than you let on, Bernardino,' she said.

'Be careful what you say. Don't you think that the Master and I know about your fondness for Febo and how often you take him to your own bed?' retorted Bernardino coldly.

Vincenza looked as if she were about to throw her knife at him so he quickly clambered out the door. He would have to warn Michelangelo about her. She was not to be trusted. It would be hard for the Master to hear this about someone from Settignano.

Bernardino let himself out of the back entrance to the house and followed the path that led to the street, the papers safely tucked under his cloak.

NINE
Rome, 1532

Tommaso stirred in his bed. The sound of knocking on the palazzo's front door echoed through the halls. He listened – someone answered the door – but he could hear no more and he buried his head in the pillow and tried to go back to sleep. He had been confined to his bed three days with a fever and sore throat, unable to take his mind off his illness.

There was a knock on the door that sounded much like that of his manservant's. The door opened at his call and his father entered, bearing a roll of papers.

'These have been delivered to you, Tommao, by Il Signore Angelini, from Michelangelo.' Giovanni de Cavalieri used his son's nickname. 'Are you feeling better today?' He drew back the bed curtains and the window drapes. Sunlight poured into the room, temporarily blinding Tommaso and making his head ache. Dust motes played in the light, dancing and swirling around him. He closed his eyes to the light and gold dust, then opened them again, hoping his vision would adjust. He had tried to get up but standing made him feel worse.

'It seems you may have some letters and perhaps sketches from the great man himself,' his father said, handing him the roll.

Tommaso struggled upright and propped himself up against the pillows. He broke the seal and unrolled it, the pieces of paper falling onto his lap.

'I'll leave you to read them. Perhaps, if you feel like it, you may come down to my salon. I shall tell the maid to prepare some lemon cordial for you. It may make you feel better. I would like to see any sketches he has given you.' His father headed back towards the chamber door.

'Why is he writing to me?' Tommaso asked, bemused.

His father stopped, one hand on the door handle. He turned and smiled. 'Perhaps you inspire him. He's a man of passion. Everyone knows he's inspired by young male beauty, it's reflected in his art. Read what he has to say. He may tell you himself.'

His father left the room and Tommaso leafed through the papers, finding letters, poems and sketches. He stopped at the sketches and studied them. They were finely executed, almost like sculptures on paper and full of meaning. The letters and poems were of heart-felt yearning, something he wasn't prepared for. He leant back on the pillow and thought about the writer. Tommaso had never been aware he could make such a profound impression on anyone, but he hadn't met anyone like Michelangelo before. He'd heard rumours about his tempers, erratic behaviour and love life. The rumours may have been true or, possibly, gossip. He had seen the great man's works and marvelled at them; how one man could create such overwhelming works of art left him in awe. Tommaso turned back to read the accompanying letters and sonnets. His heartbeat was so loud, thumping in his ears and he didn't know whether it was because of excitement, fear or love. Or, it could have been his body's laboured response to his fever. He closed his eyes and rested his mind, willing his heart to return to its steady beat. He would read the letters again, study the sketches, analyse the sonnets, ask his father's advice, and act from there.

Tommaso rang for his manservant and dressed.

~

'You are obviously better, Tommao,' said Giovanni, as Tommaso entered his father's salon. He beckoned his son to sit near his writing desk. 'You have read what the Master has written?'

'I have, Papa. I'm flattered yet puzzled. He has sent some wonderful sonnets and sketches,' Tommaso was unable to find the right words to explain and his father looked up at him inquiringly, 'but the meaning of them disturbs me. You hear so many rumours about the man. These are love letters, Father. I feel he is propositioning me. I don't want to offend or hurt him. He is a great artist and I admire his work but I feel no attraction to him. What should I do?'

'Look to your education.' Giovanni's raised his eyebrows at his son standing before him. 'He is indicating, by his poems and drawings, a pure love between men as the New Platonists taught.'

'Yes, I understand that as one drawing is of *Ganymede* and the other of *Tityus*,' Tommaso said, still worried, 'and we know the origins of those legends, and of love between men. Plato used the myth of Zeus and Ganymede to explain the love of Socrates for his students and to explain his own feelings.'

Giovanni nodded.

'If you look at the books, here in the library…' He rose to his feet and went to the bookshelf, choosing a book for Tommaso. It was by Ficino, his writings on the New Platonism, a book Tommaso remembered devouring when studying Plato. His father explained, 'This may remind you of what you learned. You know the meaning behind the exhibition of great love between men. The original philosophy by Plato has been replaced by new teachings which Michelangelo was educated in when he was at the Medici court. There is belief that the human soul is trapped within the confines of the material body. In this teaching, when the Christian soul contemplates beauty, the soul is lifted to God. The new Platonism is no longer associated with the basic love between men, but with the admiration of beauty and closeness of the beloved and how that appreciation of beauty can bring the admirer closer to God. Ficino, in his studies of Plato and analysis, tried to reconcile the pagan with Christianity.' Giovanni watched Tommaso leaf through the book. 'Beauty in this sense means goodness. It is God-given; the divine. It's not sexual. You bring Michelangelo close to God, to youth and immortality.'

Tommaso sat in the chair near his father and looked up at him. 'He must know the original ancient message in these myths? These drawings might mean he is attracted to me as an older man loving a youth.'

'Of course – he's an educated man but he's emphasising the value of spirituality associated with love that has no physical expression.'

Tommaso was still unconvinced. 'He may mean that as well. Perhaps that's what he wants me to recognise in these sketches.'

'Mmmm,' his father mused. 'His talent creates jealousy in lesser people – and there is always talk about those who succeed. Perhaps he does have these inclinations. You won't really know until you see him again and get to know him yourself. You'll have to trust your own judgement. However, you must treat him with respect. He's known as being a lonely man, temperamental and sensitive to slights and perceived threats. He is also said to relish solitude so perhaps you can bring some companionship and joy into his life. Some say he lacks joy in his relationships, which are few.'

Tommaso sighed, 'I really don't know how to approach him, how to have such a relationship with him. We have heard he's pious and abstains from sexual relations but surely he's human like everyone else? And he's surrounded by handsome young men. He uses them as models in his work. They are rumoured to be his lovers as well.'

'Perhaps he needs such relationships to enable him to create,' Giovanni said thoughtfully. 'You can respond to him spiritually with your writing, your letters, your words. He wants to use your beauty as inspiration and he wants your friendship with it. Your beauty, to him, is a conduit for his creativity. I doubt he would ever express himself physically to you. If he does, you will tell him you are not that way inclined, as politely and kindly as possible.'

'But that may offend him, Father,' Tommaso said.

'Yes, but that is the risk he and you must take. He may be offended and hurt if you rebuff him and that will be a true test of his spiritual love. He sublimates his desire and puts his passion into his art, in his poetry, yes, as he has already done so, with you. Bartolomeo has told me of this and he is a very good friend.'

'This is a challenge,' Tommaso shook his head, 'and I fear it may be beyond me.'

'Yes, it is a challenge, one you must accept and conquer. You could refuse but I think it would be to your discredit. To have his friendship and the chance of tuition from him is an honour and a gift.'

'Then you don't mind if I cultivate his friendship?'

'No. It is an honour to be his friend.'

The two men were silent as each digested what had been discussed. Giovanni looked at his son seated in his chair opposite to him and smiled.

TEN

Michelangelo waited for a reply from Tommaso, his spirit restless and longing. He had tried to lose himself in his work but was bereft and wondered if he would hear from Tommaso at all. Perhaps he had been too forward; perhaps he had made a terrible mistake.

At night, he paced restlessly until he fell into bed exhausted. He shunned the advances of one or two of his adoring apprentices who anticipated his needs, knocking on the door of his bedchamber at night when there were empty rooms just down the hall. He wrote poem after poem, interspersed with longing letters. Once Bernardino found him in the salon, his head in his arms, weeping with exasperation. When Bernardino tried to comfort him, the Master shouted and yelled at him or anyone who came within his vicinity, including two scared apprentices, sending them back to the workshop and Bernardino scuttling into the kitchen where he and Vincenza heard him bellowing from the salon.

'Why hasn't he answered me, Dino?' Michelangelo lamented as Bernardino reappeared later to inspect the sudden silence in the salon.

'Perhaps he's sick.'

'Perhaps he doesn't know what to say,' Michelangelo grumbled. 'Or has he been listening to people's gossip? I sent the letters and sketches a week ago and still there's been no word.'

'There must be something stopping him from writing. He's too polite to ignore you,' soothed Bernardino, hoping it was so.

'Tommaso is educated and refined. He would hardly attach an improper meaning to words and drawings meant in chaste love. Or would he?' Michelangelo's brow creased with anxiety. 'I have so many enemies; I don't trust anyone.'

'I could always ask Signore Angelini if he has seen the young man,' offered Bernardino. 'It may ease your mind.'

'Of course. Do that, Bernardino. It will be a relief to know one way or the other.'

~

'Bernardino, Dino! Where are you?' Michelangelo ran into the kitchen. Bernardino stopped his chores. 'Tommaso has written, he has answered my letter!'

Vincenza, amused, looked up from scraping vegetables. The Master had been acting like a schoolboy for days, moping and morose, and now he was exuberant.

'Good, Master. I'm pleased for you. Is it a good letter?' Bernardino glanced at a smiling Vincenza .

'This is what he says,' Michelangelo said, holding his spectacles on his flattened nose.

My Dear Michelangelo,

I am overwhelmed to have someone such as yourself, a great man, write to one as young as myself, and send me such exquisite drawings.

A grinning Michelangelo looked at Bernardino. 'He goes on to say that he's going to contemplate the drawings with pleasure for at least two hours a day. He's sick at the moment but when he is well he hopes to call on me to pay his respects in person, if I am agreeable.'

Michelangelo almost danced around the kitchen with glee. He put back his head and laughed, 'Bernardino, this is such good news!'

'Indeed, it is, Master. He's an honourable young man.'

'I must write to him at once.' Michelangelo disappeared out of the kitchen.

'Of course, Master. He will be waiting for your reply.'

And it will be a relief to have some peace in the house, thought Bernardino, returning to his chores. Sound drifted down the hallway from the salon. Michelangelo was singing again.

'He loves this Tommaso,' Vincenza said, with eyebrows raised, wiping her hands on her apron.

'Perhaps.' Bernardino wished Michelangelo had been more discreet in front of Vincenza.

'Perhaps?' Vincenza stared at Bernardino, her eyes wide.

~

Michelangelo, his heart full of hope, found ink and paper and drew up a chair to the table. He wrote carefully so as not to overwhelm the receiver, his love.

My dear Lord Tommaso,

The fact that you accept my drawings and letters pleases me deeply. To have my works so well thought of in your heart and soul is my good fortune. It seems I have been waiting for your Lordship all my life, yet you have lived, I think, by your wisdom and beauty a thousand times before.

He must not take the wrong meaning from my drawings. How else can I explain my feelings for him except in this way? Michelangelo thought, as he folded his letter, ready to seal it. A doubt niggled at him. Would Tommaso be influenced by the rumours about him? A frisson of fear coursed through him. He didn't want to lose Tommaso when he had come so close to experiencing such love. What about his conscience and the teachings of the Church about such relationships? His love would be chaste, he vowed to himself. He would insist to Tommaso it was chaste, and that there would never be anything more. Didn't Ficino say such love was pure and had encouraged such relationships in himself and with others? Michelangelo pushed the thoughts away. There would be no harm done to anyone, the Church or God. He would be conscious of never offending anyone and he would reassure Tommaso. Their love would be pure, entirely spiritual. A place from where he and Tommaso could lift their souls to God.

Michelangelo sealed the letter.

ELEVEN

Michelangelo stood in the doorway of his workshop watching his apprentices copy his work by sculpting, painting or sketching. He walked to the nearest youth and took the chalk from his hand, correcting the sketch the boy had done, showing him how to crosshatch and build shadows to create depth. The young men had been carrying out their tasks with as much noise as possible but, now he was amongst them, they settled into a concentrated silence.

Michelangelo sat down beside another apprentice before a plinth bearing a medium-sized block of marble. The remainder of the students were occupied.

'You have to imagine what is within the block of stone or marble you are working on, Marco. What do you think may be hiding in there?' Michelangelo ran his hand over the smooth surface lovingly. 'This is from the mountains, Marco, pushed up towards heaven from beneath the earth – and we have it here now with us, the form within waiting to be revealed. You have studied the statues of the ancient Greeks and Romans, how they created exquisite forms. You have also studied the human body from my drawings and sketches in my workbook, the musculature, the bones, and you have drawn them well. Now, it's your turn. Go. Start.'

Marco stared at the block of marble. His hands shook. Michelangelo knew that feeling – the moment before the first cut of marble.

'Come, Marco, don't be nervous.' He leaned in closer to the student. 'Look at it. Study it.' The boy turned his frightened eyes towards the marble. 'Close your eyes and run your hand over the surface. What do you feel?'

Marco, eyes closed tightly, ran one hand slowly over the marble. 'It's cold, smooth – some lumps and bumps in places.'

'Yes. What else?' Michelangelo put his arm around Marco's shoulders. Marco had been an apprentice for some time and Michelangelo had shown him all he could but the boy had to try for himself. 'You have already done many sketches and made clay and wax models of different subjects; I have seen them – they were good,' Michelangelo encouraged.

Marco was silent, his eyes still closed. He put both hands on the block.

'Use your imagination. What can you feel within the marble?' Michelangelo whispered patiently, close to his ear.

Marco's hands were still shaking. 'It's cold. It isn't alive.'

'That's where you're wrong, Marco. It's very much alive. Don't take your hands off the marble, try again.'

Marco, eyes still closed, frowned as he ran his hands over the block.

Michelangelo remembered his first carving and the sense of enormity, as if he was about to embark on a life-changing adventure. The excitement and eagerness of the first cut.

'Can you feel skin, clothing? Can you feel the contours of an arm, a leg, a foot, the features of a face, nose, eyes, forehead? The curls of hair? Can you feel the muscles beneath the skin? The tendons? The fat folds? Can you imagine?'

Marco nodded. He'd stopped frowning. Michelangelo sat still beside him and waited.

'If you can imagine all that, you can draw out the interior by shaping it as you see it in your mind's eye. It's there. What is it?'

Marco's hands stopped moving over the marble.

'Tell me, Marco, what is within the marble?' Michelangelo repeated patiently, noticing Bernardino watching and listening from the door.

'It's alive. There's something within it. Something to be brought forth, like a woman giving birth,' Marco said, with a rush.

'Yes, yes. You are right,' Michelangelo said excitedly. 'What is that you have discovered?'

'The head of a girl.'

Michelangelo smiled in relief and leant over and kissed Marco on the cheek. 'Well done. She was there in your mind all the time. You have her wax image. Now carve. Draw her out. Show me your lovely girl.'

The boy seemed to have taken no notice of the kiss but Bernardino drew Michelangelo aside. 'Master, you kissed him,' he protested.

'And why not, my friend? It's the same as I do for any of my friends, you included. You know that.' He bent and kissed his friend on the cheek. 'A token of friendship, of love, a custom, nothing more. I'm pleased with the boy's answer,' Michelangelo said, giving Marco a fond glance. 'He has learnt enough from me to create what he wants and he does show promise.'

'He's just a boy, Master, fifteen years old.'

'He's been with me long enough to attempt this. Students need a challenge to motivate them. I was younger than he when I started with Ghirlandaio and Bertoldi.' Michelangelo remembered the old man who'd taught him all he could. Il Magnifico had been fond of Bertoldi and had given him employment and a place to live.

Bernardino gave Michelangelo a slight bow and left them, Marco tap-tapping with mallet and chisel on the marble, trying to free the girl within. Michelangelo refused to see the wrong in his affectionate relationships with his apprentices.

~

The numerous rumours of what Michelangelo did with his apprentices troubled Bernardino. Vincenza did not have to tell him. Bernardino had been challenged many times in the market, carrying his trusty basket, where he was known as Michelangelo's servant. He had recently stood, as people spoke above his head, unaware he was listening.

'He has a new one, I've heard,' said the seller.

'How many is that?' asked the customer, her long skirt draped beside Bernardino.

There were several things he didn't like about being short, and one was being close enough to smell dirty feet and unwashed clothes.

This woman's skirt was stained and smelt of rancid oil. Bernardino wrinkled his nose.

'Oh, there have been several,' the storekeeper told her. Bernardino held his breath and the storekeeper hardly noticed him, adding, 'You see them out and about when they're not occupied in his workshop. You can't miss them, they're all young and handsome. He dresses them well, looks after them. One in particular has expensive clothes – and you should see the rings on his fingers.'

'So, it's true then.' The customer took the vegetables from the seller and put them in the basket balanced on her hip. Bernardino watched as she paid the seller with coins from her purse.

'Of course. After all, he comes from Florence. Everyone knows what that city is like. Another Sodom.'

Others, who had gathered waiting to be served, murmured in agreement. Bernardino felt himself go hot and cold with dismay.

'It's a sin,' the customer protested.

'And a crime. You can be executed for it, though the law is rarely put into practice. They burnt that preacher, some years back. Savonarola, I think his name was. He was against the ways of the Papacy and against sodomy in Florence. Tried to clean the city up. They got rid of him.'

'How do you know all this?' asked a man, standing nearby.

'People here frequently travel to Florence, buying and selling goods.'

Bernardino became aware of a sudden silence between the pair. Both looked down as they suddenly noticed him.

'Hey, short one,' said the stall holder, 'you work for the great artist. You may be a servant but you're richly dressed with your well-made hat, cloak and doublet. He looks after you too, I see. Though not much material would be required to outfit you. You'd be quite cheap to look after.'

Loud laughter echoed and stung Bernardino's ears.

'What do you want?'

'Some respect for my Master,' Bernardino answered.

'Does he deserve it?'

'Of course, he does. Think of all the wonderful works of art he's made. I want some fresh oranges and apples for him. I look after him and know him well. You wrong him with your gossip. Keep your mouth shut.'

'Oh, we are spirited, aren't we?' The seller winked at his customer.

'Is it true then, what he says?' The customer looked down on the short man fuming beside her.

'Nothing is true until it's proven. My Master is a pious man,' Bernardino said as he had many times before. He was dismayed to find a crowd had gathered around them. Some laughed at the news, some smiled, others nodded. They taunted him because they did not believe him.

'He has many lovers, we hear the rumours,' said the fish-monger from the next stall along.

'Perhaps you're one.' The man guffawed with his head thrown back, looking pleased with his own joke.

'I need to buy herrings, the freshest, for my Master.' Bernardino pointed to the pile of fish in front of the man in the next stall.

'The freshest for the fresh,' the fishmonger laughed, grabbing the herrings and holding them up for all to see.

To Bernardino's chagrin, the idle crowd laughed with him.

'I'm his brother,' Bernardino said, incensed that they would think such a thing about his Master. 'He has many apprentices. He teaches them, they're not his lovers.'

The man bent double in mirth. 'You? His brother?'

'Yes.'

'He usually picks pretty ones, though, doesn't he? What does he see in you?'

More laughter. The crowd had become a flight of hideous gargoyles, mocking Bernardino and Michelangelo.

The gargoyles were nothing at all like the strong statues Michelangelo carved. They were wrinkled, lined and hideous. The faces of the fruit-seller and the fish vendor contorted into grotesque satyrs. Bernardino was reminded of the one Michelangelo had painted on his father's kitchen wall when he was a boy. Michelangelo had drawn it again to show Bernardino, who had been frightened of its fierce and ugly visage. Anger rose and the market place swirled around him. He shook his head vigorously to rid himself of the devilish vision.

He slapped payment into the stallholder's palms and snapped, 'Well, he certainly wouldn't pick you.'

He grabbed his fruit and fish and swung away, avoiding the legs surrounding him as if they were trees in a forest and the laughter and whispers behind his back. Such ignorant, rude people were to be ignored. He would tell Michelangelo what people were saying and vowed that the next time, he would find another market – or send someone else to shop. Not Vincenza, she would only add to the rumours with her snide remarks. And certainly none of the apprentices, for they would be laughed at, ridiculed and accused as he had been. He frowned to himself. He would have to find someone who could shop in the market and not be recognised. But who could do it as well as he? Who knew the Master the way he did?

As long as I'm with him, Bernardino thought, trudging towards the Basilica's piazza, he will eat well. Although some interactions with the apprentices worried him, he knew the Master had no other affection and didn't know what it was to love a woman. Michelangelo considered love-making between men and women as disgusting and degrading and this had led to some odd behaviour around women. He couldn't relate to them. He had written revealing his feelings of women in general. Now, Bernardino thought, walking steadily with his load, what did he say? He searched his mind. Ah, yes, he said: "Your face is shiny like snail slime and sweeter than the tart juice of a grape. Its prettiness reminds me of a turnip. And each of your breasts hang heavily like two watermelons in a bag." Bernardino had laughed when he first heard the poem, but he knew what people would say if they read it. They only believed gossip.

'We return to Florence within a few days,' Michelangelo told Bernardino later, as the latter prepared the evening meal.

'Already, Master?'

'Yes, I must make arrangements with the De Rovere family about the Julius tomb, finish the Laurentian Library and the Medici tomb.

We will come back and live in Rome from now on. My future is here.' He looked at Bernardino closely. 'What's the matter, Dino? Have you been weeping?'

Bernardino wiped his eyes with the back of his hand. He was still smarting from his encounter in the market.

'Come, Bernardino. Returning to Florence isn't that bad and it will only be for a few months then we'll be back. Is that what's troubling you?' Michelangelo asked, with an amused smile.

Bernardino told Michelangelo about the gossip bandied around in the market. Michelangelo was silent, an appalled expression growing on his face.

'You must be careful, Master. Even Vincenza speaks of it. She really has no loyalty to you and doesn't deserve to be in this house.'

'Vincenza?' Michelangelo asked in surprise. 'Her family has been loyal to me for years.'

His heavy brows burrowed together. 'Abstinence from sex fuels my work. Why can't they see that?'

'Their minds can't see that, Master. They are thinking of themselves and how they wouldn't be able to abstain.'

'For me it's like whipping myself with a birch branch. It's painful to abstain and painful that people think such things of me. Such deprivation increases my concentration. It motivates me and drives me to artistic feats that otherwise I wouldn't think possible.'

'The rabble don't think this way, Michelangelo.' Bernardino tried to placate the anger in Michelangelo's eyes. 'You create divine works of art, surely no one should accuse you of such practices and yet, they do.' Most probably the church would take offence if they took the gossip seriously but the clergy were too busy oohing and aahing over Michelangelo's latest creation, thought Bernardino. 'It's best to ignore the gossips, pretend they don't exist,' Bernardino said, wishing he could.

'Don't trouble yourself. I will ask someone else to go to the market in future.' Michelangelo bent down and patted Bernardino on the shoulder.

'Not Vincenza, Master, not Vincenza.'

TWELVE

Vincenza finished her work for the day, removed her apron and ran a hand through her hair.

She knew Febo was in the workshop with Michelangelo; she had not seen or talked to him for a few days and missed him. Vincenza wanted to see him without attracting the Master's attention. She paused at the workshop door. Michelangelo would not be pleased to see her in the workshop. He was strict about who went into that busy place.

Determined, Vincenza pushed open the door and walked inside. Michelangelo was up a ladder chipping at a large block of marble, so intent on what he was doing he didn't notice Vincenza making her way to Febo who was busy polishing a finished sculpture. Febo turned to her then glanced up at Michelangelo who had his back to them. He shook his head at her and pointed to the Master. Unconcerned, Vincenza turned to leave. Just being there was enough. Febo would have received the message that she wanted to see him. Some of the other apprentices looked at her and it was only as she opened the workshop door to leave that Michelangelo saw her.

'Vincenza,' he boomed.

She stopped, hand on the latch, looking up at him. 'Yes, Master?'

'What are you doing here? What do you want? You know you're not allowed to come in and interrupt our work time.'

Vincenza nodded quickly. 'I was looking for Bernardino, Master. I thought he was here, with you,' she answered innocently.

'I sent Bernardino out with a message. He should be home soon.'

'Yes, Master.'

'Please don't enter the workshop again while we are working,' said Michelangelo, turning back to his work.

'No, Master.' She escaped out the door, closing it firmly behind her.

~

Vincenza waited in her room at the other end of the house from where Michelangelo and some of his apprentices slept. She knew Febo would come. He usually waited for Michelangelo to fall asleep before he crept out of bed; though lately he hadn't been sleeping with the Master, Michelangelo saying he needed time and his bed for himself. Vincenza knew it was because he had fallen in love with the nobleman, Cavalieri. She wondered what Febo would say to that. He'd told her that sex with a woman was far more satisfying than with a man but then, who was Febo to spurn Michelangelo's advances? Especially since the Master gave Febo money, clothes and jewels whenever he wanted them.

Vincenza didn't hear the tap on the door or realise Febo was in the room until she felt him climb into bed beside her. She turned to him and he put his arm over her, drawing her close.

'You wanted to see me?' he kissed her softly in the moonlight.

'Yes,' Vincenza opened her arms and drew him to her, feeling the length of his body against hers. Febo kissed her ardently, running his hands all over her body.

Something stirred between them. She melted. He climbed over her and entered her. She reached down and felt the fullness of his buttocks in her hands. Vincenza forgot time and enjoyed the moment as Febo moved above her, rhythmically drawing her in closer to him on each beat, kissing her neck, face and breasts. Somewhere, in the light of the stars and the moon, the world exploded for her and a little later for him. They lay spent, entwined.

'Is that why you wanted to see me?' Febo traced the outline of her face in the light with one finger.

'Yes and no. I have something to tell you.'

Febo propped himself up on one elbow and looked at her. 'Well, what is it?'

'The Master has a new love,' she said, trying to keep the triumph in her voice under control. Perhaps now Febo would look at her in a different light and realise that her love was definitely the best. Michelangelo had always been in the way.

Febo was silent as he digested the news. 'Do you know who it is?'

'No. I've heard him talk to Bernardino and he sent the little man on an errand this afternoon, with letters, I think, to the young man. It's been going on for some time.'

Febo turned on his back and stared into the moonlit room.

'I thought you should know because you've been his favourite for so long,' Vincenza added cautiously. 'He can't have two lovers, can he?'

'It's possible, I do.'

'Who?' Vincenza tried not to sound alarmed.

'You and the Master.'

Silence lay between them. Had she had done the right thing? Wouldn't he have learned soon enough anyway? Surely now he would see where his love lay; not in the arms of an old, craggy, temperamental man, but in one who could give him young, true love. Wouldn't he be pleased? Yet he hardly seemed pleased at all; he just seemed stunned.

Febo rolled out of bed. He bent down and kissed Vincenza. 'Thank you,' he said and he was gone.

THIRTEEN

You know who I am, Lord, and why I wanted to be close to you, so why should we wait any longer to meet? If your feelings are real, and my desire is real, we should not wait. If our feelings are stifled, they will only leave us bereft, empty and troubled. What I love in you is what you love in yourself. Our souls are falling in love with each other. My feelings are such when I see your fair face that any mortal would understand. However, to know the depth of such feelings they may have to die to experience them, that is to see the face of the divine.

Bernardino heard the knock on the door and opened it. Bartolomeo stood in the doorway and Bernardino gave him a deep bow, noticing he had someone with him. The stranger stepped from the shadows of the vestibule. Bernardino saw the strong profile, elegant features and the glow of the young man's skin as if lit from within. He could see why Michelangelo was in love. Even Bernardino was mesmerised by the young man's looks and he was not usually attracted to men.

'I have brought my Lord de Cavalieri to see Michelangelo, Bernardino. Could you tell him we are here, please?' Bartolomeo said.

Bernardino bowed again, ushered the two men into the front salon and went in search of Michelangelo in the workshop.

'Show them in, Bernardino,' Michelangelo said, stepping down from a ladder propped near the sculpture he was working on.

Bernardino sensed Michelangelo's excitement as he straightened his apron and ran a hand through his bushy, curly hair, inadvertently coating his head in more marble dust.

The men he ushered into the workshop seemed equally excited. Bernardino watched as they greeted each other with enthusiastic embraces. Tommaso's eyes were all over the room, taking in the pieces of marble cut and ready to be worked on; tables full of workbooks and paper – some with sketches, clay models of hands, feet and heads, a trestle table with chalks, coloured pigments and brushes. The apprentices stopped and stared at the three men in silence and Michelangelo clapped his hands, urging them back to work. Febo wasn't there, which relieved Bernardino – he didn't know how the young man would react to Tommaso's presence.

'Bernardino, some wine and food for our guests in the salon,' ordered Michelangelo.

Anticipating him, Bernardino was already half way out the door. He set the table in the grand salon and waited for the group to arrive. Several minutes later they sat and talked while Bernardino poured wine.

'The very best: Trebbiano!' exclaimed Michelangelo, raising his glass. 'Harvested in Settignano.' It was downed in an instant and Bernardino poured more. He waited at the edge of the room in case Michelangelo wanted something else and he observed the two men. Bartolemeo he knew, but Tommaso he had only seen from a distance when out walking with the Master. He had noticed Michelangelo's excitement then, as he espied the young man. Now, Michelangelo talked steadily to both men about his task of completing the Julius tomb and the sculptures in Florence waiting to be finished and transported down to Rome.

'I also have much to do in Florence for Pope Clement, before I can return to Rome permanently to complete the tomb. I must finish it. I will be away only a few months,' he said, looking at Tommaso.

Bartolemeo nodded and the young man sat listening to both. Michelangelo reached out and took Tommaso by the hand.

'You wish to learn to draw and paint, my Lord?'

'If you would be so good as to teach me, Master. I have drawn copies of the works you sent me, for you to look at.'

'Of course, I'm pleased that you have sketched them. Bartolomeo has told me you have talent. You are most welcome in my studio. In the meantime, while I'm in Florence, I wish you to practise drawing as much as you can. After that, I will teach you all I know.' Still holding Tommaso's hand, he added, in a quiet beguiling voice Bernardino had not heard often, 'You could be my muse, if you so wish. I wish to study you and portray your beauty in my sculptures and paintings. What do you say?'

Tommaso glanced at Bartolemeo, who nodded, then at Michelangelo. 'I'm honoured to be thought of so highly by one such as yourself, Master,' Tommaso answered earnestly.

Bernardino could tell the young man was overwhelmed to be in the presence of such a great artist. Michelangelo was as intense as Tommaso and Bernardino noticed they hardly took their eyes off each other. Tommaso's bearing was noble and he was well-mannered. When he spoke to Michelangelo his voice was musical and moderate, his Roman accent correct. Bernardino could see why Tommaso was considered by many to be the most handsome man in Rome. A true noble, Bernardino thought. Tommaso's easy smile and his eyes, large and open with the free expression of his soul, would be important to Michelangelo. It was that very beauty that had attracted the Master to Febo and all of his favourite models and apprentices. Bernardino wondered what Bartolemeo thought about this. He knew Michelangelo's friend was discreet and discretion was key to maintaining the Master's friendship over the years. There were rumours that he, too, liked young men.

Febo entered the room with only a slight knock on the door. 'Master, I have finished the sketches and I wish you to look at them...' His voice trailed away as he found the threesome at the table. His large brown eyes, which his Master so loved, settled on Tommaso, his hands clasped between those of Michelangelo. His mouth fell open.

'Tommaso, meet one of my apprentices, Febo de Poggio.'

Bernardino watched carefully. Febo, red in the face, recovered as he bowed to Tommaso and Bartolomeo and, after giving Michelangelo the sketches, he fled from the workshop.

'Another one overcome by your beauty, my Lord,' Michelangelo said to Tommaso.

Tommaso reddened and smiled at Michelangelo.

~

Later, when the house was quiet and work was done for the day, Michelangelo wrote again to Tommaso, his heart in every word, his whole being that of longing.

Tommaso, my dear Lord,

Your light is undying and unique which makes you unable to be content with anything less than that which is equal to you.

A reply came the next day:

Michelangelo, my dear and beloved Lord,

No other man has stirred my feelings as you have, and my desire for your friendship excels itself. I am proud of my judgement. The more I study your drawings, the more delight they give me.

Michelangelo wrote joyously to Bartolemeo:

Dear Bartolemeo,

I write to you, overwhelmed to see once more Tommaso and embrace him, holding him in my arms and kissing his breast and neck. Such beauty makes my soul sing. I long for time to stand still whenever I am with him.

Bartolemeo and Tommaso had left Michelangelo with a promise, by Tommaso, to visit again soon. Tommaso found himself wondering all the way home.

'Well, what do you think, my Lord? Are you ready to enter the great man's house and learn all you can from him?' asked Bartolemeo as they walked towards the Capitoline Hill.

'I am. One thing worries me. May I confide in you?'

Bartolemeo nodded. 'By all means, tell me what you think.'

'I admire him greatly and what he has achieved. I have heard so many rumours about him and dismissed them because of his talent. Now, when I am close to entering his household as one of his apprentices and, considering the drawings and poems he has given me, I am apprehensive because I feel he wants all of me. How will I react if he approaches me with such an intention?'

Bartolemeo, walking swiftly alongside Tommaso, was silent for a few moments. 'I know what you mean. As you say, there are a great many rumours that go around about him. Knowing Michelangelo, as I do, I have never had any evidence of such behaviour. There will always be rumours about those who stand out in society.'

'Even you are talked about, Bartolemeo, simply because you are a good friend of the Master.'

'Yes, I know what is said. Once again, it is only a rumour. I have known Michelangelo for many years and would do anything to please him. I, like you, admire his spirit, talent and soul. That's why I brought you together as I knew you were kindred souls.'

'I noticed that the apprentices he had in his workshop were all good-looking, especially Febo, the one who came to talk to the Master about his sketches. It did make me wonder,' Tommaso frowned.

'Well, if you are willing, you are about to take Febo's place as his muse. Michelangelo told me that Febo is leaving his household and doing messages for him in Pisa and Genoa. I'm not sure how close he was to Febo but I know he has been with him for a while.'

Tommaso stopped and looked down at the portly man beside him. 'He has mentioned that to me in his letters, and it worries me. How is Febo going to react and will he retaliate? People who are angry with such loss often do. All this makes me reticent, as much as I admire him and want to learn from him, and as much as I want to be his confidante.'

'Enter as an apprentice and take matters as they come. It's good that you are cautious about how it's going to look to lesser people. You are wise and sensible. There are many such relationships in Rome. It is not uncommon for an older man to cultivate the friendship of a youth. I'm sure you will be able to cope with him. He's demanding, volatile, temperamental and brilliant. Once you get to know him and he learns to trust you, he's the most amazing man, full of kindness, generosity, compassion and good humour.'

'His letters and sonnets are full of emotion and, dare I say "love"? Something is stopping me, I dare not love him in return unless I lose myself and my soul,' Tommaso continued.

'Have you told him this?'

'No. I don't intend to.'

'Good, because he has an extraordinary mind and heart and your rejection would break him. Just take the relationship as it comes. If there is discomfort and doubt, tell him. He may make demands on you or he may not – you will soon know.'

'The beauty of his soul stirs me and being in his company is like being in the company of the divine,' Tommaso said thoughtfully. 'No wonder some people call him "the Divine One."'

'A humanist conceit,' nodded Bartolemeo. 'He likes that.'

'His letters and poems are frequent and impassioned,' Tommaso continued. 'One after the other, full of love and hidden meaning. If I receive no word from him, I find myself stricken with intense yearning, wondering what I have done. Has he forgotten me? This surprises me about myself. And I usually write impassioned letters to him asking him about his silence, letters I regret sending as soon as I've sent them,' said Tommaso, agitation slipping into his voice.

'My Lord,' Bartolemeo said, 'I think you are what Michelangelo has waited for all of his life. He as much has told me so. I know you are wary, thinking of him having lovers in the past and perhaps he has done. He has found in you what he has been searching for, beauty, nobility, gentility, loyalty and talent. I don't think you can let this pass by. By all means, be cautious but don't close your heart to him because once he trusts you and opens his heart to give to you, it will be forever.'

'Thank you, Bartolomeo,' Tommaso bowed to him as they reached the vicinity of the Palazzo Cavalieri and took leave of one another. 'I will keep in mind what you have said.'

Bartolemeo bowed to Tommaso and walked quickly up the street away from him.

FOURTEEN
Rome

'Febo, I need you to do some errands for me outside of Rome.' Surprised, Febo turned and nodded to Michelangelo. 'For as long as it takes, Febo. You may stay in either Pisa or Genoa for some time, perhaps even go on to Venice, if you wish. I will give you money to help you on your way. I wish you to buy me a house in Genoa and some land. You never know, I may have need of it for safety sake. Times are so uncertain and I have to have somewhere to escape the clutches of those who would seek to harm me.'

Febo frowned at Michelangelo and shook his head. 'This takes me away from you, Master, for some time.' He moved towards him. 'I want to return to Rome with you and complete my studies with you. Have I not served you well?'

'Very well. Come, Febo, sit down beside me. You know that I love you as a father loves his son.'

'You are more than a father, Michelangelo,' Febo challenged. 'I have given you a good part of my life, have modelled for you, loved you, helped you with the apprentices, cleaned the workshop, shared your bed. Now everything is different? You have another love? Another muse and you want to get rid of me?'

'Sit, Febo, and calm down,' Michelangelo demanded.

Febo sat, slowly and reluctantly, on a stool beside Michelangelo's chair. The Master liked to have people below his height, especially if he wanted to intimidate them.

Febo could manipulate him but, lately, Michelangelo hadn't approached him physically. Michelangelo would rise early and disappear downstairs into his workshop, only to emerge later when Bernardino called him for breakfast. Febo, too, took breakfast with him and they ate in silence. Hurt by Michelangelo's indifference towards him, Febo would watch the artist eat hungrily before disappearing back to work, often until late at night. Carving a terracotta form in the workshop, Febo listened in surprise when Michelangelo's laughter echoed throughout the house. The Master being this joyful was a rare experience. He could be silent and morose for days, or just plain bad-tempered and objectionable. When he was like this, Febo usually disappeared until Michelangelo overcame his irascibility.

Michelangelo, happy and singing most of the time, aroused suspicions. He would burst into song as he worked. Yes, he sang rarely but now he was singing nearly all the time, a love song played in the piazza by local balladeers. Even the other apprentices were puzzled when he uncharacteristically praised their attempts at creating what he had set them to do. Usually it was a deep concentrated silence as he observed their work. Febo knew he was not the source of the Master's joy.

'What is it, Bernardino? He's treating me differently. Why?' Febo lifted Bernardino off his feet until they were eye-to-eye, pressing him against the wall in the hallway. Febo's hands flexed against Bernardino's neck. 'He has a new lover! Who is it?'

Bernardino pushed back. 'Why ask me? I'm not that much in the Master's confidence. Put me down,' he demanded, wriggling, trying to loosen Febo's grip.

'You know him better than any of us,' Febo said, taking no notice. 'You've known him since birth.'

'Being a boy and being a man are two different things. I can't read his mind, and most probably would be overwhelmed if I could. Imagine what must be in there!'

'I can well imagine,' answered Febo, peevishly. 'Has he found another lover?'

'What? A lover? The Master? He has no lovers, you know that.'

Febo laughed, his head thrown back. His white teeth glistened within the dark cavern of his mouth. 'What? You lie to protect him, and your loyalty demeans you,' Febo said, his face serious again. 'What about the poetry written for me and the sexual innuendo in the play on my name in his poems? The drawings he has made of me? My place in his bed? You know all about this. Don't pretend otherwise. What have I been to him these past years?'

'You will have to ask him yourself. I can't answer for him. You were and still are his muse, I'm sure of that.' Bernardino squirmed and twisted. Febo had a tight grip.

'Not any more, I fear. He doesn't tell me anything. Except he doesn't want me with him when he returns to Rome.'

'I know nothing of that. Put me down.'

Febo let him go and Bernardino fell in a lump at his feet. 'Well, if you won't tell me what's going on, I will find out some other way,' he snarled, glaring down at him before heading back down the hallway towards the workshop.

Bernardino struggled to his feet, pulled his rumpled tunic down over his hose and ran down the hall towards the kitchen.

~

What an undignified exhibition, Bernardino thought as he stomped into the kitchen. The Master has to be careful with the young men he chooses for his muse. He'd been alarmed by Febo's behaviour before and once again felt afraid.

Further disquiet followed when the Master requested warm water for a bath that evening, a rare occurrence, though at least it would relax him, easing the tension and hard work of creation, and he and his clothes usually smelt better for a while. The tin bath was filled with warm water, in front of the kitchen fireplace and Michelangelo climbed in and sat soaking for a few minutes.

'Thank you, Dino. The water is just right for me. My friends tell me I shouldn't bathe as it weakens the systems of the body but it's so relaxing, they must be wrong. The Romans indulged in it – look at all the ruins of the baths they left.' He let out a sigh. 'The Romans were right. You can leave me for some time.'

'Of course, Master. Just call if you need me,' Bernardino said, letting himself out into the hallway where he was immediately pounced on by Febo.

'What has he said? Anything about me coming back to Rome with him?'

'No, nothing. Don't disturb him, he's bathing and relaxing. Come with me and help me clean the workshops.'

Febo bent down to Bernardino. 'I am not your servant, nor his,' he hissed.

Bernardino, not for the first time, wished he was six feet tall. He would have liked to punch Febo on his handsome nose. Instead, he thrust out his leg to kick him in the shins as Febo made a dash for the kitchen door. Bernardino tried to stop him by getting in the way. Febo was too quick and he grabbed Bernardino and held him fast, knocking on the door over his head.

'Come,' boomed the Master.

Febo entered, his voice loud and plaintive. 'Well, Master, am I going back to Rome to be with you after I've been to Genoa? I need to know the truth now. Not knowing is torturing me.'

Bernardino decided to remove himself from the confrontation, though all throughout the house he couldn't help but hear Michelangelo's voice, low and serious, followed by Febo shouting back, his voice loud and high with rage. There came a low response from the Master which Bernardino couldn't hear. A slammed door, then running footsteps. Another slammed door further away. Bernardino sighed and returned to the kitchen at the Master's call.

'Bernardino, are you there?' Michelangelo rested his head against the bath's rim, his eyes tightly shut. 'Look after him for me. It's hard on him.'

'Yes, Master,' Bernardino closed the door and followed Febo out the back of the house where he found Febo on his hands and knees near the well.

'I have loved him, modelled for him, run errands for him,' he spluttered and sobbed. 'I worshipped him and he treated me well but now he wants to discard me. I am no longer of use to him. He has found someone else.' Febo furiously punched the flagstones he knelt on. Vincenza, alarmed, ran from the kitchen and went straight to the snivelling young man. She knelt down beside him, her hand on his back.

'What is it?' she leaned in looking at his face. 'What has happened?' Febo shook his head, too upset to tell her so she turned and looked at Bernardino who also shook his head at her.

Despite himself, he felt sorry for Febo and was at a loss as how to comfort him. He'd always known the relationship would come to this, there had been many others like Febo. There had been Urbino, Pereni and Bettini, and those were the ones he knew of. The Master lived a double life.

'It would be best if you packed your belongings and went,' Bernardino said, wondering how many more times he would have to say those words.

Febo looked up at Bernardino. 'He wants me to do an errand for him up north.'

'And you will do it, even so?'

'Even so.'

'Are you sure you will?' Bernardino knew Febo was just as likely to disappear with Michelangelo's money.

'Of course I will. I love the man.'

Febo climbed to his feet, leaving Vincenza kneeling on the ground, and made his way back into the house.

Watching him, Bernardino wondered if Michelangelo's next love was going to be dismissed as heartlessly as this one. For once, he questioned the Master's judgement. Much as he said his love for these young men was spiritual and that love helped his creativity, the physical aspect wasn't neglected, even though Michelangelo went to great pains to hide it from those around him. Even going so far as inflicting public verbal abuse bordering on cruelty at the beloved then later, when alone, in tears, begging forgiveness for his outburst and declaring his love.

There weren't many who knew him that well except those he chose to love, or those who looked after his needs and, for all his great talent, Michelangelo was just a man. A man who had lived in a masculine world since his mother's death. He hardly knew a woman. That was evident in his paintings and sculptures of women, there was no softness or femininity about them. Any woman looked like a muscly man with breasts, except for the famous *Pietà*. No one could say, when looking at this work, that the lovely lady was a man dressed in woman's clothes. She had been divinely inspired.

The only woman Michelangelo had ever seen naked was Bernardino's mother, and he'd been too young to notice. His stepmother, Lucrezia, who had died of the plague about the same time as Buonarroto, had been kind and supportive of him and he missed that, though he'd never been close to her. Even when dissecting in Santo Spiritu there had been no female corpses, there had been mainly the brothers of the monastery or male vagrants from the monastery hospital.

The house was quiet as Bernardino rose from his truckle bed, close to the floor, to prepare for the day ahead. He pulled on his jerkin, hose and shoes and walked quietly out of his bedchamber. He knocked softly on Michelangelo's door and crept in. The Master was still asleep, alone again that night. Sometimes Bernardino slept in the same room on the truckle bed, especially if Michelangelo wanted no one in his bed, or if the Master had nightmares, which were frequent. Bernardino had the task of waking him and calming him down. Not wanting to wake Michelangelo yet, he crept out of the room. The hall was in semi-darkness and no one stirred. He was surprised to find Febo in the kitchen, filling himself with fruit, cheese and bread and packing more for his journey.

'Are you going today?' Bernardino put a flame to branches and twigs and stirred the embers on the hob into life.

'Yes, the Master gave me new clothes and money. It's best I go now.'

'What will you do?'

'I will do the task he wants me to complete, then find employment in the studio of another artist while I stay there. He has given me a letter to present.'

Bernardino noticed the full bags at Febo's feet.

'What are you taking?'

'Everything the Master has given me, plus a few extras.'

Bernardino raised his eyebrows as Febo bent down to one of the bags and drew out a pile of drawings.

'You can't take those; he wouldn't like it. They belong to him,' Bernardino accused, appalled.

'They're mine. They're drawings I have done and those he has done of me. I may need them to obtain my next placement. It won't be easy, not even for a favourite of the great Michelangelo. Although, people always like to listen to a little titillation and gossip they think I will give them. That should open a few doors. Don't all the great artists love men? Leonardo da Vinci for one. Another Florentine. Only he doesn't hide it. Everyone knows,' he snorted. Febo stuffed the drawings back in the bag. 'You know yourself what is said of the Master in the streets, both in Florence and here in Rome. His education by the Medici was about love between men – pure, spiritual, unconsummated, so they say. The Master told me he was raped by Piero de Medici, Lorenzo's son, after the great man died. Men aren't strong all the time, are they, Bernardino? Despite the best of intentions and regular visits to the confessional? And what about the poem he wrote celebrating his attraction to me? Just think on that.' Febo stood up, raised his head and spat out the words. '"I was happy while Phoebus inflamed the hill. As his sweet feathers made me die, I rose upon my wings. Upon his hill I climbed, his lamp at my feet and dying, but did not rise to heaven. After thinking the hurt is still there and who will now console me?"'

Bernardino was silent. Behind closed doors he had heard the two of them reciting the poem, accompanied by loud raucous laughter. The meaning had been clear – Phoebus was Febo, described as a bird, meaning the male genitals, and the hill was the male pelvic area. Febo's bitterness was alarming, as was the harm he could do to the Master.

'Michelangelo is a good man. He goes to Mass and Holy Communion as well as confession, regularly,' Bernardino reminded Febo, trying to placate him.

'He's a hypocrite. It's easy to commit sin when you can have it taken away equally as readily,' Febo said, unimpressed.

'He's well known and liked amongst the clergy,' Bernardino insisted.

'Except when they look up at the ceiling of the Sistine Chapel and see the figures he has painted with their muscular bodies and exposed genitals.' Febo laughed, bending to collect his bags. 'They want him to get back up there to paint loin cloths on them.'

Bernardino didn't smile, he was alarmed. 'You must not speak badly of him to anyone, not after you have been so close to him.'

Febo shrugged. 'Being close to him is my advantage and I shall use it as I wish. I'm taking a horse from the local stables. It's outside, saddled ready to go.'

'Febo, don't do anything rash. He does love you and has given you much.'

'My time here is over, Bernardino. The matter is not finished. This will come back to haunt the Master and he won't be able to do anything about it.'

Bernardino frowned at the threat. I must warn Michelangelo, he thought. Febo left the kitchen and went into the hallway, donning the dark-blue woollen travelling cloak and soft blue cap Michelangelo had given him. Bernardino followed him. 'You are not without sin, Febo. You have bribed and manipulated him as long as you have lived with him. You have taken from him, sometimes without asking. He has known about it and indulged you, forgiven you. Be careful what you say to strangers. Don't malign him.'

Febo's smile was mocking as he opened the door. 'I gave myself to him in return, I was his muse. He painted and sculpted me. I am not going to be used. You know what went on. What still goes on.'

'Febo, with such a great man we all must use discretion. His greatness overcomes everything.'

'You are blind, Bernardino, but then many are. He's human like the rest of us – he just happens to be able to paint and sculpt extremely well, that's all.'

Bernardino took a step towards him as Febo went, the door closing after him. His rapid steps over the flagstones leading to the stable block were still audible when Vincenza appeared, a cloak wrapped around her nightshift.

'Where's Febo?' she looked around the kitchen.

'He just left.'

She opened the door and ran into the morning. Troubled, Bernardino shrugged and set to preparing breakfast. Several sleepy-eyed apprentices appeared.

'Who was that, Bernardino?' asked one of the boys.

'No one. No one at all.'

~

Vincenza ran to the stables, catching Febo about to mount his horse. 'You didn't tell me you were leaving,' she panted, grabbing the reins and staying the horse, who pawed and snorted at the intrusion. 'Don't you care about me? I love you. I don't want you to go.'

'I'm not going for good, Vincenza. Of course, I care about you. I'll be back; I'll let you know and I will see you then,' he said as he kissed her. She watched him ride away and, when she turned back to the house, noticed Michelangelo watching from an upstairs window. She pulled her cloak about her and went inside the house.

~

'He has gone?'

'He has, Michelangelo,' Bernardino replied.

His eyes full of proud beauty promised me so much peace but behind his pride was the intent to destroy, thought Michelangelo, sighing. Why would he humiliate me so when I have done so much for him? Why can no one see love as I see it?

FIFTEEN
Rome

Pope Clement VII's secretary, Cardinal Pier Polo Marzi, greeted Michelangelo at the entrance to the Pope's private quarters. Michelangelo bowed to the cardinal and followed him down the long light-filled corridor towards the Pope's reception room. The door was opened for him by a guard and the secretary asked Michelangelo to wait. He disappeared inside the room, the door closing on the artist.

Michelangelo waited, not looking at the guards in their colourful array which he had designed for them. That had been many years ago, in the time of Pope Julius who decided he wanted a new uniform for them emblazoned with the blue and yellow, the colours of his Rovere family. Michelangelo had taken the uniform of soldiers already seen in Europe and designed it his way. Later, Leo X added red, the colours of the Medici - colours familiar to Michelangelo. Did the guards know he had such input into the design of their uniform? He thought not.

The door opened again and Marzi reappeared. 'His Holiness will see you now, Signore Buonarrotti.'

The Pope was seated on a low dais in the centre of the large salon. His shoulders were covered in the camauro, the red velvet cape bordered with ermine and, on his head, a cap, also of red velvet, that only served to accentuate the pallor and thinness of his face. The sight shocked the artist despite the warning beforehand by Reginald Pole. The Pope nodded to Michelangelo and beckoned his old friend forward.

Clement had been in the Medici household of his uncle Lorenzo "The Magnificent" since he was six years old and was the illegitimate son of Lorenzo's murdered brother, Giuliano. Michelangelo remembered Clement, then called Guilio de Medici, being made cardinal deacon when he was sixteen years old. He had been tall and handsome, a mere child, who had no say in whether he should be cardinal or not.

Michelangelo bent on one knee and kissed the ring on the extended hand. When he looked up, he found the Pope smiling at him. Clement rose to his feet and kissed Michelangelo on both cheeks. Michelangelo was surprised, although he knew the Pope had always been fond of him. Clement was now bent and sported a long beard, grown as penance after the Sack of Rome. Popes or priests weren't supposed to grow beards. Yet, now it was considered a sign of mourning and Pope Julius had also grown one after the military loss of Bologna.

The Pope was stricken with the worries that came with office. He looked ill and was blind in one eye. His papacy had been fraught with troubles. His severing of an alliance with The Holy Roman Emperor, Charles V, in favour of Francis I of France over territory, had angered the Emperor who retaliated with the long Sack of Rome. Clement had fled for his life to the shelter of the Castel Sant'Angelo. The development of Protestantism in northern Europe had also taken its toll on Clement, who had no other option than to excommunicate England's King Henry, although that process had been stayed for the moment, hoping that everyone would come to their senses and return to Catholicism.

'Come, my friend, sit with me and tell me about yourself,' Clement said, beckoning a nearby priest to pull up a chair for the artist. 'How good it is to see you. It has been some time since we met.'

'Our paths have diverged along the way, and we have both been busy,' Michelangelo said, accepting the chair and sitting down.

Clement smiled. 'There are too many worldly worries to deal with during this Papacy. Many of my friends have been neglected. I know you have been busy with the Medici Chapel in Florence and the Laurentian Library. Are you going back to finish your work?'

Michelangelo gave the Pope his craggy-faced smile. 'Yes, within days.' Overcome with memories he blurted out, 'I remember you as a devout young man in your uncle's court. Pleasant and friendly to lesser mortals such as myself.' He wanted to add, and blessed with the Medici ambition.

'I remember you as having the talent of angels,' the Pope replied. 'I also remember when Pietro Torrigiani, another youth sponsored by my uncle, punched you in the face and broke your nose. I thought my uncle Lorenzo would go mad with anger. Do you remember?' The Pope's voice was soft and wistful, as if he were back to that time.

'Indeed, I do, Holiness.' Michelangelo winced at the memory. 'It is hard to forget,' he said, rubbing his face.

'I remember my uncle weeping for you, Michelangelo,' said Clement. 'He never forgave Pietro.'

'Perhaps I needed such assault. I was an upstart, proud and mocking because I was jealous of him.'

'You were talented; he was undermining you.'

'Or the other way around, Holiness. I certainly did not want your uncle to feel pain over what I had done. It was a mistake.'

Clement smiled. 'Perhaps you have changed,' he said curiously, his head on one side as he gazed at the artist. 'I wonder where Torrigiani is now?' Michelangelo asked. He knew the artist had left Florence in disgrace and lately was working as an artist in Rome.

Michelangelo lapsed into silence as he briefly studied the frescoes on the walls, painted by his rival, Raphael. They were as graceful and genteel as the man himself. Michelangelo studied the perfect blend of colours, symmetry and form, and the fine painting technique. A brief annoyance surfaced as Michelangelo remembered people criticising him for being aloof and solitary, not gentlemanly or sociable like Raphael. The angelic, amenable Raphael had been made superintendent of the building of the new St Peter's, ahead of Michelangelo, by Pope Leo X after the architect Bramante died. Michelangelo had felt anger and jealousy at the favour conferred on the well-liked "Raffaello Santi." However, Raphael and Bramante, both friends and relatives, had been jealous of Michelangelo's skill as a fresco painter and sculptor. They would have done anything to oust him from his work on the Julius tomb. Bramante had likely warned the Pope that it was bad luck to have one's tomb constructed while still alive. He and Raphael were always ready to undermine him. Especially Bramante.

Michelangelo was convinced it was Bramante behind Julius' decision to demand he paint the Sistine Chapel ceiling. Bramante thought Michelangelo was sure to refuse the Sistine commission because it was well known Michelangelo always insisted he was a sculptor not a painter. Pity Raphael died so young. He was no longer a rival, except when his works were displayed. Ah, Raphael and Bramante. They were everywhere in the Vatican.

Michelangelo had been in this salon before. Pope Julius had summoned him frequently at the time of the painting of the Sistine Chapel, and they had usually met in the old Borgia apartments below the new ones built for him. Julius had built this salon with its marble wainscoting and floors, eager to get away from the Borgia's stigma.

Cardinals and apostolic prelates and other priests wandered to and fro or conversed in groups, occasionally glancing in the direction of Michelangelo who recognised some of the habited acolytes.

'Reginald Pole is with us, Holiness,' he commented. 'I met him recently at the de Cavalieri's.'

'Yes, he is now within our court. Pole refused to sign the Oath of Supremacy in England. To do so, he would have had to break with Holy Mother, the Church of Rome. He had to flee. The King would have put him in the Tower of London as he has done with his brothers and so many others.'

Pole, as if aware of the Pope's conversation, turned to Michelangelo and bowed. Michelangelo, still seated before the Pope, stood and returned the gesture. Knowing someone would be timing his visit with Clement, Michelangelo prompted, 'You have a request for me, Holiness?'

'Indeed, my friend. I wish you to undertake a painting for me, something that I have held close to my heart for some time, hoping you would be able to execute it.'

'What is it, Holiness? What would you have me do?' Michelangelo asked cautiously.

Clement leaned forward so that only Michelangelo could hear – the cardinals were always hovering close by. 'I wish you to paint a scene on the wall behind the altar in the Sistine Chapel.'

Taken aback, Michelangelo was silent for a few minutes. Another painting, he thought, pressing his lips together. Didn't the Pope know he was a sculptor above all? And there was the Julius tomb still to be completed. Something stopped Michelangelo from telling Clement about the tomb. He stifled a sigh.

'Will you do that? Do it for me?'

Michelangelo was astonished by the Pope's beseeching tone. The Pope, obviously ill, wanted this done soon. 'Of course, Holy Father,' he bowed his head as he tried to hide his annoyance, 'what do you suggest as a theme?'

'Perhaps the fall of the rebel angels? Or Christ's resurrection?'

'It would take some time, Holiness,' Michelangelo replied, 'and much preparation. I would have to make drawings and drafts to be copied and enlarged by my assistants. One or two of my apprentices may be able to help. The wall would need to be prepared before I start, and I would have to study the passage in the Bible thoroughly and take advice from a priest. Yes, Holiness, it can be done, though it is a large area, and it will be a long process.'

'Oh, I bid you do it. Something to complement the ceiling.' The Pope sighed in relief. 'I know you have to finish the library and the tomb in Florence. When you are ready, show me the drawings. Make it soon. Create as you wish, a vostro modo,' he said with urgency.

Michelangelo nodded. 'As soon as I can,' he agreed, wondering when he could fit it in. 'At the moment I'm also trying to finish the tomb of Pope Julius. I must return to Florence to do this. It will be two or three months before I am back in Rome.'

Pope Clement leaned back wearily in his chair. 'Meanwhile, give me the drawings so I can contemplate and anticipate them.'

'Yes, Holiness.'

'Are the Rovere family troubling you?' Clement asked.

'No. I have been contracted and paid for the tomb sculptures, that's all. I have an obligation to fulfil the contract.'

'Michelangelo, for my sake and the sake of art, don't drive yourself too hard. Take things steadily and keep yourself healthy and vigorous. There is so much good work within you yet, my son, but it will never be fulfilled if you are dead.'

'Yes, Holy Father. I will do my best to obey you.' Michelangelo rose to his feet, bowed and kissed the Pope's ring.

PART THREE
1534

FOR THE LOVE OF TOMMASO

SIXTEEN
Rome

To Tommaso,

*When anyone looks into my face, they will find my heart, because
of you nothing shows more readily. I ask for your kind mercy and
look for the response of your kind soul. My fire, as I look at you,
is chaste, and I hope you will come closer with your grace. How
happy this would make me!*

Tommaso stood by the window of his bedchamber and, in the rays
of a sultry light from a humid Rome outside, read yet another of
Michelangelo's dedicated letters and poems to him. Just to hold the
artist's writing in his hands excited him because of the novelty of it,
he had never been close to such genius before. Meeting Michelangelo,
who had produced such works as the *David* in Florence and the *Pietà*
in Rome, almost overwhelmed Tommaso. He had heard so many
rumours, yet when he met Michelangelo, his doubts disintegrated and
he felt an opening up of his heart towards the man.

There was nothing in Michelangelo's appearance to attract him. On
their first meeting he had been soberly but decently dressed, his beard
and hair freshly washed and trimmed but it was his eyes that held
Tommaso captive, light brown with flashes of blue in the iris. They
were deeply set, protected by an overhanging brow which also shaded
his flattened nose. His smile was open, his teeth clean and intact and
his voice deep and well-modulated, although Tommaso had heard that

his voice could also be loud and raucous. He was of medium height and Tommaso could look down upon him but his body was slim and his arms and legs sinewy from constant work, his hands calloused and strong, the fingers long and sensitive. He had strong arms and hands that could create divine artworks and, here on paper, he was wanting this pampered, protected youth to accept the pleadings of his heart.

Tommaso shook his head in wonderment. He looked forward to going to the workshop again and learning from him. Yet, why was he so hesitant and, despite what he knew, full of doubts? Why was he holding back? He had never been in a deep relationship with a man before.

He knew there were laws in Rome and Florence about physical friendships. Yet, as Bartolemeo had said, these liaisons were all around him in Roman society and in Florence. Michelangelo would have much to lose if he undertakes such a relationship, Tommaso thought, with society, with the Church. He would quickly become poor if he lost commissions. As far as his private sexual life was concerned, he could easily be accused by those jealous of his success but, despite rumours, no one had. Perhaps it was because they had no proof or were reluctant to accuse because of repercussions. Likely, because of this, he reverted to his New-Platonic education and explained his relationships in those terms. Deep friendships with men, nothing more. And he was careful, couching his love in rhetoric and only having friendships with men he could trust.

The last thing Michelangelo would want was to be pulled up to the authorities for his so-called deviance with young men. His reputation and his work would be ruined and destroyed. So, as Tommaso's father and Bartolemeo had said, the development of such deep relationships was spiritual, not physical, and such love was buried in his soul and recreated in his art.

'I know nothing but hard work,' Michelangelo had told Tommaso. 'That is my life.'

Tommaso turned over the palms of his own hands and gazed at their clean softness. He did not know what hard work was. He was well protected by his father and his every need catered for. Now, through his relationship with Michelangelo, his life would change. Not only would he learn to draw, an accomplishment every aristocratic young man should have, but he would also handle marble slabs, wood and terracotta, mallets and chisels, brushes, pencils, charcoal and chalk. He would be getting dirty and covered with pigments and marble dust, he would be doing as Michelangelo requested, and his hands would no longer be soft. Tommaso's longing to learn from the artist urged him to take part in this friendship, he felt propelled by the sheer magnetism of Michelangelo's intellect and creativity.

~

To Tommaso,

I burn with longing and love you with all my heart. I will never forsake you, to do so would be to lose my soul, for you are part of that.

Michelangelo stood impatiently at the window. From there he could see the piazza close to his house, and not far away was the Palazzo Cavalieri. He had sent more letters, poems and sketches to Tommaso and the first meeting had gone well; now there was only the business of receiving the young Lord Cavalieri as his apprentice. He had received word from Tommaso that he wanted to visit and now, Michelangelo waited.

Tommaso came into view, walking down the street towards him, carrying a roll of papers. Michelangelo's heart bounded with joy. Tommaso was dressed plainly for a Roman day, a light cloak over his shoulders, his doublet and hose a rich brown, a velvet cap on his head. Michelangelo marvelled at his easy grace. As he lost sight of Tommaso closer to the house, Michelangelo turned from the window and ran down the staircase, agile as a youth. He wanted to meet Tommaso at the door.

Bernardino started to open the door, only to be pushed aside by Michelangelo who, in his eagerness to greet his visitor, grabbed it and flung it wide, revealing Tommaso framed in the doorway. Bernardino stepped aside, bowed and waited. Michelangelo stood still momentarily then recovered and bowed.

'My Lord,' he said, 'you are most welcome.'

Tommaso bowed in return and felt the customary embrace, which came quickly, with a kiss on both cheeks. The Master ushered him inside into the reception hall, never taking his eyes off Tommaso as Bernardino took his cloak then led him into the salon.

'Master, I have copied the sketches you sent me, and I bring them to you for your approval.'

With a shy smile, Tommaso held the rolled paper towards Michelangelo who took the parchment, opened it and spread the roll on the table before them.

'They are well executed, my Lord,' he said, bending to look at them, 'almost as I would have drawn them.'

'You flatter me, Master,' Tommaso said.

'No, it's true, my Lord. You have talent.'

'Please, Master, I am not your Lord. Please call me Tommao, that's what my friends call me.'

'And you may call me Angelo. That's what my friends call me.' Michelangelo smiled at Tommaso who smiled back.

'I must confess,' said Tommaso, nervously. 'I have shown them to others. I am so proud to be the recipient of such works. And when you sent me the further drawing of *The Fall of Phaeton,* which pleased me very much, I could not help but show them.'

'Who have you shown them to?' Michelangelo asked cautiously.

'Cardinal Ippolito de Medici, who came to visit us. He was most impressed with them. He asked to show them to the Pope who was also impressed, especially with *The Phaeton* and he congratulates you upon them. The cardinal wishes to have the motifs of *Tityus* and *The Ganymede* engraved into rock crystal by the engraver Castelbolognese. He truly admired your representations of the myths.'

Michelangelo nodded but was silent for a moment. 'I'm pleased the young cardinal and the Pope enjoyed them as works of art, however, they really were for you alone.' He answered reservedly – the Pope and the cardinal would know the true meaning of the sketches.

'Forgive me, Michelangelo, I never thought. I just knew they would appreciate your wonderful depiction of Greek mythology, which they did.'

'Of course, Tommaso,' Michelangelo said. 'Do you know the meaning of these drawings?' he asked.

'I do, Michelangelo.'

'The original meaning, or the new meaning of the old Platonic theory?'

'Both, Michelangelo.'

'Do you understand what I mean by these drawings? *The Rape of Ganymede* and *The Legend of Tityus*? *The Fall of Phaeton*?'

'Yes, Master.'

'That you have conquered my heart?'

'Yes, Michelangelo,' Tommaso said.

Michelangelo's feelings were in torment. Would those who admired the drawings also associate the meaning of them as to how he felt about Tommaso? They had obviously admired them for their reference to the Greek myths and they knew what the myths meant. Tommaso was silent, his eyes never leaving Michelangelo's.

'Do you understand my love for you is chaste and will remain so?'

'I do, Michelangelo.'

'These drawings explain all I feel. Here is the God, Jupiter,' he pointed to the dominant form of the eagle in the sketch, 'and here is handsome Ganymede, son of the ruler of Troy. Jupiter snatches him and takes him up to Mt Olympus. Here he becomes the cup-bearer to the gods.' Michelangelo turned towards Tommaso. 'I am Jupiter, you are my cup-bearer, my muse.'

'There is another meaning, Master, that of the sexual attraction between a man such as yourself and a younger man such as myself. That is the common interpretation.'

'Yes, I am the eagle, you are the young man,' Michelangelo said quietly.

'Or the other way, Master. I am the eagle and I have you in my thrall, forever worshipping me as divine, bringing you closer to the gods.' Tommaso smiled.

Michelangelo laughed, impressed with how Tommaso had turned the legend around. He moved closer to Tommaso as if to embrace him, instead holding onto him at arm's length. Michelangelo felt Tommaso tense under his touch and his eyes widen as he looked at the Master. 'You are so close to God,' Michelangelo continued. 'I yearn to be absorbed by your youth and beauty, to banish old age, death and decay. When I am with you and apart, I am filled with the wish to live forever. You raise my spirit from the mundane, the everyday, to the immortal. I see you understand perfectly what this sketch is about. Your beauty connects me with the divine. It is eternal, a gift reflecting the supernatural beauty of God. The more I see you, the closer we become, and the closer I feel to God.'

Tommaso was quiet at this revelation. Michelangelo was serious. He was aware he was entrenched in the ways of New Platonism and lived his life by it. The philosophy influenced even the composition of his paintings and sculpture. He wondered if this would daunt Tommaso.

'And what about *The Legend of Tityus?*' Tommaso asked.

'Tityus is a rapist and he's being punished for his sin in hell. The large bird bends over him, not an eagle this time, but a vulture, attacking Tityus's liver.'

'The seat of lust.'

'Yes. I must not commit the sin of lust,' Michelangelo said, shaking his head and looking down at the sketches, 'for that can lead to the sin of rape. It is my vow to you, that's why I gave you those sketches. To show my feelings and to reassure you that you are safe.'

Tommaso took Michelangelo's hand and held it within his own. 'I'm honoured by you and I adore you, and yes, I am safe,' he said earnestly, bending to kiss Michelangelo's hand.

Overcome with gratitude and relief, Michelangelo felt like taking Tommaso in his arms and kissing him. Instead, he stood before him, his head lowered, his heart thumping at Tommaso's tenderness –

something he had never felt with Febo.

'Thank you, Tommao. Thank you,' he said, recovering. 'My love for you rises to the sacred love of God. I become whole, peaceful and sheltered from the storms of life that surround us.'

Tommaso removed his hand from Michelangelo's. 'I acknowledge your joy, and I acknowledge your love. I understand about your soul rising to the Almighty. I know of these things. That happens to me when I see your art.'

'Come, I will show you to my workshop. There, I will draw you and then you will copy your own likeness.'

Tommaso walked with Michelangelo down the hallway and into the workshop. Some of the apprentices were working quietly in the background and Michelangelo clapped his hands and quickly ushered them out, telling them to join the sculptors in another room he had set up.

He turned to Tommaso. 'I wish to sketch you side on, from the shoulders upwards, your head slightly bent, your gaze downwards.'

'You wish me to remove my clothes, Michelangelo?' Anxiety and nervousness edged Tommaso's voice.

'Just your doublet and shirt.'

Tommaso did as he was told and stood before Michelangelo, barechested, awaiting instructions.

Michelangelo felt he would expire with desire. His whole body weakened as he gazed at Tommaso. 'Sit, Tommao, sit.' The Master hoped his feelings were not showing as he indicated a stool.

Tommaso sat and waited. Michelangelo, relieved to move himself from the intimacy of Tommaso's presence, walked to a nearby table to collect paper and chalk.

'Be still, Tommao. Do not talk. Relax yourself,' he said, returning to the chair in front of Tommaso. He sat, pulling a sketching board onto his lap, laying the paper on top, smoothing it with a clean cloth – anything to distract from his tumultuous feelings. He had never felt this strongly before.

The workshop was quiet with only the sound of Michelangelo's noisy breathing, something he had suffered from since his assault, especially noticeable when concentrating on his work and something he seemed to be unaware of. He gazed at the elegant features of the young man before him, wondering how he could capture such beauty that could only come from God. His heart pounded and he wanted to throw the chalk and paper away, bend on one knee and bury his head in Tommaso's lap. How was he going to resist the temptation to claim him sexually? But he also wanted him spiritually, which was more important. So how long could he hold out without expressing his love physically? Yet, he knew such action would lose him the young man forever; he had to tread carefully.

If there were sexual overtures they would have to come from Tommaso. His mind was in a tumult and his desires appalled him. They were sinful, completely against his faith. He would have to confess them. Yet, he loved and such love could only come from God, because before him stood the epitome of young masculine God-given beauty.

Did Tommaso feel the same? It was too early to ask, too early to know. The boy was inexperienced and more than likely a virgin.

Every feature on Tommaso's face was accurately drawn and his physical beauty was beyond compare. Michelangelo longed to reach out and touch the smoothness of the young man's skin, to run his hands over his shoulders, up the curve of his neck and under his jaw, cup the beauty of his face in his hands, feel the tenderness of his lips under his own, devour him and drown in him. He finished the drawing and relaxed, allowing the tension to leave him.

'Put your clothes back on, Tommao,' Michelangelo said. 'I shall get you some mulled wine. Here is your drawing.'

Tommaso looked at the parchment in front of him. Drawn in red chalk, his portrait was almost feminine, except for the outline of musculature beneath the skin. He was still staring at it when Michelangelo walked back into the room carrying a tray with glass cups of mulled wine and a plate of sweetmeats. 'This is perfect. I will never be able to draw that well, Master,' Tommaso said, plaintively holding out the drawing to Michelangelo.

'You *will* draw that well. You must try to draw as well as you can, whenever you can. Don't copy just this drawing, draw anything. A flower, a glass of wine, your father's face. Anything. Drawing is the key to making art. You must practise until you are perfect. Then I will teach you to grind the pigments, mix colours and paint on panel. Finally, I will teach you to model in clay and sculpt in stone, to create something from nothing. There is so much to learn.' It was hard to keep the excitement and eagerness out of his voice.

Tommaso donned his shirt and nodded thoughtfully. 'I will try my best.'

'Tommao, you have the ability. You just need to persist and that will help your confidence to grow. Come and see me often and you will quickly learn.' Michelangelo offered the wine which Tommaso took. 'Now, I will give you chalk and paper for you to draw. Remember, Tommao, you are learning. It will not be perfect, but it will be a step on the way to perfection.'

~

To Tommaso,

Whenever I look upon your lovely face, I see the promise of the divine. Nothing in life could give explanation for the joy encased in my body, other than it has already risen up to heaven.

When Tommaso left him, Michelangelo took a deep breath and found his mouth dry from nervousness and the stone-dust in the air. The motes danced in the sunlight and his thoughts immediately turned to his mother.

'Gold-dust, angel-dust,' he murmured.

Was his mother really with him now, when his feelings were in a tumult? What would she think of his new love? He put the thought out of his mind. Most probably she would not approve any more than his father would. But what they thought no longer mattered; they were not living his life.

He sniffed. The air made some of his apprentices sneeze, their eyes and noses red and running, so he had to send them outside until they recovered. Sometimes it was so bad they couldn't continue. Michelangelo was not usually challenged by the state of his workshop; now his thought was with Tommaso and he did not want his new love suffering such an indignity.

He looked around the large room with its trestle tables and ladders, macigno and marble blocks in various stages of development. There was much to be done before Tommaso returned for his next lesson. He would get Bernardino onto it – sweep and clean, make the workshop orderly. Michelangelo's head spun with excitement; the thought of seeing Tommaso regularly made him giddy and he had to sit down. He'd have to wait and be careful with those around him. In the meantime, he would write to his love, sonnets and letters. Michelangelo took up his pen. He would always write about Tommaso, write to him and love him. And he was not far away, just up the Capitoline Hill.

SEVENTEEN
Florence, 1534

My dear Lord Tommaso,

I thought you already knew from my many letters that I love you without limit. I have not written to you, not because I no longer love you. Just your name overcomes me and fills me with much sweetness and calm, and because of it I know I will see heaven.

Michelangelo stood back to examine the surface of the marble statue he had recently finished. He had polished it with pumice and emery until it reflected light – as smooth as glass. He ran a soft cloth over the marble, enhancing the translucency. His heart was in its creation. The mallet and chisel, the extension of his arm and hand, had followed the dictates of his mind and finely hewn out of stone, the even features of a young, athletic man.

Lost in longing and reveries of Tommaso's face, Michelangelo had let his mind take over fashioning the likeness of his love. It wasn't the first time he had made such a transference during creation; not the first time when the mallet and chisel seemed to work by themselves even though both implements were in his hands, obeying his pressure. Before, when he created the *Pietà,* he had experienced a trancelike sensibility he couldn't explain as he fashioned the features of the Virgin and the face of the dead Christ. Even the *David,* although a much larger work, found him lost in the beauty of his mind's eye. It was as if he stood outside of himself and watched the creation coming together by another force.

This latest image he had created was supposedly of the dead Duke Giulano de Medici, sculpted for the Duke's tomb in the Medici Chapel in Florence. Michelangelo hadn't created Giulano, but an image of his love, Tommaso. The finely hewn features, sweet lips, long neck, the musculature of the young body within skin-tight armour. He had already begun the immortalisation of his beloved, soon to stand forever within the chapel.

He reached up and touched the sculptured face, then ran his hand down over the smoothness of the body. The Medici Duke – whom he remembered from his youth – looked nothing like this statue. He wondered if anyone would realise what he had done. If anyone did, he would say he had simply made the Duke more handsome than he had been in life and that no one in years to come would know otherwise.

There was also another statue he had created in the long hours thinking of Tommaso. He left the Medici statue, strode over to the nearly finished sculpture and whipped the covering sheet off. He stared at the sculpture and once again saw Tommaso's face. The form of the young man was in an unusual twisted position, the body appearing supple and muscled, the face evenly and finely featured, the noble head turned with hair strictly curled. The face was similar to Giulano's statue. The statue's left leg was raised, and he was kneeling on the bent back of a nearly prostrating older man. *Victory,* Michelangelo called it. He focused on the youth's face then on the face below it, bearded and aged, and he gazed at his own likeness. This sculpture would belong to the *Slaves* group. Tommaso would recognise the explicit expression of Michelangelo's love in this piece.

Tommaso had conquered him and he was under his spell. A spell he did not want broken.

To Tommaso, it was as though the run of days had ground slowly to a stop; as if part of his life had died, only it hadn't. It had instead moved some miles north to Florence. His heart was there; the void was in Rome.

He wrote letters, poured out the longing within him, almost an illness. When would Michelangelo return? Some days he would lie on the floor of the Sistine Chapel, losing himself in Michelangelo's view of the Bible above: colours, movement, figures, the touch of God reaching out to Adam. It seemed Michelangelo was reaching out to Tommaso. He studied, wrote, sketched, walked, went to Mass and Communion, felt guilty, confessed, locked himself in his room, re-read Michelangelo's poems and sketched again.

To Michelangelo,

Of course, I should know that you would not forget me. I avoid all others which may please you. Come back soon; I long to see you and have my heart eased.

~

The rap upon the door was loud and urgent. Bernardino, questioning who it might be on this late Florentine afternoon, scampered down the hall to answer it. Michelangelo, from his workshop, popped his head out into the hallway, equally curious.

Suddenly afraid for his Master, Bernardino waved his hand at him to disappear. Although they had been in Florence some months, they had largely kept to themselves. The danger to Michelangelo's life was still a problem. The last time they had been here, Michelangelo had been hunted by Clement's soldiers because he'd helped defend Florence against papal troops. He had been made Florence's "superintendent of defence" and designed walls and fortifications for the city to protect it against the forces of Pope Clement and the Holy Roman Emperor.

Michelangelo had gone into hiding in a cellar beneath the Medici Chapel. It had limited light which had not prevented him drawing on the walls. Although Bernardino was still wary, all had been well in the end. Clement, ever mindful of Michelangelo's talent, had rescued him by calling off the search and telling the city's new order to treat the man with respect and kindness.

The sharp rap repeated on the door made Bernardino's heart beat faster. He opened the door cautiously, then asked in astonishment, 'What are you doing here?'

Febo stood before him, taller and broader, not as stylishly dressed as when he had been Michelangelo's favourite.

'Is there any reason why I shouldn't be here?' Febo answered belligerently. 'After all, this was my home for quite some time. I slept here, don't you remember?'

'Have you brought anyone with you?' Bernardino looked past him, afraid of who might be lurking on the street.

'No, I came alone,' Febo said. 'I have come for my wages, for the money I am owed. I want to see the Master.'

'He's busy with the apprentices in the workshop. Wait here. I will see if it's convenient,' Bernardino said, starting to close the door.

Febo smirked at Bernardino. 'With his new love, no doubt.' He put out his hand and leant on the door. He pushed it away, toppling Bernardino to the floor then he passed him without a glance, down the hall and into the workshop.

'Stop, come back,' Bernardino shouted as he scrambled to his feet and ran after him. But it was too late, Febo had disappeared.

~

'Febo, what are you doing in Florence?' Michelangelo, surprised, swivelled on his stool, mallet and chisel raised. The tone of Michelangelo's voice was enough for the apprentices to stop their work and look at the pair. Michelangelo beckoned to them to leave the room. Bernardino ushered them out of the door and into the next workroom. 'You told me in your last letter you were going to stay in Genoa,' Michelangelo was annoyed. He didn't stand to greet Febo who looked hesitant, uncertain how to approach the Master.

He gave Michelangelo a bow. 'I have come to visit you, Master. I heard you were back in Florence and I thought I would collect my reimbursement for the job you gave me. You now have a house and land in Genoa, and I also checked your workmen in Pisa regarding the shipping of marble. Something you didn't ask me to do.'

Michelangelo looked at Febo steadily. 'You did not have to call and see me about that, I gave you enough money to cover your expenses and your wages for doing so and you could have sent me a letter by messenger.' He put down his mallet and chisel and rose to his feet. 'Go into the salon, and I will come to you there.' He stripped off his apron and threw it over the stool, deep in thought, running his hands through his hair, a look of annoyance straining his face.

'Where is he, Master?' Bernardino stood panting at the workshop door.

'In the salon. Come.'

Febo turned around abruptly when they entered the salon.

'Have you eaten today?' Michelangelo asked gruffly as he turned to Bernardino. 'Some wine and food for our traveller, please Bernardino?'

Bernardino left the room and headed for the kitchen. Michelangelo turned to face Febo who looked thin and pale and was obviously there for one thing – more money. He had grown in his absence. His large, expressive eyes, which Michelangelo had so loved, were enormous in the pallor of his face.

'Master, I wish to serve you, be part of your household again; be with you. I have missed you, Master.'

Michelangelo shook his head; he was not going to give in to him. 'That cannot be. I have too many helpers and apprentices already and, when I leave here for Rome, I won't be able to afford to take you or the apprentices with me. I already have some people in Rome to help me. I'm not taking anyone with me except Bernardino.'

Febo's face hardened. 'How can you discard me so readily? I thought you loved me.'

'I do, as a son,' answered Michelangelo.

Febo raised his eyebrows at him.

'We have discussed this before, Febo,' Michelangelo continued. 'I thought you understood.'

'I hoped by now you would have changed your mind.' Febo's voice echoed his disappointment. 'I have been so much a part of your life for so long.'

Bernardino opened the door and walked in with a tray of food and wine glasses.

Michelangelo beckoned to Febo to sit and eat, which he did so readily, wolfing down cheese and bread, figs and grapes, as if he hadn't eaten in a week. Michelangelo and Bernardino, in silence, watched the food disappear. Bernardino gathered the empty dishes and left the two alone.

'Febo, you must know that although I love you, I can no longer provide for you. There are too many dependent on me already, including my brothers in Settignano and my niece and nephew. My father, God rest his soul, is no longer a burden on me. Although he has gone, I can't support anyone else.'

'I have had an offer of employment from Cardinal Biagio da Cesena in Rome,' Febo said quietly, his face serious.

'The Vatican protocol chief?' Michelangelo was alarmed. Febo had been busy.

'I would rather be in your household, Master.'

'It cannot be,' Michelangelo shook his head.

'He seems very keen to employ me. I wonder why.'

'You know why. He's my enemy. He knows you have been in my household and will want to know everything about me. He will use you, question you. He finds everything I do distasteful.'

'That's not the way he speaks about you.'

Michelangelo narrowed his eyes at Febo. He knew what da Cesena thought of him. 'Don't be fooled by him. I would rather you didn't enter his household. You know some of the things he has said about my work and about me.'

'He seems to be of the opinion that you follow your basic instincts and reveal them in your art work,' Febo said, grinning. 'That's what many people think. Is that true?'

'It's untrue and you should know that without asking. He doesn't understand my art, how I work. I just wish to demonstrate the beauty of man as given by God, nothing more.'

'You do it too well, Michelangelo. Others see the "more" in your work,' Febo answered.

'If you work for Cesena, you will never be welcome in my house again. Do you want that?' Michelangelo's voice rose impatiently.

'It feels like that already. You want to be rid of me. Da Cesena might be your enemy, I am not.'

'You are willing to work for my enemy?' Michelangelo stood over Febo. 'I have loved you ardently, provided for you, given you gifts, and yet you hate me so.'

'I have given you my body, my love and my time,' Febo shouted, jumping to his feet, knocking the glass of wine off the table.

Michelangelo stepped back as if struck, shocked at the vehemence, unable to believe the torrent of bitterness emanating from Febo. 'I will give you money, yet again. What have you got against me? Why do you hate me so, when I have done so much for you?'

'I will take your money and you will never hear from me or see me again,' Febo said, stretching his hand out.

Michelangelo reached into the pocket within the fold of his breeches and pulled out the familiar money purse he always carried with him. It was laden with gold coins.

'This means your silence, Febo,' Michelangelo roared, his temper no longer under control as he spilt gold coins onto the table, 'and it's the last you shall have from me. I never want to see you again.' He stormed out of the salon nearly bowling over Bernardino who was listening on the other side of the door.

'What are you doing, Bernardino?' he yelled. 'Eavesdropping? As if I haven't enough traitors in my life. Get back to the kitchen!'

'On my way, Master.' Bernardino ran down the hallway.

'Stop,' Michelangelo bellowed. 'See the blackmailer out of my house first and never let him in again. Mind he doesn't steal anything else from me on his way out.'

Michelangelo stalked into the kitchen and slumped on a chair; his head in his hands. He heard the front door of the house close then Bernardino's footsteps shuffle down the hall.

'Master, he's gone, and he won't worry you again.'

'I doubt that very much, Dino.'

Bernardino walked over to Michelangelo and placed his hand on the artist's shoulder. 'All will be well, Angelo. You are thought highly of by the Holy See. They won't listen to one such as Febo.'

Michelangelo reached out and put his arms around Bernardino and hugged him then sank back wearily in the chair. He had been working throughout the day on the sculptures for the Medici tomb and for the tomb of Pope Julius. Bernardino cleared the supper dishes off the table and Michelangelo, exhausted, lowered his head into his arms.

'There is nothing for me here now, Bernardino,' he said in a muffled voice. 'I have done as much as I can in Florence. The work on the Laurentian Library is underway and the Medici tomb in the sacristy of San Lorenzo is almost complete. I have nearly completed the sculptures for the Julius tomb. I have been pushed and pulled by the Popes, one after the other, although I have tried to please them. My future isn't in Florence. I can't stay here any longer.'

He gave a strangled cry. 'Now, my father and Buonarroto are dead and I miss them terribly. Buonarroto was the only brother I really loved and who loved me, and the plague's taken him and left his son and daughter for me to provide for. Febo, whom I loved so much for so long, has turned against me. Pope Clement, my friend, my patron, my supporter, is ill and some say dying. All this in only a few years. My remaining brothers have need of me. I'm still supporting them. I feel so alone.' His shoulders shook with suppressed sobs.

Bernardino put the tray on the table and went to him and laid his hand on Michelangelo's arm.

'You are not alone, Michelangelo. I'm here, and there is someone who awaits you, Master. Someone in Rome who loves and admires you dearly.'

'Yes, of course. Rome,' Michelangelo said, wiping his face with his hands.

Bernardino poured him a glass of Trebbiano. 'Have this, Master. It will restore your spirits.'

'To Rome,' Michelangelo said, downing the wine. 'I must write to Tommaso. These past months have been a trial without him.'

~

To Bartolomeo Angelini,

I long to be with Tommaso again. As you must know being parted from him tears my soul and I long to be with him every day and night. My soul is with him and my heart is here, and it is only natural that my heart should be with my soul.

Bartolomeo Angelini to Michelangelo,

My Lord Tommaso loves you as much as you love him and tells me every day that he wishes you to return to Rome. He tells me that when he is with you, he is happy and satisfied; to him you mean the world. He knows God has favoured him because of your friendship. He worships you. Obviously, he is eager for your return. Why don't you make definite plans to return to Rome?

Michelangelo smiled at Bernardino as he entered the workshop. 'Bartolemeo has delivered a message from Tommaso. He told him that when he is with me he is truly happy because he possesses all that he wishes for in this world. He loves me, Dino.'

Bernardino nodded with a smile. 'Yes, Master, he does, and now, you will soon see him.'

EIGHTEEN
Rome, 1534

Michelangelo let out a whoop of joy and urged his horse on. Bernardino followed as fast as his mule's legs would carry him. They rode down the ancient Via Flaminia outside Rome, through the Porta del Popolo, the gate in the Aurelian wall, then onwards, travelling by the Via del Corso, skirting the outer fields bordering the city.

Once they were inside the city, the stench of the busy Roman street assailed them. Rome, cradled within its walls in the wide Tiber valley, was saturated with heat which pulsed before and around them in a mirage of red, green, brown and yellow, tinged with shades of blue. Michelangelo sighed deeply with relief to be in the same city as Tommaso.

'At last,' he said to Bernardino. 'This is my home now. I shall never return to Florence.'

'Yes, Michelangelo. Here you will have a new life and here you must stay.'

'My happiness lies within these walls, Bernardino. Forever, within these walls, just waiting for me.' He turned to his companion with a grin.

'Just waiting for you, Master,' echoed Bernardino, happily returning the grin despite knowing Michelangelo could be equally as sad as he could be happy.

Michelangelo looked towards the Capitoline Hill where his love awaited him and his heart swelled with relief, excitement and longing. Only Tommaso could stir him this way.

As they rode through the narrow, unpaved streets of Rome's older quarter, they could see that the grand monuments in the Foro Romano and the Foro Imperiale, once the glory of the Roman Empire, were broken into pieces and half-covered with earth, lying where the centre of the world used to be. The city looked as if it was still recovering from the Sack and there was evidence of looting, burning and ruins in places.

Passing the Colosseum, Bernardino noticed its lower arches were now home to local foraging cattle and goats, as well as groups of homeless and Roma people. A huddle of shacks surrounded the carved Trajan's Column. They skirted the crowded, noisy Trajan Market and even Michelangelo's desensitised nose wrinkled at the overriding smell of pigs and offal. In the "slaughterhouse of crows" the air was filled with the cries and squawks of birds trapped in cages, waiting to be killed.

At last they reached the house in Macello dei Corvi, on the edge of the city, at the base of the Capitoline Hill. In the welcome shade of its wide ochre frontage Michelangelo and Bernardino dismounted then led their steeds around the side of the house to the stable. After unloading and stabling the equidae, they entered the house through the back door. The air was cool and stale, and gold dust tumbled about Michelangelo as he opened the window shutters and let the light, noise and smells of Rome in.

The repair of the house, which had been damaged in the Sack, was finally completed and Michelangelo sighed with happiness as the house folded around him in welcome. This was a far better dwelling than the other house in Florence or the one near Saint Peter's Basilica, still an area full of piles of rubble and raucous workmen. Here he could settle and create and be close to his love, Tommaso.

The house was two-storeyed with high ceilings. A large vestibule led from the entrance hall, decorated with arches and frescoes, and a wide marble staircase gave access to upstairs bedchambers. Downstairs was one large salon decorated with frescoes; a downstairs bedchamber was near a large workshop with a high ceiling. An arched hallway led to a garden atrium surrounded by a loggia. Also, there was a more intimate private salon for Michelangelo and another room that he would convert into a workshop. The kitchen and pantry were out the back with access to the basement.

It was not far away from the dun-coloured River Tiber, which was one big privy. All the drains of the city, since Roman times, entered the cloaca maxima and polluted the river and, if the wind was in the right direction, the stink was worse than the Arno in Florence, especially in the summer heat. Bernardino didn't like that; Michelangelo's broken nose protected him from the smell.

Michelangelo and Bernardino walked in the expansive garden at the back of the house. The vegetable and herb patches needed tending and Bernardino would take pleasure in that. Two fig trees, along with peach and pomegranate and a climbing grape, had grown wild and needed pruning. The stables were also there along with a forge. A crowd of overgrown jasmine, dianthus and wild roses competed for survival. Michelangelo was pleased to see the chicken coop was intact, although the chickens and cockerel were pecking their way through the long grass around the men's feet. There were also two wells in the grounds and two cottages, one for the stable boy and one for Bernardino or the Master's assistants, who rarely used it, except to get away from Michelangelo sometimes. In comparison to many houses that had been damaged and set fire to in the Sack, this one had survived and would be lived in again.

Who wouldn't one be happy living in such a house? thought Michelangelo. It was pleasant and cool, easy to live in. Ah yes! He sighed, relishing the comfort and peace despite the disrepair of Rome.

~

Sitting at one of the workbenches in his workshop, Michelangelo was busily completing the sketches he had started for the wall of the Sistine Chapel when Bernardino interrupted him.

'Master, there's news about the Pope,' Bernardino said, indicating a messenger at the entrance to the workshop. They had only been in Rome two days and already news was following him.

The messenger bowed. Michelangelo recognised his livery as belonging to the De Rovere household. 'What news do you bring?' he frowned.

'It's within the letter I was asked to give you, Master,' the messenger bowed, handing him the letter.

'Whatever could it be? I was talking to Lionardo della Rovere the day we arrived.' Michelangelo took the letter and broke the Rovere seal.

To his surprise, there was a further letter inside with the Vatican seal. 'I thought all our business as far as the Julius tomb had been arranged,' he said and began to read, frowning. 'Oh dear!' Michelangelo sighed. 'You may go.' He waved the messenger off and turned his attention back to the letter as Bernardino showed the man out the door.

Michelangelo still sat within the workshop, his head bent over the letter in his hand.

'Master, what is it?' Bernardino said as he entered the room.

'Pope Clement is dying and has asked to see me.' Michelangelo handed the letter to Bernardino. 'My old friend from Medici days. I must make haste to visit him.'

Bernardino took the letter and examined the seals and fine writing. 'Then this makes painting the wall in the Sistine Chapel even more pertinent, because that's what Clement wants.'

'Of course,' Michelangelo sighed again. 'However, the new Pope may not want it. I will have to wait until the next Pope is on the throne to find out.'

'Didn't you give Pope Clement the drawings and he approved them?'

'Yes, he saw them, and thought my idea of the fresco being about the last judgement better than his about the fallen angels or the resurrection. He liked the sketches; however, we were still in negotiations when I went back to Florence. Much has to be done to the wall before I can contemplate what to put on it.'

'Perhaps the new Pope will want something different.'

'We shall see,' answered Michelangelo.

~

Michelangelo waited impatiently outside the door of the Pope's private apartments. The guards barred him from entering and he had to wait until he was called. He was desperate to see the Pontiff before he died. He tapped his shoes on the floor, turned on the spot, paced up and down, hopped from foot to foot. The guards didn't relent.

After an interminable wait, the door opened and the cardinal secretary, Baldasarre Turini da Pescia, came out to meet him and conduct him to the Pope.

'Will the Holy Father recognise me?' Michelangelo anxiously asked the austere da Pescia.

'Yes, he is quite lucid, but he's very ill and tires easily.' The cardinal led him into the antechamber of the Pope's bedchamber then opened the large door and ushered Michelangelo inside.

The room was dimly lit, with a few candles in sconces, and the shutters were closed on the tall windows. A priest in attendance to the Pope hovered at the edge of the room. Michelangelo's eyes went straight to the figure in the high bed. He was propped with pillows, laughing and talking with a visiting cardinal who glanced at Michelangelo as he approached. Clement waved the cleric away, extending his hand for him to kiss before the man bowed and retreated from the bedside. The Pope settled from his animated conversation with the cardinal and focused his attention on Michelangelo.

He didn't look as if he was dying, Michelangelo thought, surprised how bright the Pope was and how vigorously he had been talking.

'Michelangelo, my dear friend,' Clement raised his hand in a blessing over the artist.

Michelangelo knelt and kissed the Pope's ring then stayed on his knees beside the bed. Clement, though bright, looked frail and worn, the skin stretched tightly across the bones of his face, his once full beard now thin. He reached out and took Michelangelo's hand and held onto it with a startling strength.

'Holy Father, can I send anything to you to eat or drink? We have peaches and figs in the garden I could send over,' Michelangelo said, bending to the Pontiff's hand. He was thinking of his over-grown kitchen garden that Bernardino was fossicking his way through, taking pride in weeding and replanting.

'No, no. Thank you. You have given me much in the past. Grapes, wine, figs. I appreciate your kindness. I need nothing now. I leave the world as I came into it, with nothing. I can no longer eat, Michelangelo, and can only drink a little; there is no pain, just shivers and aches all over me as my body shuts down.'

Overcome with tears, which surprised him, Michelangelo buried his head in the Pontiff's bedclothes. He was flooded with memories of their youth and how they had both loved Lorenzo de Medici. Michelangelo often thought of Lorenzo and how well he treated him. He'd had his own room, a feather bed and pillow, and a violet cloak to wear as well as a salary of five ducats. And he had the freedom to wander the impressive art filled rooms of the luxurious Palazzo Medici and take part in the stimulating conversation with Lorenzo and his friends over dinner, talking about the ancient Greeks, New Platonism, Humanism, religion and art. Lorenzo's love was like that of a father to him, more so than his own.

When Lorenzo died, he had crept into the church of San Marco where Lorenzo lay, to stand stunned near the catafalque as mourners filed past. The next day he watched the corteggio wind its way from San Marco to San Lorenzo where Lorenzo was to be buried. He had rushed to his father's house and locked himself in his bedchamber. He thought he would never recover from the grief and the suddenness of the death. The loss still hurt him after all these years.

Now, in Clement's chambers, he felt Lorenzo's presence near them, reassuring them. Michelangelo, looking at Pope Clement, was dismayed at how much this once large and handsome man had withered away. It was as if he were already dead and only his spirit remained.

'Michelangelo, look at me,' demanded Clement and, when Michelangelo looked up again, the light in the Pontiff's eyes told him he was not dead yet. The Pope grasped Michelangelo's hand tightly in his own. 'You must go ahead with the fresco on the wall of the Sistine. Please do it in memory of me and put my coat-of-arms on it. You have declined my idea of the fallen angels and rightly so, I think. Your idea about the last judgement and the sketches you have shown me please me very much. I wish I could see the finished painting, God has thought otherwise. Hopefully, I will see it from heaven. My papacy will be remembered for the wrong reasons, I'm afraid. We have lost so many of our brothers and sisters in the north, and England has become a place of apostasy dictated by the evil machinations of a tyrant king. He argues that, according to canon law, he never should have been given dispensation to marry Catherine since she was the widow of Prince Arthur, his late brother.' Clement paused. A struggle passed over his face as if he fought for strength. 'She swore the marriage had not been consummated and she was still a virgin when she married Henry. He argues that she was Arthur's widow and her barrenness, apart from Princess Mary, was an indication of God's displeasure. What nonsense! He waited a long time to find that out. Poor Queen Catherine. The excommunication has been suspended for the moment, the whole business has killed me, so it will be for the next Pope to decide on that.'

Clement gasped for breath after the tirade, as if talking about it had ridden him with pain. The attendant priest hurried to his side, supported his head and gave him water to drink. The Pope fell back on the pillows, his hand, slight and dry, still firmly within the artist's.

Michelangelo was silent as he digested the news. He knew Clement had most probably considered the fact that Catherine of Aragon was the aunt of Charles V, whom he had crowned as Emperor of the Holy Roman Empire. The Pope had been in an impossible position; in the end it was easier to offend Henry than the Emperor.

Clement gathered his breath and continued, 'The painting must show our defiance in the face of evil. It must depict the good and the bad. Christ must be at its centre and be surrounded by angels. Christ is our Church, and the painting will show that our lives are predestined as St Paul writes, so it must also depict hope.'

Michelangelo bowed his head in acknowledgement. 'I will do my very best to honour your wishes, Holy Father.'

'Yes, I know you will. My dear uncle was so right in supporting you. I remember you well, Michelangelo, so young, brilliant and handsome. I love you, dear Michelangelo. God bless you.' His grip on Michelangelo's hand lessened and he raised it in blessing.

'I love you, Holy Father.' Michelangelo, head bent, made the sign of the cross.

Cardinal Secretary da Pescia indicated the audience was over and Michelangelo stood up beside the bed. The Pope had closed his eyes and appeared to be sleeping.

'May I kiss him?' Michelangelo asked the cardinal.

Da Pescia nodded and Michelangelo bent to kiss his friend on the forehead.

Clement just lay still, his eyes closed, breathing lightly, but as Michelangelo turned to go, Clement grabbed his hand. 'Thank you for coming to see me, Michelangelo,' he said huskily. 'A vostro moda.'

The bright light after the darkened room blinded Michelangelo as he was escorted through the halls of the Apostolic Palace and down Bramante's staircase to the piazza outside. He stood in the sunshine in a daze of grief and disbelief, aware of the activity around the old basilica built over the grave of St Peter. His friend and patron would soon be gone, and a new Pope would be chosen in the forthcoming conclave. Would he want the altar painting in the Sistine? Head down, his eyes on the cobbles beneath his feet, Michelangelo shrugged his cloak around him and walked out into the piazza towards his home.

~

Later that day, engrossed in his workroom, sculpting one of the statues for the Julius tomb, Michelangelo didn't hear the heavy door knocker ram against the front door of his house. Bernardino opened the door to find a Vatican messenger standing there. He presented Bernardino with a letter bearing the papal crest, sent by Cardinal da Pescia, and

Bernardino hurried to the workroom, the messenger behind him.

'I fear bad news, Master,' Bernardino said, holding out the letter.

Michelangelo wiped his hands on his apron before taking the letter and breaking the seal. He read silently then looked at the expectant Bernardino.

'The Pope has died, Dino. My dear friend and patron, Clement, is dead. This ends my long relationship with the Medici. Forty-five years. Gone, just like that.' He snapped his fingers, then sat on his work stool, staring glumly at the letter as if hoping the message was not true. He finally looked up and waved away the messenger, who hurriedly bowed and left.

'Is there anything I can get you, Master? Wine, cordial? A posset to recover your spirits?' Bernardino was alarmed at Michelangelo's defeated attitude.

The artist shook his head. 'Just leave me alone. And that goes for everyone. Dismiss the apprentices for the day.'

Bernardino ushered the silenced apprentices away then closed the door behind him.

NINETEEN
Rome, 1534

Tommaso was elated. Armed with sketches and poems, he walked quickly through the streets down to Macello dei Corvi to visit Michelangelo. The artist had returned to Rome and already the gossip was flying. Tommaso had heard some of it, which had been repeated to his father. He had warned Tommaso to be careful as people were talking. Tommaso, though disturbed, had to see Michelangelo again. While he'd been in Florence, Tommaso had missed the stimulating conversation with him, just being within the city, breathing the same air as the artist was enough for him and now, he longed to experience the Master's presence.

The letters from Florence came regularly and when they did he read them with relief and answered them immediately, sending the messenger back straight away with the reply. His life, with the artist absent in Florence, was taken up with impatient longing for his return. This surprised Tommaso – his doubts about the relationship seemed to have eased. Now, he was on his way to see Michelangelo again and the thought of being in his company and absorbing all he had to learn from him, bubbled up within Tommaso, making him almost run. He, too, would relish his creativity and be part of his art.

The sun was barely up and the shadows were long in the street. Michelangelo would be up, either at work or on his way to Mass at his beloved church of Santa Maria Nova, ancient and crumbling, where his devotions weren't distracted by the artwork on the walls. Tommaso was prepared to wait for the Master. He saw the house, market and the old Roman Forum nearby and, in his excitement, he increased his pace, almost breaking into a run. Bernardino answered the knock on the door, bowed and ushered him inside.

'Welcome, my Lord. I shall tell the Master you are here.'

Tommaso looked around the entrance hall and noted the frescoes on the wall. At his feet were marble tiles and the early sun was beginning to shine, creating pools of bright light in the vestibule. A pleasant house, just as the Master had said. And there he was, standing before him, a welcoming smile lighting up his face. Tommaso smiled back at him and felt like running and throwing his arms about him in the joy and relief of seeing him again. Instead he stood still, suddenly shy.

'Tommaso.' Michelangelo held out his arms to the young man.

Tommaso wanted to be welcomed warmly, was it right to do so in return? Michelangelo seemed to have no qualms about the matter and walked towards Tommaso, throwing his arms about him. Tommaso felt the rough, strong pull of his embrace and then Michelangelo kissed him on both cheeks.

'I have been waiting impatiently for months to see you, and now I'm in Rome for good we shall see each other often,' Michelangelo said, pulling back and gazing at Tommaso earnestly. He reached out for Tommaso's hands and held them within his own. His hands were firm, warm and dry. Tommaso nodded and smiled. 'You inspire me so much, Tommao. There are so many sketches I wish to do of you.'

'Of course, Master, and I'm honoured and I also want to learn.' Once more in his company, Tommaso was captivated and sensed that Michelangelo really did love him deeply.

'And you shall, Tommao,' said Michelangelo. 'Have you eaten this morning?'

'I have, Michelangelo.'

'Then you are eager to start?'

'Yes, Master, very eager, and I have brought sketches for you to look at and some poems I have written honouring you.'

'I can see, Tommao, that this is going to be a very fruitful relationship.' Michelangelo smiled, putting his arm about Tommaso's young shoulders and drawing him close.

Tommaso did not pull away from the embrace. He realised, with relief, that this was what he wanted – to be in Michelangelo's arms, to be loved by the supreme artist. Michelangelo ushered him into the workshop and quickly introduced him to other apprentices working there. He pointed to a chair near a trestle table.

'Sit, Tommaso. I will have a look at your drawings.'

Tommaso pulled out his leather folio and spread his work on the table. The artist held his spectacles on his nose and carefully studied the drawings.

'These are very good, Tommaso. You have started well and have been busy, I can see, over the past months. Good,' Michelangelo said, patting him on the shoulder.

Tommaso looked around at the four apprentices in the workshop, noticing there was no sign of Febo. The youths were all busily carving various blocks of marble, making wax or clay figures or sketching. How long would it take for him to get to the stage where he was confident to tackle such tasks? His thoughts must have been displayed on his face, for Michelangelo smiled soothingly.

'First you have to learn to draw expertly and you are not far off that now. The next step will be using a paintbrush and then how to prepare different pigments and the effects that can be achieved by placing certain colours side by side. You will also learn to paint with oil paints – images of anything you choose on panels and the technique involved with fresco painting. When you are proficient, you will begin to make models and learn to sculpt. Come with me and I will show you the various types of marble we use for carving.'

Tommaso followed Michelangelo further into the workshop where blocks of marble were set out on the floor, smaller pieces on a trestle table.

'The marble I use comes from Carrara,' Michelangelo guided Tommaso amongst the blocks of marble and then along the table, 'which you most probably know. I'm very fussy about which marble I choose for statuary.'

Tommaso nodded and ran his hand over a smaller piece of marble, feeling its texture, the carving not yet finished but already glacially smooth in places. 'Which type do you use most often, Master?'

'I use a type called statuario which is particularly good,' Michelangelo continued. 'It has several grades, as you can see here,' he held up pieces of marble so Tommaso could see the difference, 'from the coarsest to the finest.'

Tommaso took the pieces and studied them carefully, turning them over in his hands. The finest was pure white.

'If I'm involved in a large sculpture,' Michelangelo continued, 'I go to the quarries in Carrara and choose the marble myself – as I did with the *Pietà*. I can usually tell the quality when the marble is still in the rockface and stone masons tell me if a particularly fine piece is found. I then hire one of them to free that particular piece, which is heavy, dangerous work, and have it carted and shipped to my workshop in Florence or, if I'm working in Rome, shipped here. I spent eight months in the quarry searching out marble for the Julius tomb.' He picked up a folio of drawings and showed Tommaso. 'These are the drawings I make of the cut marble with measurements so when they arrive, I know they are what I have ordered. Some of those blocks of marble over there,' Michelangelo pointed to the large free-standing blocks on the floor, 'I had transported down here from my workshop in Florence, so I could continue carving for the tomb of Pope Julius. As you can see, they are quite large.'

'What is this, Master?' Tommaso ran his hand over a large piece of grey-blue stone standing apart from the others.

'That is macigno, a sandstone from the quarries near my home in Settignano. It is particularly rewarding to carve and quite fine. The colours range from dark green through to blue and grey. It can be quite effective because of the varying colours of the stone. You must have seen it in buildings in Florence. Brunelleschi used it in his buildings, and it is to be used in the Laurentian Library in San Lorenzo in Florence. There are differing grades of sandstone from the finest pietra del fossato, through pietra serena to pietra forte.'

Despite being interested, Tommaso felt perplexed. 'There is so much to learn, Master.'

'You will learn, Tommaso. It takes time and practice.' Michelangelo moved to another table where his carving tools were spread out. 'These are the tools that are used. They are of various sizes depending on which part of the statue you are working on.' He picked up the largest mallet and chisel and handed them to Tommaso who was surprised at the weight of them. Michelangelo explained, 'You use those to break into the marble. A fair amount of force is needed and you work slowly. The more you carve, the better you will become. When you have been carving a while, you develop balance and rhythm and you learn to listen to the report of the sound within the stone. It will tell you if there is something wrong – if there is a flaw you can't yet detect – and you learn to respond by becoming more careful. You slow down and listen to what the marble is telling you.' Michelangelo pointed to the chisel in Tommaso's hand. 'That chisel is a punch or coarse chisel; the instruments become smaller and finer the closer you get to your subject within the marble.'

'How do you know when to actually carve the figure?' Tommaso put the mallet and chisel back on the table.

'First you draw what you want to carve and you make a model. From there on, you imagine the form within the block you are carving. You visualise the form.'

'It all seems so very hard and complex. You have to use your imagination at the same time as you are carving,' Tommaso said. He wondered how he would ever be up to the task of doing such work.

'Yes, your mind's eye is important as is the use of your imagination, as you say. Start with small pieces but first learn to make figures out of clay and wax; these figures are usually used for bronze and terracotta work and they are also useful for preparation when carving marble. It takes practice and many years of work to become proficient but that is what you are here for, Tommaso.'

Tommaso looked again around the workshop. The other apprentices were at different stages of learning. They all appeared to be busy.

Michelangelo placed a statue of a faun in front of him. He then gathered paper and chalk for Tommaso. 'Use every part of the paper – it's a precious commodity.'

'Michelangelo, may I ask a question?'

'Of course, what is it?"

'Who taught you to paint and sculpt so well?'

Michelangelo hesitated; he preferred people to think his talent was entirely God-given. After all, he was called "The Divine."

'A friend from my youth, Francesco Granacci, introduced me to Dominico Ghirlandaio and his brothers. Francesco was also their pupil,' Michelangelo said quietly so the apprentices present would not hear. 'These wonderful artists taught me in my youth. Ghirlandaio taught me the rudiments of painting on panel, fresco work and sculpture. I learnt much from him, though he became very jealous of me. Through him and Lorenzo de Medici I was introduced to the artist Bertoldo di Giovanni, who was an old man by then. He had been a pupil of Donnatello who sculpted in bronze. He taught me a great deal. They were good friends and when he died, Lorenzo was deeply grieved and he died not long after.' Michelangelo paused, the memories overcoming him. 'I am grateful to them,' he said huskily, 'but this is my secret and it shall remain just between you and me.'

'It is our secret, Michelangelo. I will not tell.' Tommaso felt honoured. He had heard that Michelangelo never revealed the origin of his skills, which created numerous rumours.

Tommaso looked from the statue and down to the paper, then he began to draw. Michelangelo walked back to his carving. Tommaso studied the shape of the faun. He peered over at Michelangelo who, as if summoned, turned to look at him. They smiled at one another.

~

Tommaso sat near the window in his father's salon, Ficino's treatise on his lap, one book of eighteen written by Ficino on the subject of New Platonism. He had spent the morning going through the book, refreshing and absorbing the work in his mind.

He longed to be with Michelangelo, all the time. Unanswered questions tumbled through his mind. Is he thinking as much about me as much as I think about him, or am I just another dalliance? Dare I give into my feelings only to have them laughed at, dismissed as he had others?

When he was away from Michelangelo waiting for the next letter, poem or note, his whole being was filled with yearning. He devoured the poems and letters as soon as they arrived, reading them over and over again, locking them carefully away in his scrivania. What would Michelangelo be doing right then? What was he saying, what marvellous works was he creating? The feeling of being whole, impassioned, complete only came to him in the presence of the man. The days seemed brighter, the sky bluer, the clouds whiter, the birdsong more joyous. The Master had turned Rome into a place of wonder.

Michelangelo's great soul and intellect, at times, made Tommaso feel inadequate in his presence. The poignant *Pietà* he had created had almost made Tommaso weep when he saw it for the first time. The painting in the Sistine Chapel, so far above their heads – how the artist had struggled physically to render perfection in a place almost high as heaven was a marvel. Yet, the challenge of loving and being loved by Michelangelo's intellect almost overwhelmed him.

For a moment, he came close to panic. Michelangelo overpowered him. A man, not a woman. Such love was frowned upon by the Church and part of him was worried by that uncertainty which never went away when he was on his own, yet when he was with Michelangelo the uncertainty disappeared. In his presence anything seemed possible. Although Michelangelo's yearning was couched in poetry and his sketches indicative of passion, such a desire was a human thing, a longing for completion. Had he been sent by heaven, as Michelangelo himself suggested?

Amused, Tommaso smiled at the thought. He was full of human weakness and pride. Sometimes heaven seemed far away. He wanted Michelangelo to hold him, protect, enjoy, support and share his mind, his life and love. Tommaso was only satisfied when he was with him, when he saw the light in the Master's eye as he looked at him, when he felt his worth grow within Michelangelo's presence. This satisfaction also puzzled him. How could he feel this way when he had been taught love and desire between men was wrong? Tommaso knew he should hold back, keep his emotions in check, instead he found them running away from him whenever he was in the artist's presence. Was this love? Was it just idol worship? How could anything considered so wrong, feel so right? Would he be ready for intimacy at the highest level? Would he be able to go through with it?

Tommaso had known neither man nor woman. Would there be such an act? Michelangelo assured him not. Tommaso was not convinced. When he searched his soul, he found he wanted closeness and a physical expression of this love,and, he suspected, so did Michelangelo. The artist held back to keep the relationship sacred, physically at a distance, to let the desire fuel his work. Was it possible? And what would it be like, this consummation of minds and hearts and bodies? Was it inevitable? Could he really reconcile his love for Michelangelo with the teachings of Ficino where the mind and soul rose to God in the other's presence? Or with Ficino's attempt at reconciling the pagan with the Christian? They were human as well as spiritual beings.

What would his father say?

His father should not know. He needed to talk to someone who could answer his many questions.

Tommaso put the book back in the bookcase, grabbed his hat and cape and left the salon and the peace of his father's house. His heart beating fast, there was only one person who might be able to help and reassure him.

~

Tommaso stood at the kitchen door. Bernardino and Vincenza were preparing food for the Master's supper.

'I did not hear you come to the front door, my Lord.' Bernardino grabbed a cloth and wiped his hands.

Tommaso shook his head. 'I came around the back of the house.'

Vincenza lifted her head from her cleaning task and Tommaso saw her eyes sweep appreciatively over him.

'The Master isn't here.'

'It's you I have come to see, Bernardino.'

'Me, my Lord? Come with me.' Bernardino ushered Tommaso out into the hallway. He opened the salon door and closed it quietly behind them, indicating a chair for Tommaso. 'How can I help you, my Lord?'

Tommaso hesitated. 'You know the Master better than anyone, you are one of Michelangelo's oldest friends and most loyal to him.'

'I have that privilege.' Bernardino nodded, a puzzled look on his face. 'Go on.'

'The Master writes to me often, as you know. His letters are full of praise and love. I find myself responding in kind because of his genius, his warmth, and I'm flattered that one so gifted would want the company of one so young and inexperienced. I find a part of me is holding back and another wants to give myself wholly to him. When I'm with him my feelings are out of control and I feel love and admiration for him,' Tommaso blurted out to Bernardino, his face colouring at revealing his innermost thoughts.

Bernardino did not smile. 'You have not told the Master this?'

Tommaso shook his head and was relieved. The Master's confidante took his concerns seriously. Tommaso twisted his blue cap in his hands as he looked at Bernardino.

'If I give my heart and my soul, as he has given to me, I'm afraid of what may happen. I may lose my heart to him along with my soul, yet how can I deny him? Does he feel this way about me or am I just another muse, one he may abandon in time?'

'Ah,' Bernardino smiled at last. 'I have known Michelangelo since we were boys. There have been attachments, however, I have never seen him as overcome with anyone as he is with you. He doesn't expect anything from you except your loyalty and devotion.'

'He doesn't expect physical love, only spiritual?' Tommaso asked.

'He has never said so, only indirectly and through his poetry,' added Tommaso quickly. 'Yet I know what he desires and it's far from spiritual. He hides his real desire in the new Platonism theory.'

Bernardino nodded.

'If I love him as he wishes,' Tommaso continued anxiously, 'where does that leave me? If he falls in love with someone else and turns from me, how can I reconcile that? I know there is that risk in the future, even so, I find it difficult to reject his rhetorical advances. His sketches challenge my learning and awaken my soul to his genius. Is it right to give him my heart and challenge my soul? And if I do, will I lose my soul?'

'Only you can decide upon this,' Bernardino answered. 'Of course, there's always a risk that he will turn to someone else. Life itself is not without risk, my Lord. If you give your heart and soul to Michelangelo and you are trusted as his muse, his insight and his inspiration, then you will never leave his heart. That's how he is.'

'How many lovers has he had?' Tommaso asked frankly. 'There are many rumours that go around about him. Am I just one of many?'

Bernardino's eyebrows shot up. 'The Master has had many apprentices in the past and, being young and impressionable, many have fallen in love with him. As far as I know there has never been anyone he has loved and admired as he loves you. He has said that to me himself. Yes, some of them have shared his bed at the end of a long day, but that sharing has been only for sleep. He is more like a father-figure to many of them.'

'Then, he truly loves me?'

'Yes, I believe he truly loves you, and only you,' Bernardino answered, without calumny.

Tommaso bowed his thanks and walked out onto the busy street, pulling his cap over his head. He would act appropriately if the need arose, whatever that need may be. He hummed happily to himself as he made his way home. The uncertainty had disappeared. He would be with Michelangelo soon.

TWENTY
Rome, 1534

Michelangelo heard the heavy pounding at the front door as Bernardino ran to open it.

Light flooded the entrance hall. Beyond the light were brightly coloured forms, like a background to a painting. The doorknocker, a Vatican guard in his colourful uniform, stepped inside.

'Who is it, Bernardino?' boomed Michelangelo, walking into the hallway from the workshop.

Bernardino stood silent with a shocked look on his face.

'Tell your Master that his Holiness, Pope Paul III, is here to visit him.' The Pope's guard gave Bernardino a push with his foot as if to wake him up.

Bernardino turned on his heel to be met by Michelangelo standing, staring at the guard.

'Tell the apprentices we have a visit from the Pope.' Michelangelo said, gathering his wits, concerned about the untidiness of the workshop and his busy apprentices.

Bernardino scuttled off.

Michelangelo found himself surrounded by men in scarlet robes and other clergy in attendance to the Pope, as they invaded the hallway.

The Pontiff entered the hallway and stood before him. Michelangelo knelt in his presence and kissed the feet of the new Pontiff, then kissed the ring on his finger. The man he had formerly known as Cardinal Alessandro Farnese, a senior member of the Sacred College, was now Pope Paul III.

Popes usually did not visit the homes of artists, but apparently this one did.

'Holiness, you do me a great honour by visiting me,' Michelangelo said, as he looked up at the man standing over him, clad in white and gold, the red velvet camauro edged with ermine draped over his shoulders. The Pope's face was youthful yet he had a full white beard and he was bent over and clutched a walking stick in his hand. Although Alessandro had been a cardinal since the age of twenty-five, it was well known that he had fathered four children before taking Holy Orders and now had five grandchildren. He was also ambitious for his sons in the Church. This man was highly intelligent, eager for reform, determined to have his way and stood no nonsense.

'Perhaps we should have notified you first, my son,' said the Pope. 'I have been waiting to hear from you about your latest project for the Sistine Chapel.'

'Forgive me, Holiness, I had intended to ask for a meeting in the formal way as usual. In my haste getting settled and working again, I had put it off.'

The Pope indicated for him to stand and Michelangelo rose to his feet.

'Holiness, please come into the salon and be seated and perhaps we can discuss it further.' Still in shock, Michelangelo was unusually polite.

One of the clerics rushed to the aid of the Pope who was having difficulty moving, although he was only fifty-seven, younger than Michelangelo. The ten cardinals, accompanying the Pope, were ushered into the salon after him while the guards took their places outside the front door of the house and the door of the salon. The mass of red cassocks parading through his house dazzled Michelangelo. Their robes brightened the room's dark interior. The Pope took his place in the room's one good chair, while Michelangelo stood nearby. He was unused to entertaining a Pope in his home and, when he was invited to social occasions in the Vatican, he was carefully polite and withdrawn.

Usually, in his dealings with Popes, apart from Clement, he had found himself at loggerheads with them. Julius was the worst. His rages and bullying ways, as well as his war experiences, led him to be called

"Il Papa Terribile," a title which had suited him – Michelangelo had conceded at the time. Julius, the "Warrior Pope," had been first and foremost a soldier. Although this new Pope appeared to be different and had been highly regarded as a cardinal, Michelangelo was still wary.

'The wall over the altar in the Sistine Chapel is to be painted, Michelangelo. Have you done any more work towards this? Are you painting what Clement asked for, or something else?' asked Paul III.

'Holy Father, I wish to be released from this contract as I have to finish the Julius tomb for the de Rovere family.'

His face flushed with annoyance, Pope Paul stood up from his chair and leant on his stick fixing his penetrating brown-eyed gaze on Michelangelo, who fell onto his knees.

'What did you say? I have waited thirty years to be able to ask you to do something for me. Where is this contract? Give it to me, I will tear it up! You would rather oblige the de Rovere family than add to the chapel of the Pope?'

'No, Holiness, that is not the case,' Michelangelo replied quickly, surprised at the Pope's vehemence. 'The late Pope and I had discussed the altar wall of the Sistine Chapel. Nothing was decided upon. Pope Clement came up with some ideas, including "The Resurrection of Christ" or "The Fallen Angels", which I thought were not suitable and I suggested a fresco on "The Last Judgement", and he saw and approved the sketches. That was as far as we planned. The wall is prepared and plastered, almost ready. At the moment, I'm greatly taken up finishing the tomb for Pope Julius which I have been trying to complete for some time. The de Rovere family, especially the Duke of Urbino, are impatient to have it completed. I have to do this work which I have already been paid for, before I can start anything else.'

The Pope's eyes flashed with anger. He brandished his walking-stick at Michelangelo who was immediately reminded of Pope Julius. He too had threatened him with a stick. Just as well it wasn't a sword or he would have been dead years ago.

'I have some sketches, cartoons and plans for the wall, Holiness. Would you like to see them?' Michelangelo, thinking fast, tried to calm the Pontiff down. He didn't want to get on the wrong side of this man so early in his papacy.

Paul shook his head as he calmed down and resumed his seat. 'I will not be thwarted. I want you to start on the fresco in the chapel as soon as possible. I shall speak to the Duke de Urbino and the de Rovere family so they do not bother you anymore. We will get others to finish the tomb. I believe you have already finished some statues for it? You must do this painting – for me and in memory of our dear departed brother, Clement.'

Michelangelo, still on his knees, stared at the Pope then bent his head in subservience. 'Would you like me to fetch the plans we have done so far, Holy Father?' Michelangelo was still on his knees. The Pope's wish overrode everything.

'Indeed, my son, I would. Pope Clement spoke in praise of your ideas. I wish to see anything else you have here; the statues for the Medici and Julius tombs and any other sketches or paintings.'

Michelangelo scrambled to his feet, bowed to the Pope and left the room. He found four cardinals had already made their way into the workshop and were looking at the apprentices' work. There was much animated talk amongst them as they studied the clay models for the Medici tombs and the statues themselves, as well as the half-completed statues for the Julius tomb. Michelangelo gathered the sketches and cartoons together and headed back to the salon.

The Pope was talking to Cardinal Biagio da Cesena, now the Pope's secretary, someone forever ready to demean Michelangelo, who was immediately reminded of Febo. He wondered if Febo was indeed in this man's employment – if so, what was he telling the cardinal? And what was the cardinal telling Pope Paul?

Both Pope and cardinal looked with interest at the sketches in Michelangelo's hand. Michelangelo waited until the cardinal had bowed to the Pope and to the sculptor and backed away, leaving the two alone to talk, although the groups of chattering cardinals would still be watching him and Pope Paul closely.

'Show me,' the Pope said, stretching out his hand and pointing to the sketches. He rose slowly to his feet and followed Michelangelo to the table where the plans were spread out. The Pontiff stared at each of the sketches then the cartoons. He was silent for so long that Michelangelo grew worried he might be displeased.

At last the Pope lifted his head and looked at the sculptor. 'This is astonishing. The ideas I am familiar with, of course.'

'Luca Signorelli's *Last Judgement,* Holiness?'

'Indeed, yes. His frescoes in the San Brizio Chapel in the Orvieto Cathedral – I have seen them.'

'I am still developing ideas. Signorelli's frescoes of the *Last Judgement* have inspired me,' Michelangelo paused. 'This is only a suggestion, Holiness. I admire the way he included the damned and the saved into a seething mass with avenging angels flying above them. Although I have started on the drawings, they are by no means ready and the final painting will be different to Signorelli's fresco.'

'He used Dante's work in his painting. Do you intend to use Dante's vision of hell in yours?' the Pope said, leaning on the table and looking up at Michelangelo standing beside him.

The Pope was clearly well-informed about the artwork in Orvieto, however Michelangelo had other ideas about the wall and how he wanted to paint it.

'I am influenced by Dante's depiction of judgement and damnation, and some of the images he invokes in *The Divine Comedy*, especially the *Inferno,* I may use.'

Pope Paul nodded slowly. Some cardinals, including da Cesena, stood closer to them and listened. Michelangelo would not reveal any more since the knowledge would be passed on to his rivals and enemies, especially the Friar Sebastiano del Piombo, once his friend but now an enemy. He and Michelangelo had once banded together in their envy of Raphael, that prolific, talented painter. However, since Raphael's death, Sebastiano had started to rival Michelangelo in his artworks for the Vatican and they could no longer be friends.

'Did Pope Clement see these?' Pope Paul glanced at Michelangelo.

'Yes. He too queried my ideas. When I explained to him my vision, he was delighted and gave me leave to do as I wish. "A vostro moda" he said, several times. Unfortunately, the Duke of Urbino pestering me about the Julius tomb has distracted me from doing further work on the wall project. There is still some work to be done preparing the wall, Holiness, before I can start.'

'One of your friends, the painter, Fra Sebastiano del Piombo, has suggested the work should be completed in oils and wishes to prepare the wall as such.'

Michelangelo felt a lurch of annoyance and raised his eyebrows at the Pope. 'Prepare the wall for oils!' he said, horrified. 'Why was I not told of this? With all due respect to Fra Sebastiano, Holy Father, I insist on painting in fresco. The effect of oils can add depth with rich colours, but fresco is a faster method and creates an effect that lasts well.'

'It's a difficult art form to execute,' the Pope suggested.

'Yes, it is. I managed that art form on the ceiling without too much bother. This will be far easier for me because I won't be continually painting above my head.'

The Pope nodded. 'A vostro moda, then fresco it shall be,' said Paul. He would be aware of the rivalry between Michelangelo and Piombo. The Pope rose to his feet. 'Now, show me the statues for the Julius tomb.'

In the workshop, the completed statue of Moses was surrounded by the cardinals who were stunned into silence as they studied the carefully constructed portrait of the prophet. They stepped to one side for Pope Paul who looked at the statue in amazement. He turned to Michelangelo. 'This statue alone is worthy of gracing Pope Julius's tomb. He looks so real, almost alive, ready to speak to us.'

'I have done two more, Holiness,' Michelangelo said, leading the Pope to other statues. He removed their covers and the Pope gasped with delight.

'These are magnificent.'

'I still have three more to do,' Michelangelo beamed.

The Pope turned to Michelangelo, his face full of pleasure and wonderment. 'I will discuss this with the de Rovere family. You must be released from this contract to continue your work in the chapel.

When that is finished you may return to your work on the tomb. What do you think of that?'

Michelangelo didn't know what to think – except that the de Rovere family would not be happy – as he acknowledged the Pope's suggestion with a bow.

The Pope leaned towards Michelangelo and lowered his voice. 'The times are bad for Mother Church. I wish the painting to depict a *newness*, a *freshness* within the Church. It is to be a warning that we all shall account for our sins on the day of judgement, including those who have abandoned the Faith. Augustine said that heaven is reserved for those who follow Christ; only they will be saved and, when they choose this path, they are entitled by the first resurrection. So, when we reach the stage of the second resurrection, before the judgement of Christ, only those true to Christ's teaching shall be saved, as judgement of the souls has already been made.'

Michelangelo looked fixedly at Pope Paul and nodded.

'We have been badly put upon, the Church is endangered,' Paul continued. 'We must reform. I wish this painting to be part of a renewed Roman Catholic Christianity. There is hope that the Protestant cause will diminish and we will be able to welcome those who have strayed back into the fold. So, this painting must tell a story of predestination, renewal, and the story of Christ's mercy and forgiveness and of his judgement during the last of our days.'

'Holiness, I will please you to the best of my ability.'

'Then I cannot ask for more, my son. Keep me informed.' The Pope stood and extended his hand to Michelangelo, who once again fell to his knees, his head bent to kiss the ring on the Pope's hand.

With Bernardino behind him, Michelangelo bowed to the departing Pontiff and cardinals as they paraded out of the house, and watched as the Vatican Guard quickly surrounded and escorted them to their coaches.

'It's going to take years to do this fresco,' Michelangelo said as he solemnly watched the departing entourage.

'Master, think how wonderful it will be.'

'We hope so, Bernardino, we hope so.'

PART FOUR
1534–1535

RAPTURE

TWENTY-ONE

Cardinal Biagio da Cesena fell to his knees before the Pope.

'Come, Biagio, rise. What is the matter?'

'Michelangelo is the matter,' said Cesena. 'I have reason to believe that the painter is not as pious as is thought. A recent addition to my household has told me of his private life. Is it wise to give a man who likes to bed youths, the task to paint a spiritual theme?'

'You are questioning my wisdom?' Pope Paul raised his eyebrows in annoyance.

Cesena shook his head. 'No, Holiness, I'm not. Michelangelo is known to have lustful imaginings which he expresses in his art and in his letters and poems. The men he depicts in his drawings and paintings are all handsome and nude. He reveals his impure soul in his work. His painting in the chapel will be full of nudity, as is depicted in the ceiling he painted. It is hardly Christian to paint such images in a chapel where Mass and ceremonies take place.'

'This is art you are talking about,' Pope Paul said, eyeing the uneasy cardinal kneeling before him. 'The human body is God's gift to us. You surprise me with your worries. Did you express them to Pope Clement?'

'I did, Holiness, and I suggested that the nude paintings on the Sistine Chapel ceiling should have loin-cloths painted to cover their nakedness.'

'And what did Clement say?'

'He was astonished and said this is art. He told me that Michelangelo, for all his depiction of the naked body, was a good and pious soul who believed in the beauty of the human body, as designed and made by God.'

'That is so,' nodded the Pope. 'Michelangelo was educated by the finest Greek scholar in Florence, Father Marsilio Ficino. In Ficino's theory, male beauty was worshipped as a divine gift, reflecting the supernatural beauty of God and bringing the observer closer to God. Michelangelo has been educated in the humanist and classical traditions from ancient Greece and Rome, which idealised the male body, hence the depictions in his art. He knows the meaning of right and wrong and his depictions of the human body, in all its naked glory, is the result of his education. He knows chastity is important in this love. He is making us aware of each other as perfect and vulnerable, just as God has made and sees us, and as God is.'

'Holiness, we are flawed and have been since Adam and Eve. Not everyone understands the human body is something to be worshipped, as Michelangelo presents it. They see only the erotic. His paintings and depictions of the male body are lewd. Do we really want this on the wall of the chapel?'

Pope Paul frowned at the cardinal. 'You obviously have been in the chapel looking at the painting when I have expressly forbidden it. Don't do that again. The artist will give us an artwork that will last centuries and remain unsurpassed. It will be the culmination of his work on the ceiling and will make the chapel complete. He must be allowed to express himself freely, that is the essence of his artistic genius. Even Pope Clement said a vostro moda.'

'Forgive me for saying so, Holy Father,' da Cesena persisted, unconvinced. 'I don't share your confidence in the artist. His morals appear flawed. He is bound to paint something along the lines of the last judgement with everyone in it, including Christ, completely naked.'

Pope Paul smiled. 'I understand your concern and no doubt there will be many critics, now and in times to come. Surely, Jesus at his crucifixion would have been naked when he was nailed to the cross? Tell me, Biagio, what worries you about the nude depiction of the human body? Isn't it what God gave us before the sin of Eden? It is our sinful ways that require us to wear clothes, to cover what has become our shame. Michelangelo will depict us bare, without adornments just as when we rise from the dead for the last judgment.'

The Pope's face remained expressionless as he eyed the red cassock and lace surplice adorning the shameful form of the sharp-faced cardinal. 'We, you and me and Michelangelo, all who live now, all who have lived before us and all who are to come, we will be the same on the day of the last judgement. We will rise naked to greet the Lord, for our clothes will have rotted away and perhaps our bodies too. He will resurrect us as the supreme body the Lord has made. That is what Michelangelo will paint.'

The cardinal was silent.

'Why are you so worried about this? Look to yourself, Biagio, to your own heart and soul, before you judge others.'

'Yes, Holiness,' bowed the cardinal.

The Pope waved him away in dismissal.

TWENTY-TWO

To Tommaso from Michelangelo,

There is nothing else in this world that comes up to you and your beauty. When I am away from you, sadness fills me, drains me, weakens me to death. You are my life. But I still must toil and live because you are so good, you would not wish to despoil me.

From Tommaso to Michelangelo,

I avoid all that spoils my soul. You are my only love and only with you do I feel it.

Tommaso watched Michelangelo as he climbed a ladder close to one of the statues for the Julius tomb. The artist quickly became absorbed in his work, as if Tommaso was not there. Michelangelo had dismissed the other apprentices but allowed Tommaso to stay and watch him while he worked. He was already captivated by Michelangelo's drawings of the proposed statues.

'Which one are you carving Michelangelo?'

'Leah, from the Old Testament,' came the voice from above. He had his chisel and mallet in hand and pieces of marble and dust fell from around the upper part of the marble.

Tommaso saw the chisel applied deeply then turned on its side and tapped gently, turned again, cutting into the form visible in Michelangelo's mind and starting to take shape under his hands.

'I left many works in Florence but this, and one other, I had shipped down here. I will continue to work on them if I get time,' Michelangelo explained.

Tommaso saw the head and face of the statue forming. Michelangelo was consumed within his task as, with dust covered hands, he clasped the mallet and chisel and carefully chipped, his eye on the outcoming form.

Tommaso sat in silence. He felt at ease now with Michelangelo and relished his company and knowledge. The Master was gentle, yet strong with Tommaso, and the young man's heart opened more towards him. He loved being with someone whose soul he understood because it was similar to his own.

~

Michelangelo and Tommaso went for walks and explored the old Forum of Rome and many churches around the area. Tommaso listened as Michelangelo explained the history of the churches and the artworks inside.

'This church is built over a pagan temple.' Michelangelo looked around the interior high upon the Capitoline Hill, lit by high windows and the soft glow of votive candles from the side altars. Tommaso had led him to the Church of Santa Maria in Aracoeli. 'This is where the Tiburtine Sybil appeared to the Roman Emperor Augustine,' Michelangelo added.

Tommaso nodded as if he already knew. 'My relatives are buried here, and one day I will be too.' Tommaso looked around the cool dusty interior, the outside noises of street goers and wagons hardly audible.

Michelangelo reached out his hand to him and touched him gently on the shoulder. 'Not for a long time and well after me, Tommaso.'

Tommaso had been in this church for the burial of his brother and his mother. He genuflected to the high altar. The deep cut of grief still hurt. He led Michelangelo over to the family chapel.

'Who lies here?' Michelangelo asked.

'My mother, brother and grandparents. Everyone else lies in Florence.'

'It is a beautiful chapel, Tommao. And look at this Roman sarcophagus,' Michelangelo ran his hand over the carved marble's lid and side. 'It's *The Fall of the Phaeton.*' A subject he had drawn for Tommaso. 'Do you come here often to pay your respects?'

Tommaso nodded.

'Do you miss them still?'

'Yes, all the time,' Tommaso's voice was thick with tears.

Michelangelo put his arms around him. Tommaso did not pull away. To have the comfort of someone who understood his grief was a relief. His father never spoke of his loss. Michelangelo sat beside him in front of the chapel altar and Tommaso took his hand and held it tightly. They sat for some time within the church, their minds as one. Tommaso's felt his heart open completely towards Michelangelo.

~

They were alone – the apprentices dismissed into the next workshop for the afternoon. Tommaso stood still, half-turned to Michelangelo, who was busy sketching him. Although Michelangelo had built the fire in the chimney in the corner of the workshop, the heat barely penetrated to Tommaso, half-naked, in the centre of the room.

Michelangelo, as he sketched, added musculature, concentrated on the regularity of form then captured the straight profile and purity of Tommaso's face while Tommaso shivered.

'Are you cold, Tommao?' Michelangelo said, alarmed. 'I'm nearly finished. Here, cover yourself with this.' He grabbed a light cloak one of his apprentices had abandoned and put it gently over Tommaso's shoulders.

Tommaso wrapped himself in it.

'I shall call Bernardino to fetch us some warm cordial.' Michelangelo strode to the door and opened it. 'Bernardino, Dino!'

Running footsteps from down the hall stopped at the doorway.

'Bernardino, we need some warm drinks.'

The footsteps scampered away again.

'Tommao, forgive me, I was lost in my work. I didn't realise you might be cold,' Michelangelo said, drawing his stool closer, 'Are you warmer now?'

'Yes, Angelo. May I see the drawings you've done?'

'Of course.' Michelangelo held up the sheets of paper in front of Tommaso.

The young man bent his head and looked closely at the fine lines conveying his likeness. He let out a sigh. 'Is this really me?'

'It is you. How I see you.'

'I look almost like a woman.'

'You are more beautiful than any woman could be,' answered Michelangelo softly.

Tommaso lifted his head. Michelangelo sat close to him, his deep-set eyes alight, his flattened face open and soft with love.

'You are as I have drawn, Tommao. These drawings are going to be part of the fresco in the Sistine Chapel. You will be immortal.'

Pride and awe followed by trepidation swept through Tommaso. Michelangelo leaned toward Tommaso and brought his hand to his lips and kissed it. Tommaso, breathing fast, was overcome.

'I never draw anything from life unless it is exceptionally beautiful, don't you realise that?' Michelangelo said in earnest.

'What you say overwhelms me, Angelo,' Tommaso said, feeling the heat rising in his face.

Michelangelo smiled and bent closer to him, putting his arm about him. 'You know how I feel about you. You fill my days and nights and I long for you when you're not here. I am bereft if I think I'm not going to see you for some time – my days are empty in your absence. When I look at your lovely face, my soul rises up to God.'

There was a knock on the door and Bernardino came in. He placed glasses and a carafe of warm cordial on the work table.

'Tell one of the apprentices to fetch more wood, Bernardino,' Michelangelo ordered.

Bernardino disappeared out the door and Michelangelo handed

Tommaso a glass of cordial and helped himself to one. They waited in silence as the apprentice appeared with an armful of wood, accompanied by Bernardino who stoked the fire, sending flames roaring up the chimney.

'It looks like snow outside, Master. The sky is so heavy you can almost touch it,' Bernardino said, wiping his hands on his apron. 'My Lord Tommaso may have to leave soon to avoid the fall.'

'Yes, Bernardino, we shall keep that in mind.' Michelangelo did not take his gaze off Tommaso.

Bernardino and the apprentice bowed and left the room.

'You receive my poems and letters; you know how deeply I care about you,' Michelangelo said quietly.

'Of course, Master. I know. It just overwhelms me at times and I am honoured by it.'

'Not disturbed?'

Tommaso shook his head. 'No, Angelo, your love doesn't disturb me. I relish it. I feel the same way about you.'

'You don't mind being immortalised? People will recognise my muse, they are bound to.'

'I am honoured. They can imagine what they like. I'm never happier than when you express your love for me.'

Michelangelo brought Tommaso's hand to his lips and kissed it. 'You are always in my heart. Always, now and forever.' Reluctantly he let Tommaso's hand go. 'Shall we go on? Do you mind if I draw some more? Or do you want to leave soon because of the snow?' Michelangelo said, shifting his stool away from his subject.

'I don't have far to go, and my father knows I'm with you. I'm happy to stay until you complete your drawing,' Tommaso said happily.

'Are you warm enough now to remove the cloak?'

Tommaso let the cloak drop and lifted his eyes to the artist who was looking intently at his smooth, bare chest.

'Lean forward, Tommao. Turn your head to your left and look down and raise your right hand above your head as if in chastisement. Your left foot forward, your right foot back, like so.' The artist went over to

Tommaso and arranged his limbs the way he wanted them placed.

'Which person am I to be in this fresco?' Tommaso said as he settled into the pose.

'You will be a number of people. This sketch I'm doing now will be of the Christ.'

Tommaso was startled. 'Oh, Angelo, this worries me. I am unworthy.'

Michelangelo went over to him and lifted Tommaso's face. 'You are young and innocent. That, and your beauty alone, make you worthy. It's not that long since you were with the angels before you were born. God has sent you to me for this purpose. This is what being a muse is about and there is no doubt you are mine.' Michelangelo bent and kissed him on the lips.

'That's why I'm not worthy, Master.' Tommaso felt the touch of Michelangelo lips on his own. He returned the kiss. 'Because you love me like no other,' he said, with a catch in his voice.

'God has given me this great love. It's not to be wasted. God knows you are worthy,' Michelangelo said, resuming his seat and sketching rapidly, looking at him, then back to his drawing many times. Tommaso watched him and mulled over his words.

At last Tommaso said worriedly, 'I'm astonished that you would do this. Does the Vatican know I'm sitting for you? What would the Pope say?'

'They don't know, and the Pope is not painting the fresco, I am.'

Tommaso smiled with relief at Michelangelo's confidence. What would his father say to his depiction on the wall of the chapel? He was not going to tell him.

'Don't smile, Tommao. The Christ is stern in this painting. He is condemning the wicked to hell and sending the holy to the joys of heaven. And sit still.'

Tommaso tried to control himself but the funny side overcame him and he let out a whoop of joyous and relieved laughter.

Michelangelo looked at him, chalk poised over paper. 'Whatever is so funny?' he asked wryly.

'The prelates are going to be amused to see me sitting in judgement.'

'They won't be too amused – I'll be putting them in the painting too.'

'Heaven or hell?'

'Hell for one or two of them,' Michelangelo laughed.

Tommaso laughed with him, leapt from his stool and ran over to Michelangelo.

'Tommao, what are you doing? If you don't sit still I'll never get this done.' The artist looked up at the merry-faced, semi-naked man before him. Tommaso bent down with a smile and kissed Michelangelo on the lips, then turned back to his stool.

Michelangelo stared down at the sketch. Tommaso, as he slipped back into the same pose as before, noticed Michelangelo's flushed face – how easy it was to stir the man.

'I can't have you as I want you,' Michelangelo said.

'I know that, Angelo, I just love you, that's all,' Tommaso said softly, aware of Michelangelo's conflict. 'Don't worry, whatever happens within these walls will never be known without.'

'If only I could have you as I wish,' said the artist wistfully.

Tommaso, beguiled, smiled at him. 'Who would know?'

'I would know and you would. Your beauty would be defiled.'

'Would it? Or would you love me more?' Tommaso smiled. 'I would only love you more,' he said, amazed at his own daring. He had this celebrated artist in his thrall.

'I don't want to take the risk. The last thing I want is your disapproval of me. I could not live with myself. I must keep the physical expression of my love in abeyance, for your protection and mine. Not to mention the passion it inspires in my art. We have talked about this.' Michelangelo's voice was troubled.

'How can I be an inspiration if I'm that much of a threat?' queried Tommaso.

'A wonderful threat and an inspiration. You have taken my heart completely and the threat intensifies my feelings for you.' He turned back to his drawings.

'I don't want to go home tonight.'

'You can stay, Tommao. Have a meal with me and we shall sit by the fire and I will tell you about the Medici court and read some of my poems to you.'

When I looked at you, I found the divine and everlasting peace in your beauty, but saying that such love ascends to God. The eternal is not found on earth among the mortals who only decay and die, but in the observation of God's beauty on earth. Our friendship is perfect here on earth. Rampant desire deadens the soul, but our love creates and we, us two, live perfectly. In time we will be together in heaven.

This time Michelangelo put his arms around Tommaso, drew him close and kissed him on the cheek. For a moment Tommaso rested his head on Michelangelo's shoulder, thrilled to feel the love.

~

The house was dark and hushed with the fall of snow. Tommaso had been given a bed in a spare room. Bernardino, for once, was in his own room. Tommaso woke and stared into the darkness. What had woken him? His eyes adjusted to a sliver of light through the window shutters and he rose and walked to open them. Snow was falling thickly; he felt the cold air and closed the shutters. Then, in the silence of the house, he heard the echo of a cry.

Michelangelo sat up in bed. Tommaso was standing over him, holding a lamp.

'Angelo, wake up, you are having a bad dream.' Tommaso shook him by the shoulder.

Michelangelo fell back on the pillows, his breathing coming in rapid gasps. The rape by Piero de Medici was all too real once again.

'What is it, Angelo? What scared you so? You woke me. I was asleep when I heard you scream through the walls. Even Bernardino heard you and his bedchamber is further down the hallway than mine.'

Michelangelo became aware of Bernardino in the shadows behind Tommaso.

'Was it the same rape dream, Michelangelo?' Bernardino's face appeared a grotesque mask in the lamp's reflected light.

'Yes, the same,' Michelangelo shuddered, the horror still with him.

'It's alright, Michelangelo, I shall sit beside you until you sleep again.' Tommaso placed the lamp on bedside table then drew up a chair.

Bernardino left the room and Michelangelo settled into the comfort of his bed. He looked at Tommaso sitting beside him and closed his eyes.

How could he inflict such an abomination on this young man? The thought horrified him. That was not the way to love someone – to abuse and terrify them. There were other ways he knew of, hoped for, longed to experience with Tommaso. The temptation to love Tommaso physically alarmed and frustrated him. He had never felt such intensity before. I mustn't lose him, or I will be stripped of my power to portray beauty, he thought. His mind reeled as he sighed.

'What happened, Angelo?' Tommaso asked gently.

'It was so long ago, yet it's still real to me. I was in bed in the Medici Palazzo and I heard him enter my room. He forced me onto my front and took me, pressing my head into the pillow. I could not breathe. I bled for days. I left and went to the monks at Santo Spiritu, they looked after me. I eventually returned to the palazzo and kept my distance from the man and I left soon after.'

Tommaso reached out and took his hand and held it firmly. 'It's all over now Angelo. Sleep and you will feel better.'

Exhausted, Michelangelo slipped into sleep and awoke hours later to find himself alone, the house silent, the light through the shuttered windows muted. The dream was still with him, colouring his mood and the day. He climbed out of bed and opened the shutters. A blast of cold air made him shiver as he stood at the window, hoping the chill would wake him properly and banish the dream from his consciousness. He peered out the window and saw that Rome was covered in snow.

'Bernardino,' he called, as he strode to the bedchamber door and opened it. 'Dino,' he shouted again down the hallway.

Bernardino came running up the staircase. 'Yes, Michelangelo?' he panted.

'Get me something to eat. I shall be down shortly. Today is a good day for more sketches to be done for the wall. Where's Tommaso?' He felt the horror of the dream still with him.

'He returned home earlier this morning when the snow stopped falling.'

'I can do without him today. I will use some of the apprentices for models.' Michelangelo stopped and looked at Bernardino. 'I might even use you.' With his head tilted to one side, he looked at the short man and his large head.

'Like you did on the chapel's ceiling?' asked Bernardino eagerly.

Michelangelo had drawn him side-faced, front-faced, looking down, looking up. He had changed the shape of his head, softened and regulated his features, curled the hair on his head where there was none, then straightened his body, lengthened his legs and arms, and given him muscles in all the right places along with a set of compact genitals.

When he saw the depiction, Bernardino couldn't believe it and cried. It was a stirring rendition of how he felt inside. The Master had captured his soul perfectly.

'In the ceiling you were handsome. I don't think you will be as handsome in this painting.'

'Oh,' Bernardino was unable to keep the disappointment out of his voice.

Michelangelo disappeared into the room to dress.

'Will I be redeemed, Master?'

'Let's put it this way. You will either be in heaven or hell,' came the muffled reply.

Bernardino made his way down the stairs to the kitchen. 'Let's put it this way,' he mimicked, 'I deserve heaven.'

TWENTY-THREE

Febo straightened the drape on the tall window of Cardinal da Cesena's salon to keep out the draught.

'Febo, I wish to speak to you,' said the cardinal from his seat by the fire. Glad to get closer to the warmth, which didn't reach the rest of the room, Febo went down on one knee before the cardinal. The man seemed to favour him before the other servants in the house, because he'd been a favourite of Michelangelo.

'Tell me all about Michelangelo, that ugly, crude man – the one who sleeps in his clothes and loves boys,' said da Cesena.

Febo concealed his amusement as he looked at the aged face of the cardinal with its dull flesh and webbed, broken lines. In comparison to this man of the church, Michelangelo was handsome.

'I have already told you all I know. He works very hard, has great talent and employs apprentices to help him.'

'Yes, yes,' the cardinal said, impatiently tapping his fingers on the arm of the chair. Febo looked at the pectoral cross the man was wearing; the rubies in it glinted red in the firelight. The cardinal gave him a steady stare. 'You have not told me what goes on in the privacy of his bedchamber.'

'He sleeps,' Febo answered quickly.

The cardinal sighed, 'You know what I mean, Febo. Tell me what goes on exactly.'

'He goes to bed late, often too tired to take his clothes off, or his boots. He sleeps in them.'

The cardinal raised his eyebrows at Febo. 'And…?'

'He snores, loudly. His squashed nose, I think. Then he gets up to take a piss in the pot and goes back to bed again.'

'How do you know about this?'

'I have slept in his room but only that, just slept.'

'Nothing else happened?'

'Not that I'm aware of.'

'Who else shares his bed?'

'Usually, no one. If he and the apprentices have been working late, sometimes one of them does.'

'Ah,' the cardinal gave a satisfied sigh, 'I knew it.'

'Nothing happens.'

'Nothing happens? Nothing happens! Are you sure?' Da Cesena was astonished, his eyebrows raised.

'Going from my own experience, nothing happens.'

The cardinal took one of the rings off his finger and turned it to the light, it flashed bright red in Febo's vision. A ruby! Febo's heart leapt. The ring was for him if he told the cardinal what he wanted to hear but he hesitated. As disappointed as he was by Michelangelo, he still loved him. The artist had been good to him, giving him a home when he didn't have one and he missed him. Febo didn't want to be the harbinger of wrong-doing, and that was what the cardinal was about. The pectoral cross on the cardinal's chest glinted at him again.

'He only wanted company,' Febo said hesitantly.

Da Cesena grinned. 'And?'

'That's all. Company.'

'Company! A red-blooded male such as himself?'

'He said if he touched me, his inspiration and my beauty would be defiled.'

The cardinal glared down at Febo kneeling beside him. 'Do you expect me to believe such nonsense?'

'It's what happened, Eminence. He didn't use me – he just loved me, looked after me, protected me, taught me.'

'You were with him for so long. Was it the same throughout your stay with him?'

'While I was his muse, Eminence.'

'And what about now. Who is his muse?'

'A Roman nobleman. I don't know him,' Febo lied.

The cardinal still held the ring between his thumb and forefinger in Febo's line of sight. The ruby flashed red as blood. 'Then find out for me, Febo, and find out everything else that goes on. Here are some gold coins for your informant.'

'Yes, Eminence.' Febo bowed his head slightly. The ruby dropped into the palm of his hand along with the suede pouch of coins.

'There's more of the same for you, especially if it suits me. You may go.' Da Cesena waved him away with his hand.

Febo rose to his feet and walked deliberately to the door of the salon. He let himself out, clutching the pouch, the ring pressing into the palm of his hand. Once safely outside the salon he leaned against the wall and let out a long sigh of relief, then walked softly down the marble hallway whistling under his breath.

~

Febo stood in the darkness near Michelangelo's house. He needed to contact Vincenza. The windows were shuttered but a faint light edged around the side of the house. Silently, he walked down the flagstone path to the back garden. The kitchen was lit with a lamp and candles and he could see Vincenza preparing supper. He watched and waited for a few moments, hoping she would lift her head and see him. He raised his hand to knock on the window. She saw the movement and, hand to mouth, screamed.

Bernardino, followed closely by Michelangelo and Tommaso, ran into the kitchen.

'What is it? What's wrong?' Michelangelo shouted.

Febo turned and ran.

'A man, outside, in the garden. I don't know who it is.'

Febo heard footsteps behind him and increased his pace but he was outrun by Tommaso who caught him down the pathway. Tommaso grabbed him roughly and shoved him against the wall of the house.

'Who are you? What do you want?' Tommaso cried, holding Febo fast.

Febo, hidden by the dark, refused to answer but he quickly reached around his back and drew out a small sword he had taken to wearing for safety. Tommaso stepped back and loosened his grip at the sound of the sword unsheathing.

Febo leant forward and held it up to his face. 'How I would love to scar your pretty face,' he hissed.

A window opened upstairs and Febo, surprised, glanced upwards. Tommaso knocked the sword from his hand and it fell to the ground with a clatter. He stepped back just as Michelangelo tipped a full chamber pot over Febo. Drenched, he ran away from Tommaso, down the path and into the darkness of the street.

~

Vincenza served the men supper. They were all shaken by the suddenness and ferocity of the attack. Vincenza returned to the kitchen, sobered and frightened. She had realised, as Tommaso rushed out the door, who it was but pretended she didn't know. Febo wanted her for something. They had been meeting clandestinely in the market and he had asked her to spy on Michelangelo and Tommaso, telling her it was someone high up in the Vatican who wanted information. This immediately scared her but he had shown her gold coins so she believed him. He promised her some if she co-operated.

'Who do you think it was, Vincenza?' asked Michelangelo as she ladled soup into their bowls.

'I don't know, Master,' she lied. 'He gave me a fright.'

Bernardino, who was pouring wine for the two men, looked at her and raised his eyebrows. She avoided his glance. She would have to tell Febo not to come to the house again.

Tommaso held the sword in his hand and showed Michelangelo who turned pale at the sight.

'Febo!' Michelangelo leaned across and took Tommaso's hand. 'He could have killed you, my Lord. That sword I gave him as a gift, I recognise the engraving on the hilt,' he said, a tremor in his voice.

Vincenza did not wait for Tommaso's reply. She left the room.

TWENTY-FOUR

Michelangelo spread a part of the large cartoon of *The Last Judgement* painting on the floor of the workshop. His four apprentices and Tommaso crowded around.

'This is not the scale of the whole work,' Michelangelo said. 'It will be much larger than this, and when I'm ready to start painting in the chapel, you will see the size for yourselves.'

He walked around the drawings on the floor. 'This gives you some idea of what I have in mind. I will need you for models – mainly faces and gestures. Later, some of you may help me apply the half-inch layer of plaster, the intonaco over the rough layer of plaster or arriccio and then the cartoons. After this, I will quickly paint a light glaze of the pigments to the intonaco before it dries.'

Tommaso gazed at the drawings. The figures were massed together, those who were saved and those condemned. He knelt and studied the works. He recognised some faces and his own scattered throughout the work – including the one in the centre. He stared at it intently. The likeness was good in the drawing and it would be even better in the painting. Everyone would know it was him. Yet, he was still uncertain if he liked that or not, even though Michelangelo had tried to reassure him.

Michelangelo walked over to Tommaso and stood beside him. 'What do you think?'

'The idea of a condemning Christ and the tortures of the damned is readily apparent. It's disturbing, almost horrifying.'

'Good. That's one interpretation. Look closely. Christ is half rising from his seat, he is about to start the judgement. Only some angels are sounding their trumpets, as it is the beginning of the judgement. If you look at it that way, it is not of condemnation, but of hope.'

'Hope, Master?' Tommaso was puzzled.

'Above the dead is an angel with the Book of Life, ready to announce those who are saved and those who are not. Here are the names of everyone since the beginning of time, since creation. Our lives are predestined, St Paul says, and that is our hope. Have we lived as we should have done, or followed another path? It seems like awe and terror, however, central to it all is Christ's mercy as mankind faces predestination.'

'You have studied passages from the Bible and had some priestly advice,' concluded Tommaso.

'Yes, I have studied St Paul's writings and marked them in my Bible. My friend Father Fattucci has helped me interpret the scriptures.' Michelangelo picked up a well-worn Bible on a table nearby. Flipping the marked pages open, he showed Tommaso.

'It's in Italian, Master,' Tommaso said as he read the fine script.

Michelangelo nodded. 'This I can understand. My knowledge of Latin is lacking, which frustrates me. I only have myself to blame. I was not interested at the time and left school before I could become interested.'

He went on to quote from scripture. 'Paul says … "The Lord himself will descend from heaven with a cry of command, with the archangels' call, and with the sound of the trumpet of God. And the dead in Christ will rise first; then we who are alive, who are left, shall be caught up together with them in the clouds to meet the Lord in the air." That is what I am going to paint. That is what you will see.' Michelangelo closed the book.

Tommaso and the apprentices were silent.

Michelangelo said quietly, 'Don't look so troubled, all of you. This painting will also be a depiction of the soul of man. My own soul is revealed which, despite my fervent prayers, attendance at Mass and frequent confession, is often tempted by sin, and I end up disturbed and angry at my weakness. Those who look at the painting will find terror if they have led sinful lives but, if they are good, they will see hope.' He gestured at the papers covered in black chalk drawings. 'This is just the beginning. Those figures are going to fly in a vortex in the firmament, against an intense blue background and the dead will arise and be clothed in flesh again and many will be saved and many will be damned.'

'It looks like a painting of anger, Michelangelo. Christ's anger,' Tommaso said, trying to keep the doubt out of his voice.

'Well, some will interpret it like that. And perhaps this is what Pope Paul wants at this time in the Church. The ones who have left the fold must be made aware of what they have done. So, the painting must also depict the anger of the firmament, the admonishment of the angels and the devils' greed. There is also redemption. In the centre is the peace and calm forgiveness of Christ and his blessed Mother who, as you can see, almost turns at the horror of the damned. Christ does not turn away. He holds his hand aloft to those who have lived bad lives as he looks down upon them. At the same time, his gesture is upward for those entering heaven. His bodily expression is broad and open as he lovingly receives those who look to him and have served him well. Those with hope look upon him in awe and love and others, who have turned their backs on his love and mercy in pursuit of their own earthbound desires, realise their destination.' Michelangelo put his arm around Tommaso's shoulders. 'When it is finished, Tommao, you will see what I mean.'

'When will that be? How long will it take?' Tommaso felt the subtle pressure of Michelangelo's body against his. Temptation in the warmth bound them together. Surely the other apprentices must notice his fondness, his closeness, the softly spoken voice for him alone? It didn't seem to worry Michelangelo and the apprentices, used to his ways, appeared not to notice.

'Many years perhaps – it's a large area to paint. You will see how it grows and all the while, I will listen to you and take your advice.'

Tommaso was surprised. 'My advice, Michelangelo? I am so inexperienced and ignorant about art.'

Michelangelo smiled at him. 'You know more than you realise. Your inbred good taste, education and knowledge are all a help to me. And especially your love and attention.'

Michelangelo never took advice from anyone if he could help it and for him to accept it from Tommaso astonished the youth. However, it was too late to have doubts about the relationship. His love was already pledged to the man, even in writing.

Tommaso ran his eyes over the large drawings. 'My advice would be scant. It is you who has the talent, skill and knowledge.'

'You can help me with the cartoons and painting and I want and need the image of your face to paint from, not to mention the perfection of your body so close to mine,' Michelangelo whispered gently so the others could not hear.

Tommaso shook his head in wonderment. 'I will be there for you when you need me, Michelangelo.'

The room buzzed with the apprentices and Bernardino talking as they looked at the drawings. Michelangelo reached out and touched Tommaso on the arm. 'Thank you,' he said.

Later over supper, Tommaso asked Michelangelo how he came to know about the anatomy of the body. He had noted, looking at the drawings and cartoons, how real and muscular the figures looked.

'I had a very good friend in the monastery of Santo Spiritu, Prior Niccolò Bichiellini who helped me. Leonardo da Vinci had learnt about the human body there, through the generosity of the Prior. He made available to me the corpses of the recently dead monks or patients in the hospital and I spent many nauseating nights dissecting them. I learnt the structure of bones and muscles and everything else about the body and I am grateful to the dead. It was horrifying work and sickening. I spent most nights with my head in a pail but I did learn. The experience was most valuable.'

'I hope I don't have to do such work, Angelo,' Tommaso said, his face pale with the thought.

Michelangelo laughed. 'No, you can learn from my sketches, Tommao.'

Tommaso was relieved.

'I shall give you my sketchbook and you can start copying them.'

'The Prior must have been a generous man to allow such activities,' murmured Tommaso. 'What about the Church authorities then, was it allowed?'

'Yes, the Church at that stage was not ambivalent to it because it expanded knowledge about man. The Prior was a good man, he looked after me until I felt better when Piero assaulted me and he knew my brother. In gratitude I carved a wooden crucifix for him which is in the church to this day.'

'Perhaps we shall see it together one day, Angelo.'

'Yes, perhaps, one day.'

Febo stood in the closed doorway. The sloping street was dark, the flagstones shining wet in the light of a wall torch. Below he could see Michelangelo's house and, to the right, the ghostly outlines of the ancient market, Trajan's Column and the Colosseum. Vincenza would come – she'd been clandestinely meeting with him in the market for some time, always with news of Michelangelo and his latest paramour. He had rewarded her richly so it wasn't hard to get information out of her. Febo had asked to see her at night with no one around and now he wrapped his fur-lined cloak about him, the one Michelangelo had given him, pulled his hat further down his head and waited.

The wind whistled up the hill, making the torchlight gutter and flare then gutter again. The house looked deserted, the shutters closed with no light visible. Michelangelo and Bernardino would likely be in the kitchen, with Vincenza finishing her work for the day. He hopped from one foot to the other to stop his feet from freezing. He stopped as he heard a footfall. He swung around, half-expecting a sword at his throat. To his relief he found a woman bundled up in a cloak standing beside him with a shawl over her head.

'I was afraid you weren't coming.' He grabbed her and pulled her into the darkness of the doorway.

'What have you got for me then?' She held out a hand covered in a mitt.

'Nothing unless you tell me what I want to hear.'

'There's nothing to tell,' she whispered. 'If I'm caught, Michelangelo will send me back to my family in disgrace. You gave us all a nasty fright. The Master doesn't know who it was at the window, though he has a suspicion. You should be more careful.'

'He tipped the piss-pot over me, I stank for days,' Febo moaned. 'Cesena wouldn't let me near him until one of the servants filled the bath and I had to soak in that.'

'You might have known they would see you.'

'It was a risk but I had to see you soon instead of meeting in the market. I need more information. Cesena says he will reward us well. You know what they say about Michelangelo,' Febo said, 'tell me what's going on with his new lover.'

'Nothing as far as I'm aware. He's in the house most of the time. Nearly every night he returns home.'

'Is he there at the moment?'

'No, only Michelangelo, Bernardino and the apprentices.'

'Have Michelangelo and Tommaso slept together?'

Vincenza was silent. Febo fumbled under his cloak. He lifted the pouch out of his jerkin's pocket, heavy with coins and swung it back and forth in front of her.

'Tell me!'

'Yes,' she admitted.

'When? How many times? How do you know?' Febo was excited despite himself, a mixture of lust and jealousy writhing through him.

'You forget, I help make the beds and wash the linen,' she said. 'I see them together. When Tommaso is with him, everyone in the house is banished from their presence. Except Bernardino, of course, he's involved with everything that goes on with the Master and he protects him. Michelangelo is mad for Tommaso and keeps him close most of the time. He writes letters to him and poetry, like he did for you.'

Febo felt a punch of hurt in his chest and pushed her further into the blackness of the doorway, his face close to hers. 'You must get me some of those letters, some poetry, anything that incriminates him,' he said, his breath hot on her face.

'Why? Why are you doing this?' Vincenza was alarmed. 'You were with him for a long time and he was good to you.'

'He loved me once and tired of me. I'm no longer of use to him and I gave him much, my heart, soul and body. I must fend for myself now. He's a snob, pretends he's of noble blood. You know that. Tommaso is of ancient nobility. That's why he likes him.'

'Michelangelo is of noble stock too,' Vincenza answered indignantly. 'Everyone in Settignano knows he comes from ancient families on both his mother's and father's sides. His mother was descended from the Rucellai family. His father was the mayor of Caprese when he was born. He owns land, a villa and a quarry. The Buonarroti are well-liked and looked up too. You're acting out of jealousy!'

Febo pressed her further against the closed door, his grip strong. 'You've gone soft on him. I thought you disliked him. I've paid you well enough. I will pay you even more if you find me his letters and poems.'

'He never leaves his papers lying around,' she said hotly, pushing him away with both hands. 'He locks everything of note in the sealed trunk in his salon. Anyway, you know I can't read or write. That's the only reason they trust me. I won't know what I'm looking at even if I do find them. And he'd soon know if anything went missing.'

'He has a locked scrivania and there is a way of getting into it,' Febo remembered. 'He has a key hidden under the window seat for the scrivania in his bedchamber where he usually keeps his poems. That's where he kept those he wrote for me. If you find the poems he has written for Tommaso there, you will be rewarded twice as much as what I give you tonight,' Febo insisted.

'There is a risk,' answered Vincenza. 'If I'm caught he will tell me to go. He's very suspicious and so is Bernardino.'

There was a footstep behind them; again he pressed her into the darkness. He bent down and kissed her firmly on the lips so she would not speak.

The steps of a passer-by receded. Febo pulled back and looked at her face, barely visible in the dim light. 'Here, take this and we will meet in a week when you will have evidence for me.'

Febo gave Vincenza the pouch of coins and walked away into the street. When he turned to look back, she had disappeared.

PART FIVE
1535–1537
CREATION

TWENTY-FIVE

Michelangelo stared up at the wall as it loomed above him. Forty-six by forty-three feet covered in a seven-storey scaffold, it jutted out from where the previous wall had been, as he had ordered. Windows walled up, the painted works of Pietro Perugino – *The Assumption* and *Coronation of the Virgin Mary* – had been destroyed. Other works including those by Michelangelo himself had gone as well. The wall had been chiselled and changed, bricked until it sloped, then a rough coat of plaster applied. Now the wall slanted to the floor; this would help prevent dust sticking to the fresco. It would also tower over the Pope and the cardinals when they said Mass. They would look up at the consecration and see the image of Christ above them. The work satisfied Michelangelo and wiped out Sebastiano's pre-emptive preparation for oil painting which had so infuriated him. Fra Sebastiano, eager for the lucrative commission, had stepped in and prepared the space. Most probably da Cesena had been behind it. Without a word to the Pope or Sebastiano, Michelangelo, maddened, quickly replaced the Friar's work with his own plaster preparation.

'Perugino's frescoes and your two lunettes and *The Four Popes* have gone, Angelo,' Tommaso said, dismayed, looking up at the wall.

'Yes. Sometimes you must sacrifice your work to create others. The space would not have been large enough otherwise.'

'You said that Fra Sebastiano suggested oils,' Tommaso said.

Michelangelo shook his head indignantly. 'That was the silly friar's idea. He suggested it to Pope Paul. As far as I'm concerned, oil painting is for the leisurely, for idle women and people like Sebastiano – those with plenty of time. This is to be fresco. Fine true fresco. The use of this technique gives an impression of infinity and power. Only fresco will do, as it has been done on the ceiling above us.'

'You don't like oil painting, Master?'

'It is not my preferred medium though I have used it in the past. Oil painting can be colourful and add depth but I like to bring out the sculptural quality in the works and make it active and alive. When this is finished, people will want to observe and watch. There will be so much movement in the painting, if the observers blink, the figures will move. The figure of Christ is to be in the centre with all the important figures close by and around him. Because the wall is positioned as it is, when the light shines through the upper windows in the chapel, the figures will stand out.'

'So, what happens next?' Tommaso stared at the height of the wall. 'It's going to be an enormous painting,' he added, dubiously.

Michelangelo stood, hands on hips, head thrown back as he studied the space. 'Yes, it will be large but it will be done in stages.' He turned to Tommaso who appeared transfixed at the size of the wall. 'The intonaco will be applied and smoothed over. That's the first step. You can help me with that, then the cartoons will be pounced out. I will begin to paint each section in a light glaze before the plaster sets.'

'I don't understand, Angelo. Isn't the plaster too wet to paint over?' Tommaso asked.

'Ah, my dear Tommao, that is the secret of fresco. The technique goes right back to Crete in the second century. With the plaster still fresh, I paint with additional pigment. It's a technique called velature a secco. The coloured pigment is mixed with animal glue. Only pure pigments are used; I don't use mixed colours and this technique allows me to build layers and shadows with more time, which is needed for this work. As the plaster dries, it binds with the applied paint so it will last a very long time.'

'How long do you think?'

Michelangelo smiled at Tommaso. 'Much longer than you or I. When you are a very old man you will come and look at it and remember and it will look as good to you then as if freshly painted.'

'You would have to work very fast to get it done before the plaster dries,' Tommaso added.

'Yes, that's important. I paint with a brush in each hand. The area is broken up into sections. That's why I can only paint a section at a time, a gionata, which is done in a day. The sections are all in my mind and in my drawings and cartoons. I know exactly where to put them.'

'The figures in the cartoons are massed, they appear to overlap each other.'

'Yes, they do, but that's the effect I wish to create, a large swirling mass of good and bad. After all, there is not just one of us on this earth but masses of us.'

'Where do we start? How can I help when I am so inexperienced with this?' Tommaso asked.

Michelangelo turned to him. 'I could not work without your presence and support. You are one of my abler apprentices and are amongst those I choose to help me. Also, some of my friends from Settignano may be called upon, as they were for the ceiling — I may need them to help at the beginning.'

Tommaso bowed to the artist in acknowledgement. 'I feel daunted by the task, though I admire your resolve.'

Michelangelo put an arm about Tommaso's shoulders. 'I have every faith in you, Tommao. We will start tomorrow.'

'Tomorrow?'

'Yes, first thing in the morning. At dawn, you and I will come here and apply the first layer of intonaco, then I will place the first cartoon. I will teach you how to pounce it onto the plaster. When that's done I shall start to paint. It will take some time as I build layers and shadows. First, we must get it on the wall. You will help me, Tommaso, along with my other apprentices, who will come later. Together, you will grind pigments and place cartoons and generally assist me. You may stay in my house tonight as we will be up before dawn.'

Michelangelo sat by the fire in the front salon of his house and spread his poems across the table.

Tommaso watched him. 'You have written to me again, Angelo? Even though I am here with you?'

'It's the only way I can express how I feel about you. How much you mean to me.'

Tommaso took the paper Michelangelo handed him and read it silently.

If love chaste and pure brings together two lovers, the two souls fly to heaven as they become one in spirit, there they remain forever as one. Only doubt, cynicism and distrust can break them apart.

His head bent, Tommaso sat staring at the page. 'This is so perfect, Angelo. You love me so much, you take my breath away.'

'You mean everything to me, Tommao. I would be bereft and heartbroken if I lost you because of rabid gossip. And there has been much gossip and it gets back to me. Please, I beg you, don't listen to the foolish, malevolent crowd who accuse me of wrongdoing.'

Tommaso moved over to where Michelangelo sat and put his arms around him, burying his head in Michelangelo's chest. 'You will never lose me,' he said passionately, lifting his head, his warm breath brushing Michelangelo's face. 'I am your love for as long as you live and for as long as I live. I will be faithful and true to you and admire you, because you are divine. No one can take your place.'

'There are those who would taint my name with many accusations because they don't understand my inspiration is beauty,' Michelangelo said huskily.

'Michelangelo, there will always be some people who think the worst of others. People who are blind to the workings of a great mind, who cannot appreciate what it is to be inspired. They must be ignored and treated with disdain for the sake of your art.'

Michelangelo, unguarded, bent and kissed Tommaso on the lips.

Tommaso felt the rough pull of Michelangelo's sinewy body as the artist put his arms around him, holding Tommaso's body close to his own. 'Just to feel your loving, breathing life and warmth within my arms is wonderful. It's something I have always longed for and sought and have now found. You are all I ask for, Tommao,' he whispered, 'all I ask. Your presence gives me love and hope. Don't leave me as so many I've loved have. You are young and will not die soon as others have. Stay with me.'

'I will, Michelangelo,' answered Tommaso sincerely. 'You will always be in my heart.'

'These poems are for you, Tommao.' Michelangelo gestured at the pages.

'I will treasure them.' Tommaso leafed through them. Some he had read before but many were new. Tommaso knew Michelangelo's heart was captured, and his love was deep and lasting.

If I do not love you with all my heart and feel for another, I will lose my soul.

Michelangelo put his hand on Tommaso's shoulder. 'Come with me,' he whispered, holding out his hand and bending to his ear. Tommaso slipped his hand into Michelangelo's and they walked to the door. In the dimness of the hall, Michelangelo drew Tommaso to him, holding him gently. How could anyone so strong, be so gentle?

'Come with me we will spend the night in each other's arms.'

~

'Bernardino. Dino. Where are you?'

Bernardino was stoking the oven in the kitchen. He put down the poker and sighed, running a hand wearily across his eyes.

'The Master calls, Bernardino.' Vincenza had her arms in a bowl, kneading dough.

'Bernardino!'

'Coming, Angelo.' Bernardino fled from the kitchen into the hallway. 'Where are you, Michelangelo?' Bernardino stopped and listened.

'In the front salon.'

Bernardino ran into Michelangelo's salon and found him pacing the floor.

'Last night, I left letters and poems on the table addressed to Tommaso. Where are they? Have you shifted them?'

Bernardino shook his head. 'No, Master. I haven't.'

'Someone has taken them.'

'Perhaps Tommaso took them, Michelangelo. Is he still here?'

'No, he went home.'

'I should say they would have gone with him.'

'Yes, perhaps. I'm going to the chapel. I will see him there.'

Bernardino, relieved the anxiety was no more than missing letters, walked back down the hallway into the kitchen.

Vincenza, her hands and arms covered in flour, looked up at him. 'What was the matter?'

'Missing poems and letters.'

Vincenza patted the mound of dough in her hand as she floured the table and tipped the dough onto it. 'I will soon need the skillet, Bernardino, to put the rolls into the oven,' she said as she kneaded the dough.

Bernardino turned to his task, slipping the large, flat skillet onto the hot glowing coals of the hob.

'Did you find the letters?' asked Vincenza.

'There were no letters there. Lord Tommaso may have taken them.'

'Was he here?'

'Yes, last night. He left before dawn to go to the chapel, I think.' Bernardino waited patiently with the pan still in the oven.

'It's ready,' answered Vincenza. Bernardino lifted out the pan and slipped it under the flattened rolls. As he slid it into the oven, she added, 'That will be ready for the Master this evening, and rolls for his dinner tomorrow.'

'I don't suppose you have seen the Master's letters?'

Vincenza ran a hand over her face, spreading flour everywhere. She shook her head.

'How would I manage that? He locks his writings away, you know that. I came straight to the kitchen after dawn and there were no letters here. They are of no use to me anyway because I can't read. Anyway, he wouldn't be that careless.'

Bernardino shrugged. 'Well, he's in love and sometimes love makes a man careless.'

'How do you know Bernardino? Have you been in love?' She raised her eyebrows at him. Her tone was mocking and she ignored Bernardino's discomfort. 'He's always losing something. They will turn up,' Vincenza said pragmatically, turning away from his enquiring gaze.

Bernardino frowned as he often did in his encounters with Vincenza. No, he had never been in love and she need not have emphasised his plight. If only he could love someone. Who would love such an insignificant man, all three feet and six inches of him? Only his mother, God rest her soul. He blessed himself.

Vincenza continued to watch him with a look of amusement. If only Michelangelo would listen to him and get rid of her! His loyalty to those from Settignano was unrealistic. Just because they came from his hometown! He shook his head as he thought how naïve Michelangelo could be sometimes.

~

Pope Paul looked at the letters and poems in his hand and recognised Michelangelo's handwriting.

'Where did you get these, Cesena?' the Pontiff asked, looking up at the sharp-faced cardinal standing in front of him.

'From a reliable source, Holiness. There is incriminating evidence about the artist – something many of us have long suspected. He is obviously in love with this young man, Tommaso de Cavalieri.' Da Cesena was hardly able to keep the triumph out of his voice.

Leaning on his stick, the Pope tapped away from him to stand in the light from the window and read the poems. He turned and glanced over at the red-clad cardinal. 'This nobleman Cavalieri comes from a family known to us. I would be surprised if there was anything physical in this relationship. The young man is very educated and good living.'

'And handsome.'

'His looks are a gift from God. Just gazing at him is a pleasure for Michelangelo and a tangible link with God, according to the New Platonists, anyway. This is what affects him as an artist. His reasoning is based on the New Platonism – the unconsummated love between men.'

The stubborn cardinal was already aware of the reasoning but Pope Paul was repeating it again to reinforce it, if possible.

Da Cesena was silent for a moment. 'There are those who say it is physical, as he has had many such relationships in the past: Mini, Perini, Urbano, Poggio…. From all accounts this one is special. You saw the poems gifted to my servant Febo de Poggio, they were full of double meanings, and the sketches Michelangelo gifted to Tommaso de Cavalieri were full of meaning obvious to me.'

'Yes, I saw the poems to de Poggio, silly playful nonsense, and I remember the sketches to Tommaso. Exquisite rendering of the Greek myths, nothing more.' Pope Paul walked away from the cardinal and sat down in the nearest chair.

'The meaning of the sketches has been noticed and talked about by others,' da Cesena continued.

'Enough!' the Pontiff held up his hand. 'It's all rumour and speculation. I'm surprised you believe these tales.' Paul frowned at the cardinal. He stood and walked to Cesena and deliberately encroached upon him. The man was annoying him. He stared into the cardinal's deep-set eyes. 'Michelangelo honours the beauty of the human body in the only way he knows how. He glorifies it, as he should, in his art.'

'I'm not the only member of the clergy, Holy Father, who has these concerns,' Cesena persisted, staring back. 'That is why some of us would have preferred the Friar Sebastiano to decorate the chapel wall. At least…' he challenged, 'we would know the angels and saints would be wearing clothes.'

The Pope shook his head.

'No. Sebastiano is a fine painter. He paints in oils which takes a very long time, since you have to wait for each layer of paint to dry before painting the next one. Michelangelo's method of fresco is the best for this assignment and it lasts better. Look at the ceiling.'

Pope Paul returned to his chair and sat down. Impatiently, he asked, 'What are you trying to do, Cesena? Destroy the man?'

'I'm thinking of the Church, Holy Father. We live in bad times; our integrity is challenged. What must it seem like, to those factions who oppose us, to have such paintings in the Sistine Chapel? It is a special place, the Capella Magna, where the College of Cardinals congregate to discuss Church business many times during the year. It is where you say Mass. We are already under attack by those who have split from us. Surely it gives the impression of immorality and indecency to allow this exhibition, and only confirms their opinion that the Church of Rome is corrupt!'

The Pope frowned as he handed the sheaf of papers to da Cesena. 'You offend me, Cesena,' he said, brusquely. The cardinal flinched and bowed to Paul in apology. 'You speak of this as if I know nothing about what goes on. Mind yourself and your manners. The Church will survive. This is art. Michelangelo's painting itself will be a lesson to those who have left us. His painting is of the last judgement, which we all must face — loyal and disloyal, sinner and saint alike. Those who have left us will look at the painting and see for themselves where they are placed. I instructed Michelangelo as to what theme to express and it is based upon the epistles of Saint Paul. It might be in order for you to re-read this part of the Bible before you make any more accusations,' the Pope said, quietly incensed, as he waved the papers at Cesena. 'Here, take these papers and give them to your informant, and tell him or her, from me, that these letters and poems must be returned intact. Michelangelo must not be accused of anything improper. He must not be upset. He must not know I have seen these letters and poems. There will be no more word of it, from you or anyone. He can be difficult, however, this is often the sign of greatness. He must be left in peace to accomplish his vision and finish his work.'

The Pope held out his hand for da Cesena to kiss his ring. The cardinal knelt before him to do so. 'Go quickly, Biagio,' the Pope concluded with a wave of his hand. 'Return the papers before he realises they are missing. And look to your own conscience.'

The house was quiet. Michelangelo, Tommaso and the apprentices were at the Sistine Chapel.

Vincenza, out in the kitchen garden, was feeding the chickens, her hand scattering seed and bread on the grass and gathering eggs in a basket looped over her arm. She heard a noise inside the house and ran back through the loggia and into the kitchen. Everything was quiet. The noise came again, this time closer. Someone was inside the house. A door slammed.

'Bernardino, is that you?' Vincenza half-hoped it was Febo who would know she was alone. She walked quickly down the hallway, opened the front salon door and her mouth dropped open in surprise. Before her stood Cardinal da Cesena.

'Eminence, you startled me.' Vincenza bowed to him, then bent to kiss the ring on his outstretched hand.

'I have come expecting Michelangelo to be here. I wished to see his drawings for the chapel again,' the cardinal said.

'Everyone is in the chapel, Eminence, and his drawings are there too. I believe the work is coming along well from what I have been told.' Vincenza ushered him into the hallway. 'I'm sorry I didn't hear you knock, Eminence. I was in the garden.'

The cardinal shrugged. 'I took the liberty of letting myself in. I will go to the chapel and see for myself.' He looked askance at the servant then swept past her into the hallway. Vincenza followed his billowing red cloak out the front door. A pale hand rose in blessing as his coach juddered away. She blessed herself, gave a quick curtsy then turned and raced back inside. She entered the salon. Her eyes widened and she gasped, covering her mouth with her hand. On the table were the Master's poems and letters that she had given to Febo. Afraid to touch them, she ran down the hall to the kitchen and closed the door behind her. Leaning her back against it, she concluded she would have to pretend she'd found them. She wondered who, besides the cardinal, had seen them. With a sickening lurch in her stomach, she realised there was only one person who could have ordered them to be sent back.

TWENTY-SIX

Michelangelo stood in the centre of the Sistine Chapel, contemplating the far wall. The first scaffolding and draping had been erected and behind them lay the beginning of his vision. His apprentices and workers, including Tommaso, were high above him, grinding pigments and using powdered charcoal within one of the lunettes to pounce the outline of a cartoon shape onto the intonaco.

He had already painted some of the shapes in the lunettes and the colours stood out brightly, the nude angels flying in a blue firmament, vibrant in the dusty late afternoon air of the chapel. The men's voices echoed around the ceiling's vault as they discussed the placement of the central section of the left lunette close to the wall.

From where Michelangelo stood, the lunette figures looked to be in the right position. Soon he would have to go up and join the men to begin painting.

The climb to the top level he now found arduous and tried not to think about it. Years ago, when he had painted the ceiling he had thought nothing of climbing ladders and working at a great height on the wooden scaffolding. He had been surefooted and safe enough and had never suffered from vertigo or a fall. He hoped this time it would be the same and that he would soon finish the higher part of the fresco and move down to a lower level.

He desperately wanted to paint the figure of Christ, so he could place the other figures in the scene around Him. But he wouldn't start yet on Christ or His Mother, situated beside Him in the upper centre of the wall, until the lunettes were nearly finished. He was staring so hard at the wall and visualising where he was going to put his figures that he didn't hear the chapel door opening or the footfall behind him.

'Signore Buonarroti.'

Michelangelo whipped around and found, to his dismay, it was Cardinal da Cesena.

'Eminence.' He recovered with a bow and kissed the cardinal's extended hand. 'If you will pardon me, how did you get into the chapel?' Surprise and annoyance edged his voice.

'The guard let me in, of course.'

Michelangelo scowled. 'They have had strict instructions about not letting anyone in. Even the Pope has to ask permission.'

'I'm here on behalf of the Pope,' said da Cesena.

Michelangelo did not know whether to believe the cardinal or not. 'And what does the Pope want to know?'

'How the painting is evolving.'

'Slowly, Eminence, slowly. It's going to take some time. The area is large.'

The cardinal tipped back his head and screwed up his eyes as if to see the wall better. 'I see some of the figures you have painted so far in the lunettes are nude.'

'Indeed, Eminence. They are angels, and angels have no human form. What form they do take is perfection. How else can we, in our earth-bound humanity, recognise them except by their beauty of form and features?' Michelangelo knew which way the conversation was heading. 'You have a problem with the naked body, Eminence?'

'In a place of worship, yes. You even sculpted a statue of Christ nude some time ago. It's blasphemy.' Cesena removed his gaze from the painting and directed it at Michelangelo.

'It's not blasphemy, Eminence. It is art. You must remember that I was educated in the Humanist tradition where the human body, especially the male, is idealised. God gave us this form and that is to be revered, naked or not. Aren't we made in His image? It's also part of my style to express God's glory through the human body, so nothing less than perfection results.'

'The body should be covered,' insisted da Cesena, his brown eyes glinting in the subdued light. The prelate faced Michelangelo. 'We all know you like young men, Michelangelo,' he said quietly. Michelangelo almost heard the hiss of a snake in his voice. 'And we know that you paint them, and some of them can be very fine indeed. They would be even better with their clothes on. These figures you have drawn so far are male and nude. Angels are sexless, and I believe all yours are male.'

Michelangelo screwed up his face in annoyance. He found it difficult to tolerate the cardinal's opinions. 'And you, Eminence, are you never naked and admiring of the body God gave you?'

Cesena looked at him coolly. 'I do not glorify my body, Michelangelo. There will be others who will say these figures should be covered, as do I.'

'Then let them say it. Did God really intend for us to be strung up to our necks in clothes?' Michelangelo felt the tight knot of impatience in his stomach wind itself tighter.

'God expected us to be content and not display what we should not,' came the even answer.

'Have you ever seen a naked man, Eminence?' Michelangelo gritted his teeth.

'Yes, of course.'

'What was your reaction?'

'Embarrassment. I felt offended by his display, the way I feel when I see nudity in statues, the way I feel when I look at your paintings.'

'Did the Holy Father tell you to come and interrogate my painting skills and ideas?' Michelangelo was exasperated.

Da Cesena shook his head. 'Indeed, no. These thoughts are my own. This chapel, the Capella Papalis,' the cardinal made a sweeping gesture to encompass the whole space, 'is precious to the Holy See. It is where the majesty and the power of the Church is demonstrated to people who come to visit us. Therefore, only something uplifting, aesthetic and holy should be depicted, and all figures fully clothed.'

Michelangelo thought he heard another hiss and turned to find Tommaso sliding quickly down the uprights of the ladder in his soft shoes. Michelangelo suddenly wished he hadn't arrived, not with da Cesena here. Tommaso, looking agile and young, his face flushed and hair tousled, jumped down the last few rungs and walked over to the pair.

'One of your helpers, Michelangelo?' The cardinal clasped his hands in front of him as he turned to the artist with a sarcastic sneer.

Michelangelo felt his body tense and his face flush. 'Yes, this is Tommaso de Cavalieri, one of my apprentices,' he answered, curtly. Tommaso bowed to the cardinal and knelt to kiss his ring.

'Well, very nice,' da Cesena said, head on one side, as he surveyed the young man in front of him. 'Is he teaching you well?'

Michelangelo would have liked to wipe the smirk off his face. Tommaso looked from the cardinal to Michelangelo then back to Cesena and nodded. 'Your father will be most pleased about that,' da Cesena said.

'Indeed, he is, your Eminence. If you will pardon me…' He turned to Michelangelo. 'Master, one of the apprentices needs your help in placing the cartoon in the right place.'

'Please excuse me, Eminence, I must get back to my work.'

The cardinal opened his mouth to reply. Michelangelo had given him enough time, so he bowed to him and walked quickly away towards the ladder leaning against the scaffolding. He didn't look back as he climbed steadily upwards. Tommaso, after bowing to Cesena, followed Michelangelo up the ladder and into the scaffolding, further away from the fuming prelate still standing in the middle of the chapel floor. If Michelangelo looked down on him, he would be tempted to tip a full bowl of paint over him.

'Go,' he boomed from the top platform. Still he didn't look down. His workers glanced over at him and Tommaso.

'What did the cardinal want, Michelangelo?' Tommaso asked.

Michelangelo was still angry. 'He wants me to put clothes on everyone,' his loud reply echoed throughout the space.

'Is that what the Pope wants?' Tommaso asked, just as loudly.

'I doubt it. He has left me to paint as I wish, just as Clement did.'

Michelangelo yelled at the top of his voice to let the cardinal know. 'A vostro moda.'

They heard rapid footsteps echoing as the man crossed the marble floor and then the bang of the closing door reverberated through the chapel.

'I suppose he will go straight back to the Pope now and tell him the painting is going to be full of nudes,' Michelangelo concluded. And he will certainly tell him that the handsome Tommaso de Cavalieri is helping, the artist thought bitterly.

Tommaso broke into his thoughts. 'Perhaps you should get in first, Michelangelo. Go and see the Pope and complain about Cesena.'

'I think the Pope already knows about da Cesena,' Michelangelo muttered.

~

Bernardino, standing on a chair, scrubbed down the wooden kitchen table. Michelangelo, the apprentices and Tommaso would soon be home for supper.

He wondered about the lost papers Vincenza said she'd discovered in Michelangelo's bedchamber. They hadn't been there earlier when he had gone through the rooms dusting and sweeping and he was sure Michelangelo wouldn't have left them there. The woman had seemed agitated as she told him.

'I went into the large bedchamber to change the linen and put some away, when I saw them on the table near the window,' Vincenza had lied, words spilling from her mouth in a rush. 'I thought the Master must have been writing there and I presumed they were the missing papers.'

Bernardino frowned at her. He could tell she was lying; her face was red and her actions quick as she avoided his gaze and busied herself, clanging copper pots and pans as she searched for a pot for the vegetables.

'What did you do with them, Vincenza?' he asked.

'I left them there,' she said without looking up.

Bernardino's frown deepened. 'I'm glad they've been found. He was worried as to where they were. He doesn't want them to get into the wrong hands. They are sensitive and really for no one else but Tommaso de Cavalieri. Was there anyone in the house at the time?'

Vincenza shook her head. 'Just me. I'd been out in the yard feeding the chickens before I went upstairs and found them.' Vincenza kept her head down, still unable to look at Bernardino as she peeled and chopped vegetables for the evening meal. 'There was a visit from Cardinal da Cesena,' she added, with what Bernardino deemed was false nonchalance.

'What did he want?' Bernardino was suddenly wary.

'He just wanted to know how the painting was going in the Sistine Chapel and wanted to see the drawings again. I told him as far as I knew it was going well and the Master was there at that moment. Then he left.'

'Da Cesena is against the Master. You didn't say anything to him?' asked Bernardino suspiciously.

'Nothing, apart from what I have told you.' Vincenza added the vegetables to the cooking pot.

Bernardino climbed the stairs to Michelangelo's bedchamber. He saw the papers and immediately knew they had been tampered with. They were rolled into a bundle, whereas the last time he'd seen them, when Michelangelo and Tommaso had been here together, they were lying flat. He smoothed the papers out with his hands, so they lay as flat as possible and he left them there. Michelangelo would soon find them.

TWENTY-SEVEN

Michelangelo walked across the room to greet Pope Paul III. The artist was tired and unkempt, his gait slow and unsteady. He had requested an audience with the Pope who knew what it would be about – da Cesena no doubt. Why the cardinal was so against him, Pope Paul didn't know. Michelangelo's priest friend, Father Fattucci, at Santa Maria Nova, was full of praise for him and assured the Pope of his piety and regular attendance at Mass and the sacraments.

'Dear Michelangelo, how good it is to see you again. I believe the work in the chapel is progressing satisfactorily?' the Pope said, as Michelangelo bowed and knelt to kiss his ring.

'Yes, Holy Father. It will be some time before it's finished.'

'Quite. That is to be expected. It is a large work. You do have helpers to assist you?'

'Yes, one or two at the moment. They are trustworthy and do most of the preparation of the wall and help with the grinding of pigments for the paints.'

'I have been told that Tommaso de Cavalieri is one of your apprentices.'

Michelangelo was taken aback and momentarily could not speak. 'Yes, Holy Father, he approached me about taking him on as an apprentice and I have done so. He is trustworthy, intelligent, eager and talented.'

'He is also a good-looking young man. Is he one of your models?' the Pope asked congenially.

Michelangelo glanced at the Pope and thought yes, da Cesena had been to see him. 'Sometimes. It depends. I try and capture his beauty on paper. It's perfect to an artist's eye and I will only draw and paint from life those who are truly beautiful.'

The Pope nodded. 'Of course. You must look after yourself, my son. Take things quietly if you can. Don't be stressed by talk and gossip.'

'Pope Clement did utter a similar plea, Holiness, but I find it difficult to take things quietly when I'm besieged by a trouble-making cardinal who complains about nudity in my art and tells me to cover the figures in the painting. He wants to stifle my creativity.'

'Yes. Yes. I have already had words with the cardinal in question. Da Cesena. He shouldn't trouble you further, if I can help it.'

'I would prefer he was not allowed into the chapel at all until the work is completed, or nearly complete,' Michelangelo sighed. 'He has a horror of nudity in works of art, because he misinterprets them. He tells me this constantly. I think of the viewers and how they understand the message in the painting.' Trying not to raise his voice he explained, 'My art practice is entirely different to what has gone before in the past, with the carefully placed figures, fully clothed and static. My paintings are full of movement. The figures I am painting on the wall express the state of the human soul and people can relate to that. I should be allowed artistic freedom and that should be expected.'

'Quite. You must create and paint as you wish. Da Cesena will not worry you again.'

'On the threat of excommunication, Holiness?'

Pope Paul looked closely at Michelangelo. He did not admonish him for insolence. Michelangelo had reduced Pope Leo X to tears with his obstructive behaviour and this was known throughout the papal court. It didn't matter if it was Pope or Prince, Michelangelo spoke his mind when it suited him. He knew that Paul would not take offence because he wanted the fresco completed.

'I shall not go that far, Michelangelo.'

'If I were Pope, I would,' the artist grinned wryly.

'Well, my dear son,' Paul returned the smile, 'perhaps that is why you are not the Pope.'

Michelangelo chuckled. 'The Curia would have a hard time with me, Holiness,' he said as he bowed to the Pope.

Pope Paul nodded with a smile and extended his hand to him. As the artist bent to kiss the papal ring, the Pope said, 'Don't let lesser people worry you. Banish them from your thoughts. Concentrate on your task. I will make sure you are not bothered again. Do as Clement said you must… a vostra moda.'

~

To Tommaso

Your eyes reveal a light I will never see, one invisible to me. You see for me, and your feet walk for me, because my burden is too heavy. I fly upon your wings and in your mind I see heaven. If you are cold, I feel warmth; if you are warm, I feel cold. We are combined. What you wish, I wish too. My thoughts are yours and your voice is mine. Above me is the moon forever lit by the sun as our souls as one are forever lit by God.

Tommaso and Michelangelo sat at the salon table eating their evening meal.

'Your father doesn't mind you staying with me?' Michelangelo asked.

'It's better that I'm here with you while we are working in the chapel. He knows where I am if he needs me.'

The Master nodded. 'That's not what I meant.'

Tommaso glanced at the Master. 'He has said I am my own man now. I am twenty-six. He wishes for my happiness and is pleased you have taken me on as an apprentice and are teaching me all you know. I love you, Michelangelo. I want to be here.'

The artist looked weary, although he had tidied himself up since being at home and scrubbed the paint and plaster from his face and hands. *The Last Judgement* was taking its toll on him. He was nearly sixty and finding the days of painting gruelling, the concentration tiresome and the scaffold climbing trying, and he was also disturbed by the accusations of da Cesena. The man suspected he was having an illicit relationship with Tommaso and was trying to influence the Pope to break his contract.

'I will tell my father to inform Cardinal da Cesena that nothing is wrong. Try not to concern yourself, Michelangelo,' Tommaso assured him.

'I do worry, and for you, your reputation. Da Cesena has always questioned my work. He's dangerous. He cannot understand why I paint as I do, why my subjects are nude.'

Tommaso left his place at the table and pulled his chair over towards Michelangelo. He reached out and took the hand of the Master. Michelangelo saw love in his eyes. He trembled at his touch.

'You must not let da Cesena worry you. The work you are producing is a marvel which will be revealed in time,' Tommaso said earnestly.

'Your father, what does he think?'

'He knows and respects you. He admires you. He thinks only good can come of my relationship with you and I agree with him.'

Michelangelo felt the warmth of his companion's hand over his own and, reaching over, put his arms around Tommaso and kissed him on the cheek. He found solace and comfort in the young man's attention and his beauty continued to overwhelm him. Fully aroused, he found Tommaso's mouth and felt the firm young lips under his own respond to his kiss. Suddenly the men were standing. The chairs tipped to the floor with a loud bang.

Michelangelo could feel the strength and youth of the man in his arms and wished it for himself. 'If I lose myself in you, I will find myself,' he whispered. 'What is wrong with such love?' Michelangelo felt a surge of desire rush through him and knew what he wanted and what he dared not have. He wanted Tommaso to stay unsullied, always close but out of reach. If he took him for himself, the divine would disappear and Tommaso would be like any other young man, a shell prone to mortality. By loving Tommaso physically, he would be giving into his own weakness. In spite of his reasoning, he felt the heat of lust flood him and he shuddered.

Michelangelo pulled back and looked at Tommaso's flushed face. The early growth of his night beard darkened his unlined skin, his eyes were languid, the pupils large with diminished light and pleasure, the eyelashes like fans, even longer in the shadow of the candlelight. Michelangelo ran his hands over Tommaso's face, tracing the structure of the bones beneath and marvelling at the perfection as his fingers stroked the soft skin. He stopped and let his hand drop.

'I'm sorry, Tommao, I didn't mean…'

'It's alright, Angelo. I know what you mean. I want that too. I'm desperate for an expression of our love. How can we stay apart, even though it's better to be so, for your sake, for mine, and for the sake of your work?'

'It must be that we remain apart,' Michelangelo said plaintively, almost tearfully. 'It pains me that I will never have you as I wish.'

Tommaso put his arms around the Master. 'You will always have me, Angelo. Always, until the day I die and in heaven thereafter.'

Michelangelo felt the warmth and the stirring of Tommaso's body, alive, strong and vibrant within his arms. He pressed the young man to him, revelling in the feeling of love and youth. It was overwhelming, disturbing, damaging. To his faith, it was a sin. With the surety of youth Tommaso did not seem disturbed, he was straight and strong within Michelangelo's arms. The last thing Michelangelo wanted was belittlement. Tommaso would never do that to him and the thought of such loyalty almost made him weep.

Michelangelo pulled away from him. 'Good-night, Tommao,' he bowed slightly as he made for the door. 'I shall be going to the chapel at six o'clock in the morning. You don't need to come with me at that time if you don't wish. You can join me later.'

He bowed to Tommaso again and walked out of the room. He closed the door behind him and, heart beating fast, leant his head against the wall trying to control the desire surging through him. He wanted nothing more than to have Tommaso in his arms all night. They had already slept in the same bed. Nothing had happened but, it wouldn't last that way.

'Are you alright, Master?' Bernardino came upon him on his way upstairs to bed.

'Yes, I'm alright, my friend.' Michelangelo, glad of the interruption, put his hand on Bernardino's shoulder. 'You must come to the chapel with me tomorrow, Bernardino, and I will show you where I have put you in the fresco.'

They climbed the staircase together, their soft shoes making no noise in the night air. Holding the lamp high to light the way, Bernardino looked up enquiringly at Michelangelo.

'Are you using many people you know in the fresco, Angelo?'

'Some, Bernardino, some. There's one person I will definitely put in the painting, on the border of heaven and hell, being banished to hell, his ugliness for all to see.'

'Who is that?' asked Bernardino anxiously.

'Da Cesena.'

Bernardino smiled and breathed a relieved sigh. He'd thought it was going to be him in all of his ugliness. He gave a soft laugh. 'The honourable gentleman will not be pleased with that.' He paused at the top of the stairs and held the lamp high so the two men were in a pool of yellow light. 'The papers you misplaced have been found, Master.'

'That's a relief. Where were they?'

'Vincenza found them in the bedchamber upstairs where they still are. She also had a visit from da Cesena the same day.'

Michelangelo stood still and frowned down at Bernardino. 'Why am I suddenly suspicious?' Wariness edged his voice.

'Because, Michelangelo, there's something to be suspicious about.'

'Is Vincenza involved in this?'

'Master, I suspect she is but there's no proof.'

'Watch her, Dino. As soon as there is anything untoward, she goes.'

TWENTY-EIGHT

The Sistine Chapel door opened and Michelangelo, up on the third level of the scaffolding, felt the draught. Annoyed, he was sure it was Bernardino bringing him food and drink far too early. He was not ready to stop to eat yet; in fact he didn't care if he didn't eat at all, except Bernardino insisted.

Michelangelo was beginning to paint the plight of the damned on the right of the wall, the left being for the saved rising up to heaven and that, too, would be completed soon. He rose from his stool and put down his brush near the paints on a nearby table.

Tommaso, working nearby layering paint, glanced over at him. Michelangelo looked down into the cavern of the chapel to tell Bernardino to wait until he was finished and was surprised to find it wasn't just Bernardino standing on the marble floor below him, there was also one of the Pope's cardinals.

'Master, you must come down. Cardinal Romano wishes to meet with you,' called Bernardino, his voice carrying and echoing in the vast chamber.

'Can't you see I'm in the middle of something important here?' Michelangelo shouted. 'I don't like to be interrupted in my work.'

'Master, this is important. It's a message from the Pope,' Bernardino protested.

The cardinal held up a letter showing the large seal of Paul III.

Michelangelo's heart skipped a beat. Surely the Pope didn't want to give him another assignment?

This one was taking all his time, he had none left for anything else.

And as soon as this was finished he had to return to sculpting the figures for the Julius tomb. So, perhaps the Pope had finally listened to Cardinal da Cesena and was intent on ousting him? Staying where he was wouldn't answer his questions and so he threw the paint-stained rag in his hand onto the scaffolding floor and wearily made his way over to the ladder, climbing down to the next level, and the next, and the next. Finally, he descended from the lower rung onto the altar floor and walked down the steps to the chapel floor.

He knelt and kissed the ring of the cardinal who bent and helped him to his feet.

'We were unsure when to give this to you, since you are always busy, Michelangelo. Pope Paul insisted that it be given to you as soon as possible.' The cardinal handed him the document. Michelangelo broke the seal and opened the letter, then his mouth dropped open in surprise as he stared at the cardinal.

'The Pope would like to see you, Michelangelo. He has appointed you as Supreme Architect, Sculptor and Painter of the Apostolic Palace, and wishes to personally confer the honour upon you.'

Michelangelo, for once, was dumbfounded as he looked from the cardinal and back to Bernardino. 'When does His Holiness wish to see me?'

'At his next audience with the cardinals, bishops and priests next week on Tuesday afternoon.'

'They're all going to be there? Is that necessary?' Michelangelo asked, in dismay.

'It is a great honour which he wishes to bestow upon you publicly for several reasons. Can I tell the Holy Father that you will accept and will be present on Tuesday?'

Humbled, Michelangelo hung his head. 'Of course, Eminence.'

The cardinal held out his hand then bowed to him. In silence Michelangelo and Bernardino watched the tall, red-clad figure leave and, as the door of the chapel closed, he let out a loud sigh, still staring at the letter in his hand. Bernardino, red-faced and excited, bowed and left the chapel.

Tommaso climbed down the scaffolding ladders. 'What is it, Michelangelo? Is everything alright? You look as if you have received a shock.'

Michelangelo gave him the letter to read. 'Such an honour and I haven't even finished the fresco.'

'Michelangelo, you should be pleased at this.' Tommaso glanced at the artist, standing stolidly beside him.

There is so much to do, Michelangelo thought. 'I am', he answered. 'One thing bothers me. Through this honour I will be controlled by the Church, even more than I already am. My conscience will be sharpened even further. Why has the Pope done this now?' He turned to Tommaso. 'The last time this position had been offered I was passed over for Raphael and, the time before, for Bramante.' Michelangelo lapsed into silence. He's done it to stop me from sinning, to stop me from loving Tommaso, he thought. He dared not express his feelings to Tommaso, not in this holy place which to him at that moment, gazing at his beloved, seemed to be part of heaven itself.

Tommaso watched him with gentle eyes.

'Perhaps, Master, the Pope realised that you hadn't been recognised before and now is your time.'

~

Michelangelo waited on his own in the long hallway before the door of the Sala Regia, one of the audience halls in the Vatican. Guards stood on either side of the large double doors as he waited.

Hearing a footfall, he turned to find Cardinal Romano walking towards him. He bent and kissed the cardinal's ring. For once, on Bernardino's insistence, Michelangelo had taken time with his appearance. His black hose and doublet were clean and fresh and his cape was of deep-black velvet, expensive and rich, something he wore only on special occasions. He had even had a bath. His hair, showing streaks of grey, was freshly cut and curled about his face and his beard was trimmed carefully and forked in his usual fashion. Yet he felt jittery with nerves as he looked at the cardinal who smiled at him benignly.

'His Holiness will see you now. Come with me.' The cardinal took Michelangelo by the arm and led him to the door. He nodded to the guards to open the doors and the pair entered an antechamber, passed through another guarded door and, at last, were in the salon.

The room was recently started by Paul III. It showed promise of grandeur with its high ceiling, marble floor, balanced on either side by equally spaced dominant double-doors. Beyond that there was the Sistine Chapel. Michelangelo's glance immediately went to the large window high above his head, designed by Bramante. Michelangelo was familiar with most of the new rooms in the palace but this one almost took his breath away. The window let in a shaft of light that intensified the colours on the floor and gold dust motes swirled in the air as he moved. God's gold, Mama's angel dust.

Pope Paul was seated opposite the entrance door on a raised throne with cardinals, prelates, priests and dignitaries on either side of him and ranged down the length of the room. Michelangelo knew some, but not all. He also saw other dignitaries and ecclesiastical officials, standing, watching, including Giovanni de Cavalieri, Tommaso's father.

The Pope beckoned him forward and, with Romano beside him, Michelangelo advanced towards the Pope's throne and knelt in front of him.

'Welcome, my son. I have great pleasure in bestowing this honour upon you. Please rise,' said the Pope.

Michelangelo stood, and Pope Paul opened the rolled document in his hand and read it aloud. '"In honour of our son, Michelangelo di Lodovico di Buonorotti Simoni, Count of Palatine, we confer this honour. You are now Supreme Architect, Sculptor and Painter of the Apostolic Palace. May you grace the beloved St Peter's Basilica and the Apostolic Palace with your talent for many years to come. You are now a member of our household with all the favours, prerogatives, honours, duties and preferences that are enjoyed and can be, or are, enjoyed by our families."'

Michelangelo took the rolled parchment from the Pope with its heavy seal and bowed again to the Pontiff who started clapping. Cardinals and dignitaries joined in and Michelangelo turned and bowed in acknowledgement as they moved to crowd around him. Pride, astonishment and bemusement surged through him at being given this honour and he wondered what his father and uncle and Buonarroto would have said if they'd been witness.

Afterwards, Reginald Pole approached him, drawing him aside from a clutch of congratulating cardinals.

'At last, Michelangelo, you have received this well-deserved honour. Congratulations,' he said, bowing to the artist.

'Thank you, my Lord, I have waited a long time for this. I never thought this honour would be mine,' Michelangelo answered.

'I wish to speak with you on an important matter. May I come to your home sometime?'

'Of course, you are most welcome anytime,' Michelangelo bowed, wondering what the cleric wanted.

'I will send you a message and inform you before I come,' Pole said. Michelangelo bowed again and Pole took his leave.

TWENTY-NINE

Bernardino stood on the platform next to Michelangelo and gazed at the painted figure in front of him. He felt honoured. Now, no one was allowed near the fresco while Michelangelo was painting, not even his apprentices, apart from Tommaso. Yet, he helped Bernardino, his old friend, to climb the ladders on the scaffolding, to view up close the image he said was a painting of him. At this close proximity, the figures in the lunettes, so far executed in detail, were enormous.

The one depicting Bernardino was larger than life, flying through the painting, his arm wrapped around a column. Bernardino was one of the nude angels or ignudi which, when the painting was completed, would be above and to Christ's left. The figure was muscular and strong-looking, anatomically detailed to perfection, as only Michelangelo could do.

'Master, that looks nothing like me,' he said, looking up at the artist.

'That is you, Bernardino, your face, your eyes, your expression.'

'You have depicted me as perfect. My body and face are far from that.'

'Bernardino, you are perfect as you are. That is your soul you can see. It shines through any imperfection.'

Bernardino was overwhelmed with tears. 'I don't know what to say, Michelangelo, except, thank you.'

'Don't weep, my friend. That is how you are and it's how I see you, Dino.' Michelangelo placed his hand on Bernardino's shoulder. 'If you look closely, on the edge of the figure you will see some marks. Tip your head and they will come clearer to your vision.' Michelangelo pointed to the upper part of the column the angel was supporting. Bernardino tipped his head and, eyes screwed up, focused on the area Michelangelo indicated. There he saw it, a light, lengthy scrawl blended into the painting's shading, so from an upright angle it could not be read. It was unmistakably Michelangelo's hand. *Bernardino Basso*, it read, *my friend*. If you didn't know where to look you wouldn't realise it was there and, you would have to look very closely. Michelangelo often encoded his frescoes, usually things no one could pick up at first, or even second glance.

Michelangelo lifted Bernardino and put him in the lowering basket. 'Hold tight, Bernardino, and go home and make my supper. My Lord Tommaso will be joining me this evening.' He leaned over the bar of scaffolding and slowly lowered the small man in the basket to the floor.

~

To Tommaso

As the fire burns I will burn too if I don't love you truly as I should. My soul would suffer if it does not feel as it should. If I am taken in love by any other, may I forget and destroy that which intrudes. If I don't love and adore you, may my thoughts and my mind become dead in sadness. How could I feel joy? When my love for my lover is damaged.

Tommaso, on his feet, his head held high, looked at Michelangelo, sitting opposite him and lifted his wine glass in a toast. 'To the newly appointed member of the papal court, the Supreme Architect, Sculptor and Painter of the Apostolic Palace, Michelangelo Buonarroti Simoni. Long may he reign.'

Michelangelo smiled. They had finished their meal and Bernardino had cleared the dishes with help from Vincenza.

'The Pope has paid me well for my services,' Michelangelo said. 'He has granted me an income of one thousand two hundred scudi a year for the rest of my life. He has made sure I will never starve. He has also freed me from finishing the Julius tomb. As much as I want it done, I will not be able to do both. The three remaining statues for the tomb will be done by other sculptors. The de Rovere family were not happy about it but they couldn't refuse the Pope. I will finish my sculptures for the tomb when I have completed the fresco.'

'He truly supports you, Michelangelo. This gives you much scope for your art and architecture. The new basilica will be your work,' said Tommaso. 'The painting in the chapel is wonderful even half-finished. It will be regarded as a wonder and I am proud to be part of it, to be in your confidence, to share your creation and spirit.'

Their love had grown over the past months as both men worked side-by-side and were in each other's company for most of the day. Carrying their wine glasses, they rose from the table and sat beside the fire.

'Yes, that's true. Although I am grateful to the Pope, he has tied my hands and I wonder why he should do that.'

'It's because he doesn't want you to commit yourself too fully to other commissions that may come along.'

'He's controlling me.'

'In one sense, but he's also honouring you and supporting you. You deserve this honour, Michelangelo. It has been long in coming to you. He also wants you to be the artist who will help the Church in the changes he is keen to establish.'

The wine and warmth from the fire had brought heat to Tommaso's face. Michelangelo was gazing at him; his face full of love. He would have liked to reach for chalk and paper and to do a quick sketch of Tommaso yet again, as he did when he was so moved. Tommaso also knew Michelangelo was more than likely aroused and that his desire was conflicting with his conscience. The Master would be controlling a strong impulse to reach over and kiss him ardently, which Tommaso would welcome.

Michelangelo looked embarrassed and disturbed. He shifted in his chair, stood and moved to the other side of the room, feigning interest in a book lying on the far table. Tommaso, now familiar with Michelangelo's moods, knew how he felt. In this state, Michelangelo would do anything to distract himself and take him away from Tommaso's ever-present temptation. Now, Tommaso too was even more aware of his feelings than he had been at first. His wariness of Michelangelo had disappeared a long time ago as he had grown to understand and respect the artist. And the understanding and respect developed into love – Tommaso's first. He knew love was there, out in the world somewhere, but to experience this feeling with such intensity was a revelation. Michelangelo's soul and intellect were perfect but he was lonely, bereft of close companionship and love. Michelangelo was constantly searching for something elusive – which Tommaso knew he could provide.

Michelangelo had his back to Tommaso and the young man walked over to him and put a hand on his shoulder then put his arms around Michelangelo, hugging him around the waist, pressing his body close to the artist's. He felt the Master's body tense and, through his hands, Tommaso felt Michelangelo's heart thudding – and the artist's dilemma. Tommaso decided he'd answer the question for him. He quietly turned Michelangelo to face him and embraced him, holding him firmly against his body. He felt Michelangelo relax and return his embrace. Emotion surged through him and he surrendered to his desire as he held the artist 'I have never before felt such love,' Michelangelo whispered. Tommaso's lips were on Michelangelo's and they clung together in a long passionate kiss, until they pulled apart, breath coming in short gasps. Michelangelo looked almost tearful, agonised over the intensity of his feelings. Tommaso knew Michelangelo wouldn't want to ruin their relationship or offend his faith. Yet he would be desperate to consummate their love. Tommaso reached out a hand and stroked his face tenderly.

Michelangelo took his hand and kissed it. 'It cannot be,' he whispered.

Tommaso went on pretending he had not heard, kissing him again. This time impatiently and hard. Michelangelo kissed him back, their bodies locked together. Tommaso felt every inch of Michelangelo's body, as the other man could feel his. They knelt together on the floor, still within their embrace. They were both enraptured, desperate for relief.

The door opened. Vincenza stood in the doorway, a stunned look on her face. The two men broke apart and Tommaso sprang to his feet and turned his back to her.

'Vincenza, what are you doing here?' Michelangelo barked, climbing to his feet.

'I came to check the fire before going to bed myself, Master. I thought you had retired. I didn't mean…' Her voice failed and she bobbed a hurried curtsy and left the room, closing the door behind her.

Michelangelo sank into the fireside chair and Tommaso knelt beside him, his head on Michelangelo's lap.

'That is the last possible thing that should have happened,' Michelangelo said, stroking Tommaso's hair, misery making his voice shake. 'She's bound to go and tell someone and it will get back to the Pope, or the courts and I may be put on trial. I could lose everything.'

'We weren't doing anything but embracing, Michelangelo. There's nothing to tell.'

'It's what it implies. People are ready to criticise me and already do. I'm sure this isn't the end of it. And what about you, Tommaso? What will people think?'

'I'm unafraid of what people think. We are not doing anyone harm; a physical outlet is unavoidable. The intensity of our love is beyond us. People always talk, Michelangelo.'

'For my soul, and yours, I have to avoid it. I remember hearing Savonarola railing against such love when I was young at the Medici court. I believed in many of his ideas – not only about the sin of sodomy, which was rampant in Florence, regardless of Church teaching, but also about the Church and her shortcomings at the time. My brother was in the Dominican monastery. I even remember wanting to join them, become a friar. Everything Savonarola preached made sense to me. I admired him, he wasn't afraid to stand up to the decadent society in Florence. I can still hear his voice in my head as he preached his fiery sermons. He criticised the Papacy as being corrupt and immoral, practising simony and nepotism, especially under the Borgia. He was so strong he fascinated me.' Michelangelo stopped speaking for a moment, staring into space as if transported back in time. 'Savonarola felt it was his duty to protect the Church,' Michelangelo continued, appearing to bring himself back into the present. 'After all that's why the Dominicans were formed. He was burnt at the stake for heresy. I still have copies of his sermons and writings. How can I give in to my baser instincts now, after all this?' Michelangelo said, turning to Tommaso and holding his gaze. 'It's not that I haven't loved before, I have. My physical weakness has made me sin. Though the love I experienced then is nothing to what I feel for you now but to give into my feelings with you will take away the beauty of our relationship. It is your physical beauty I prize and you are like the divine to me, like the angel I knew was within the block of marble when I carved *David*. I love your mind, your knowledge and wit. You inspire me, encourage me, support me. You love me. I love you. To spoil that is sin alone.'

'Michelangelo, you are too hard on yourself,' Tommaso frowned and wrapped his arms around him. 'You are human and you deserve love, a relationship, not only spiritual, but physical. You are so alone, Michelangelo, but I'm here for your comfort,' Tommaso whispered tenderly. 'I will always be your friend and always love you.'

Michelangelo bent down and kissed Tommaso on his curly head of hair. A knock came on the door and Michelangelo called enter while Tommaso leapt to his feet.

'At least you wait for us to answer before barging in,' said Michelangelo as Bernardino came into the room with mugs of mulled wine.

'Who barged in, Master?' he asked, surprised.

'Vincenza, of course. She burst in on us without knocking first. Did she say anything to you after she found us together?'

Michelangelo took the glasses off the tray and gave one to Tommaso.

'She knows better than to talk about you to me, Master. I did sense something wasn't right because she came into the kitchen flustered, then rushed upstairs to her bedchamber.'

'We may have to let her go. See if you can find me another maid, someone reliable, good at what she does and who doesn't gossip.'

'You are asking for a miracle, Master,' said Bernardino, head on one side.

'As usual, Bernardino, as usual.'

Bernardino nodded and left the room, closing the door quietly behind him.

THIRTY

Michelangelo lay in his bed wide awake, wondering where his father was. He'd been here a moment ago. He had pulled him from sleep and told him again that if he became an artist he would no longer be his son. The dream had felt real; now reality claimed him. Anything to do with his father was always dark. No, his father was dead, no longer able to criticise, abuse or demand money and support. That was all Lodovico had done during those last years in Settignano.

Michelangelo remembered, Lodovico pestering him for attention, love and protection from his younger brother, Giovansimone, who abused the old man badly. Michelangelo had gone to his aid, protected him from further assaults, and threatened his brother with dire action if he continued. He had also been impatient with Lodovico. He didn't want his father near him and rarely visited him and when he did, Lodovico cried, which made him feel guilty. Lodovico said he was sorry but he still was not happy about his son being an artist, despite the *David*, the *Pietà*, and the success of the Sistine Chapel ceiling and his lucrative earnings from the Della Rovere family for the Julius tomb. It had been his art that had supported Lodovico and his younger brothers on the farm and enabled them to buy more property and set up their own business as wool merchants. Michelangelo had easily become cross with him – in fact he was still annoyed.

"Honour Thy Father and Thy Mother." That was all very well. What about another Commandment: "Honour thy Children and do them no harm." Moses should have added that to the Ten Commandments.

Michelangelo studied the dark room and the shadows on the wall. Was his brother, Buonarroto, nearby? He called but there was no answer, just a shifting next to him in the wood-framed bed. Of course, Buonarroto was dead. How could he have forgotten? The brother he'd loved above all others had died in his arms and broken his heart. Oh, yes, he had become impatient with Buonarroto too, but that had been some time ago, long before his brother's death.

Lucrezia too had died, and he remembered her kindness and still mourned her. She had helped protect him from his father's beatings and reasoned with Lodovico that his son had talent which needed to be nurtured. His father had, at long last, taken notice so when Michaelangelo's friend, Francesco Granacci, who was already an apprentice to the great artist Ghirlandaio, suggested to Lodovico and Lucrezia that Michelangelo should learn from Ghirlandaio too, Lucrezia agreed and his father relented.

When Lorenzo di Medici took Michelangelo into his home so he could have the education and training as an artist, Lodovico was so overcome he relented easily to Lorenzo, who also promised to find him an income rather than depend on his farm in Settignano. His silly father, so subservient to Lorenzo, asked for a humble position instead of one more lucrative. His lack of ambition had annoyed Michelangelo, and amused Lorenzo. He sighed, the memories came back to him far too easily these days.

His father was no longer around but his other brothers, Giovansimone and Sigismondo, were still there and occasionally pestered him. He also had Buonarroto's children, a nephew and a niece, to worry about. Would his worries never end? He let out an exasperated sigh which sounded more like a sob. There was the movement in the bed again and the form next to him turned over.

Tommaso rolled over in bed. He had been sleeping but Michelangelo's movements had woken him.

'Michelangelo, what is it? You have been dreaming again? You made a noise. Are you alright?'

Michelangelo turned to face Tommaso in the dim light.

'What is it?' Tommaso whispered again. 'Can I help?'

'I was dreaming, that's all.'

'Another bad one?'

'Sometimes, apart from you, I think my whole life is one bad dream.'

'Let me help.' Tommaso shifted over in the bed and put his arm about him.

Michelangelo kissed him on the forehead. He revelled in the warmth, comfort and closeness. This was what he longed for, this intimacy, this love. They lay together quietly in each other's arms.

'What did you dream about?' Tommaso asked.

'I dreamt I was a child again, in our house in Caprese when my father was Podesta of the region. It was a vivid dream, full of colour, yet very dark. I was about six. My father woke me.' Michelangelo turned away from Tommaso, not wanting to relive the pain of the scene.

'Tell me, Master. You must tell me,' Tommaso said as he turned Michelangelo back into the warmth of his arms. He held him firmly so he could feel the full length of his body, something he knew the Master liked. Michelangelo relaxed in his arms.

'It was so long ago. I was only a child and I thought I had forgotten. Memories come back easily to me now. There was a time when I pushed such memories from me, thinking I would be able to forget them eventually. That isn't so, they are alive inside me, even more so, just waiting for a moment of weakness to show themselves in all their lurid glory. It was the day my mother died. I remember it clearly, I made my baby brother cry and it woke my mother. I knew she was dead yet she sat up and admonished me. I was terrified.'

'Wasn't she dead?' Tommaso brought Michelangelo back to the present.

'Yes, she was. I was imagining things. I was scared. This was my dream, my mother's sorrow, my father's punishment. My dream is also of loss, never to feel the softness of her touch again, or smell her perfume, never to see her loving smile. It still haunts me, even now. I often dream about that night. The dream still scares me,' Michelangelo sighed. 'I have never loved a woman, apart from my mother, Tommaso,' he continued. 'Never felt the tenderness or touch of a woman in love. It is as if my sense of love was halted when she died. Our stepmother was a good woman and looked after us boys, and that must have been difficult because we were a boisterous, unruly lot, as far as my father was concerned, anyway. I never again felt a mother's love. The normality of it. Lionardo and Buonarroto were the same, they felt the loss as I did and we were close. We comforted each other. Lionardo blamed our father for Mama's death, for making her pregnant yet again. He was a year older than me. I don't think he ever forgave Papa. He had no respect for him. When he was about eleven he was raped by a teacher called Raffaello Canacci. It had a bad effect on him. He withdrew into himself, became silent and morose. Later, he joined the Fra Savonarola's Dominican monastery and became a Friar. Our father did his best with us but he disciplined us harshly. He knew no other way. There was no love anymore. Now I'm older, these memories are very clear and real to me. Incidents I thought I had forgotten, trouble me and give me nightmares.'

'They are dreams, Michelangelo. The past is over, nothing can harm you now.' Tommaso reached out and caressed his lover's face, soothing the lines, releasing the stress. He kissed him tenderly. 'Sleep, dear Angelo, sleep.'

Michelangelo fell asleep, wrapped in Tommaso's embrace. When he awoke Tommaso was still there, sleeping soundly beside him, his arm stretched across Michelangelo's chest. It was not yet dawn and the artist, forever mindful of time's passing, needed to go to the chapel now if he was to get a full day's work in. He shifted gently, so as to not wake Tommaso, and removed himself from the bed.

~

A rapid pummelling and shouting boomed from the kitchen door. Bernardino, about to open it, was squashed behind it as it opened in a rush.

'Where is she?' yelled the man at the door.

'Where is who?' Bernardino scrambled around the side of the door. 'Who are you?'

'Vincenza's brother. I have come to deliver her from this house of immorality!'

Bernardino gaped as the man, a grubby apron over his clothes, stormed out of the kitchen and into the hallway, shouting for Vincenza. Belatedly, Bernardino recognised him as the owner of a grocery store near Trajan's Market.

Vincenza poked her head over the railing from upstairs.

'What do you want?' she called.

Her brother leapt up the stairs two at a time and grabbed her roughly, pulling her downstairs after him, her arms full of folded linen.

'Stop! Stop! What are you doing?' she protested. He was oblivious to her cries.

'What is this all about?' Bernardino demanded, as the pair landed at the foot of the stairs.

'I'm taking her from this place. We have known Michelangelo for many years but this time he has gone too far and I don't want her near him.' He set off down the hallway, pulling a struggling Vincenza after him.

'What have you heard?' Bernardino followed the pair through the hall to the front door. Vincenza turned and thrust an armful of linen at Bernardino who caught most of it.

'You know what goes on here,' the grocer snarled. 'She's leaving.'

The outside door slammed shut. Bernardino picked up the linen from the floor and stood for a moment, thinking. Thank the Lord that Michelangelo was in the chapel and not in his workshop. And at least he didn't have to dismiss Vincenza but what had her brother heard that caused him to suddenly barge in and demand her to leave?

PART SIX
1535–1537

TREACHERY

THIRTY-ONE

Cardinal da Cesena paced the marble floor of his apartment. Febo had not yet arrived in response to his summons. Da Cesena was annoyed he had to submit to the Pope, yet again, regarding the nudity in Michelangelo's paintings and his behaviour with young men. Everyone knew about it and the Pope tolerated it because he wanted the artwork in the Sistine Chapel finished. Da Cesena paced and fumed.

Where was Febo?

Da Cesena had a duplicate key to the Sistine Chapel lock and had sneaked in two hours before dawn when the chapel was unguarded. He had stood at the foot of the altar and held his lantern high to see the painting, parts of it finished and other parts yet to be painted. He headed towards the ladder on the right-hand side of the scaffolding and began to climb, despite knowing it was against the Pope's and Michelangelo's orders. In the lamplight it was hard to see the painting but, as he'd suspected, the finished section depicted muscular nudes as they twisted, turned and swirled in various poses all over the heavens. The figures' accurate anatomical detail amazed and horrified him. How could such nudity be tolerated in this holy chapel?

Some of the figures were grotesque and horrifying, although there was still much work to be done. The painting was only completed in the lunettes at the top of the wall and the figures immediately below. He climbed down the scaffolding and onto the chapel floor, walked towards the entrance and let himself out quietly. No one would know he'd been there, apart from the guards at the gate of the Papal Palace.

Da Cesena completed yet another parade through his chamber.

Where was Febo? The young man seemed to be avoiding him – doing his household duties as directed but never telling where he'd been at night or who he'd been with. Despite the valuable ring given to Febo and gold coins to bribe the informant, he had heard nothing in return. Da Cesena turned sharply at a rap on the door. Febo entered, walked over and knelt before him.

'Where have you been? I've been waiting for you for days and have hardly seen you,' the cardinal snarled. Protocol forgotten, in his anger he failed to extend his hand to Febo, instead he towered over him, ready to strike. 'Well? Where is this information you were supposed to get me?'

'Apologies, Eminence, I have been occupied with my duties and unable to contact my informant. I have just come from the market hoping to see her. The place was crowded so it took some time for me to get away from the mob and make my way here.'

The cardinal walked around Febo, sniffing the air. The servant was well-dressed as usual, wearing a dark-green velvet cape and doublet and, in his hand, he held a soft cap decorated with a feather. His clothes looked clean but there was a definite whiff of fish or some other undesirable market smell about him.

'Well, have you found out anything more about the artist and his latest lover?'

'There is much to tell, Eminence. Unfortunately, my informant, who was a maid living in the house, has been forbidden by her brother to work there anymore,' said Febo.

'Then you must find someone else to spy on him. We need to know exactly what he gets up to with Cavalieri. His family is well-known and noble. It surprises me that he would be in such a relationship. Does his father know what's going on?'

'I believe so, Eminence. The young man is of age, so he can please himself.'

'Is Michelangelo teaching him art?'

'Yes, and he's reputed to have talent. He's helping the artist in the Sistine Chapel with the latest work.'

Da Cesena paced. 'The Pope has forbidden me to worry him about the indecency of Michelangelo's art but if I can get stronger evidence of the pair, then His Holiness may be forced to censure the artist and get him to make his paintings decent. He may even take him off the painting and replace him with Fra Sebastiano.'

Febo raised his eyebrows.

'He would paint everyone with clothes on, which would be much better,' da Cesena continued. He swung around and eyed Febo, still kneeling. 'I need a witness. Why can't you do this? He knows you?'

Febo shook his head. 'He would make sure I didn't know anything. I am not welcome in his house. He doesn't trust me.'

The cardinal paced again, head down, away from Febo. He didn't trust him either. How could the Pope allow Michelangelo so close to the Holy See and tolerate his indiscretions? Perhaps it was because Paul was a father himself, and a grandfather. Perhaps that gave him patience, understanding and tolerance? Virtues Cesena did not possess and, in this case, could not understand.

Febo was still on his knees before the cardinal. 'I believe there is a way I may find out, Eminence. I will need more gold coins, or one of your valuable rings to bribe my friend into confessing what she has seen.'

Da Cesena studied Febo, who had his face turned up to him, his eyes wide, brown and innocent. Da Cesena thought he recognised the young man from some of Michelangelo's paintings and could see why the artist had used him. Febo was handsome, youthful, his skin smooth – he was almost feminine in his appearance, much like de Cavalieri. But another part of him wasn't feminine and that part had been portrayed and sculpted with gusto and accuracy by Michelangelo. Looks can be deceiving and Febo was no angel. The cardinal had reports of him visiting the whores near the market, and, of course, he was prone to squandering money on valuable velvets, satins and silks. Yet, he had refused to reveal any intimate detail about his life with Michelangelo apart from the poems the artist had written to him. The Pope had recognised Michelangelo's writing when da Cesena showed him the poems. If shocked, the Pope had not shown it. He chose to ignore the sexual innuendos within the poems for Febo, just passing them off to da Cesena as good work.

The cardinal went to the drawer of his desk and removed a large topaz ring set in diamonds.

Febo gasped. The cardinal asked, 'How much do you give the informant, Febo?'

'As much as I think is necessary.' He eyed the ring.

'You get me the information I want and you shall have this ring.'

'I need something now so I can get the information out of her,' answered Febo.

'I will give you some more gold coins and once you have information, you will have the ring.'

Febo stood and bowed. 'I will do my best, Eminence.'

The cardinal reached into the deep pocket of his red soutane and brought out a pouch of gold coins. Febo was no fool but the cardinal needed proof and information. Michelangelo had to be stopped.

Febo took the coins, knelt and kissed the cardinal's ring.

'Don't be too long about it, Febo,' said the cardinal.

Febo turned at the door and bowed again then left, closing it behind him, leaving the long figure of the cardinal standing in the centre of the salon.

The smell of the market wafted around Febo. Revolted, he lifted his arm and pressed his sleeve to his nose. Customers bustled past him as he stood at the entrance of the grocery store. He had been there many times before, sometimes buying for Bernardino when he had felt unsure of tackling the unruly mob. Now the ripe smell of spices, fruit and vegetables filled the air, making him wrinkle his nose.

Where was Vincenza? He turned and went around the back of the store, down the side alley littered with rotting vegetables, empty wine caskets and feral, scrapping cats. The back of the store stank more than the front but he had to find her so he crossed the yard and went to the back door, which was slightly ajar.

It was dark inside the storeroom and he could see Vincenza as she scooped flour into bags to be bought in the shop. He stole up to her and grabbed her by the arm. She squealed in fright and he put a hand over her mouth. She dropped the flour bag, spraying the contents over the floor. He held her firmly and dragged her outside to the yard and towards the brick ruins of the old market. There he shoved her roughly into an alcove then followed her, pressing himself close to her so they were out of sight.

'What do you want?' she asked, wide-eyed and frightened.

'I need more information about the Master and his lover, de Cavalieri.'

'I have already told you what I know.'

Febo reached into the pocket of his doublet and held up a pouch of coins. He had taken his share out. He jingled them under her nose. It usually worked. Her eyes were fixed on the jangling pouch.

'Why do you want more information?'

'A good friend of mine needs to know, that's all.'

'And it's worth all these coins?'

'Perhaps even more if the information is worth knowing.'

'You know I don't work there anymore. My brother took me from the house. I'm not going back.'

'Why did he take you away?'

'He doesn't want me working in such a place. I have never before been exposed to such debauchery. He thinks it would only do me harm.'

'Has he only just discovered what goes on with the Master?' Febo was astonished.

'Of course not. We've known Michelangelo for years, ever since we grew up in Settignano, and we decided to ignore the talk because we needed the money. Then my brother heard rumours about de Cavalieri from people coming into the store and it was too much.' Vincenza squirmed under Febo's fierce grip, avoiding his scrutinising gaze.

'Look at me, Vincenza. What did you see?' He shook her. 'Tell me, what's been going on?'

A noise came from the back of the store. 'Vincenza!' called her brother. Vincenza tried to move but Febo pinned her to the brick wall, his hand over her mouth. They could hear her brother growling and mumbling to himself in the storeroom.

'Tell me what you saw and I will let you go and give you the gold,' Febo hissed, taking his hand from her mouth.

'He'll beat me if I don't show myself.'

'He can't beat you if you're not there.'

'I walked in on them in the dining salon. They were on their knees and in each other's arms and kissing passionately.' Vincenza's words tumbled out of her mouth, as if she was eager to get rid of them.

'Have you seen them in bed together?'

'No. I don't start work until Michelangelo has gone to the chapel. But when I sleep in the house I know de Cavalieri is there and I have heard them talking in the Master's bedchamber. There is much talk and laughter. The Master seems constantly happy when de Cavalieri is around, so he has him with him nearly all the time.'

Febo frowned. 'I need more information, more poems, letters,' he said urgently, pocketing the coins again. 'Anything to incriminate him.'

'How can I do that if I'm not there?' Vincenza asked, puzzled.

'Find a way. Make an excuse to go back to the house. Do it when the Master isn't there and Bernardino's not around. Watch the place.'

'Sometimes in the evening Bernardino takes a meal to the Master in the chapel if he works late,' she murmured.

'Where's de Cavalieri then?'

'Usually with the Master. He's been helping him.'

'Find a time to bring me more evidence: letters, poems, anything. If you do, you will get more than gold,' Febo promised.

He bent and kissed her on the lips, this time a soft, lingering, persuasive kiss, and ran his hand over the rise of her breast.

'I miss you, Vinnie,' he whispered, his mouth close to her ear. 'I need you. Do this once for me and that will be the last. I will leave da Cesena and we will be together.'

They broke apart and Febo poked his head out to check if the way was clear then left her in the alcove, her back still pressed against the bricks.

~

Vincenza hid amongst the ruins near Michelangelo's house, watching carefully between chinks in the stone. She really didn't want to do this anymore but the thought of Febo made her succumb to his wishes. He was handsome and well-dressed enough to enamour any woman and Vincenza wanted him for herself. She could impress him now. She gathered her cloak around her against the cold of evening and watched the house for signs of life. Michelangelo wasn't there. He would be at the chapel until late, although she had seen apprentices lingering within the house, walking around the side of the building to the back entrance. She was unsure if Bernardino was there. Horse-drawn carts rumbled past and people moved to and from the market, baskets laden. Taking a chance, she emerged from her hiding place with her head down, stepping quickly across the road and around the side of the house towards the kitchen garden. It didn't matter if Bernardino was there, she would say she had come to collect her belongings.

The garden was empty and there was no smoke from the chimneys of the two cottages on the side. The stables and forge were deserted, apart from the steady eyes of Sheba, Michelangelo's horse. Vincenza sneaked around the side of the garden and entered the loggia where she tried the kitchen door. It was open, so she let herself in carefully and stopped to listen. Silence, apart from the noise of the apprentices in the back workshop.

She tiptoed through the kitchen and into the hallway where she stopped again. The house was quiet. She called Bernardino lightly, knowing if he were there he would appear promptly in the hall. There was no answer. She ran down the hallway into the vestibule and up the marble staircase, her hard-soled shoes clackety-clacking all the way. If anyone was in the house they would have heard her. Instead of heading towards the servants' rooms at the back of the house, she stopped at the door leading into Michelangelo's bedchamber.

She would find his poems and letters in his scrivania and knew where he kept the key. After using the key in the past following Febo's instructions, she had put it back in its hiding place. Hopefully it was still there.

Her heart beating fast, Vincenza opened the salon door and closed it behind her, turning the key in the lock. The bed-chamber was half in darkness, with a musty man-smell, and the bed was rumpled and unmade. The room itself contained the scrivania, a large wardrobe, a credenza and two chairs. They had clearly not found a maid to replace her yet. She went straight to the window seat, quickly found the key and unlocked the scrivania.

A pile of paper with Michelangelo's writing stared up at her. Illiterate, she couldn't understand the wording. She quickly rifled through the pile, finding those that looked like letters, poems and sketches. She looked at one of the sketches and gasped, a hand to her mouth. There was one explicit sketch of an enlarged erect phallus and below it was written the name Tommaso. There was also another similar with the name Michelangelo written beneath it. Both were signed by the two men. Those words she could recognise. Her hands shook as she took the sketches and letters and what looked like poems. She locked the scrivania and slipped the key back in its hiding place. Hopefully, the Master would not realise some of his work was missing and that she could return it later.

She tucked the papers into one of her apron's voluminous pockets and slipped from the room. Her heart pounding, she was eager to escape the house with the burden of the incriminating evidence. She would come back the next day for her belongings.

Removing her loud shoes, she checked for any stray, wandering apprentices then ran down the staircase, through the vestibule and hallway, out the back door and into the garden, unseen. Noise echoed from the workshop as she raced past the windows and out of the kitchen garden.

Febo would be pleased, for the letters and poems were sure to be incriminating, not to mention the sketches. Perhaps he might even love her enough to take her away from her bullying brother. She stayed still for some minutes, calming herself, before slowly returning through the shadowed streets to her brother's shop.

At least, she thought, when I was with the Master I had a good bedchamber, clean air and a decent bed, not a smelly truckle on top of a grocery shop.

~

At midnight, Febo waited at their designated meeting place in the street. Vincenza, papers still in her pocket, stuck to the shadows as she slunk toward him. He stepped out of the doorway, grabbed her hand and pulled her with him into the shadows.

'Did you get what I asked for?' he asked, gruffly.

She nodded and pulled the sheaf out of her pocket.

'Good.'

'What about my gold?' she held out her hand. With enough money she could leave her brother and fend for herself if Febo let her down.

'Not yet. I must show them to the person concerned. Only if they are pertinent will I give you the coins.'

'I have done my share. I demand the rest of my payment,' Vincenza declared, heatedly. 'You'll find they are what you want.'

Febo held her at arm's length. 'No. No reward yet. Meet me back here tomorrow night at the same time and I may have your gold for you.'

'What are you going to do with them?' Vincenza asked, fear in her voice, still alarmed at what they contained. 'It was difficult for me to get the letters and if I'm found out I'll be punished,' she whined. 'I don't know who would punish me but I know it would happen somehow. Perhaps I had better go to a priest to confess?'

'Don't worry. I have told no one where I get my information from. No one knows. Be patient. Tomorrow.'

He kissed her again, opening her lips, his tongue darting into her mouth. He lifted her skirts, finding his way to the place he knew best and pressed his body against hers, then abruptly pulled away and was gone.

THIRTY-TWO

Reginald Pole sat before Michelangelo in the black robes of a cleric within the Vatican court. His only claim to colour was a long deep blue mantelleta over his black soutane. Bernardino had placed Pole's biretta on the table in the salon then poured them both a glass of Trebbiano.

Pole's habits were abstemious and he sipped the liquid slowly, savouring its texture and aroma as he studied Michelangelo. He waited until Bernardino left the room before he spoke.

'Pope Paul has agreed to a group of cardinals, priests and myself to discuss church politics and reform for the future – we will be named "The Spirituali." I asked him if you could be included because you have much to offer and it is good to have a secular person, yet one who knows the workings of the Church.' Pole gave Michelangelo an inquiring look.

"How exactly is this reform to be brought about?' asked Michelangelo.

'It is to be reformed from within through argument and persuasion,' said Pole.

'I'm hardly worthy to contribute to argument and persuasion, impatience is my failing. I'm not worthy,' Michelangelo said. 'My specialty is art. I'm unsure if I can contribute to work of reform in religion. I have no knowledge of theology and my Latin is poor.'

'You have a fine mind and have studied Humanism and have been taught by the finest minds in your youth. Your ideas would be welcomed.'

'No one would take me seriously. Rumours abound about me.'

'They are rumours, Michelangelo.'

'You never know, they might be true,' Michelangelo said with a smile. 'I have no wish to join any political faction, my Lord,' he added warily.

'Indeed. You would not be obliged to, but you may be interested in the people we have amongst us and what we have to say. Your thoughts on different matters would be enlightening and may help us.'

'Mmm. I understand but I doubt I would be of use.'

'Just to have your fine company would be of use, my friend, and would save us getting bogged down in too much dogma.'

'There is that risk.'

Pole smiled at him and nodded. 'The Church is in quite a state because of past happenings within its walls, and reform is needed. The Pope is rightly worried and looks for advice; that is why this group has been formed. Pope Paul intends to summon another council about reform later. This is preparation for it. The Marchioness de Pescara, Vittoria Colonna, also belongs to the group. I am her spiritual advisor. She is a wise and saintly person and she has great respect for you and wishes to meet you.'

Michelangelo nodded. 'Yes, I know of her. I've heard she is well-known for her intellectual thought, illustrious family and wealth,' he answered. 'My friend, Bartolemeo Angilini, believes I should meet her. I have done some work for her. I produced a design for a Noli me Tangere which she has received with pleasure but I have not met her. She is talked of as being a woman with the brain of a man because she is said to be able to converse on any subject.'

'Yes, that is true,' Pole agreed. 'She is interested in the reform of the Church and is distressed at the rupture in the north. There is much talk that if Pope Leo X had taken notice of Luther's ninety-five theses, perhaps the overwhelming schism might have been avoided.'

'True. He should have taken notice of the friar.'

'It has been thought for some time that the ones who have fallen from us might come back into the fold but it does not seem to be happening. It has made the Pope hesitate on many issues,' answered Pole, thoughtfully.

Michelangelo nodded; he too had heard such talk.

Pole leant forward and looked at the artist earnestly. 'It is settled then? You will come to one of our meetings?' he asked, a note of relief in his voice.

Michelangelo thought for a moment. 'Yes, I will. And I thank you for asking me. I am honoured.' He smiled at Pole. 'I suppose one day there will be a red hat for you, my Lord?'

'I doubt it. I am not looking for it. I am not even an ordained priest.'

'That has not stopped the system before,' Michelangelo commented, thinking of Guilio de Medici, Pope Clement, a cardinal at sixteen.

'Yes, that is one of the things we need to consider, for the Church's future – the ordination of priests before they ascend to high office. I can see, Michelangelo, you are going to be of great use to us.'

Michelangelo smiled and inclined his head to Pole. 'Tell Madame Colonna that I would be honoured to meet her.'

'You shall hear from her in due course and I am sure you will not be disappointed by this dear lady. There is one thing I haven't mentioned. Everything discussed, even the group itself, must remain in the strictest confidence of those involved. No one must know what we discuss. I'm sure you understand.'

'I understand, my Lord,' agreed Michelangelo.

Pole stood from his chair. 'I will take my leave,' he said, bowing. 'I am so pleased to have you with us, Michelangelo. You shall hear from us and I am sure you will not be disappointed.'

THIRTY-THREE

Tommaso sat quietly beside Michelangelo and watched him work, steadily filling the cartoon of the figures on the wall, applying the glaze in stages, bringing out shape and form.

'Tell me, Michelangelo. Is this how you painted the ceiling?'

Michelangelo nodded. He didn't like talking while he painted. He also preferred working on his own, without interruption, but Tommaso was an exception.

Intently and quickly, with a brush in each hand, Michelangelo applied the brushwork, moulding and sculpting figures out of paint by gradually building up layers, deepening shadows and cross-hatching. As he painted, he stood back occasionally to judge the overall effect. The figures were coming to life before Tommaso's eyes.

'The figures look as if they are flying. They are weightless,' Tommaso commented.

'They are in the process of being judged whether they proceed to heaven or hell. The dead will rise, ready for the judgement. Some will be condemned, so their faces will be devilish, their bodies twisted as a result of their earthly sins. Those who are saved will have the goodness of their lives glowing from their faces.'

'It will scare people, Angelo,' Tommaso said.

'It may scare some but those who study the scriptures will understand. We Christians are of God's elect.'

'We have no certainty of that.'

'No, you are right. We have only our belief and that is why we are torn between what we want to do and what God wants us to do. It is this uncertainty which worries me most of the time. It makes me chastise myself when I sin, makes me want to avoid sin yet, miserably, I succumb. That uncertainty drives me to ask God for forgiveness. Yet, sometimes when I'm here or alone with you, the uncertainty disappears and belief in my faith diminishes. I long for God's grace, but I also long for you. If I love you, even with a chaste heart, will that mean I am damned in the sight of God? Or am I to be redeemed? Is that part of my predestination?'

Tommaso went to Michelangelo and put his arms around him, holding him closely. He then took his hands in his and bent and kissed them, the palms, the back of his hands, and reached up and kissed his lips.

'Come, Tommao, we must continue,' Michelangelo said, reluctantly pulling away.

~

The chapel, except for where they were situated on the scaffolding, was quiet and dimly lit. They were surrounded by candlelight and lamplight and the light from the top windows. Michelangelo had also rigged the drapery near where he was painting so that light reflected off it onto his work. Tommaso ground more pigment which Michelangelo mixed into animal glue, then settled into painting again, working fast, concentrating hard as he crosshatched with colour to create depth and form before the plaster dried.

Gradually, the outside light disappeared and they were in darkness, except for the ring of light surrounding them. Michelangelo looked over at his muse, curled like a child on a bed of drapery, sound asleep. Michelangelo had been so intent on his work he hadn't even noticed the young man had quietened. He walked over to him and bent down to study him in the candle-light.

Tommaso's face was relaxed and oblivious to the older man's admiration. Michelangelo looked at the profile and long eyelashes that cast a shadow over Tommaso's cheeks. His beauty was so great it made Michelangelo's heart ache. He bent and traced a finger over the high, straight forehead, lightly over his cheekbones and down to the strength of his jaw. His skin was taut and velvet-soft except for the shadow of his beard over the jawline.

Michelangelo was overwhelmed with love. He wanted to take him and make him his own. Even standing next to him aroused Michelangelo. He revelled in his warm emotions yet, at the same time, he was torn; his faith told him it was wrong. He bent and kissed the smooth cheek and forehead, the lovely upturned full lips, always ready with a smile, and the smooth paint-stained hands. Tommaso stirred and woke. He reached up and put his arms around Michelangelo, drew his head back down to him and kissed him on the lips.

'I ache for you, my dear,' Michelangelo whispered. 'Long for you. Come to me.' He knelt down beside Tommaso who sat up and kissed him ardently.

'My dear,' said Michelangelo, after a time. 'My dear,' he repeated, his heart thundering in his chest, conscious that his whole being was excited by Tommaso's presence and touch. 'It's time to go home.'

~

Febo let himself into the palazzo belonging to Cardinal da Cesena and walked rapidly down the hallway to the cardinal's salon. He knocked and waited until he heard the call to enter. The cardinal was at his scrivania, writing, and looked up as Febo knelt beside his chair.

'Well?' da Cesena put down his quill and looked at the smooth-faced man.

'More letters, Eminence. More letters, poems and sketches. He's definitely in love with de Cavalieri. I think you will be impressed with the sketches.'

The cardinal took the papers and rifled through them, bringing one out and reading it carefully. He pulled out a sketch from the pile and covered his mouth with his hand.

Da Cesena's face went red. 'This is proof enough of what's going on. You have received these from the same source as before?' he asked Febo.

'Yes, Eminence. A most reliable source.'

Da Cesena smiled to himself. 'This is excellent, Febo.'

The cardinal reached into a drawer in his scrivania and brought out the large topaz ring set with diamonds. 'Your reward, Febo. No one must know.'

'No one will, as far as I'm concerned,' Febo said. 'I do need more coins for my informant because I was not sure if this information would be sufficient for you.'

Cardinal da Cesena nodded, reached into another drawer and brought out a pouch of coins and handed them to Febo. 'Go,' he said, 'this has never taken place.'

Febo bowed to the cardinal, kissed his ring and left the room. There was just one thing left to do. Glancing over his shoulder as he walked down the hallway, suddenly nervous, he took the wide tread of the marble stairs two at a time and headed for his bedchamber.

THIRTY-FOUR

To Tommaso,

I have always longed to see lovely things of this world and the next. It helps my soul to reach God; such a radiance draws us back to God. Here on earth it is called love. My heart sees only one face to find the way, my eyes possessed by those stars.

'Tommaso, I wish you to stand in front of the prepared plaster, just here.' Michelangelo indicated a bare patch on the upper middle section of the wall where he'd already arranged white drapery to reflect light from several lamps. 'No clothes,' he added.

Tommaso stripped quickly, accustomed to the request. Often Michelangelo would ask him to take off his clothes just to admire the perfection of his body. The pleasure of looking at him bare overcame the artist once again as he admired the strength and length of his body – his broad shoulders, strong hands, taut abdomen and the swell of his torso above the groin. The exact features he had used in the *David*. Here, the perfection of *David* was in front of him. Tommaso's legs were long, straight and muscled, his feet large enough for his size.

'You truly are a perfect image of the divine,' Michelangelo said in wonder.

'How do you want me to pose?' Tommaso smiled at him.

Michelangelo had already drawn him kneeling, one arm raised, producing several sketches from various angles and detailed studies of the limbs. He would have to draw him again here, in the place where the painting would be painted, without any distractions around them. He asked Tommaso to go down on one knee and hold out his right arm. The artist began to draw. After a moment, he went over to Tommaso and gently took his arms and hands, placing them in certain positions and, again, recorded them.

'Stay on one knee, then move your body as if you are about to rise up onto your feet.' Tommaso did. 'Now, place your right arm up, bent at the elbow as if you are about to admonish someone. And look towards your left, your head inclined downwards.'

Michelangelo walked over to Tommaso. He put both hands on either side of Tommaso's face and adjusted the pose, then bent down and kissed his lips. The young man didn't move. Michelangelo returned to his sketch.

'Can you hold that pose a little longer?' Tommaso did while Michelangelo sketched. He placed a lamp in front of Tommaso then stood back to watch the effect. The outline stood out already pounced, but the light on the wall enlarged the area further. Michelangelo walked quickly behind him and, with a stylus, pressed the new outline onto the fresh plaster.

'Thank you, Tommao. Relax for a few minutes.' Michelangelo sorted through the sketches. 'Again Tommao, please,' he said and Tommaso reverted to the previous position. Michelangelo placed Tommaso's left hand across his body. 'Hold that for a few minutes.' He sketched Tommaso's bent arm, then went behind him and added to the larger outline of his body on the plastered wall. 'Thank you,' he said at last and the young man got up and stretched, relieving his muscles.

Michelangelo stood back and surveyed the sketched image. It was much larger than life-size to create the impact he wanted. Michelangelo went to the edge of the scaffolding and called for one of his apprentices, who was waiting on the chapel floor, then told his patient sitter, 'You can get dressed now.'

Tommaso disappeared behind the drapery as the apprentice started climbing the ladder.

'Matteo, I wish to use your dear face for the image of the Virgin.'

Used to his Master's unusual requests, Matteo nodded benignly. Tommaso, fully clothed, appeared from behind the drapery and sat on the nearest stool to watch as Michelangelo arranged Matteo's body. The apprentice sat on a stool, half turned away and positioned slightly to the side of the central sketch on the plastered wall.

Again, this wasn't Michelangelo's first time drawing Matteo's face for the scene, he had already done several sketches, but he wanted to draw him here in this place. He put his hands on either side of Matteo's face and gently moved it to the right position, then told him he had to look modest with his eyes downcast. He drew out of a basket some material he had brought for the purpose and draped it over Matteo's head and body, watching where the folds fell, looking intently at Matteo's features which were, because of his young age, still adolescent and feminine. Michelangelo would soften them more to create an image of the Virgin Mary. The boy sat still for Michelangelo as he sketched.

'Now, turn your face more to the left and look slightly downwards,' he said. Matteo obeyed instinctively. 'Bring your arms up against your body and cross them at the wrist like so.' Michelangelo demonstrated the position. Again, the boy complied. When Michelangelo had finished sketching, he placed the lamp in front of Matteo and told him not to move and went behind him, as he had done with Tommaso and, with a stylus, he traced the enlarged line from that already pounced.

At last, he said, 'Thank you, Matteo, you can go now. Please tell Bernardino that Master Tommaso and I will be late home.'

Matteo deposited the drapery back in the basket, bowed to both men and disappeared down the ladder towards the floor of the Sistine Chapel.

'Now, I can start to fill in the central piece, Tommaso.' Michelangelo sighed with relief as he gathered paints and brushes and arranged them on his work table. He mixed the lightly pigmented glaze onto his palette and immediately applied colour to the form on the wall. Even with the lightest glaze, it began to take shape. It was obviously going to be lighter in colour than the surrounding figures he'd already painted.

Mesmerised, Tommaso asked, 'Is this the figure of Christ, Michelangelo?

'Yes.'

Tommaso was silent as Michelangelo set to work, already sculpting a basic image with paint. 'I know how you feel, Michelangelo, and I'm honoured that you consider me worthy but it still troubles me.' Tommaso gazed at the large figure, filled with glaze, growing under Michelangelo's brushes.

'You are worthy, Tommao. You are one of God's perfect beings. There is no one else who could possibly be my model for this. Your looks and bodily beauty will outshine the rest of the painting, as they should. As Christ outshines mere mortals.'

'Michelangelo, I am a mere mortal. My soul is not pure, as you know. How can you use me like this, to represent the divine?'

'Christ was also mortal in his humanity. Yes, you are mortal but your looks bring you close to the divine. You reflect the glory of God in heaven. I see in you immortality, a vision of heaven, a glimpse of God.'

Tommaso conceded defeat. 'How can I help you, Michelangelo?'

'You already help me by your cooperation, your willingness to understand what I'm trying to achieve. Your presence inspires me. That alone is a help. If you want to help with the painting of these images you can fill in the shape of the Virgin Mary for me. Here, take this pigment and brush and start with a light glaze, all over.'

The two men painted quietly together, Michelangelo giving Tommaso instructions now and then. The light diminished until, at the end of the day, when darkness filled the chapel and lamps were the only light, they stood back and surveyed their work. The forms, now completely filled in with the basic glaze and the application of coloured pigment, towered over the men. The Virgin Mary's form was to the side and positioned lower than the Christ figure. Tommaso could already see the strength and dominance in the expression of the Christ form he had posed for.

Michelangelo turned to Tommaso and put his arms around him. 'Bravo, Tommaso. Bravo.'

~

Michelangelo gently lifted Tommaso's arm from his chest and rolled out of bed, then turned and looked back. The young man hadn't stirred and the sight of him fully stretched out awakened Michelangelo's senses. The desperation of wanting him flooded his whole being again, an emotion he was trying to control, although it was persistent in the back of his head. Defamation of his beloved no longer concerned him and belief that the consummation of their love would threaten his artistic soul had disappeared. His concept of love had evolved into another sphere. It had been some time since he had been embraced in physical love. The last time was with Febo who was unsatisfactory. He had always waited for Febo to demand something from him, like his father used to. Now his desire rested only on Tommaso.

Guilty about that desire and the weakening of his will with Febo, he had gone to see Father Fattucci and, in humble penitence, laden down with sin, had confessed. Now, in the hour before the sun appeared over the horizon, there was only one thing he wanted. The opportunity and beauty of his beloved innocently asleep overcame his doubt.

He did not even think of chalk and paper, as he usually did when moved, his beloved was well imprinted in his brain. He wanted nothing more than to express his love with the young man.

Michelangelo walked across the floor to the closet, placed the chamber-pot on a stool and relieved his bladder. He finished and turned to find Tommaso propped on one elbow watching him, his body in a full state of arousal.

'Come to me, Angelo.' Tommaso held out his arms. Michelangelo crossed back to the bed, lifted his night-shirt over his head and stood naked above him. Tommaso smiled, drew up his legs and arched his back in desire, holding out his arms to Michelangelo, who thought he had never seen anyone look so enticing in his life. He climbed into bed beside him and put his arms around him, the young man's body resilient, smooth and firm under his touch.

Michelangelo lay with the length of his body pressed to Tommaso's, as their lips locked in a long, tight embrace. They held each other, face to face, gently moving against one another, their bodies as one. This was what Michelangelo wanted, they would not commit the sin of sodomy.

He pulled back and ran his hand through Tommaso's curly hair. He started kissing Tommaso's chest, the softness of his neck, his firm abdomen, running his hand down and around and up until Tommaso moaned with desire and ecstasy. Michelangelo was desperate and greedy and now he'd started, he wanted nothing more than contact and release.

Tommaso leaned forward and clung to Michelangelo. Their bodies became inseparable, their movements frenzied yet rhythmical, the contact as close as possible, biting, kissing, hugging, shifting, yet fastened until they reached the point of starburst. Michelangelo clung to the moment of ecstasy, wanting it to go on forever, his whole being entrenched in the love of the young man within his arms and legs. They fell apart, drenched with sweat. Michelangelo rolled out of bed and Tommaso lay panting, looking at him in the early light.

'We have just done what we said we would never do,' Michelangelo said, walking over to the wash basin in his room, finding a cloth and washing his body.

Tommaso smiled at him. 'And how wonderful it was.'

Michelangelo put the cloth back and returned to the bed and gazed at him in adoration. He put his arm over Tommaso who turned into the curve of his body, making an even stronger love for Tommaso surge through him.

'I have never been happier, Tommao.' Michelangelo stroked the young man's skin, feeling pleasure just by touching him.

They lay together quietly and when Tommaso fell asleep, Michelangelo roused himself and made ready for the day.

THIRTY-FIVE

Vincenza stood in the shadows, waiting impatiently for Febo to show himself.

When she met him in the market his message had been brief and terse. She was to meet him in the usual place and she was to bring some belongings with her. Excitement crept through her. She'd rummaged through the clothes she wanted to take with her and bundled them into a large scarf, tying it firmly. In the surrounding darkness of night, she had slipped out the tenement's back door and headed away from the market, now black and empty.

Distant fires illuminated the Colosseum's arches. She doubted those sheltering there would see her this far away. She kept to the shadows, walking quickly up the slight rise.

Michelangelo's house looked deserted, although Bernardino would be there, and the artist along with his lover. Everyone knew about Michelangelo's affair with Cavalieri; people laughed about it in the market and in her brother's store. There was gossip about where the lovers went in the evenings after they had finished in the Sistine Chapel and rumours flew as to the subject being painted there. Someone knew someone who knew someone who had seen the half-finished project and declared it full of naked men. Vincenza wondered who had set the rumour mill going.

Febo appeared before her and she jumped. He took her hand and led her beneath the overhang of the nearest building.

'Don't talk. Just listen,' he hissed. 'I have to leave Rome. This situation is getting too dangerous for me; I know too much. There are men close to the Pope who want to oust Michelangelo and his art. They are eager to discredit him, eager to bring him down. Have him arrested for his actions with Cavalieri. I have been used, and my life is in danger.'

'The papers?' Vincenza asked in a whisper.

'They are in the hands of someone who will go to great lengths to destroy the Master.'

'I'm scared, Febo. About what I have done,' she said, blessing herself.

'Yes, we are in danger. We must leave. You must come with me. We will go to Venice. I have contacts there and I should be able to find work.'

Febo took Vincenza's hand and opened it. Coins fell into her palm. 'This is your payment.'

She squeezed the coins in her palm and ran her finger over them; they were heavy enough to be made of gold.

'Come.' Febo put his hand over hers. Vincenza's eyes widened as she noticed the flash of diamonds in the topaz ring on his finger, reflected in the light of the street torch. She nodded, gathered her bundle and, with Febo beside her, slipped into the darkness of the Roman street without looking back.

PART SEVEN
1537–1541
CONSUMMATION

THIRTY-SIX

Cardinal Biagio da Cesena bowed before the altar. He was assisting at the Pope's Mass in a private chapel situated not far from the Sistine Chapel. Behind him were various members of the household and other cardinals. Before him, Pope Paul faced the altar reading the liturgy of the Mass, which was part said and part sung, with the cardinal assisting and joining in or responding when necessary.

Despite himself, Biagio found his attention wandering. He had requested an audience after Mass, wanting to speak to the Pope, yet again, about Michelangelo. He wondered if the Pope would agree to meet him again about the artist but he knew that he had to keep him informed of what was going on in the artist's house.

The Mass over, the Pope and cardinal moved into the sacristy.

'There is something on your mind, Biagio?' asked the Pope, after they had removed their vestments and the sacristan was putting them away, ready for the next Mass.

'Yes, Holiness. Once again it is about the artist.' Biagio was aware the sacristan could hear them talking.

'Come with me,' the Pope dismissed other priests and cardinals who had entered the sacristy.

Biago followed the Pontiff as, leaning on his stick, he walked down the corridor into his private office. There he stood in the centre of the large room, staring intently at Cesena.

'You still persist with this, Biagio.' A frown of annoyance clouded the Pope's face. 'Well?' he demanded.

'Holiness, I have yet more letters, sketches and poems to show you. The young Cavalieri is constantly with Michelangelo while he is working in the chapel and he is also at night in his house – I suspect committing sodomy.'

'Are you sure of this? Quite sure?' the Pope queried, his head on one side.

'There are witnesses, Holiness,' returned the cardinal. 'There can be no mistake about it.'

Pope Paul frowned. 'Show me your proof,' he said, waving his stick at Cesena then limping to his desk to sit down.

Da Cesena placed the letters before the Pope, who perched his spectacles on his nose and held the papers to the light and read all of them thoroughly. The Pontiff hesitated at the sketches, his frown deepening, face impassive. The cardinal waited. The Pope leant back in his chair.

'How old is Tommaso de Cavalieri?'

'About twenty-six, Holiness.'

'How long have they been friends?'

'Many years, Holy Father.'

'How long has Cavalieri been staying with the artist?'

'I'm unsure of that but I know they have been together recently.'

'It's about time the young man was married. I will give you a letter to deliver from me to his father. No one else must know.'

'And Michelangelo, Holiness?'

'Leave him alone and let him finish the work he is doing. Take these letters, poems and sketches and give them back to Michelangelo. We are all human, Biagio. I don't want to hear any more about this. Do that much, then let it be.'

Pope Paul handed back the papers and waved his hand in dismissal at Biagio as the cardinal kissed his ring, bowed and left the room.

~

Biagio waited in the vestibule of the Cavalieri Palazzo. It reminded him of Michelangelo's house in Macello dei Corvi but much larger – in fact, the whole house was on a grander scale, with high frescoed ceilings, marble-lined floors and wainscoted walls. He knew Tommaso's father, Giovanni, through the nobleman's association with the Vatican court and had been here many times on social visits, usually with other cardinals.

Upon arrival, Biagio had been admitted to the atrium by a servant then ushered across the forecourt and into the house proper, where the servant went to announce his arrival. He heard a door opening and closing further down the hallway and an older, thinner version of Tommaso came toward him, a long, blue silk coat over his doublet, breeches and hose, a cap on his head.

Giovanni bowed to the cardinal and knelt to kiss his ring. 'You wished to see me, Eminence?'

Da Cesena bowed in return. 'Yes. Thank you for seeing me so promptly.'

'Please come into the salon,' said Giovanni.

A servant in attendance opened the door and the pair walked through. The room was almost cavernous, softened by fine furnishings, glass lamps and mirrors from Venice. Several works of art adorned the walls and there were marble plinths with sculptures. The cardinal recognised all the artists. Giovanni offered Biagio a chair and sat down opposite him. The servant poured each of them a glass of wine then left the room.

Biagio studied the walls. 'I see, my Lord, you have no works of art by Michelangelo here.'

'I have several sketches given to my son, which you already know about.'

The cardinal nodded, thinking of the sketches of Tityus and Ganymede.

'I hope to obtain a work from the great man before too long,' Giovanni continued.

The cardinal gave him a long, studied look as he took a sip of wine. 'Fine wine,' he said, and Giovanni nodded, drinking only a sip himself. Silence settled around the two men.

'You wished to….'

'I have come to….'

They both spoke at once, then looked at each other and smiled.

'Eminence, please continue,' Giovanni nodded.

Biagio placed his wine carefully on the marble table beside him. 'Are you aware, my Lord, that your son, Tommaso, is Michelangelo's lover?' he asked bluntly.

Giovanni did not answer immediately. He turned pale at the cardinal's words and appeared to mull the words over in his mind. Cesena watched him carefully. Tommaso's father was shocked.

'I am aware they are in a relationship, one of mutual good-will and friendship that is quite chaste,' Giovanni said carefully.

'Are you sure it is chaste?'

'I trust my son. He's an honourable young man. He supports and befriends the artist who teaches him drawing, sculpting and painting.'

'You are aware of the rumours that circle around Michelangelo and his apprentices, how he loves being surrounded by youths and uses them as models?'

'I am aware of rumours, yes. Tommaso has modelled for him, I believe.'

'This does not worry you?'

'Up until now I have had no cause for concern. My son tells me where he will be. Sometimes, as the situation is now, the days are long for them both. Tommaso helps him with the painting of the Sistine Chapel, he's the only one Michelangelo trusts to do as he wishes. Sometimes, when they finish late, Tommaso goes to Michelangelo's home and has a meal, rather than coming here and waking servants to let him in.'

Biagio frowned at de Cavalieri's trust and naivety. 'Michelangelo is a lover of young men,' he said irritably. 'His artworks prove that; he idolises the male form and I believe your son is the most handsome among men. One of the best.'

'He is blessed that way.' Giovanni nodded, then raised his eyebrows at the cardinal. 'What are you trying to say, Eminence?'

Biagio stood up and walked away from Giovanni and took a deep breath, afraid of Giovanni's reaction to what he was about to say. This man was generous towards the Church and a good practising Catholic as well as a society favourite. He turned and faced Tommaso's father, sitting in the chair, seeming outwardly relaxed and unconcerned, much more so than Biagio felt.

'I have reason to believe that Tommaso and Michelangelo are sleeping together. They love one another,' Biagio said.

Tommaso's father smiled. 'Really, Eminence, I don't think that is the case. I know my son is fond of Michelangelo, he admires him for his brilliance and creativity and Michelangelo has taught Tommaso much about art. It seems my son has talent and the Master wishes to foster that. Knowing the man as I do, knowing that he is straightforward, honest and pious, I find it difficult to believe there is anything sexual in their relationship. They have a high regard for one another. Michelangelo appears to resist sexual encounters with men, although he is fond of many, and expresses that fondness with letters, poems, and gifts of food and wine from his garden and from his property in Settignano. I'm sure you too have been a recipient in the past. We have often been graced by such generosity, as indeed have the popes he has been close too. Surely you are aware of this?'

Biagio was not impressed. 'With due respect, my Lord, I think you have been misled and are naïve about the relationship. I have seen letters and poems between the two. It is hard to imagine them not having a sexual relationship when there is so much passion involved and expressed.'

'I know they correspond if they can't see each other for some time. Lately with the work in the chapel they have been constantly together. I also know that Michelangelo writes sonnets to Tommaso. I have seen some of them. Tommaso is Michelangelo's muse, and helps him to create art of a high order,' Giovanni insisted. 'My son has explained his Master's thinking to me. He believes in the chaste love of another man. He believes that through his gaze on perfection he is brought closer to the divine and he lives his life through the beauty of another, which grants him a sense of immortality. This is the way he thinks, the way he creates. He submits his will to the beauty of the beloved but he does not touch. To touch is to defile. To touch would mean the end of genius. There is a fine balance to be maintained here,' Giovanni said gruffly, his voice impatient and annoyed.

Biagio frowned. Giovanni's loyalty and stubbornness were exasperating. 'I am familiar with the New Platonism and how Ficino tried to align it with Christianity,' he answered haughtily. 'I don't agree, of course. The root of it is paganism. And, as Ficino wrote about chaste love between men associated with the new interpretation, it was rumoured in Florence at the time that he was not so pure in his relationships. However, I admire your loyalty to Michelangelo.'

He reached into the pocket of his cloak and pulled out a roll of papers. 'I must show you; I have letters, poems and sketches written by both.' He handed them to Giovanni. 'I want you to read these then tell me what you think.'

Tommaso's father looked at the papers in surprise. He opened the roll and spread them on his lap. He recognised Michelangelo's and Tommaso's writing immediately.

'Read those,' Biagio said, returning to his chair to sit opposite him again.

'Where did you get these from? These are personal papers,' Giovanni asked, his face ashen, registering horror.

'I have my sources,' answered the cardinal abruptly.

'I had no idea they were corresponding to this degree.' Giovanni looked disturbed, handling the thick layer of paper.

'You will find some of those poems are written to someone else, who happens to be in my household. He too slept with the artist, although he denies it. He was Michelangelo's favourite for a long period until your son came along. Then he was dismissed.'

Tommaso's father quickly scanned the poems written to Febo, and then the poems, letters and sketches for Tommaso; his expression changing to annoyance, surprise, shock and incredulity and finally, realisation.

'I had no idea,' he frowned, looking up at the cardinal. 'These letters by Michelangelo are certainly impassioned and those from my son, equally so. And these sketches are explicit. Is the Pope aware of the relationship?'

'He is aware both are working on the paintings in the Sistine Chapel. He knows that Tommaso is often in Michelangelo's company. He is also aware of the gossip surrounding the relationship and knows what is said about Michelangelo. Like yourself, he thinks, or hopes the attraction between an older man and a young man is part of the New-Platonist sensibility, nothing more. However, saying that, he has written a letter to you which he has instructed me to deliver.' Biagio handed Giovanni the Pontiff's letter.

His hands trembling, Giovanni took the letter from the cardinal. 'What do you think, Eminence?'

Biagio hesitated. He did not wish to further upset this nobleman who had many friends in the Vatican and amongst the nobility. However, Biagio had challenged him this far and was not going to back down. 'Going by the tone of the works and the emotions expressed in them, and by what I have been told about Michelangelo by people who have known and served him, I am convinced the relationship is a sexual one.'

Giovanni was silent for a few minutes. 'I trust my son,' he said finally, 'and I am surprised and sad that this is going on. I will speak to him.'

'Admirable. Sometimes trust can be broken, my Lord,' Biagio said, moderating his tone. 'Tommaso is a man with his own ideas and desires and he no longer, by rights, is answerable to you. Sometimes it is hard for a parent to realise that.'

'Are you speaking from experience, Eminence? Or are you admonishing me for being faithful towards my son?' asked Giovanni.

Biagio looked at Giovanni de Cavalieri, keeping his face blank and unapologetic. 'I just think you should be aware of what is being said about the artist and Tommaso.'

'You have achieved that, Eminence. With both men involved in such a mammoth task, naturally they would be close and at this point it would be destructive to Michelangelo's creativity to interfere in their relationship. Don't you agree?'

The cardinal nodded. 'Perhaps. There is also something I must show you,' he persevered. 'To do that we have to go to the Sistine Chapel when both have finished for the day. A journey at night, perhaps?'

'Do you think that's necessary?' Giovanni protested, staring at the unopened letter.

'To convince you, yes.'

'Then I will wait for your message and meet you where you wish.'

Da Cesena bowed to de Cavalieri. 'You will not be disappointed.'

~

The Basilica was in darkness and the gates to the Apostolic Palace locked but well-guarded.

'Who's there?' one guard cried, standing in the darkness, a long black cape over his person as he held a halberd drawn across his body. He peered at the two men waiting outside the gate, the guards' solitary lantern forming a pool of light.

'It is Cardinal da Cesena and friend.'

'Step into the light,' came the command.

The two men did as they were told and the guard looked to be studying the pair. He pointed to Tommaso's father. 'Who are you?'

'Giovanni de Cavalieri, friend of Cardinal da Cesena and of Pope Paul.'

'What is your business here?' barked the other guard who, up until now, had remained in the shadow of the guard box. He emerged now under the light, his black cape smothering his uniform, his sword clutched in his hand as if ready to strike.

'Grave apostolic business in protection of the Church,' answered the cardinal, unfazed.

The guards examined the pair in the light and, after recognising da Cesena, opened the gate. They both walked quickly into the entranceway. One guard opened the door for them and they found themselves at the foot of a high staircase leading to the Apostolic Palace.

The cardinal fetched two lamps, lit them with a flint and gave one to Giovanni. 'Follow me,' he whispered.

Giovanni had been in the Apostolic Palace before but it had always been well lit or in daylight. Now, as they walked up the shadowy staircase and down darkened corridors, he was disorientated. He would never have found his way to the Sistine Chapel on his own. Giovanni shivered in the dark as he followed the cardinal who looked like an avenging angel holding the lamp before him, his red cloak flaring out from behind his form. They arrived at the entrance to the Sistine Chapel and da Cesena pulled out a key.

The lock opened with a click so loud it could have woken the Pope, and they slipped inside. Giovanni instinctively looked up, as he always did when he entered the chapel. He was aware of God and Adam somewhere in the darkness above him. The two men held the lamps high and Giovanni could see the far wall covered in scaffolding.

'Follow me,' the cardinal whispered to Giovanni. The cardinal walked quickly to the scaffolding and began climbing one of the ladders up onto the first level, above the altar. He waited for Giovanni to join him then proceeded along the platform to the next ladder.

Giovanni glanced at the wall as they advanced upwards. It was astonishing how much work had been done. Figures floated above him against an intense blue background and even in the dim light of their lamps he could see many of them, jostling and moving against one another. Far above were more figures, supposedly angels, without wings or halos or other angelic trappings. They all looked like strapping, sexually strong young men, their bodies painted in detail and somewhat exaggerated, much like the ignudi on the ceiling.

'As you can see, Michelangelo is obsessed with the male form but that is not what I have brought you here to see,' said Cesena. 'Come with me to the centre of the wall.'

Giovanni followed him carefully; they were a long way up from the floor. The cardinal held his lamp high, lighting first the Virgin Mary, fully painted, and then beside her, a large floating incomplete figure in the centre of the wall.

Giovanni gasped.

'This is what I wanted you to see, to convince you. This is his painting of Christ.'

Giovanni, shocked, knelt on the platform before the painting, awestruck. 'This is my son,' he said, at last, staring at the figure before him.

'Now you can see why I have been concerned,' da Cesena told him. 'It's your son, representing Christ, and it's your son who is the artist's lover.'

Giovanni rose to his feet and recovered himself, still staring at the painting. 'No one need know it is my son.'

'Everyone who knows your son will recognise him in this portrayal of Jesus.'

'This is the divine, the inspiration that Michelangelo talks about,' Giovanni said, staring at the painting. 'He has used the human beauty of my son to portray the divine.'

'Not everyone will see it that way.' Da Cesena held the lamp closer to the figure. 'He has painted Christ without any clothing, physically perfect, beardless and uncorrupted.'

'He is awe inspiring,' said Giovanni.

'And very naked.' The cardinal lifted the lamp to show the rest of the finished painting rising above them. 'They are all naked and the anatomical accuracy of the bodies is distinct. The damned are writhing in their agony trying to avoid hell. Perhaps,' he murmured, his eyes on the floating bodies above him, 'it is Michelangelo's soul that is expressed in the painting. The torture. Perhaps he is afraid of being damned by his desires and he expresses it in this way without realising.' He turned back to Giovanni, his dark eyes glittering in the lamplight, his face distorted and shadowed. 'Those who don't know your son may not be offended but those who know him and know of the relationship between the pair, may call it blasphemy.'

'I'm not sure what can be done about the situation of the relationship, if it is from Tommaso that Michelangelo gets his inspiration,' said Giovanni.

'There is one thing that can be done to diffuse the relationship problem as far as the Church is concerned – one that has been suggested by Pope Paul in his letter. Now that you have seen our concern, you must do what the Pope asks of you.'

The cardinal was ordering, not asking. Giovanni did not like the look on the man's face. In the half-light he looked almost demonic, his face long and hollowed, his eyes and ears upward slanting, creating long shadows on the painting behind him. Giovanni realised he wanted to be miles away from the cardinal and from the chapel.

~

Giovanni paced within his library, fuming with anger and betrayal. After walking home alone from the Apostolic Palace, his thoughts in a turmoil of dismay, he had waited a day to see Tommaso. When his son hadn't returned from Michelangelo's house by evening, he sent a terse message asking for Tommaso to come home.

He stirred the embers in the fireplace, lit a lamp and sat down to think, only to be startled by a knock on the door and Tommaso entering the room.

'Papa, you wished to see me?' Tommaso removed his cloak and trailed it over the back of a chair. 'Are you well? I was worried when I received the note. You don't usually demand I come home.'

His father was lost for words. Tommaso looked tired and a little ill-kempt, compared to how he usually looked, but he was also relaxed as he arranged his shapely limbs over one of his father's plush chairs. Giovanni went and stood in front of him.

'I have received a visit from Cardinal da Cesena,' he said bluntly. 'I have also seen the painting in the Sistine Chapel. Particularly, that of the Christ.'

Tommaso sat upright in his chair, his face pinched and white, his hands clasped in front of him, eyes wide, fastened on his father's face.

'Da Cesena accuses you of sleeping with the artist and says it has to stop.'

Tommaso opened his mouth and closed it again.

'He has been to the Pope about his concerns regarding the painting and about you helping the artist as you do. The Pope has sent me a letter, which Cesena delivered to me. He also gave me many letters, poems and sketches to look at, which you must return to Michelangelo.' Giovanni walked over to a table and picked up a pile of papers and handed them to Tommaso. 'These papers betray both your feelings. The man is in love with you and you with him. This must stop; it bears a bad reflection on our family. You must know this. I have not brought you up to betray your station in life.'

Tommaso, shocked, looked at the papers in his father's hand. 'How did he get hold of these?'

'I don't know and don't want to know. There are spies everywhere. What have you got to say for yourself?'

Tommaso slumped in the chair and covered his face with his hands. 'I'm sorry, Papa, I didn't mean to hurt you or anyone.'

Giovanni still stood over him. 'Of course, you have hurt me and your faith. You don't deny your love for the man and that you have slept together?'

'No. I love him in every way. Our being together is just an outward manifestation of that love. You can't deprive him or me of that.'

'I can, and you must deprive him. You are always in his company. No wonder rumours are rampant. Regardless of whether it is true or false there will always be those who talk and make mischief about others, especially if they are successful or affluent.'

Tommaso, dumbfounded, shook his head. 'To be part of such a creation is overwhelming for me. It makes me very happy to be there, to be part of it. I can't deny him. My presence by his side helps him to achieve his dream. He needs me.'

'Nonsense,' huffed Giovanni. 'You shock and dismay me with your immaturity and naivety. I told you to be careful in your dealings with him. He obviously has you under his spell. Remember, he was creating before you were born. Have you asked him how many lovers have helped him in this way over the years?'

Tommaso, his face still covered, shook his head.

'The Pope has seen the papers, including the drawings, which I am ashamed of. Look what he has seen!' Giovanni said, showing the sketches to Tommaso, who quickly hung his head. 'Here is the Pope's letter for you to read. Return Michelangelo's papers to him, tell him you no longer can help or visit him.'

Giovanni dumped the Pope's letter on Tommaso's lap. Tommaso opened it and read it hurriedly. He gave the letter back to his father quickly as if it was contaminated.

'I will put it in safe-keeping. Don't upset the man any more than you have to. This is upsetting enough. Now go from my sight before I whip you.'

THIRTY-SEVEN

Tommaso stood in the salon's doorway. Michelangelo knew by the look on his face the news was not good. He hadn't heard from him for days and had been beside himself with anxiety, thinking he was ill. Michelangelo had sent notes to the Palazzo Cavalieri, only to have them returned unopened. Worried, he had tried to concentrate on his work in the chapel.

'Come in, Tommaso, come in. Where have you been? You have something to tell me?'

Tommaso didn't answer. He walked over to where Michelangelo sat and knelt at his feet, lowering his head.

'What is it? Why are you so disturbed?' Michelangelo needed to know, yet was afraid of the answer. Tommaso hadn't greeted him with his customary fond kiss and embrace and Michelangelo already felt worse.

'Come, tell me,' Michelangelo put his hand on Tommaso's head, wanting desperately to love him again.

'First, forgive me for loving you as I did. I never should have. I know what this can do to you and how it can affect your work,' Tommaso said quietly. 'Please forgive me.'

'It was as much my desire as yours. We are only human, Tommaso. I have already confessed, the sin is no longer.' Michelangelo leaned forward and took Tommaso by the arms, pulling him close. 'Come, sit on a chair near me and tell me what else is troubling you, for I fear it is not just our ill-judged lovemaking.'

Tommaso climbed to his feet and sat on the chair Michelangelo indicated.

'Was our lovemaking the reason you have kept away from me?' Michelangelo said, thinking of the long and lonely days he had suffered through. He carefully studied the ill-at-ease, unhappy face before him.

Tommaso shook his head and averted his eyes from Michelangelo's gaze. 'I couldn't think how to write to you. I couldn't put down on paper how sorry I was that I gave in to my baser instincts,' Tommaso answered, his voice shaking. 'I wanted to love you, to feel your tenderness and to comfort your great soul.' Tommaso looked up at Michelangelo. 'I have been walking the floor for days. My father knows of my plight.'

'He knows?' Michelangelo was surprised and wary.

'He received a visit from Cardinal da Cesena, and a letter from the Pope that suggests I should be married.'

Michelangelo was stunned. 'The Pope wants you married?'

Tommaso nodded. 'To put paid to the rumours. I protested but I know Father must obey the Pope and I must obey Father. Michelangelo, I don't want this, but it must come about. The Pope thinks it will take me away from you. It never will, dear Angelo. You will always be close to my heart. I will always love you. Always,' Tommaso said, brokenly.

Michelangelo pushed himself out of his chair and strode away from Tommaso, red in the face, trying to control his rage. 'How dare anyone interfere in our lives to such a degree,' he said, whipping around and looking at Tommaso who was kneeling, bent over, his expression pained, his arms wrapped around himself. 'How dare they! How dare da Cesena and the Pope, and your father conspire against us!' He walked over to Tommaso and looked at him. 'When are you to be married?' His voice was strangled with anger.

'The date has not been set. We have been betrothed since we were children. Father has been trying to get me to commit to a date for our wedding for some time. It isn't time yet, she still has some growing to do. I am older than her by many years. I hardly know her. Her name is Lavinia della Valle.'

'There used to be a cardinal by that name. Is she related?'

'Yes, she is of the same family.'

'You have met her?'

'Occasionally. I like her. She's bright, intelligent, pious and young but she will make a good wife.'

Michelangelo was silent. Tommaso had not mentioned Lavinia or that he was betrothed to her the whole time he'd known him. But then he would not have wanted to know. A familiar feeling of betrayal ran through him.

'I'm sorry, Michelangelo. I know I should have told you sooner, but I didn't know how. This is very painful for me because I truly love you. There is no reason why we can't remain friends. I would be bereft if I lost your friendship. Please forgive me. My father has been concerned recently that I haven't been eager to marry Lavinia, now that she is starting to grow up. I have been too occupied and happy in your company to even think it. Lavinia's family is honourable and it will be a good marriage, I do know that.'

Michelangelo took a big breath and let it out slowly. 'Does Lavinia know of our friendship?'

'Yes, she and her parents know I am your muse. They are honoured.'

'So, all this has been going on since our last meeting?'

'Yes. As I said, it had always been a possibility. Now Father has put pressure on me. He said I am at a marriageable age.'

'You mean the Pope has put pressure on your father.' Michelangelo covered his face with his hands, his whole body shaking. 'Did you tell your father about our lovemaking? I do not want to lose your friendship and love. Does he think less of me?' he murmured, lifting his head and looking at Tommaso.

'No, it's the Pope's letter that has upset him. The fact that the rumour of our relationship has reached him. He is worried that it may be reported to the authorities and we may be imprisoned.'

'There is no proof. Not even in our letters.'

'Vincenza caught us together. She could be called as a witness.'

Michelangelo stared at Tommaso. Vincenza. Bernardino had warned him. She was no longer around. Rumour had it that she had run away with some brigand, according to her brother who had come to see Bernardino on the off-chance he knew what had become of her.

'This is so hard for me to grasp. I thought Pope Paul was my friend and patron.' Michelangelo sank heavily into his chair, devoid of strength.

'Perhaps it is because he's your friend that he has worked this way. He wants to save you.' Tommaso went over to Michelangelo, knelt before him again and looked up into his face. 'Michelangelo, because you are so talented, it means you have many enemies who would have the world think less of you.'

Michelangelo, incensed, was not listening. 'Your father listened to that rat, Cesena?' Something exploded within him. 'Cesena has been against my work right from the start, but to carry it this far? The Pope's interference surprises me. Why is it that people are always eager to think the worst of me? People talk too much, even to the Pope. I thought the Pope was my friend,' he moaned.

'Father heard that da Cesena has talked about how much he dislikes the way you depict the male form in your paintings, and how nude images shouldn't be seen in a place of worship such as the chapel.'

Head in hands, Michelangelo groaned.

Tommaso continued, 'Father was annoyed. He doesn't think much of the cardinal, but he knows how careful you have to be in dealing with him. Da Cesena even took my father into the chapel and showed him the painting of Christ. Father immediately recognised the likeness to me. He thought the painting was wonderful and he has nothing but admiration for you and your work. He just thinks that me marrying will quench the rumours going around at present,' Tommaso said.

Michelangelo, a little calmer, sat back in his chair. 'Why am I surprised?' He wearily rubbed his hand over his face. 'Our lovemaking was a sin and I knew Cesena had employed Febo, who had been with me as an apprentice for quite some time. He did that for only one reason, to find out about me.'

'You must not take any notice of anyone's talk, Angelo. You must continue to create as you always have. Your works are going to last forever and I am proud you have loved me,' Tommaso said, a catch in his voice.

Michelangelo could not speak for the constriction in his throat.

Tommaso rose to his feet and reached to touch Michelangelo's shoulder, then pulled Michelangelo towards him, putting his arms around him briefly. 'I will always love you, Angelo. Always.' He reached into a pocket within his doublet. 'Father gave me the letters and papers he has seen, to give to you.' Tommaso put them on the table.

Michelangelo gazed at them, speechless. Da Cesena and the Pope had seen them, his sketches and personal papers. Now, they knew his soul. He moaned. 'These papers are my business alone. How did Cesena come by them? Was it Vincenza?'

'That I don't know,' answered Tommaso. 'He didn't tell my father.'

There was a knock on the door and Bernardino walked in, carrying a tray with mulled wine. He stopped and looked at the two men. 'A nightcap for you both?' he queried, as if nothing were amiss. 'Do you wish for anything else this evening before I go to bed?'

Michelangelo, unable to speak, shook his head. Tommaso kissed him on his forehead, on his lips, then took his hands and kissed them too. Tears fell from Tommaso's face as he turned and walked out of the room.

'Michelangelo, are you alright?' Bernardino was alarmed at the finality in Tommaso's leaving and Michelangelo's dejected state. He put the drink on the table beside him and left him alone.

An hour later Bernardino heard a crash coming from the workshop; the sounds grew louder as he approached the door. For a moment he was afraid to open it. Michelangelo was in one of his terrible rages. He pushed the door open and stared.

Michelangelo had thrown marble forms and statues to the ground and he was standing over them beating them with one of his heavy mallets.

'Master, what are you doing? You're destroying your work,' Bernardino cried in horror.

Michelangelo raised the mallet and for a moment Bernardino

thought he was going to strike him. But he stopped and dropped the mallet and collapsed in a heap on the floor. Bernardino went over to him and sat beside him.

'Master, this does no good. Tommaso does love you.'

Michelangelo moaned and shook his head. 'I loved him, I still do. How can I go on without him? Not only that, I may have ruined my reputation and my life. The Vatican, the Pope could decide to punish me. My life could be ruined. No more commissions, I will be poverty stricken. I could even find myself in court and end up imprisoned.'

Bernardino put his arms around Michelangelo's shoulders. 'Nothing like that will happen. There are many relationships like yours in the city and no one is punished. Tommaso is a kind and gentle soul, and he loves you. He would never do harm to you.'

'The Pope already knows through that devil Cesena, and he was informed by Febo, whom I also loved,' moaned Michelangelo. 'Febo! Where is Febo? He's answerable to all this, him and Vincenza!'

'Most probably it was those two, though we will never know. The Pope admires what you do, Master. He wants the mural finished and he is a man of the world. He knows of love and begetting children. He also knows people will destroy others selfishly. He will not be harsh,' Bernardino said quietly, his arms still around Michelangelo. 'Come, go upstairs to bed. I will bring you a warm drink.'

He helped Michelangelo to his feet and, avoiding the broken marble, they made their way out of the workshop. Bernardino helped Michelangelo undress then went downstairs to the kitchen to heat a cup of milk. By the time he went back to Michelangelo's bedchamber, his Master was almost asleep.

'Master, have this.' Bernardino put the cup to Michelangelo's lips. He drank the warm milk and closed his eyes and Bernardino did something he had not done for some time. He undressed and climbed into bed beside Michelangelo. He put his arm around Michelangelo and slept beside him.

PART EIGHT
1537–1542–1564
CULMINATION

THIRTY-EIGHT

To yearn intensely for one beautiful to the sight is not always a cause of sin. Love enlightens us and from that love of beauty we rise to meet God. This love is of the highest, the chaste love of man for man. To love a woman is apart from that, a difference that sullies the heart and debases the soul of a man. The first draws towards heaven and the other is of the earth. So, one is soul bound, the other is base and is of the senses which can lead to pleasures undesirable.

Michelangelo was lonely. It had been months since Tommaso had appeared with the news that he was to be married and that their relationship would end. Though the letters and the yearning kept coming, they never saw one another, only wrote. Their letters were delivered faithfully by Bartolemeo who was concerned for the two. There had been no punishment from the Vatican or the city fathers although many would know of his indiscretion.

Michelangelo's days and nights were work-filled but his heart and soul ached with emptiness and shame. How could he face Pope Paul again? Despite this, his painting in the chapel progressed well. Every day he lost himself in the work, shutting out all memory of Tommaso, keeping a screen before the image of Christ so he would not be reminded.

He worked from early morning until night. He missed Tommaso's company, his sense of humour, his light-heartedness, his undiluted admiration and the pleasing vision the young man always created in his eye. He waited each day for Tommaso to appear but there was only an empty space.

The days tumbled one into the other. Michelangelo was up before dawn, home long after sunset, sometimes staying late into the night to finish the day's work. Every day felt the same, as the painting grew under his hand. His soul was raw, exposed in the work, painted all over the chapel wall.

He missed Tommaso intensely. His suffering released, appeared before him as he painted. The figures jumped out at him as soon as he completed them and the damned screamed at him in their horror and torture at the realisation of hell before them as they writhed in their torment. The evil heads of the devils he painted with minute, animalistic precision. Every devilish line created depth and foreshortening, close ups and distance, until, in the tired haze of his head, the devils appeared to leap at him from the walls, contort and twist above and around him, threatened to grab him and pull him down towards Charon.

Dante's words from the *Inferno* were present in his mind. And there, in the lower right-hand corner, stood …

Charon, the demon, who upon his boat, glared at the fallen with fire-filled eyes. He pushed all those before him, and any that were slow, he struck with his oar.

Horrified at the vision conjured up in his mind, he had to stop painting. He closed his eyes and rubbed his face with his hands to eliminate the images from his sight. His slips of sin with Tommaso, their nights of love had ruined their relationship forever, as he had known it would. Why had he given in to his desires? What he had feared had happened. In nights of love, the muse had gone. One afternoon, addled with sorrow and despair, the lines of the *Inferno*, playing over and over in his head, he painted an upright devil.

The sinners' hands were tied with snakes and bound behind

*their backs. The tails and necks of the snakes entwined upwards
between the buttocks. The ends formed knots up front, and gaped
to grasp the genitals.*

Michelangelo concentrated intently as the image emerged under
his hand, the half-animal, half-insect face, the pointed donkey ears,
and then the snake crawling up between the devil's legs, grasping his
genitals in its open jaws, biting down, emasculating him.

The light flickered around Michelangelo. Had he offended
Tommaso that much? Knowing Tommaso, he thought not, but he had
offended God. The Christ, in Tommaso's image, hovered over him and
admonished him in Tommaso's likeness, which was why he kept it
covered while he painted.

*God with his great power and might, brings down a maelstrom
of revenge!*

Michelangelo's heart broke as Tommaso had seemed to discard him
because of the expression of their love and, most of all, because of his
forthcoming marriage. How could Tommaso ever be friends and still
love him if he was married?

Another sinner appeared under Michelangelo's brush – one eye
covered, the other eye wide with realisation and despair at his fate.
The horrified eye penetrated Michelangelo's soul. Was it his reflection,
staring back at him?

*The sinner shocked at his fate, fixes upon me one staring eye, full
of despair.*

Dante's *Inferno* was all around him – within him, above him, below
him, in front of him, at his back. The damned yelled at him, screaming
their cries of disbelief. He was going mad. Was this his soul he was
painting? Was this the ruin of him?

The vision of the judged on their way to hell leaped from the eternal lapis lazuli of the painted sky. He had painted the rising of the dead, the trumpeting angels and those angels about to sound the horns signalling the beginning of judgement. Good and evil, they swirled in a vortex, flying in the air; the good rising, or readying to rise; the bad tumbling into the abyss of diabolical torture. Christ looked down, His arm raised in admonishment for those who had sinned, and in encouragement for those virtuous enough to enter Paradise.

For Michelangelo, there was no Paradise, only his torn heart, numb with sorrow. How could it continue beating when he didn't have Tommaso's love? How could he carry on creating? But, he had created before Tommaso, and he would continue to create after him.

Michelangelo worked doggedly, painting the saints. Saint Lawrence sat below Christ, looking up at him, waiting for judgement. Saint Bartholomew had risen, skin whole, yet he looked warily at Christ, wondering if he was good enough to enter the Kingdom of Heaven. His old skin hung in his hand, as if he or Michelangelo didn't know what to do with it, and he showed Christ the knife that had been used to flay it from his body. Christ eyed the knife. Michelangelo contemplated the flayed skin. His own skin that he had imagined would be occupied by Tommaso. Michelangelo studied it. Would it be his? His life and sacrifice were now empty. Tommaso would never be one with him. There was no sign that it belonged to Saint Bartholomew; it was blank, limp and lifeless. Michelangelo hadn't finished that part of the painting.

Tommaso was now in the painting, many times. All of him, parts of him, in various poses and facial expressions. Michelangelo painted him over and over, unwilling to dismiss his visage from memory. Tommaso was never once a devil. Always angelic. Although Tommaso was no longer beside him, Michelangelo would always have him in the Sistine Chapel. All he would have to do was to come into the chapel and gaze at his image.

'Michelangelo.' A voice from below startled him.

Michelangelo looked down to the chapel floor. Pope Paul stood there with one of his clerics. The artist put down his brush and made his way along the scaffolding to the ladder and climbed down. He felt the heat of embarrassment flood his face. He wondered if the Pope had come to chastise him in person. He greeted the Pope with a bow and knelt to kiss his ring.

'My son, I have come to see how you are.'

Michelangelo looked up at the Pope then lowered his head and beat his breast. 'Forgive me, Holiness for my indiscretion. I am well, thank you,' he wondered if this was the real purpose of the visit.

The Pope turned and waved his attendant away out of earshot. 'You are forgiven, Michelangelo. Don't worry about that. I needed to see you. You have obviously been working very hard on this mural. What I have seen so far is wonderful. I didn't come to talk about that but I have been disturbed by the rumours among people that have made their way to me about you and your muse, the young Cavalieri.'

Michelangelo stiffened. 'There has been too much talk, Holiness.'

'I didn't want to see you upset about the de Cavalieri betrothal, yet I felt it was the only way to stop the gossip. The young man is agreeable, I believe, and the marriage will go ahead as planned.'

Michelangelo bowed to the Pope in deference.

'What I am wondering, my son, is how you are and how this loss has affected your work.'

Michelangelo shook his head. 'It has made no difference, Holiness,' he lied, wishing to scream – yes, it has ruined my soul, my life. I am empty without him.

The devils on the wall were about to devour him.

'Are you still in contact with him?'

'No, Holiness. I have not seen him for some time now'. He did not mention the letters.

Pope Paul looked at Michelangelo and smiled, as if with relief.

'Good. That's the way it should be, considering he is to be married.'

Michelangelo nodded.

'I want you to look after yourself,' the Pope said, looking at him steadily. 'You work far too hard. Your health is important to us all.'

'The painting needs to be finished, Holiness, and it soon will be.'

The Pope nodded and looked up at the mural crowding out from the wall above his head.

'There has also been much talk about the nudity being depicted, my son, but I, myself, don't find it offensive. I understand it is how you express your artistic vision. It is as God made us.'

He moved closer to peer at the lower right side of the painting, examining the devil whose genitals were being devoured by a snake. He turned and smiled at Michelangelo. 'A good likeness, my son, a good likeness.' He walked over to Michelangelo again. 'I would be most pleased if my name is associated with *The Last Judgement.*'

Michelangelo nodded but did not verbally agree. It would be associated with Pope Paul III's papacy, but he would paint Clement's coat of arms into the fresco, not Paul's.

The Pope bid Michelangelo good-bye and left the chapel with his assistant.

Michelangelo looked up at the wall. There was still much to be done, finishing the last figures, and painting over areas of the mural with oils for depth and shine. Had the Pope noticed his broken heart in the work? His sinful soul? He climbed the ladder again and looked up at the painting of Christ. Had the Pope noticed it was covered from view?

Time moves fast and skins me alive, as death and soul battle on my road to finality.

The words reverberated in his head. He had written them some time ago, battling with thoughts of old age and death. He looked at the flayed skin of Saint Bartholomew and started to paint.

~

'The young man was here,' Bernardino said, placing a bowl of soup and rolls in front of Michelangelo.

Exhaustion crowded down on him as he looked up from his supper, not daring to hope. Surely it was not Febo, who seemed to have disappeared.

'Which young man?' There were so many, Michelangelo felt a stab of shame.

'Master Tommaso.'

'Tommaso? What did he want?'

'He didn't say. He seemed upset and wanted to see you.' Bernardino sat down with Michelangelo.

'He said he didn't wish to go to the chapel while you were working. It would set people talking and seeing him might upset you and you would stop for the day. He said it's important that you continue.'

Michelangelo pushed the plate away wearily. 'Is he going to come back or am I supposed to get in touch with him?'

'He didn't say.'

'No doubt he will be in touch in time. I'm exhausted. Going to bed.' Michelangelo pulled himself to his feet and walked out of the kitchen.

THIRTY-NINE

Tommaso knocked on the door, unsure how he would be received. It had been months since he had seen the Master face to face. Unable to bear Michelangelo's hurt, bewilderment and humiliation, Tommaso had kept away. Now he was tempted to see him again, though he knew that for Michelangelo, he would still be temptation. However, he still loved him and pined for him and could stay away no longer.

The street behind Tommaso, as he waited, was busy with people, carts, and riders on mules and horses. People were going to or returning from the market. Beyond them the Roman ruins were more visible since the Pope had ordered the shacks around the Trajan Column dismantled. Rumour had it the timing was to do with the arrival of Emperor Charles V in pageantry and glory, celebrating his victory over the Turkish admiral at Tunis. The Sack of Rome seemed forgiven and forgotten.

Michelangelo had viewed the pomp wearily, according to Bartolomeo. 'These people always have to boost themselves for their own glory,' he had said. 'One minute they're the enemy, the next minute they're friends. It depends whose side they wish to be on.'

At last the door opened and Bernardino bowed to Tommaso and ushered him inside.

Tommaso removed his cap. 'I would like to see the Master, Bernardino. Do you think he will see me?'

Bernardino closed the door on Rome behind him. 'Please wait here, my Lord. I shall tell the Master you are here.'

Tommaso watched as Bernardino headed towards the workshop. He could hear noises of tapping and hammering and Bernardino soon reappeared, beckoning him in. Tommaso hesitated, not wanting their meeting witnessed by the apprentices, but he was relieved there was no one else in the room. Michelangelo was seated on a ladder, working on the sculpture of *Rachel,* from the Old Testament, for the Julius tomb. Tommaso waited to be acknowledged and bowed. Michelangelo eyed him cautiously.

'You have come to see me at last, your Lordship,' he climbed down from his ladder and walked over to Tommaso.

'Please forgive me for not writing to you or coming to see you. There's so much going on about my marriage and I'm thoroughly ashamed of myself for hurting an esteemed person such as yourself.' The words came out in fits and starts as he twisted his green velvet cap in his hands. 'I couldn't bear to witness your hurt. Forgive me. It was cowardly of me.'

Michelangelo stood with his hands on his hips. 'Of course, I'm hurt. I love you. I still want and need you, Tommaso. I miss seeing you and having your company. Your jokes and laughter, your conversation, your interest in my ideas and what I do. Your encouragement. Your letters. And most of all, your love and attention, your loyalty to me. And I miss you helping me in the chapel. Bernardino comes to help sometimes. He's not as attractive as you.' He smiled then shook his head. 'Of course, I'm hurt.'

Tommaso knelt before him. Michelangelo stepped back, astonished.

'What are you doing? Don't kneel to me. Get up.'

Head bent, Tommaso couldn't look at Michelangelo. 'I have missed you with all my heart, missed your talk about art, religion and humanism,' he said quietly. 'I have missed your mind and beauty of thought, your creativity. I don't want to lose that, Michelangelo. I still want to be your friend.'

Michelangelo knelt level with him, his arms around him. Tommaso felt the strong, sinewy body pressed closely to his.

'I want you to be my lover and my friend,' Michelangelo growled fiercely under his breath. Tommaso shuddered within the strong grasp of his arms. He wanted that too but wouldn't say so.

'Just once, then no more,' said Michelangelo.

Tommaso pulled back and looked at the artist. Michelangelo's eyes were bright and he looked hungry for love. Tommaso wanted to unite with him in one final act of true love. The love he would experience with his wife would be different, a necessity for procreation. No doubt he would come to like it, and come to love her too.

'We are only human, Tommaso. I have never experienced with anyone what I have experienced with you,' Michelangelo pulled Tommaso gently to his feet, 'and I have missed you dreadfully. Come, love me.'

Michelangelo and Tommaso made their way upstairs to Michelangelo's bedchamber. The room was quiet and dimly lit, the shutters on the window closed against the light and noise outside. Michelangelo closed the door behind them and locked it. He did not want Bernardino barging in.

Michelangelo looked at Tommaso spread out before him on the bed. He shed his clothes without ceremony, lay down beside Tommaso and gazed at him. How long had they known each other? About ten years and, in that time, the slim young man had grown in maturity and masculine beauty. He was perfect: his limbs long and straight, his torso slim yet muscular, his abdomen tight. Michelangelo ran his hand over Tommaso's body with relief at touching him again. This most exquisite specimen was waiting to be taken and glorified as only Michelangelo could, through the love he bore for him in his heart.

Michelangelo bent over Tommaso, caught his face between his hands and kissed him ardently on the lips. He ran his hands over Tommaso's chest, arms and shoulders, feeling the strength and flexibility of youth beneath his touch. Aroused, he bent and kissed Tommaso's firm young cheeks, neck and chest.

Tommaso wrapped his arms round Michelangelo's back, their bodies locked in the length and strength of their kiss. Michelangelo savoured Tommaso's firm body against his own, longing for his own body to return to such a state as his lover's. Now, his muscles were rigid from overuse, strong and taut, and his joints stiff. He pulled back and once again kissed Tommaso all over. He ran his hand over the swell of Tommaso's groin, and kissed him there to feel the rigid response he wanted. Tommaso writhed with ecstasy under his touch and moaned as Michelangelo caressed him. Suddenly Tommaso pushed himself on top, delighting Michelangelo with his strength, pushing him back into the bed, covering him with kisses, fondling him, moving against him vigorously and greedily. Once again, they clung together, legs locked as one, their movements growing faster and more frantic. Sweat poured off them. Michelangelo was swept along with the fury. They peaked together. The power of their rapture unleashed itself in devilish spasms of blinding intensity. Wrapped in each other's arms, they were reluctant to let the moment pass but eventually kissed and fell apart, exhausted with their efforts.

It would be the last time they would show their love.

The light through the shutters dimmed. Tommaso removed himself from the bed and walked to the basin to wash. Michelangelo watched him wash then dry himself with a towel. He came back to lie on the bed. He was so enticing Michelangelo could have ravished him again.

'The last time, Michelangelo.' Tommaso leaned down and kissed him. 'I will always love you.'

He dressed quickly, unlocked the door and was gone.

Michelangelo turned on the bed, curled himself into a ball and wept.

FORTY

Father Fattucci laid out vestments in the sacristy of the church of Santa Maria Nova in preparation for Mass the following morning. The church, built on the Roman foundations of a temple to Venus, was frequently being fixed. The crumbling walls struggled to hold up the roof and there were workmen's tools and ladders in the sacristy and part of the nave. The priest was patiently waiting for the work to finish but, every time he came down from Florence, he never saw much progress.

A door banged somewhere in the empty church, startling the priest; he'd thought he had locked the church for the night. He picked up the lamp on the sacristy table and ventured into the dim interior, but the nave was empty and the many side altars in darkness. Some statues, covered in dust-sheets, resembled ghostly forms. Two candles glowed on the altar and a red light signalled the presence of Christ in the tabernacle. He held the lamp up to see past the pool of light. The nave disappeared into darkness near the entrance.

'Who's there?' He hoped for a reply only to be met with silence. He genuflected to the altar then turned and walked slowly down the empty nave, holding the lamp high. A bundled-up figure knelt on the marble floor, head down with arms wrapped around it as if in self-defence. Fattucci recognised the man immediately and sighed. Yes, it would be Michelangelo here at this hour in this state.

'Michelangelo. You startled me,' he said, rushing to the stricken figure and putting his hand on the artist's shoulder. 'What's the matter, are you ill?'

Michelangelo looked up at the priest and held out his hand. The priest grasped it and helped the man to his feet.

'Come, tell me what's wrong.'

'I have sinned, Father, and I have to confess. I'm tormented by my wrongdoing. You must hear my sins and relieve my soul.'

Father Fattucci eyed the artist. This was not the first time he had come to him to confess. He looked as if he had come straight from work at the Sistine Chapel, smelling of sweat, paint and plaster, and his dishevelled clothes had a fine layering of plaster dust over them. His eyes were bright and feverish in the lamplight and his face, spotted with paint, was even more gaunt looking than usual.

'We can talk in the sacristy where there's light,' he said, going to the door in the entrance to lock it. When he turned around, Michelangelo was already half-way down the aisle of the church. The priest followed him and watched in alarm as the man fell to his knees before the altar, then lay prostrate on the marble floor. Above him silver-shimmering mosaics of prophets, an ox, an angel, a lion, and an eagle looked down on him. Michelangelo appeared to be in agony.

A ripple of fear ran through the priest. Had the man committed some terrible deed like murder? He had enough enemies and was constantly besieged by them. His bad temper was well known and he could fly into fits of rage, which he had confessed to often enough. He just couldn't seem to find any peace. Father Fattucci had never seen him in a rage, only as a penitent parishioner, dejected, and pious. The artist was often at Mass, not only on Sunday but during the week as well. He would often slip in to hear the dawn Mass before starting work for the day, always carrying his rosary with him and often reading the prayers from his book.

He had told the priest he prayed anywhere at any time, especially when he was painting or sculpting, or just out in the garden, or on the back of his horse. God gave him strength, joy and love, yet he continued to let God down. He confessed regularly and had great faith but he was troubled by doubts and fears and tortured by his desires. The priest crouched beside the prostrate figure.

'Michelangelo, you must tell me what ails you,' he said anxiously. 'I will give you a blessing and your soul will be eased.'

Michelangelo remained motionless, his body stretched out in the shape of a cross, his head resting on the dusty marble floor.

'Bless me, Father, for I have sinned,' he murmured.

The priest sat back on his heels and waited. Michelangelo lay in silence.

'When you are ready, Michelangelo, I will be in the sacristy.' He rose to his feet.

Whatever had happened, whatever he had done, he needed time. The priest entered the sacristy, leaving the lamp on the table. He found a chair and settled down to wait.

Ten minutes later Michelangelo stood at the door as if afraid to enter. The priest beckoned him in and the artist walked over, ignored the offer of a chair and knelt before him.

'I have sinned as I never thought I would again. I believed for the sake of Jesus and my art I would be able to keep myself free of sin. The very thing I vowed would not happen, occurred again the other night. I have been in agony since. . .' Michelangelo's voice trailed away. The priest looked down at Michelangelo's curly greying hair streaked with splashes of paint.

'I'm here to listen to what you have to say, so tell me,' he said gently. The last thing the artist needed was chastisement.

'I'm sinful because I let myself be swayed by the teachings of Ficino who said that love between men was a good and noble thing. But relying on this knowledge to appease my conscience was sinful. Ficino's theories became my excuse for sinning. I allowed myself to be led by it and I was carried away. I did not use my sense of reason. With others I have loved I have confessed and then forgotten my sin, but this time it was different. Perhaps it is because I am older and not as resilient. I feel deep shame for what I have done and for all my sins as well. You know, Father, this is not the first time.'

'There is no such sin if you don't touch. One can love without touching,' the priest said, shaking his head. 'Yes, you let your humanity get in the way and you succumbed to temptation.'

With his head bent, Michelangelo related what had happened the day before. He explained in fits and starts the consummation of his love.

'Did you commit the sin of sodomy?' asked the priest.

'No,' Michelangelo said, his head still bent, too ashamed to look at the priest.

'And what of the young man? Was he a willing partner?'

'Yes, very.'

'The sin is his also,' said the priest. 'He must go to his confessor. Have you seen him since?'

'No. I have been working on my own in the chapel. I really don't want to see him, I am too ashamed. What do I do, Father?' pleaded Michelangelo. 'I still love him intensely. Just to look upon his face brings me joy yet, at the same time, he is a temptation like no other. He gives me solace, comfort, kindness and companionship as I have never had before. Am I to live my whole life without such love because of the danger of sinning? Am I to banish him from my life even though he brings me closer to God? Without him my life is empty and hollow. I am desperate, Father. You see. . . we had an understanding, no sexual activity, but we lapsed – our love for each other is too powerful. The inspiration that he invokes within my soul is extraordinary. How can I walk away?'

'Michelangelo, we are all made in God's image. You must pray for strength and guidance. God has given you great talent which you have never wasted. He has also given you this young man for love and companionship. Perhaps even to test you. You can still have a relationship with him but you cannot, without sinning, physically love this man.'

Michelangelo held his head down.

'Do not be too hard on yourself, and remember that Jesus is merciful.' The priest reached out and rested his hand on the artist's shoulder. 'You have a yearning for love which is insatiable. Like all of us, you are a human being and we are presented with temptations all the time. It's a pity you have not found a woman to love as intensely as you do this young man. Love between man and woman, in the eyes of the Church, is the proper, God-given love; love between man and man is an anomaly that dates back to the pagan world. Yes, you have done wrong, but God loves us dearly. Christ Jesus forgives us our sins because we were created by God and he knows our weaknesses. You glorify God in your art, sculpture and poetry, and you know your own strengths and weaknesses and are eager to ask God forgiveness of your sins. Once again, ask his forgiveness and he will forgive you. This must not happen again. "You shall call and the Lord will answer; you shall cry for help, and he will say, Here I am. . . then your light shall rise in the darkness and your gloom will be like the noonday."'

Father Fattucci placed his hands on Michelangelo's head. 'I absolve and bless you, dear Michelangelo, in the name of the Father and of the Son and of the Holy Ghost. Amen.'

Michelangelo blessed himself. 'I will do as you say, Father. I beg God's forgiveness. I vow never to love another man as I have…this man.' Fattucci helped him to his feet and gave him a chair to sit on. Michelangelo looked haggard. The priest poured him a glass of wine.

'Here, drink this to fortify yourself. And in future it might be wise to keep away from the young man. He perhaps may be regretting it also.'

Michelangelo nodded. 'I have been lucky I have not been pulled before the justices of the city and the Pope who, I'm sure, knows the nature of our relationship, and for that I'm grateful,' Michelangelo said with shame in his voice.

'It has been a good lesson, my son.'

He finished his wine and Father Fattucci let him out of the church through the sacristy door.

'Forgive yourself, Michelangelo. God is all merciful and has already forgiven you. God is all love and He loves you dearly. Despite what you have done, God knows your heart and mind. Look at the gifts He has given you. You are forgiven.'

'Even after all my sins?'

'Even after all your sins.'

Michelangelo thanked the priest for his compassion. He knelt on one knee before him and kissed his hand. Fattucci helped him to stand and watched as the artist walked away down the path beside the church.

FORTY-ONE

Michelangelo watched as Bernardino laid out the clothes on the bed. Bernardino then dressed the artist carefully.

'A new shirt to impress the lady.' Bernardino held up a fine linen shirt. Michelangelo shrugged himself into it. 'Your new black breeches and black hose.' He handed the artist the garments.

'Where did you learn to dress so grandly?' Michelangelo asked. He eyed the breeches with suspicion, then struggled into them. 'They're too big,' he growled at himself in the mirror, clutching the seat of them in his hands.

'You must eat more and not work so doggedly. It makes you lose weight. Turn around, Master, and I will adjust the laces at the back.'

Michelangelo did as he was told. 'I can't dress like this every time I go to see the Marchioness,' the Master grumbled, catching sight of himself in the mirror and frowning.

'Well, knowing the grand lady only by reputation, I think she would be unfazed at the sight of your work apron, but she is a lady of worth and deserves her guests to be dressed accordingly.' Bernardino firmly adjusted the breeches laces, then fastened the legs of the breeches over the hose covering Michelangelo's legs.

'How do you know? And I can do that,' Michelangelo growled at his industrious servant.

'Master, it would take you all day,' Bernardino said mildly, handing him a dark-blue doublet.

'Well, I can button this up, so go away,' he said, waving Bernardino away.

Bernardino raised his eyebrows and fetched a dark-blue cape and hat from the clothes chest, holding them out to Michelangelo who took the cape and swirled it around and over his shoulders.

'A handsome hat, for a handsome man' Bernardino said. 'You should dress like this all the time.'

Michelangelo's brow creased in a deep frown. 'Very practical for working with paints and marble,' he grumbled as he put the hat on his head. He surveyed himself in the mirror. Apart from his flattened nose, he was a handsome brute. What would Madame Colonna think when she saw him? As much as he wished to meet her, Michelangelo was unhappy at the thought of being a part of such a group, even with Reginald Pole's reassurance. As for being around a woman of quality, from an illustrious family, he was dumbfounded. How would he relate to her?

He groaned. 'I am not worthy for such company. I don't want to go.'

'Michelangelo, this is an honour and you are worthy to join their company.' Bernardino smiled. 'Relax and enjoy yourself, Master.'

~

The Marchioness de Pescara smiled warmly at Michelangelo as Reginald Pole introduced them.

'I have heard great things about you, Signore Buonarroti, and have looked at your artworks with awe. At long last we meet.' Vittoria held out her hand to Michelangelo who bent and kissed it.

'It is my pleasure to meet you, my Lady.'

He looked down at the slight woman in her expensive finery and deep-blue velvet gown. Her dark hair, starting to turn grey, was done up and caught under a fine white muslin veil. She looked to be in her early fifties. Her face, the skin smooth, exhibited a serenity and peace that surely reflected the quality of her soul. He would like to draw and paint her. He felt surprised as he never thought that of anyone unless they particularly moved him with their beauty – and they were usually male. He looked at her more closely; she was not a conventional beauty.

'Come, Michelangelo, I will introduce you to the other members of our group.' Vittoria led him and Pole into a large salon where several prominent church members were seated talking.

Michelangelo glanced at Pole. 'I had heard a rumour, Eminence, that you had refused the "red hat."'

'The rumour is correct but I am being persuaded otherwise. I am still not ordained. That will come later.'

Michelangelo had heard that Pole, now head of the Spirituali, had refused the honour outright. He was not ordained and felt unworthy. Also, there was still the possibility of marrying the Princess Mary Tudor, which made him hesitate. It was thought, when she came to the throne, that between the two of them they would be able to restore Catholicity to England.

Vittoria immediately set about introducing Michelangelo to everyone. Unused to esteemed company, especially with a woman involved, he immediately retired into himself. Michelangelo nodded at each introduction but said little and was relieved when they were over. Reginald Pole sat in the chair next to him. The only other members of the group he knew were Cardinal Gianpetro Carafa and Cardinal da Cesena. Carafa was the Founder of the Theatines, a strict, newly-formed orthodox religious group; a sect which encouraged virtue in laity and religious. There were rumours that one day Carafa would be Pope. Michelangelo eyed him warily, hoping it would never happen. Carafa was also someone, along with da Cesena, who disapproved of his artwork.

Michelangelo watched the men in their priestly robes talk amongst themselves until he became aware of Madame Colonna looking at him. For a woman, she was exceptional. She spoke to him and the other men as if she had known them for years, drawing Michelangelo out, making him answer her questions, including him as part of the conversation. Despite himself, his wariness lessened. She was a well-known poet; what would she would think of his poetry?

'Tell me, Michelangelo, how progresses the painting in the Sistine Chapel?' Vittoria asked.

'Slowly but well, Madame.'

'I look forward to seeing it when you have finished.'

Michelangelo became aware of the priests looking at him.

'As you may or may not know, this group has been formed to talk about reform in the Church at the behest of the Pope,' Vittoria continued. 'He knows what we are doing and everything we discuss is reported back to him. In time there will be a council of cardinals to change matters in the Church. I, for one, am in great favour of reform. Saying that, I am still Catholic and will remain so,' the Marchioness said. There was a general nodding of heads around the table. 'Now, with our honoured guest, who will become part of this group, we hope, we will commence our discussion and, perhaps, find some answers.'

Later, as supper was laid for the group, Cardinal Carafa and Michelangelo took Pole aside. Pole had contributed to the conversation and ideas in the group but appeared strained and reserved, unwilling to comment on some matters that had been raised. The group talked about the English problem for some time, for Pope Paul had carried out the excommunication of King Henry that had been suspended by Clement.

'Eminence, have you had any word lately about the state of the Church in England?' Cardinal Carafa asked. 'I have heard there is much strife?'

'Yes, it is too late to rescue Catholicism in England,' Pole shook his head. 'It is not the safest place to be if you are a Catholic. People are abandoning the Faith to save their necks. My cousin, the King, has taken leave of his senses, all for the want of a male heir. Madness! He already has a daughter.'

'You know the King well, my Lord?' Michelangelo asked.

'Yes, since childhood. I have always been fond of King Henry, and my mother looked after him in his household. As much as his father was ambitious and ruthless, he did have respect for the Church and its teachings. I don't know what he would say if he knew that the Church has been torn asunder because of Henry's whims. His reign began with so much promise but now all that has gone. It is a sorry business and something that is going to have repercussions for the future of England and its people.'

'How do you know what is happening?' asked Michelangelo.

'I know all the facts but often weeks and months later, depending on the source.'

'How so?' asked Michelangelo.

'I have my informants in the court who go to great pains to tell me the state of things. I have a faithful messenger who goes to and fro. Everyone is at risk, of course. They are men of noble families who have followed the King and signed the Oath of Supremacy but secretly remain Catholic.'

'How can they? Won't they eventually be discovered and punished?' asked Carafa.

'Perhaps. They take the risk. Henry has insisted that everyone around him sign the Oath of Supremacy, which they have done to save themselves and their families. They urge me to return so they can have a leader to guide England back to the true faith. I will not sign the Oath and I can't go back yet, not until it is safe. Only then will I return in the service of the Pope.'

'You must be a threat to King Henry,' Michelangelo said.

'So it is rumoured but that is nonsense. I am not a threat to Henry. The only threat to Henry is Henry himself.'

FORTY-TWO
1541

Michelangelo stood back and surveyed his work. *The Last Judgement* was nearly complete. He needed to add only the finishing touches.

The figures towered over him; he found his reflection in every devil's eye and, in Christ's turned head, there was only censure. Had he made the figure of Christ too reproachful? Was he, Michelangelo, going to be cast down to the devils at the base of the painting? Were they waiting ready to seize him? Father Fattucci had said no, so he tried not to think about it.

He was working on his own in the chapel, as he did most of the time these days. When he coughed, sang or prayed, the sound echoed eerily around him. He no longer needed help to finish the figures and, if he did, he asked Bernardino who came willingly enough to grind pigments and bring food and drink. The work he did now was directly in front of him, which he was grateful for, since he didn't have to suffer strain throughout his body as he had all those years ago when painting the ceiling. He had aged since those days and the stiffness in his legs and hips made climbing the scaffolding a challenge.

Apart from the Pope, no one disturbed him, allowing him to work steadily, building layers and adding detail, filling in the blue background with lapis lazuli pigment from Persia, covering up the joins in the giornate. He was pleased with the effect of the blue vault of heaven. Losing himself in the scene, he became part of it.

'Michelangelo, it is I, Cardinal Pole.'

Michelangelo turned, startled by the sound. He'd not heard the chapel door open or the soft footfalls of the tall man in his red robes, gazing up at the wall. How long had the cardinal been there before he'd eventually called him?

The cardinal knelt on the altar steps, gazing up at the scaffolding and drapes and what he could see of the art. Pope Paul had, some time ago, insisted that Pole accept the "red hat," because Pole was needed in the Church hierarchy to help bring the institution into enlightenment. Even so, the usual run of annoyance ran through Michelangelo. Why did these confounded cardinals think they could come into the chapel whenever they chose? Michelangelo turned and waved to the cardinal and returned to his painting to finish the section he was working on. After a while, he felt he was being watched. He turned and found Pole still there. Michelangelo put down his brushes and climbed down the ladder until he was on the altar steps. He walked over to the praying cleric, ready to admonish him for coming into the chapel but Cardinal Pole was looking up at part of the painting as if mesmerised. He rose to greet Michelangelo, who bent down on one knee and kissed his ring.

Michelangelo, on his feet once more, looked at the cardinal whose haggard appearance disturbed him; he would not reprimand him for the intrusion.

'I have heard you have been unwell. Are you better now?' he asked. Michelangelo had learned of the beheading of Thomas More and Bishop Fisher in England. Pole's family, his brothers, Lord Montague and Lord Exeter had also been executed and his mother, the Countess of Salisbury, had been imprisoned in the Tower of London. All that grief would make anyone unwell.

'I have come to tell you about our next meeting at the Palazzo Colonna,' the cardinal said.

'Of course, I will be there. You could have sent a message for me rather than trouble yourself.'

'Forgive me, but I needed to see your painting. I need a burst of faith and I thought by looking at it, my soul would rise up from its depths.' Pole sounded anguished.

'You are suffering, Eminence?'

'Mightily. My faith has diminished with the passing weeks. I accept Pope Paul's appointment of me but feel unworthy. And I have yet to be ordained. I have to return to England for the Pope at some stage, but to enter the kingdom at the moment is a risk.'

'It would be dangerous for you, knowing the times?'

'Yes. I cannot go yet.'

'What has happened, Eminence?'

Cardinal Pole was silent for a few minutes as if mulling over just how much to tell Michelangelo. He shook his head. 'News from England. I received it last week. My mother, Lady Salisbury, has been executed,' Pole said, his face turning pale, his voice strained.

Shocked, Michelangelo instinctively put his hand out to the cardinal, taking him by the arm and sitting him down on a chair in the chapel. He pulled up another chair and sat beside him. The cardinal had aged. It was sobering to meet someone directly involved with the troubled nation's executions.

'My sympathy, Eminence.'

Cardinal Pole nodded in acknowledgment. 'It was a brutal slaying. The executioner missed his target. It took eleven strokes to kill her. People who witnessed it were horrified at how much she suffered.' Pole could not continue.

Michelangelo waited until he could speak again.

'She was a good and saintly woman, my mother,' he said eventually. 'She never spoke ill of the King; in fact, she reprimanded me if I ever criticised him. She still remembered Henry as a boy and youth. She loved him as a son. She wrote me many letters condemning the treatise I wrote for Henry about the Faith and how he was permitting evil and wrongdoing to enter the governing of the country. Henry could not punish me so took out his anger on my family. How could he claim to be God's representative on earth and cause so much chaos?' Pole asked anguished. "My mother wanted me back in England to make peace with the King. It was impossible. He would not listen to me. He would kill me. Now, all I can do for my mother and brothers is pray.'

'We will pray together, Eminence. I will remember them in my prayers. They are martyrs.'

'You must pray for me too, Michelangelo.' Pole shook his head sadly. 'I may have contributed to their deaths. The last time I saw King Henry in England, I went before him hoping to mediate and help him through this problem with the Church, but he would not listen to me. He stopped me from speaking and when I persisted, telling him he should not disrespect the teachings of the Church and that he should listen to the Pope, he shouted at me. I went on, saying he must not risk losing his soul, which would surely happen, if he continued to follow the path he had chosen. He leapt to his feet and shouted again, drawing a dagger he always carries, and threatened me with it. Cursing me, bellowing in my face. Holding the dagger to my throat. This cousin, I loved! I fled from his company and his fawning courtiers, the fear of their own lives revealed in their white faces when they witnessed the scene. I collapsed outside his privy chamber overcome with tears. Once he would have made me Archbishop of Canterbury, now he would kill me. Later, he sent a messenger asking me to write to him, telling me of my views, and I did. I urged him to listen to the wisdom of the Pope. However, I knew, even as I wrote to him, that it was too late. He had started on this path and there would be no return. He has influential men around him thinking of their own prosperity and advancement, especially Thomas Cromwell. Henry takes notice of him.'

'I am sorry for your pain, Eminence, and I will pray for you and your family,' Michelangelo said gently. Cardinal Pole nodded to him and both men rose and walked to the altar steps and knelt. Michelangelo raised his eyes to the mural. From where they knelt Christ was visible, suspended in the blue element of heaven.

After some time, Michelangelo rose and asked the cardinal's forgiveness. 'I have to continue with my work, Eminence, but stay if it eases you.' He left Cardinal Pole kneeling at the altar.

FORTY-THREE

To Tommaso,

When I look upon your lovely face, my Lord, in this life no words can explain. Though still within this mortal frame, my soul is transported. Often have I risen to God just by being in your presence.

Michelangelo and Tommaso continued to write to one another, their letters and poems still impassioned. Once, when Michelangelo had been busy and hadn't answered one of Tommaso's letters, he received a plaintive letter asking why he had been forgotten and was Michelangelo offended by something he had done? The artist had smiled and answered the letter; he had been busy, that was all. Tommaso loved him and that was all he needed now.

Michelangelo gathered his brushes and cleaned them with an oiled rag for the next day. He'd need a few weeks more or maybe a month to complete the work. He grabbed his coat off a stool, put it on and stepped back to survey his work; satisfied, he turned to climb down the ladder to the floor.

A board on the lower scaffolding broke under his weight. He slipped and fell heavily through the gap, shearing the skin off his leg on the jutting piece of wood. He tumbled onto the altar step, rolled down the steps and hit the floor with a thump and a yell. Gold dust whirled around him in the late light coming through the upper windows. Pain shot through his leg and hip, then up his back.

'Mama,' he moaned. He lay on the marble floor in the semi-darkness unable to move, looking up at his painting, the ceiling as high as the Temple of Solomon in Jerusalem, so far away, yet so close. He used to dream about his figures in the firmament above him, merging with the stars and whirling in his vision. Lately he'd been dreaming only of devils; the damned beings pushed into hell by the fiendish clan, as in the *Inferno*.

He too was capable of being damned and, now he was older, closer to death, that fear had become more pronounced. Eternity had presented itself to him before when he was a young child. Now, instead of angels' wings, he could see only eternal flames. A change had come about after committing himself to the love of God, never to sin again. Whenever he entered the chapel to paint, he knelt before the altar and prayed; before leaving at night, he genuflected and blessed himself, thanked God for his successful day of work and prayed again. This time he hadn't even had the chance to give his thanks.

'Just like me to die in here,' he murmured. Then he shouted at the ceiling figures, 'Why not take all of me? Most of me is in this place, anyway. My soul is here, why not take my body as well?' He yelled to the ignudi, the nudes from the golden age of Rome, the prophets and the sibyls — prophets of angels, to Noah in his drunkenness and to God and Adam and everyone else floating above him, gazing down in surprise or horror at their creator sprawled on the floor.

The ceiling whirled about him as pain seared through his leg and he panted, trying to keep himself conscious as his ears buzzed. He had an overwhelming sensation that the ceiling would come down to crush him and he'd be smothered by his own creation; the figures of his imagination would take him up amongst them and forever hold him ransom. Not for the first time, he wondered how he had painted it. What God-given energy had possessed him to create on such a massive scale? Pope Julius had died four months after the chapel had been opened to the public to crane their necks and admire or hiss at. It wasn't Julius who had sustained him to complete the ceiling but sheer doggedness on his part – anything to prove to his enemies what he could do.

Julius had not been called "Il Papa Terribile" for nothing. The Pontiff had once asked Michelangelo when he was going to finish the work. Michelangelo had retorted, 'When I can.' He really didn't know. Julius, impatient and enraged at the passing of time, succumbed to his weakness and hit him with his walking stick. He also threatened to have him thrown off the scaffolding. So much for a pious Pope.

'Was it you, Julius? Did you push me?' Michelangelo shouted over the stabs of pain, the sound reverberating back at him. 'Are you punishing me for my sins? But you have sinned too!'

His breath caught as spasms silenced him. He wondered if he had broken a bone. He rolled painfully onto his knees and stayed there for a few minutes, breathing hard. He inspected his wound. The skin had been partly sheared off the calf of his leg and was hanging loose, his hose and breeches were torn and blood ran onto the floor. He had a dirty paint-covered rag hanging off his belt but decided against using it to stop the blood. He climbed to his feet and swayed. The room whirled and he put his head down until the spinning stopped. He made his way painfully to the chapel door, dripping blood. How would he walk home?

An hour later he limped into the house and found Bernardino worried he hadn't returned at the usual time.

'I was about to go looking for you.' The servant pulled at the sleeves of his coat, catching it as it slid off. 'Oh, Master, what have you done?' Bernardino was horrified at the sight of Michelangelo's blood-stained hose and breeches.

'Nearly killed myself. I blame Julius,' Michelangelo sank into the nearest chair.

'Julius?' Bernardino was puzzled.

'Revenge. He's spoken to the good Lord himself and told him of my sins.'

'Well, if you ask me, Master, Julius was no saint. I don't think the good Lord would listen to him.'

If he hadn't felt so bad, Michelangelo would have laughed at Bernardino's insight into the Lord's mind. Instead he moaned, 'Dino, I need my bed.'

'Lean on me and we will go upstairs.' Bernardino took Michelangelo's hand and placed it on his shoulder. 'Then, when you are settled, I will get you something to eat and drink. First, we'll fix your leg.'

—

Bernardino helped Michelangelo remove his outer garments, breeches and hose and, with some effort, rolled him into bed. He was shocked at the sight of Michelangelo's leg. It was badly torn and he was in intense pain. Bernardino sat Michelangelo up on pillows and fed him vegetable and beef broth he had made for him. Michelangelo's face was filmed with sweat and pale with shock and exhaustion. The leg still bled, soaking Bernardino's bandages, so he took them off and applied more, tying them firmly around the wound.

'I should get the doctor to see you, Master.' Bernardino lifted Michelangelo's leg and placed it on a pillow.

Michelangelo let out a yell of pain. 'No, no. I don't want a doctor. It will heal in a few days. I just need rest.'

Bernardino made his way downstairs. After a time, he took a posset of hot milk, a freshly poached egg, water and fruit up to him and fed him as much as he would take. Michelangelo thrashed in pain.

'The doctor,' insisted Bernardino.

'No, no doctor. I don't want people to know I'm ill. They already think I'm too old to be doing my work,' he groaned. 'Anyway, doctors always make you worse with their plasters, potions and cuppings. Leave me alone.'

Bernardino was not convinced. He pulled out his truckle bed in Michelangelo's bedchamber to spend the night with him but was kept awake by the Master's moaning. He tended to the wound with fresh bandages and fed him warm honeyed milk through the night but Michelangelo could barely move with pain.

Two days later Michelangelo was still in pain and had developed a fever. In the morning Bernardino fed him broth and gave him water to drink but Michelangelo barely roused and slipped into a restless sleep as soon as he had eaten.

Bernardino was alarmed. Michelangelo had hardly recognised him and was burning with fever, his wound still oozing and beginning to smell. When Michelangelo was asleep, Bernardino crept out of the room and headed downstairs. Desperate, he decided he would disobey the Master and get the local physician.

The morning was cold, the light dim and the streets quiet as he made his way towards the physician's house. In the market, long shadows stretched across the cobbled roads. Bernardino came upon the doctor's house and found it deserted. The house was closed up with shutters over the windows and doors locked.

Bernardino panicked. Without proper treatment, Michelangelo could die. There was but one solution – the Palazzo Cavalieri, ask Tommaso to fetch their physician.

~

Bernardino hammered on the door of the palazzo. Footsteps, and the door opened to reveal a servant girl. She looked down at him with a frown.

'What do you want?' she asked brusquely. 'You are making enough noise to wake the dead! The two Masters are not yet awake. Go away.'

'I need to see my Lord Tommaso urgently.' Bernardino put his hand on the door in case she closed it on him.

'What do you want with my Lord, at this hour?'

'It's none of your business. My Master, Michelangelo Buonarroti, is ill and I need a physician. It's urgent.'

'Wait here,' she shrugged and started to shut the door but Bernardino put himself in the way.

For a moment he worried she would push him out of the doorway, instead she turned into the house. Bernardino waited for what felt an age before Tommaso appeared, a cloak over his nightgown. He was sleepy-eyed, his hair tousled. Bernardino was relieved to see him.

'What's the matter? Why are you here at this hour? Is something wrong?' Tommaso rubbed the sleep out of his eyes.

Bernardino quickly told him how ill Michelangelo was and how he couldn't find a doctor.

Tommaso's face folded into deep concern. 'Wait for me to dress and I will take you to our physician, Baccio Rontini. The Master knows him; he won't object.'

Bernardino wasn't so sure of that, given how stubborn Michelangelo could be, especially with anyone in authority. Maybe Tommaso could persuade him.

Ten minutes later they walked through the straight streets of the affluent part of Rome in the early morning sunshine. Tommaso knocked on the door of a free-standing house. They were ushered into the front salon and waited for Rontini.

By the door, Rontini listened to Bernardino recounting Michelangelo's hard work in the Sistine Chapel and his injury. The doctor proclaimed his admiration of the man, although he had heard of the Master's unsociability and stubbornness.

'Go back to the house, Bernardino, and I will be there within half an hour,' Rontini assured Tommaso and Bernardino, showing them out the front door.

'I will not go to see him yet, Bernardino,' said Tommaso. 'My presence may upset him. I will call on him later.'

Bernardino bowed to Tommaso, thanked him, and headed quickly back down the street to Michelangelo's house.

Marisa, the new servant girl, opened the door. He called behind him as he ran up the stairs and informed her that the Master was ill and there would be a physician coming to see him soon. The Master was babbling in delirium, so he quickly stripped him and bathed him but didn't touch his leg. The smell was now stronger. Bernardino tried to get him to drink but the Master pushed the cup away and abused him heartily.

At last, Rontini was shown into the room. He assessed Michelangelo and looked at the wound. Marisa, standing at the end of the bed, heaved at the smell and, hand-to-mouth, fled. Bernardino helped the doctor remove the bedclothes and Michelangelo's night-shirt.

'Get me a bowl of tepid water; we have to bathe him to get his fever down. Then I will attend to his leg. He also needs to drink, so bring up fresh drinking water.' Rontini opened the shutters and window to let fresh air in.

They bathed Michelangelo then put fresh linen on the bed and dressed him in a clean nightshirt. Barely aware of what was happening, Michelangelo was compliant – to Bernardino's relief. Once Michelangelo had drunk some broth and water and had been attended to, Rontini, his expression blank, examined the wound.

'Could you get some boiled water?' the doctor asked. 'Then let it cool and give it to me in a clean dish. I will also need some fresh water to wash my hands and clean cloths to wrap the wound.'

Bernardino hurried downstairs to do the doctor's bidding. Later he assisted Rontini as he cleansed the wound and stretched the skin back into place, binding a linen dressing pasted with garlic and honey onto the wound. Michelangelo lay quietly, slipping in and out of sleep, his body exhausted from the fight for his health and from his work. Bernardino sat beside him and watched as the fever gradually subsided. By evening the Master was more settled in his sleep.

'You did well, Bernardino, to fetch help. He could have died,' said Rontini. 'I will stay here as long as he needs care to make sure he's recovering. He should be alright in a week.'

'Will I be able to finish my work?' Michelangelo asked from the bed. They both turned to him – he was not asleep!

'Yes, Michelangelo,' Rontini answered. 'First you must get well. The chapel will wait.'

'I'm glad "Il Papa Terribile" isn't here,' mumbled Michelangelo, before he fell into a deep sleep.

~

Later, Rontini took Bernardino aside. 'I have arranged through Tommaso for the Master to be taken to the Palazzo Strozzi as soon as he's strong enough to walk. There he will be looked after by myself and Luigi del Riccio. Roberto Strozzi has given permission for him to recuperate in the palazzo until he is better.'

'Will I be with him?' asked Bernardino plaintively. He did not like Michelangelo ill and him not being there.

'Of course, Bernardino, we will need your help. You are to come too. But you cannot look after him on your own.'

Bernardino was relieved and he knew Tommaso would be too.

Later, Tommaso crept into Michelangelo's bedchamber. A dull light issued from the half-shuttered window. The outside noises of the market and street were muffled. Tommaso stood by his bedside and looked at the man he loved. The Master was sleeping peacefully on his side, his head buried in the head-sheet over the pillow. Tommaso wanted to bend and kiss him awake but he also did not want to disturb him.

Bernardino whispered that he was recovering, his fever gone. Tommaso knelt beside the bed and watched the steady breathing. He would always be grateful for him and always would be his friend. Head down, he prayed with gratitude and love and, when he lifted his head, Michelangelo's eyes were open.

'My love,' he said, reaching out and grasping Tommaso's hand. 'Thank you for coming to see me.'

Tommaso leant forward and kissed him. 'You will always be in my heart. You can always call on me. I will always be with you.'

Michelangelo fell asleep, his hand still in Tommaso's. Tommaso stayed for a while then, bending, he kissed the Master and left the room.

FORTY-FOUR
Rome, 1541

Head thrown back, Michelangelo knelt at the foot of the altar and gazed at the mural, his arms outstretched. He had given himself body and soul to this creation and the work had become expiation for his sins. His Christ appeared to leave the wall and come down to hover before him, so close the depiction seared itself into his brain. He thought of Tommaso and of the overwhelming love that nearly devoured them both. Michelangelo doubled over as if in physical agony. He struck his breast. 'Mea culpa, forgive me, forgive me, forgive me,' he murmured to the image. When he looked again the image was back on the wall.

The scaffolding, ropes and drapes had been taken down and the noisy workmen gone, carting everything with them and leaving the wall bare, looming over him, bright and startling. He had created another masterpiece, regardless of the controversy it would create. Pope Paul was impatient to see the finished work, but Michelangelo had to be sure that it was perfect. He had spent the last two weeks adding the finishing touches. Now, the angels whirled above his head while devils crushed the bodies of the damned below, forcing them to journey into hell, and for once they did not crowd down on him.

After six years of work, Michelangelo was exhausted. He had seen little of Tommaso for some time, except at social occasions at the Cavalieri's – where he was still invited – and, on occasion, at Pope Paul's gatherings of nobility and clergy. Tommaso still greeted him warmly, love standing in his eyes, treating him as a friend and writing to him frequently. Michelangelo still loved him and rejoiced whenever he saw him or heard from him. There was a sadness for times past within him now but also a calmness he had not experienced before. His passion for male flesh had dissipated, that part of him had gone. He was older and knew there would never be another love like Tommaso. Now all he wanted was to merge his soul, not with earthly love but with the love of God. He wished to exile his soul from the material world around him and concentrate on his love for Christ and His Holy Mother, Mary.

Michelangelo's faith in Mother Church was stronger than it had ever been. Although Tommaso would always be a loved friend, Michelangelo was at a new phase in life. Vittoria Colonna was now a dear friend he was grateful for. She cared for him and about him, enchanted him as no woman ever had, stimulated his mind, amused and challenged him and asked for his opinion and advice. She was always eager to listen and she openly admired him. They shared letters, prayers and poetry. His love for her was different. They saw each other frequently, along with other Church members like Cardinal Pole. Their associates were eager for Church renewal although Michelangelo, much as he enjoyed the enlightened discussions, disassociated himself from the politics.

Father Fattucci had placed all of Michelangelo's sins before God and given him the blessing of forgiveness. The artist was relieved, thankful and peaceful. And now this work was complete, he could return to the statues for the Julius tomb. The sins of the flesh would not bother him again.

His fresco would be open to the public within a few days but he would not be in the chapel to witness their reaction. He would hear the criticism and praise soon enough.

The figures on the wall danced before his eyes, the saved and the angels rejoicing in resurrection.

In the top centre was Christ wrapped in an aura of light, floating against the deep-blue firmament, standing out in all His glory; handsome, muscular, energetic, strong, naked and clean-shaven –

Tommaso. This depiction would cause concern and perhaps derision. Tommaso had been his inspiration, had triggered his creative energy, and was now immortal. The Virgin Mother beside Christ, turning aside from the depiction of the raised and the damned around her, appeared submissive to the will of her Son, just as Michelangelo wished her to be. Below them all, the damned and the devils hovered and sank into the River Styx as the demon Charon challenged them from his boat with his oar before the fires of hell.

Michelangelo walked back to the centre of the chapel to observe the effect of his work. The scene merged together seamlessly. Larger figures stood out from a distance while the upper figures, close to or inside the lunettes, added depth to the fresco with their obscurity.

He stepped further back; the drama was even more pronounced, drawing him forward to study each figure and its individual story. He had completed the fresco exactly as he'd wanted it done, a privilege not afforded to him when he painted the ceiling. Pope Julius had been impatient to see it completed so Michelangelo had stopped painting before it was finished. Julius later told him to finish it but putting the scaffolding up again deterred Michelangelo. Even now, the unfinished part still niggled him every time he entered the chapel. But he was satisfied with the painting on the wall.

The door from the papal apartments opened, jolting Michelangelo out of his reverie. He felt slightly disorientated and self-conscious. Pope Paul, accompanied by two cardinals, da Cesena and Carafa, entered the chapel. He knelt before the Pope. He knew both cardinals would disapprove of his work. They stood in silence, their postures stiff and faces unreadable as they looked at the fresco. What would da Cesena say?

'My son, Michelangelo,' said the Pontiff as Michelangelo went down on his knees and kissed the Pope's ring. 'I could not wait any longer to see your work. Although it will open this week, I had to see it before then. Come, rise up.' The Pope helped the artist to his feet.

The cardinals looked at each other in silence, then back at the wall. The Pope approached the altar, leaning heavily on his walking stick.

He looked intently at the painting, then knelt before it in homage, opening his arms and holding them up while he tipped his head back.

'Lord, do not charge me with my sins when you come on the day of judgement,' the Pope prayed. Michelangelo, with eyes closed, trembled at hearing the spontaneous prayer from the Vicar of Christ.

The Pontiff lowered his arms and prayed silently as he examined the fresco. His eyes started at the top with the lunettes and progressed downwards. He absorbed every aspect. Michelangelo worried that something was wrong; that the Pope was displeased. When he approached the Pontiff to explain the work, he found him weeping.

'This is a miracle, Michelangelo,' the Pope said. 'What talent God has given you. Thank God for you. It is like looking into heaven itself,' the Pope added huskily and lapsed into silence. After what seemed a long time, he turned to Michelangelo. 'I am so lucky that God has spared me to see this masterpiece.'

Cardinal Carafa helped raise the Pope to his feet. Pope Paul bowed to the artist. 'Thank you, Michelangelo, for all your hard work.' Michelangelo wondered about Pope Clement's coat-of-arms depicted on the painting. If Pope Paul noticed, he didn't say. He just seemed pleased and relieved.

Michelangelo bowed to the Pope and once more kissed his ring. He then bowed to the cardinals and they to him before they walked out. Neither of them had commented on the work; da Cesena held his head high and did not look at the painting again.

Michelangelo smiled to himself as the three men left the chapel.

~

Da Cesena stood before Pope Paul in the papal apartments and brayed his unhappiness to the highly amused Pontiff.

'He has ridiculed me!' The cardinal, his face red, waved his arms furiously. 'He has painted me as a devil at the entrance to hell, my genitals being devoured by a snake! And he's added donkey ears to make me look a fool! I am not a bad man but in this painting I am on the way to hell. I want you to order Michelangelo to paint that image out; I don't want to be remembered in such a way!'

Pope Paul smiled. 'Well, Biagio, you know that I have some influence in heaven and on earth, but I have no such authority in hell. You must be patient if I cannot liberate you from there.'

FORTY-FIVE
All Saints' Eve, October 31, 1541

Bernardino dressed carefully. This was an important day; the unveiling of the fresco with pomp and ceremony. Along with an invited multitude, he was going to see the newly finished painting in the Sistine Chapel.

He wore deep-blue hose and knee breeches, a blue velvet doublet and black cape and, on his head, a black velvet cap. He presented himself to Michelangelo in the workshop where the artist was busily chipping away at a large statue of another Old Testament woman, *Leah*, to accompany his statue of *Rachel* for the Julius tomb.

'Do I look alright?' he asked and Michelangelo looked up, his spectacles perched on the end of his nose.

'Wonderful, Dino. No one will be looking at the wall, they will all be looking at you.'

Bernardino laughed. 'Master, you should come with me and hear what people say about your work.'

'I will hear soon enough.' Michelangelo turned back to his work. 'What they say doesn't really interest me. What's done is done. It must be accepted. The official unveiling will be in December. I'm sure you will come home this afternoon with many tales, Dino.'

'Will you celebrate this evening, Master?'

Michelangelo shook his head. 'No, I will have an evening with Vittoria Colonna and some friends. The Pope has given me the task of painting his personal chapel and the Lady Colonna wishes to see the sketches.'

'*The Crucifixion of St Peter?*' Bernardino had already seen the sketches.

'Yes, and *The Conversion of St Paul.*'

Bernardino bowed to Michelangelo and went out into the Roman day. The sun was shining and the streets were busy with foot traffic, horses, coaches and carts. The crowd thickened the nearer he came to St Peter's Basilica. He was caught up with people heading for the chapel. When he finally arrived, the Sistine Chapel was full, and the air was abuzz with talk. Some people stood far back to look at the mural, while others were right up close to the altar, looking upwards. Many had their heads tilted back, comparing the work on the ceiling to that of the altar wall. People arranged themselves in groups to comment on the painting, although there were the solitary silent ones, unsure what to make of it.

A rush of pride overtook Bernardino, who pushed himself through the crowd to the front to see the wall clearly. It was a magnificent painting, majestic and disturbing all at once. It shone like a huge jewel. Bernardino stared into a deep-blue, endless space in which nearly four hundred figures floated and jostled. Like the ceiling above, Michelangelo had created his own miracle. Bernardino's heart swelled; he wanted to shout that it was he who looked after the great painter. Instead he walked between the hosed legs and long skirts of the nobility, the long black capes and cassocks of the clergy, between and around the red and purple cassocks and capes of the cardinals and prelates of the Curia, who were milling about, talking and gesticulating in the direction of the wall.

Everyone was excited, talking in hushed tones that gathered through the chapel into a soft roar.

Some looked appalled; others stared at the work in wonderment. Many were on their knees, praying, and some were weeping, overcome by the masterpiece. The shocked ones stood silently with hands to mouths, staring at the arrangement of bodies in a vortex of nakedness whirling around a naked Christ.

Bernardino wished Michelangelo was here.

Bernardino was also part of the work, so he tipped his head back to find himself as one of the angels. He squinted – it had been some time since Michelangelo had shown him his angel. One of many, high above, but he still felt proud. This is how God sees me, he thought, this is my soul. Thank you God, and thank you Master.

He moved from the front of the altar and stood beside a group of cardinals and eavesdropped.

'It's wonderful,' exclaimed an enthusiast. Bernardino looked up and recognised Cardinal Cornaro who had appeared with Pope Paul in Michelangelo's house all those years ago. 'If Michelangelo would give me a painting of just one of the figures in the mural, I would pay him whatever he asked,' he said, awestruck.

Nearby, another cardinal butted in, his nose screwed up in distaste. 'The painting has too many lewd figures to be placed in a chapel of all places.'

'It is art,' said Cornaro, haughtily, but with some dismay as he took note of the speaker.

Bernardino now recognised the speaker as Cardinal da Cesena.

'Michelangelo paints like no one else has painted before,' continued Cornaro. 'His figures have movement and expression. They look normal and natural. And there is no decoration or adornment, no scene behind them to distract the viewer. He glorifies the human form and uses it to display the state of the human soul. They are wonderful.'

'Yes, but this is a chapel,' came the answer. 'It is a place for prayer and Holy Mass, for meditation and contemplation. This fresco is supposed to lift the soul up to God. The figures don't look normal, they are exaggerated – we see nudity, anguish and devils – and a Christ who looks like Apollo, a pagan god. It is a most dishonest act in a respectable place to have painted so many naked figures, immodestly revealing their shameful parts. It's not a work for a papal chapel but for a bathhouse or a house of ill-fame.' Biagio da Cesena's loud voice carried to those around him – cardinals and clergy and members of the public, who turned to look at him.

Cardinal Carafa nodded with an indignant sniff. 'It is indecent. The figures should be clothed. It's not right in such a place.'

'Pardon, me, Eminence,' said another cardinal near da Cesena, 'isn't that your likeness in the lower right-hand side of the mural, painted as Minos, already with one foot in hell?' He indicated the devilish figure in the lower corner among the damned, his face turned to one side, his genitals being devoured.

The cardinal glanced away from the figure. Da Cesena and Bernardino met one another's eyes briefly. The cardinal, who had seen Bernardino with the Master many times, frowned at him until Bernardino stopped staring and scuttled away, disappearing into the crowd and trying to keep from guffawing out loud. The surrounding cardinals and citizens who witnessed the conversation moved closer to the wall for a better look. Bernardino watched with amusement as they turned to da Cesena, commenting on the likeness. The cardinal turned red in the face and left the chapel.

All around Bernardino came positive and negative remarks. Some people stood mouths agape, stunned. Others looked horrified at the vibrant show of bare skin, or terrified at the apocalyptic vision. Some appeared guilty, stealing one look, then hurrying from the chapel. Bernardino realised that many might think they were being judged just for being there.

A group of priests standing together studied the mural; Bernardino sidled up to them as they animatedly discussed the work's meaning.

'"And who shall abide on the day of coming, said Isaiah, the prophet. And who shall stand when he appeareth?"' uttered one priest in awe.

'Christ is beardless. He always has a beard,' another priest complained.

'He's also too young and too naked,' added a third priest. 'He's broad and muscular and he reminds me of the *Belvedere Apollo*, the sun god.'

'The figures look as if they are flying around Christ and he is in the centre, just like the sun,' agreed the second priest.

'Everything is revolving around him. He is lit as if he is the sun himself; he glows,' said a fourth priest. 'Do you think Michelangelo has been influenced by Copernicus and his theory of the earth revolving around the sun?'

The second priest nodded. 'It's part of the platonic sensibility. The sun is a deity. Michelangelo is well known for his adherence to Plato's theories as described by Ficino. Yes, Christ is depicted here as if he is the centre of the universe, like the sun, and all the other figures fly around him in a vortex, as Copernicus has written.'

The priests turned and looked at him in surprise.

'Have you read Copernicus' writings? It's seen as heresy. Pope Clement studied it, as did some of the cardinals and, although they couldn't find a conflict with the Church's teaching,' the third priest said, 'I have also heard the argument that it is against the teaching of the Old Testament. Do you really think Michelangelo has been influenced by the theory that earth revolves around the sun, rather than the other way around, as we are taught? He must have heard about it in his conversations with others; they say he's close to Pope Paul.'

The second priest shook his head. 'Just a theory, nothing more.' A frown furrowed his brow. Head tilted back, he looked up at the painting and continued, 'He is chastising the wicked with his arm raised like that: "Depart from me you cursed into the everlasting fire burning for Satan and his angels." That's what he's saying.'

'Surely the depiction of such nudity is a sign of human weakness on the part of the artist. It's a sign of sinfulness and demonstrates what man is capable of – and what is in Michelangelo's mind. Should that be portrayed here?' asked priest number four.

'He's obviously used living people as models and has not copied the ancient statues,' the third pointed out. 'That's a sin in itself.'

'He hasn't copied statues for some time,' said the first priest. 'Neither has Leonardo, if you look at his works.'

Bernardino found their comments becoming more interesting and heated. He listened intently to hear everything so he could tell Michelangelo.

'To me, the painting conjures up Dante's *Inferno*,' said the first priest. 'He's borrowed from it. Can't you see that? The angels are helping the dead to rise.'

'Is that what they're doing?'

'I don't like the devils. They look as if they deserve the flames.'

'Well, the painting has succeeded in that regard,' the third priest added.

'And the angels don't look like angels. They don't have wings or halos.' The first priest pointed to the lunettes.

'The ones below are blowing their trumpets to sound the last judgement,' explained the fourth, indicating the upper part of the wall with his hand.

'Not all of them are,' commented the first priest. 'Perhaps it's just the beginning of the judgement?'

'Yes, perhaps. If you look at Christ, He is not yet judging, that is why only some of the angels are blowing their trumpets,' said the third priest.

'Why isn't He judging?' The first murmured.

'Look to Paul's epistles to the Thessalonians. Our lives are already prejudged in the Book of Life.'

'Then Christ is not condemning?' said the third priest.

'No, his upraised hand doesn't mean he's condemning. It is raised because He is about to judge. Michelangelo's message is not only about the eternal fire for the devil and his angels, but also about St Paul's message of hope in predestination,' the fourth priest explained. 'Michelangelo is reiterating that the Church's teaching on the afterlife is to be found in the scriptures, in St Paul.'

'The dead are rising out of their coffins. Some look like skeletons, some have shrouds, or are naked or fully clothed,' bleated the second priest.

'Their bodies are being reconstituted as it says in Ezekiel in the Bible. They are at all sorts of stages of decomposition and are re-fleshed as they rise to heaven,' the fourth answered.

One of them said, 'It disturbs me, just the depiction of it.'

'Yes, the scene is horrifying but there's also hope there, ' said the first priest.

'The activity of the figures, the blending of colours and the creation of depth are wonderful,' commented the fourth, as he stared at the painting.

'And whose skin is Saint Bartholomew holding? It doesn't look like his,' asked the third. 'There's nothing of him on it.'

'You're right. I think it's a portrait of the artist,' said the first priest. 'What! Michelangelo?'

'Yes, look closer. The skin shows hair on the head while the saint depicted is hairless. It looks like Michelangelo.'

'There's St Peter holding a large set of keys out to Christ. He looks dubious as to whether he is worthy of them,' commented the third.

'And who's that on the left? St John the Baptist, perhaps?' asked the fourth.

'The figures are huge. Larger than Christ,' added the third.

'Yes, artists tend to exaggerate their models. A large size means virtue and power,' said the fourth.

'There's St Sebastian holding the arrows that killed him; and there's St Lawrence, holding his gridiron,' said the first.

'It's an astonishing work of art. It's a pity it's so obscene,' said the third.

'He should have put clothes on them,' agreed the first.

'I think this painting is beyond our humble minds,' added the third thoughtfully.

'I agree,' said the fourth. 'I think we have to look to the scriptures again to understand it and the answer, I think, is in Thessalonians: "For you alone are all sons of the light and sons of the day. We are not of the night or of darkness… For God has not destined us for wrath, but to obtain salvation through our Lord Jesus Christ."'

Amused, Bernardino left the group of priests trying to come to terms with an advanced state of art they had never witnessed before and he moved through the throng to the front of the altar, where he knelt amongst others. He held the spectacle of the created work in his vision and heart and thanked God for it, then rose to his feet. He made his way out of the chapel and stopped when he saw Tommaso. He was standing alone, apart from the throng. Strong looking and handsome in his well-cut clothes of black velvet, Tommaso held his head high, looking all over the wall, taking in the gestures and facial expressions of the contorted flying figures before him. Bernardino watched him as he walked closer to the altar and knelt before it. He blessed himself with the sign of the cross then bent his head in prayer.

'There's Tommaso de Cavalieri, Michelangelo's muse,' a man nearby said to his male companion. Bernardino moved closer to the pair.

'And his lover, so the rumour goes,' added the other man. 'And there he is on the wall.' He pointed up to the figure of Christ hovering above them over the altar. 'Do you think he is praying to himself?' he said, suppressing a laugh.

'He is recently married, so perhaps he wasn't Michelangelo's lover.'

Bernardino did not wait to hear more. He dodged and darted between people and made his way out of the chapel. He would head home to tell Michelangelo all the good things he had seen and heard. He would talk about the crowds of people, the priests and the cardinals, tell him he had seen Tommaso and how overcome the young man was looking at the finished painting. He would not mention that Tommaso knelt as if in adoration before his own image, when truly, he did not. Michelangelo's devotion to his Faith was deepening, and Tommaso belonged in a part of his life he had put aside. And for that, Bernardino was pleased.

Later that day, Michelangelo watched as Bernardino laid out the clothes he was going to wear to dinner at the palazzo of Vittoria Colonna. Michelangelo looked forward to it. He was no longer wary of her, had no more doubts about her. Their friendship had deepened to a spiritual love.

Bernardino prepared a bath for Michelangelo then massaged his feet, neck and shoulders.

'How do you remember Tommaso, Master?'

Michelangelo, relaxing in the bath under the massage of Bernardino's strong hands, thought for a moment.

"I loved him; he inspired me, and no one will ever take his place," he said. " I still love him, and he loves me. He will always be with me.

I will always be his friend. My love for him was a splendid sin. One I will not commit again."

'Do you believe in the theory of Copernicus that the earth revolves around the sun?' asked Bernardino.

Michelangelo was silent, for once without an answer. Where could a simple manservant have obtained such knowledge? Perhaps he had been around him too long. Smiling, he turned to Bernardino and raised an eyebrow.

Bernardino smiled back.

FORTY-SIX
Rome, 1564

He traced the figure in the air, his hands crooked, fingers bent, nails long. The outline was clear as if suspended in the firmament, for that was how he thought of his beloved, amongst the stars. He remembered the large eyes fringed with long, dark lashes. Another quick dash and there was his straight nose, another, the upturn of his sweet lips ever ready to smile.

'Tommaso, I love you,' the old man sighed. 'Where are you, Tommaso? *Tommaso?*' The cry from the bed was urgent and anguished. The rheumy eyes stared unknowingly at the man bending over him.

'It's alright, Michelangelo, I am here.' Tommaso leaned further over so Michelangelo could see him. He took the flailing hand in his and held it firmly.

Trapped in his ailing body, Michelangelo remembered every detail of the young man's face and body. And there he was looking at him. Michelangelo held out his other hand, wanting to grasp Tommaso's face and crush it to him, to hold him forever.

Tommaso would make him young again, immortal. It had been hard for them to keep apart as their love intensified. The old man sighed, a long, drawn-out sigh that made his carer look hard at him. Was this the end? Michelangelo's grip on Tommaso was fierce and, with the other hand, he was still sketching in the air, trying to make the ephemeral real. Their love had been impossible but it was still real. Such beauty. Such inspiration. Michelangelo had nearly died of longing then, wondering how he would keep himself pure and apart, because the love only deepened, lashing him with its temptations. He couldn't remember, but wasn't there a time when the longing had tortured him so badly he had succumbed? He confessed, he went to Mass and holy communion and vowed never to let it happen again. But it did. Despite all, he was still human. He still loved Tommaso after all those years.

Light shifted around Michelangelo and figures paraded before him; paintings done, statues he had carved. Even the frightening satyr he had painted in childhood confronted him – with horns and hairy body and a man's face. He yelled at it to go away. The image disappeared and other figures paraded before him, the sybils, the prophets and God giving life to Adam. But it was the ignudi, in their erotic poses, an outward manifestation of his passion for the male nude, that disturbed him. His desire had produced such beauty.

The conflict between love for his faith and love of the male body had torn him in two, threatening him with madness, tearing him from the teachings of the Church. Yet they were there, all the time, persecuting him from the ceiling, on the wall, and in his statues. The expression of his mind made tangible. Their beauty mocked him.

The figures whirled in his vision; he shut his eyes to block them out. He opened his eyes again only to be confronted with the risen dead from *The Last Judgement*, helped from their graves by angels while other angels blew trumpets to announce the presence of Christ – the formidable Christ, everlasting, merciful, loving, beardless, bare on the sloping wall. The turgid risen and damned revolved around Him. The devils, half-animal, half-insect, were there with their ugly bodies, faces and long ears, grimacing as they dragged the screaming damned into hell. He could hear the shouting, screaming and moaning as they tumbled towards the abyss.

'God forgive me!' he cried, his heart thumping in his thin chest. He batted the images away with his hand until only the merciful Christ remained. Michelangelo stared at Him. He was close, bending over him saying, 'I'm here. I'm here. You are forgiven.'

Michelangelo, suddenly lucid, moaned. 'They have covered my works on the wall. They said they are too nude. Pope Paul disapproved.

The fourth, not the blessed third. That Neopolitan Carafa was always against me.'

'The wall is as glorious as it ever was, Michelangelo, and Carafa is five years dead,' Tommaso soothed, still holding his hand.

'It wasn't only Carafa – da Cesena, Contarini, Politi, Cirillo, Aretino. They were all against my art, my *Last Judgement*.'

'It is over now, Angelo. They can't hurt you; *The Last Judgement* will last forever,' Tommaso said gently.

Rain had persisted all day and now it had stopped. A muted light shone through the windows. Michelangelo's vision cleared a little and dust swirled in the light. What had Mama called those golden flecks when he was a boy? Golden stars. Gold flecks from God. Gold dust. Angel dust. If he saw gold flecks in the light, it was by the grace of God and she would always be with him, she had told him. How old had he been then? Six years old, he remembered it clearly. And it was true, she had always been with him. Was she standing at the foot of the bed now? Was she there? He reached out for her. 'Mama…'

The reply came, the echo of her soft voice. Angel dust. 'Michelangelo,' the voice soothed him. It was a man's voice not his mother's. Another vision. Was it Bernardino? No, he had gone some time ago. Bernardino had been his other half, his helpmate, the one person always by his side, who understood him and anticipated his wishes. The other half snuggled in his mind. The small man, Bernardino, his faithful friend and servant – ever in his vicinity, always with him, sometimes in front of him, sometimes behind him. Whispering in his ear, prompting him. Always around him. How could Michelangelo survive when his other half had gone? There was an emptiness, a void.

The vision turned into his father. 'Don't beat me, Papa,' Michelangelo called. There was no answer. Was that Lodovico standing in the corner of the room, waiting for him? 'Papa,' he cried, but his father disappeared into the mist. Was he, Michelangelo already in heaven? Where was he? Am I not in my workshop like always? He would feel better if he were watching his apprentices and helpers, knowing he was working as he had done for nearly eighty-five years, even up until the last week. He had spent years working on another *Pietà,* this time in the round, chipping away constantly until it was almost mutilated, and yet he could not stop. He had to free the vision within. Why would it not reveal itself? He wanted it to decorate his father's tomb where he himself wished to be buried. He had to show his father one last time how talented a sculptor he was and how honourable it was to have such talent. Hadn't his father's disapproval driven him all his life?

He'd spent the previous Saturday on the sculpture until his hands refused to cooperate; reluctantly he had climbed down from his stool, rubbing his eyes to clear the mist. His eyesight had been deteriorating for some time although he could hear well enough, considering he was nearly ninety. He could still paint and draw, if not as well.

He reached out his hand again and called out, his voice echoing in the large, sparsely furnished room. The vision came again. The face close to his. The large eyes, the smooth skin, and the dark shadow of his beard, for the vision was no longer the young man but a mature man, with a wife and two sons living a happy, stable, affluent life. The loss pained Michelangelo even after all those years.

'Master, dear Angelo,' the lips hovered in his familiar smile.

Michelangelo touched Tommaso's face, hoping it was real and would not disappear into the gathering mist in the room's edges, a mist gradually moving to encircle him, a mist that blocked out all light. The face was still there. It was real. He grasped it in both hands and pulled it to him. 'Tommaso,' Michelangelo whispered. 'My only love.' Tears spilled out of his nearly sightless eyes. The mist came closer. 'Don't go from me,' Michelangelo said, 'always love me.'

'I am here, Michelangelo. I am with you. I have been here all along; I will not go. I will always love you,' answered Tommaso, his voice muffled in Michelangelo's nightshirt, his face pressed against the artist's bony chest.

Michelangelo whispered, the effort of talking too much. Tommaso lifted his head and listened.

'Painting and sculpture were my life and always calmed my tortured soul but now, art does not matter. I am close to the divine love who died on the cross for us. Soon He will open His arms and take me into his embrace.'

Tommaso continued to listen but Michelangelo's breathing had become stertorous. Tommaso lowered his head again.

The night had closed around Michelangelo. The afternoon had passed and the hour was near dusk. Tommaso pulled away and sat holding the sculptor's hands in his own. He studied the fine bony hands, the joints enlarged from overwork, the translucent skin revealing bones, veins and tendons, the fingers thin and long, the skin hardened at the tips, the nails short. Such marvels those hands had wrought! The light had gone from Michelangelo's eyes and his grip lessened. Tommaso still sat by his side, watching the Master slip in and out of consciousness, his breathing slow, rattling intermittently.

It stopped and started again. Then it stopped.

Tommaso kissed the lined forehead, the lips, loosened Michelangelo's hands and kissed the palms, the backs of his hands, then laid them gently on the bedcover. He bent over Michelangelo's forehead and leant his own head against the warmth of the sculptor as if wishing to absorb his spirit.

The hovering priest, standing at the foot of the bed, made the sign of the cross over the departed soul. He had given Michelangelo the last rites earlier in the day and had stayed at Tommaso's request. Throughout the day, they had both read passages from the Bible to him.

'He was a good and saintly man,' said the priest. 'He has gone to a high place in heaven.'

Tommaso, overcome with grief, could not speak. He looked at the depleted body lying on the bed before him and pushed his chair back from the bedside.

'There will never be another like him,' said Tommaso, finally, his voice breaking. 'He was extraordinary. And I loved him.'

NOTES

This is a work of fiction based on only part of the life of the extraordinary artist, Michelangelo Buonarroti Simoni.

He was dedicated, determined, obsessed and a perfectionist in his artistry. The novel mentions a few of Michelangelo's works of the time portrayed in the novel, that is, *The Last Judgement* and the *Tomb of Pope Julius,* although there were others at this time. His creativity and output over the years was astonishing. Michelangelo's life was intense and full of artistic endeavour and this period of his life was no exception. I have kept to the correct time frame as much as possible throughout the novel.

To create fiction based on fact about the rest of his life, works and accomplishments, friends and enemies, churchmen and Popes would take many novels.

This novel is based on fact and created around the love affair between Michelangelo and Tommaso de Cavalieri, the structure of Michelangelo's artistic endeavours during this time, and how this relationship affected his emotional and spiritual life and contributed to great works of art. Especially the painting of *The Last Judgement* in the Sistine Chapel.

While Michelangelo was an apprentice, between the ages of fourteen to seventeen, he was taught by Ghirlandaio and Bertoldi under the patronage of Lorenzo de Medici. He completed the sculptures, *Battle of the Centaurs*, the *Madonna of the Stairs* and *Hercules* during this time. He had decided that sculpture was the art form he wanted to follow and perfect. He also learnt how to paint frescoes from Ghirlandaio and how to sculpt from Bertoldi, Ghirlandaio's and Lorenzo de Medici's friend.

He left Florence, sensing trouble brewing with the "unfortunate" leadership of Piero de Medici and the oncoming invasion of Florence by the armies of Charles VIII. He arrived in Rome after some time in Bologna and Venice and sculpted the *Bacchus* and the *Sleeping Cupid*. In 1498, in Rome, he was commissioned by the French Cardinal, Jean Bilhères de Lagraulas to create the *Pietà*. He also completed the *Tondo Taddei* and *Tondo Pitti* and was commissioned for the *Bruges Madonna*. Michelangelo began the sculpture of *David* in Florence. This was completed and placed in the Piazza del Signori in 1504.

In 1505 Pope Julius II commissioned Michelangelo to design and sculpt his tomb. His relations with Julius were fiery as they were both volatile, obstinate and strong-willed characters. Julius stopped providing money for the tomb, frustrating Michelangelo. He called Michelangelo from Florence, where he was busy sculpting Julius' tomb, to Rome, to paint the Sistine Chapel ceiling.

He returned to Rome from Florence to commence the painting of the Sistine ceiling, which was completed in 1512. Julius died in 1513 and was succeeded by Leo X, the son of Lorenzo de Medici, whom Michelangelo knew while he was under the patronage of Lorenzo in Florence. Leo X gave Michelangelo the title of Count of Palatino in 1515.

Michelangelo returned to Florence to carve the tombs of the Medici. Leo X died in 1521. In 1523, Pope Clement VII, Lorenzo de Medici's nephew, was elected. He was close to Michelangelo. During this time, with a commission from Pope Clement, Michelangelo commenced carving *Dusk* and *Dawn* for Lorenzo's tomb and drew plans for the Laurentian Library in Florence.

The Sack of Rome occurred in 1527. Michelangelo fled Rome for Florence. He became involved in planning the city defences against the Medici. Clement sent troops to round up traitors to the Medici regime but Michelangelo hid and Clement spared him anyway. In 1531 he received a commission from the Marchesa Vittoria de Colonna for a

Noli me Tangere. About 1532 or 1533, in Rome, he met Tommaso de Cavalieri. In 1534 he left Florence for good to live in Rome.

After the death of Pope Clement in 1534, the new Pope Paul III asked Michelangelo to paint *The Last Judgement* on the altar wall of the Sistine Chapel. This was finished in 1541. He went on to produce the statue of *Marcus Aurelius* in the *Campidoglio* in Rome, the paintings in the Pauline Chapel in the Vatican, and completed the tomb of Julius II, amongst other works and became the chief architect of the new St Peter's Basilica.

Tommaso de Cavalieri remained a lifelong friend and was with him when he died in 1564. His friend Gianfrancesco Granacci who introduced him to Ghirlandaio, was also a successful artist and remained a lifelong friend.

Michelangelo was a difficult character, obnoxious and suspicious of other artists to the point of paranoia. He was untidy in his person and anti-social. Yet, he was able through focus, determination and persistence to create sublime works of art, which are still admired today, five hundred years later. He had a strong sense of religion and his Roman Catholicism was important to him, though he was not blind to its shortcomings. The strong spirituality which he experienced through his faith, is obvious in his works and this created a conundrum for him. Not familiar with women, from early childhood he only felt confident and at ease amongst men. His longing for a deep relationship that he could only find in a male companion caused strife in his spirituality. He was torn between his sexual inclinations and the love of his faith. He had many male associates and a few good friends who understood him. He also had the companionship of his apprentices, some of whom were probably his lovers. His conscience was acute and loving feelings for men created a continual spiritual struggle for him. Before his death he was supposed to have destroyed many letters, poems and sketches. Why? What did they contain? Were they incriminating?

The relationship with Tommaso de Cavalieri is factual. They remained good friends right up until Michelangelo's death. However, for the first year of their relationship, there is no written record of their activities. What happened during this time? Whether this relationship was ever consummated, no one knows. Considering the frailty of human nature I have fictionalised that it did.

Most of the characters who appear in this novel are based on historical figures who Michelangelo would have known in his lifetime, with the exception of Bernardino. He did know the real Bernardino who was from Settignano and was the son of Mona Basso, Michelangelo's wet-nurse, and born about the same time as Michelangelo. He was not Michelangelo's servant and was not a "short-person" as far as I am aware.

Vincenza existed and worked as a maid for Michelangelo and her brother did pull her roughly out of Michelangelo's house with a cry of dissolution. Febo also is factual and he was close to Michelangelo for some time. The relationship between Vincenza and Febo is fiction.

The books I have used in research I have listed in the bibliography. For further intensive reading of this remarkable man I recommend: *Michelangelo,* by George Bull, *Michelangelo: A Tormented Life* by Antonio Forcellino, *Michelangelo: His Epic Life,* by Martin Gayford, *Young Michelangelo: The Path to the Sistine* by John T. Spike, *Michelangelo: A Life in Six Masterpieces* by Miles Unger and *Michelangelo: The Artist, the Man and His Times* by William Wallace.

The sonnets written to Tommaso I have reworked in accessible twenty-first century prose using translations dated 1904 and 1905. For further reference I have studied the work of Anthony Mortimer's book *Michelangelo, Poems and Letters,* which has been invaluable and also translations of Michelangelo's poems by James M Saslaw from *The Columbia Anthology of Gay Literature Readings from Antiquity to the Present Day.* Other books I have referred to are tabulated in the bibliography.

GLOSSARY

Arricco: The rough first coat of lime and sand in fresco painting. (Merriam-Webster.)

Credenza: Sideboard

Gionata: Gionate (pl): A day's work. A session of painting over the intonaco before it dried, carried out in a day. *The Last Judgement* took four hundred and forty-nine gionate. (Gayford)

Ignudi: Seated male nudes in the Sistine Chapel ceiling fresco.

Intonaco: The final thin layer of wet plaster on which a fresco is painted. This wetness allows the pigment in the paint to penetrate into the plaster.

Noli me tangere: A depiction in art or statuary of the meeting between Christ and Mary Magdalene after the resurrection when Jesus says 'Touch me not' (John 20:17).

Sack of Rome (1527): A military mutinous event when troops of Charles V, the Holy Roman Emperor, against his wishes, invaded and wrecked the city, killing citizens and forcing Pope Clement to hide in the Castel Sant'Angelo.

Scrivania: A writing desk.

A vostro moda: Do as you wish.

BIBLIOGRAPHY

Alighieri, Dante. *The Inferno.* Translated and edited by Robin Kirkpatrick. Camberwell: Penguin, 2006.

Barkan, Leonard. *Michelangelo: A Life on Paper.* Princeton: Princeton University Press, 2011.

Beck, James H. *Three Worlds of Michelangelo.* New York: Norton, 1999.

Buonarroti, Michelangelo. "Poems to Tommaso de Cavalieri." *The Columbia Anthology of Gay Literature: Readings from Western Antiquity to the Present Day.* Translated by J.M. Saslow, edited by Byrne S. Fone. New York: Columbia University Press, 2001.

Buonarroti, Michelangelo. *Poems and Letters, selection, with the 1550 Vasari Life.* Translated and edited by Anthony Mortimer. London: Penguin, 2007.

Bull, George. *Michelangelo: A Biography.* New York: St Martin's Press, 1997.

Calvesi, Maurizio. *Treasures of the Vatican: St. Peter's Basilica, the Vatican Museums and Galleries, the Treasure of St. Peter's, the Vatican Grottoes and Necropolis, the Vatican Palaces.* New York: Portland, 1986.

Chapman, Hugh. *Michelangelo Drawings: Closer to the Master.* New Haven: Yale University Press. 2005.

Condivi, Ascanio. *The Life of Michelangelo.* Translated by Alice Sedgewick Wohl, edited by Helmut Wohl. Oxford: Phaidon,1976.

Condivi, Ascanio. *The Life of Michelangelo.* Translated by Charles Holroyd. Introduction by Charles Robertson. London: Pallas Athena, 2006.

Corsini Collection: A Window on Renaissance Florence. Installation, Auckland Art Gallery /Toi o Tāmaki, New Zealand, 2017-2018.

Coughlan, Robert. *The World of Michelangelo 1475-1564.* New York: Time Life Books, 1972.

Cresti, Carlo and Claudio Rendin. (Photos: Massimo Listri). *Pallazi of Rome.* Cologne: Könemann, 1998.

Crompton, Louis. *Homosexuality and Civilisation.* Cambridge MA: Howard University Press. 2003.

Duffy, Eamon. *Saints, Sacrilege and Sedition: Religion and Conflict in the Tudor Reformations.* London: Bloomsbury, 2012.

Forcellino, Antonio. *Michelangelo: A Tormented Life.* Translated by Allan Cameron. Cambridge: Polity, 2009.

Gayford, Martin. *His Epic Life.* London: Figtree, 2013.

Graham-Dixon, Andrew. *Michelangelo and the Sistine Chapel.* London: Weidenfeld and Nicolson, 2008.

Hall, James. *Michelangelo and the Reinvention of the Human Body.* New York: Farrar, Straus and Giroux, 2005.

Hibbard, Howard. Introduction by Michael Levey. *Michelangelo.* London: The Folio Society, 2007

King, Ross. *Michelangelo and the Pope's Ceiling.* New York: Walker and Co., 2003.

Liebert, Robert S. *Michelangelo: A Psychoanalytical Study of His Life and Images.* New Haven and London: Yale University Press, 1983.

McDonald, Jesse. *Michelangelo.* London: PRC. 2002.

Murphy, Caroline P. *The Pope's Daughter.* London: Faber and Faber, 2004.

Müntz, Eugene. *Michelangelo.* New York: Parkstone, 2012.

Néret, Gilles. *Michelangelo 1475-1564.* Cologne: Tashen, 2004.

Norwich, John Julius. *The Popes: A History.* London: Vintage, 2012.

O'Connor, James. *Michelangelo and the Death of the Renaissance.* New York: Palgrave MacMillan, 2009.

Ormiston, Rosalind. *Michelangelo. His Life and Works in 500 Images.* London: Lorenz Books, 2010.

Partridge, Loren. *The Renaissance in Rome.* London: Laurence King, 2012.

Partridge, Loren, Fabrizio Mancinelli, Gianluigi Colalucci. *Michelangelo: The Last Judgement. A Glorious Restoration.* Translated by Lawrence Jenkins. New York: Abradale, 2000.

Richmond, Robin. *The Creation of the Sistine Chapel.* London: Beutha, 1992.

Spike, John T. *Young Michelangelo: The Path to the Sistine.* New York: Vendome, 2010.

Stone, Irving and Jean Stone. *I Michelangelo Sculptor: An Autobiography Through Letters.* Translated by Charles Speroni. London: Collins, 1963.

Unger, Miles J. *Michelangelo: A Life in Six Masterpieces.* New York: Simon and Schuster, 2014.

Wallace, William. *Discovering Michelangelo: The Art Lovers Guide to Understanding Michelangelo's Masterpieces.* New York: Universe, 2012.

Wallace, William. *The Artist, The Man and His Times.* New York: Cambridge University Press, 2010.

Wallace, William. Introduction by Marcia B. Hall. 'Michelangelo's Last Judgement: Resurrection of the Body and Predestination.' *Selected Scholarship in English. The Tomb of Julius II and Other Works in Rome.* New York: Washington University, 1995.

Zöllner, Frank and Christof Thoenes. Preface by Benedict Taschen. *Michelangelo: Life and Work 1475-1564.* Cologne: Taschen, 2010.

Online Sources

Buonarroti, Michelangelo. *The Sonnets of Michael Angelo Buonarroti,* Translated by John Addington Symonds. Second Edition. London: Smith, Elder and Co. New York: Charles Scribner's Sons. 1904. Cornell University Library:

https://publicdomainreview.org/collections/the-sonnets-of-michelangelo-1904-edition/

Buonarroti, Michelangelo. *The Sonnets of Michelangelo Buonarroti.*

Translated by S. Elizabeth Hall. London: Kegan Paul, Trench, Trubner and Co., Ltd. 1905:
>   https://archive.org/details/sonnetsofmichela00michrich/page/n8

Cardinal Reginald Pole. 1500-1558.
>   http://www.luminarium.org/encyclopedia/cardinalpole.htm
>   https://archive,org/?./details/sonnetsofmicheloomichrich

Ficino, Marsilio. *Platonic Commentaries*
>   *Commentary on Plato's Symposium on Love.* Translated by
>   Sears Jayne (Spring Publications) second revised edition:
>   http://www.wordtrade.com/philosophy/renaissance/
>   ficinoplatoniccommentaries.htm

When Philosphers Rule. Ficino on Plato's Republic, Laws and Epinomis.
Translated by Arthur Farndell. (Shepheard-Walwyn) June 2009:
>   http://www.wordtrade.com/philosophy/renaissance/
>   ficinoplatoniccommentaries.htm

Fraiman, Jeffrey. "James M. Saslow on Sensuality and Spirituality in Michelangelo's Poetry" The Metropolitan Museum of Art, New York. 2018:
>   https://metmuseum.org/blogs/now-at-the-met/2018/james-
>   saslow-interview-michelangelo-poetry/

Hooker, Richard. *Renaissance Neo-Platonism.* Washington State University:
>   https://hermetic.com/texts/neoplatonism

Lessons from Michelangelo. Part Three.
>   https://caerusartresidency.wordpress.com/2013/02/21/lessons-
>   from-michelangelo-part-3/

Lindley, Geraldine, and Maria Amesbury. *Vittoria Colonna and Michelangelo*. Bath Royal Literary and Scientific Institution:
   https://brisi.org/events-proceedings/proceedings/24922

Michelangelo: Biography:
   http://www.Michelangelo-gallery.org/biography.html/

Michelangelo:
   https://www.uis.edu/gendersexualitystudentservices/michelangelo/

Norton, Rictor. *Gay History and Literature: The Passions of Michelangelo*.
   http://rictornorton.co.uk/michela.htm

Nothing Too Trivial. "Did Michelangelo design the uniforms of the Vatican's Swiss Guard? In short: no way":
   https://jackiefox1976.wordpress.com/2015/04/26/did-
   michelangelo-design-the-uniforms-of-the-vaticans-swiss-
   guard-in-short-no-way/

Phillips, Edith Carolyn. *Does Michelangelo's poetic veil shroud a secret Luther?* Thesis: University of South Florida Scholar Commons, Graduate School. 2009.
   https://scholarcommons.usf.edu/etd/2143/

Saslow, James M. "Michelangelo's Gifts to Tommaso" *The Gay and Lesbian Review. Worldwide.* May-June 2018:
   https://glreview.org/article/michelangelos-gifts-to-tommaso/

ACKNOWLEDGEMENTS

Thanks to Cloud Ink Press: James George, Annabelle Grierson, Thalia Henry, Mark Johnson, Dione Jones, Helen McNeil. Thanks for great support, encouragement and diligence.

Critique Group: Denise O'Hagan, Debbie Haworth, Dione Jones, Suzanne Laidlaw, Gillian Roach, Lorraine Marson. Thanks for companionship and wonderful advice.

Thanks to Michael Giacon and Arriana Elliot for advice on Italian language.

Suzanne Laidlaw, MFA, MCW for reading the manuscript and checking the art processes.

Anna Gailani — Copy Editor.

Rachel Stevens — Cover artwork.

Craig Voilich — Graphic Designer.